Nightmare's Disciple

The Stars Are Right ... for Murder!

More Titles from Chaosium

Call of Cthulhu® Fiction

Encyclopedia Cthulhiana, 2nd Ed.
The Azathoth Cycle
The Cthulhu Cycle
Cthulhu's Heirs
The Disciples of Cthulhu, 2nd Ed.
The Dunwich Cycle
The Hastur Cycle, 2nd Ed.
The Innsmouth Cycle
The Ithaqua Cycle
Made in Goatswood
The Necronomicon
The Nyarlathotep Cycle
The Shub-Niggurath Cycle
Singers of Strange Songs
Lin Carter's The Xothic Legend Cycle
Lord Dunsany's The Complete Pegana
Henry Kuttner's The Book of Iod
Richard Tierney's Scroll of Thoth

Pendragon™ Fiction

The Arthurian Companion
Percival and the Presence of God

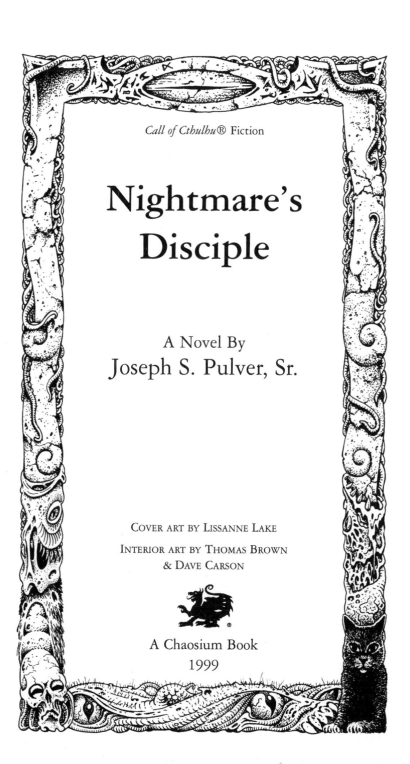

Call of Cthulhu® Fiction

Nightmare's Disciple

A Novel By

Joseph S. Pulver, Sr.

COVER ART BY LISSANNE LAKE

INTERIOR ART BY THOMAS BROWN
& DAVE CARSON

A Chaosium Book

1999

Nightmare's Disciple is published by Chaosium Inc.

Nightmare's Disciple is ©1999 by Joseph S. Pulver, Sr.; all rights reserved.

"Bang a Gong (Get It On)" words and music by Marc Bolan; ©1971 Westminster Music Ltd., London, England.

Excerpt from "Byzantium" reprinted with the permission of Simon & Schuster from *The Poems of W. B. Yeats: A New Edition*, edited by Richard J. Finneran; ©1933 by Macmillan Publishing Company; Copyright renewed 1961 by Bertha Georgie Yeats.

"Muskrat Love" by Willis Alan Ramsey; ©1971 Wishbone Music, all rights reserved. Used by permission.

"Can I Play with Madness" by Adrian Smith, Bruce Dickinson, and Steve Harris; ©1988 Iron Maiden Publishing (Overseas) Ltd. Administered by Zomba Music Publishers Ltd. All rights reserved. Used by permission, Warner Bros. Publications U.S. Inc., Miami, FL 33014.

"The Blimp" by Don Van Vliet; ©1971 EMI Unart Catalog Inc. All rights reserved. Used by permission, Warner Bros. Publications U.S. Inc., Miami, FL 33014.

"Never Tell Your Mother She's Out of Tune" by Jack Bruce and Peter Constantine Brown; ©1969 Bruce Music Ltd. (PRS), administered by Chappell & co. (ASCAP). All rights reserved. Used by permission, Warner Bros. Publications U.S. Inc., Miami, FL 33014.

"Highway 61 Revisited" by Bob Dylan; ©1965 by Warner Bros. Music., copyright renewed 1993 by Special Rider Music. All rights reserved. International copyright secured. Reprinted by permission.

All material concerning Shudde-M'ell and Cthonians, and all other inventions of Brian Lumley as portrayed in his works, specifically *The Burrowers Beneath,* are used with his kind permission.

All material concerning the *Massa di Requiem per Shuggay*, Q'yth-az, Baoht Z'uqqa-Mogg, and/or the Tick Tock Man, as created by Scott David Aniolowski, are used with his kind permission.

Succeeding permissions and acknowledgments starting on page 399 are an extension of this page.

Cover image by Lissanne Lake. Cover layout by Eric Vogt. Editing by Janice Sellers. Interior layout by Shannon Appel. Editor in Chief Lynn Willis.

Please address questions and comments concerning this book, as well as requests for notices of Chaosium publications, to Chaosium Inc., 950-A 56th Street, Oakland CA 94608-3129, or by email at chaosium@chaosium.com. Our web site is at http://www.chaosium.com.

FIRST EDITION

10 9 8 7 6 5 4 3 2 1

Chaosium Publication 6018.

ISBN 0-56882-118-2

Printed in Canada.

❦ Dedication ❦

For the spirited masters who held me—willing, and
always hungry for more—in their web:

Robert Bloch, Lin Carter, and Brian Lumley.

Inspiring sages all,
who were kind enough to show a young
pilgrim the many roads to dreamland.

And to J,
who gave me time to dream
in my own small way.

"A belief in a supernatural source of evil is not necessary; men alone are quite capable of every wickedness."
— Joseph Conrad, Part 2, Chapter 3, *Under Western Eyes*.

"Can I play with madness — the prophet looked and he laughed at me.
Can I play with madness — he said you're blind too blind to see."
— Iron Maiden, "Can I Play with Madness."

❦ Prologue ❦

"Iä! Kassogtha! Infinite doorway of pain, I hunger. Sister and mate of our dormant monarch, Lord Cthulhu, I hear your cry." *Most exalted and hallowed Holy Mother, your agonies scream in my skull. Your hate splits the night wider than the abyss.*

Tightly framed in swirling snow and the shadows of a refuse-strewn alley the blurry figure shivered.

Hidden in the folds of your skin lies the pain of a thousand rending teeth. Incestuous slut of abomination, queen of dark aeons spent suffering undead. I hear, I feel, I follow. "Most royal and holy mistress of debauchery, I, your servant, prepare the way for your blessed liberation. I cover your altar with the blood of their whores, that you may bathe in a thousand degradations. *Iä! Kassogtha! Bininc Cau Mo! Neleh Cau Mo!* Holy Mother, grace the faithful with your return!"

Echoing off weather-cracked brick and mortar, Gregory Bradshaw Marsh's partially screamed prayer issued from lips spattered with frozen spittle. His hissed litany merged with the harsh, high-pitched blur of the wind as he ejaculated on the marred torso of sixteen-year-old Angela Shire.

Green-eyed Angela Shire, a pale lily too early shorn of its fragrance, a bent human crucifix. Her once enticing form now lying desolate on the blood-splattered snow like a discarded doll, empty arms outstretched and grotesquely angled. Tormented, wistful, Angela Shire, her full plum-colored lips parted, perhaps to grant a kiss, or whisper a lover's endearment none would ever partake.

Weak light from a street lamp shone on snowflakes, which lay like cold tears around the hooded, unfocused eyes of the young woman's whitening face. The open wounds where her fleshy breasts had been now steaming in the brittle air of a shabby alley that even city's rodents neglected.

❦ Chapter One ❦

Howling winds weren't the only thing ripping through the city of Schenectady this winter. Death, dyed a sartorial red, and the murderous talons of despair had also begun preying on the Electric City.

Out there somewhere walked a monster whose heart was colder than the bitter winds wintering in the gray city. A societal abomination, many quickly stated, trying to rationalize the carnage, born of a turbulent childhood, from hatred's hard fists and anger's bitter squalls.

Half-cocked theories and accusatory looks flew like snow from an embedded Nor'easter.

Who is he? You? Him?

That guy sure looks crazy enough!

Maybe one of those scummy homeless people. If they could live like that, they could . . . .

There's so much slime out there. Baby-rapers and . . . .

With all the layoffs at the plant, I'm sure someone might . . . .

I heard that one's into drugs. Crack could make someone crazy enough to . . . .

I heard it's an angry pimp who . . . .

The quick guesses piled up like overnight snowdrifts. Perhaps the monster hid behind the seemingly timid eyes and aspirations of an office worker frustrated by the shackles of an unrewarding civil service career. Perhaps the demon lay camouflaged underneath the curt grunts of a blue-collar worker fearing for job security in an economic ghost town of lies wrapped in the bright paper of hollow political promises. Such were the assertions of downtown's daylight inhabitants as they traded self-embellished hearsay in the coffee shops and diners of Erie Blv. before filing into architecturally uninspired constructions for their paychecks.

For once the police were in concurrence with the city's populace. He could be anyone.

This was the second year of the monster's fevered bloodletting. A year of triumphs spurred by bold ambitions. Five prostitutes butchered since the eighteenth of November—two in the latter part of November, another pair before Christmas, and the latest victim, sixteen-year-old Angela Shire on New Year's Day.

Last December the butcher had been flexing, measuring boundaries. The results of his experiments had been discovered with frozen and forgotten mounds of garbage in darken alleys off Albany Street, both young prostitutes slain in the same brutal manner as this winter's star-crossed prey. Each mutilated victim presented the police with the same problems: few clues, no arrests, and, worse, no suspects. Now the beast had risen from his summer hibernation and the slayings had started anew. Schenectady was fast becoming a ghost town in more ways than one.

The currently unpopular mayor and even less popular city council members of upstate New York's faded jewel were demanding an instant resolution to this bloody plague of butchery-spawned terror. This was, after all, an election year, and if the politicians couldn't find the means to protect the agitated electorate, then it would be the incumbents who'd find themselves being butchered at the polls, ten months hence.

After the local economy, quickly being orphaned by General Electric, the major concerns of Schenectady's population were the Hamilton Hill drug epidemic, a debilitating cancer that was rapidly spreading into the city's better neighborhoods, violent crime (domestic violence was up 28% from last year, rape 17%), and the seeming inability of the city fathers to govern responsibly, let alone effectively. And if the recently renewed, year-old, empty promises of city hall didn't create enough noise, the citizens of Schenectady and four surrounding communities, as well as the print and electronic media were calling for a declaration of war on this unknown butcher, whom Jack Beckett at the *Times-Herald* had dubbed "The Mastectomist."

Beckett would have loved to call him something else. The butcher was, after all, severing his victims' breasts, for God knows what hellish purpose, after he slit their throats. Beckett had a dozen other names for the killer; unfortunately, they weren't appropriate for the hometown paper. There were, after all, limits to what this conservative blue-collar community of seventy thousand would allow in print.

* * * * *

The Mastectomist. The appellation lay on the Mayor's tongue like a mantle of ashes as he recalled the silky firmness of his wife's left breast and the doctor's hesitant, but all too candid, pronouncement.

"It's developed too far. I'll have to remove the whole breast."

Tony Ivanelli's impotence as husband, lover, and mayor mocked him. He couldn't bring himself to touch the only woman he'd ever loved, and his police department couldn't cut out this human cancer.

This has to stop. It has to stop now! he thought, violently butting the morning's fifth cigarette. His anger roared in his ears as his mind fixed on an image of his youngest daughter, now college age and as well developed as her mother had been before the surgery.

After mentally ranting his way through another pair of stale-tasting cigarettes, his thoughts shifted to the harsh politics of his now-too-pregnant-to-conceal crisis. As much as he'd like to spread the blame around, it was his head on the political chopping block.

The opposition, "those cocksucking, tight-assed liberals", were giddy from the effects of the media firestorm aimed at city hall. The Republican stronghold cast a harried, war-torn appearance since the butcher had resurfaced and the Democrats were already popping the corks of champagne bottles in anticipation of victory.

It was time to light a bonfire under Police Chief Michael Carroll's ass. A big one.

Ivanelli cursed the economics of this manhunt: Just the overtime was breaking the city's police budget. *Christ, why did I ever take this job. These atrocities are about to go national. Damn it! Next CNN, the national rags, and all those fucking TV news magazines will be camped outside my door.*

He saw the ravenous media horde, their sharp questions and Cyclops-eyed cameras brandished like weapons, all leveled at him. Their broiling desire for first blood seared his harried fears. From an imagined net of their logos, the mayor saw letters separate and declare **Ineffectual Mayor Out**. He held up a shield of anger and screamed "LIE!" at the bold attack.

Other New Yorkers had had their shot—Cuomo, Stratton, Rockefeller. For years he'd wanted a chance to be in the national spotlight, but not with his pants down, caught unaware and lacking. Tony Ivanelli wanted to ask if anyone understood, but the words wouldn't come. Confused, he tried to spin away from the pack's harsh barks. He winced, his ears flooded by the unanswerable interrogation. He cursed his luck, the wandering loyalty of the electorate, and the police. Most of all he cursed the cold microscopic revelations of the media.

That's not the kind of coverage I want. No need! *Not if I want to be sitting in the governor's office in ten years. Face it, Tony, you're fucked . . . .*

* * * * *

"Results, Mike. I don't give a shit about anything else! Your ass is in the same sling as mine. Damn it, try magic if you have to. Get one of those psychics or a crystal ball, but make something happen. And make it happen now!" Ivanelli dropped the phone in the cradle and looked up at the ceiling toward a god he really didn't believe in. "How about a little help on this one?" he asked, like a well seasoned politician covering every base.

"Powell! Get Stewart! Tell him I want him sitting in that chair in twenty minutes or I'll be using his balls to tee off with this spring," Police Chief Michael Carroll barked at his assistant. *Fuck Ivanelli! That son-of-a-bitch isn't the only one being fried in the press. Don't those bastards at the* Times-Herald *ever take a break? I'm not a magician, but Stewart better be. It's everyone's ass. His first.*

* * * * *

Seventeen miles away from Carroll's office, hidden behind deep walls of visually impenetrable pine and leafless maples on a thirty-two-acre lot in the town of Clifton Park, sat a white mansion with wide terraced parterres, built in the '50's for baking czar Herbert Walters. Beneath it, in a basement room he believed was a gateway that led to fantastic regions outside the reaches of time and space, Gregory Bradshaw Marsh admired his latest trophies.

Five years ago he had hired a series of contractors, angrily firing one after another, to build the huge underground chamber, which was attached to the original basement by an underground tunnel. It was from here, away from questioning eyes, that he would use the secrets he'd acquired to bring the deities he served through the portal. It was here, in his sacred chamber, that the goddess Kassogtha,

Holy Queen Mother of the Holy Ones, would shortly arrive to shower him in her dark glory.

Before the next full moon, due on the twenty-fourth, he'd be ready to release Kassogtha from her aeons-old prison, a black hole in the constellation Monoceros. Liberated from shackles of damnation imposed long before man's tenuous footfalls padded the verdant Earth, the perfect and complete power of Kassogtha's dominion would rain in blistering, sweeping arcs across the face of Earth like scarring acid.

In less than two weeks he would don the sacrificial vestments and hold her rite of deliverance. Once she arrived, she would bring the dholes, a race of behemoth-sized wormish nightmares, here from the Algol system near the constellation Perseus where they were imprisoned, and set them to their appointed task—preparing the basin of a once great prehistoric lake which had covered much of upstate New York. In its center Kashkash, the hideous jewel of blasphemy, would be rebuilt. Over the aeons, movements in the Earth's crust and forestation had retaken and destroyed the blasted desolation where her otherworldly city of incomprehensible constructions and turbulent nightmares had once stood. It was from this sacred site that Kassogtha would raise R'lyeh, her beloved Cthulhu's sunken prison. Then, side by side, they would begin—for the second time—their rule of this planet.

"'That is not dead which can eternal lie, and with strange aeons even death may die'," Marsh recited an orgasmic slur. "Soon, My Queen! Very, very soon." *Your teeth will gnaw on their bones, grinding the races of man to your holy will. Soon, your crimson-splattered visions will rend fetid furrows in the dreams of these upright cattle. Six billion souls to rip from the light of hope. The glory, the dark sweet glory.*

Such were the thoughts and fantasies of Gregory Bradshaw Marsh as he masturbated on his collection of breast skins. Fourteen large skins, four black and eight white; the two newest ones he was dying red. Anointing the skins properly was critical to the holy ceremony he would shortly conduct. He would need to obtain the final four very soon.

Zipping his jeans, he walked upstairs to gather his instruments of fear. *It's time to fan the flames*, he thought. *The cattle feel too at ease.*

* * * * *

Cursing silently, Detective Sergeant Christopher James Stewart, the primary investigator on three of the seven grisly homicides, sat at the counter in Pat's Boulevard Grill. Last stool, next to the kitchen door. It was the farthest seat from the cash register and most of the customers. It was also a quick way out the back to the parking lot if needed.

Chris loved the smells that flowed from behind that worn old door. *Pat's Grill* was the last decent place in the city to get a steak sandwich and almost the only place in the city, except home and Laurinda's flat, to get a cup of his beloved Earl Grey. Patrick Price kept the Earl Grey on hand just for Chris. Pat couldn't stand the stuff, but if it pleased Chris, it pleased Pat. Chris didn't believe it was possible to think properly on an empty stomach, so he ordered the works, peppers, extra onions, and cheese. Pat would make damn sure no one bothered him while he tried to eat.

Patrick Price counted family dearer than anything, and to Pat, Chris was family. Brothers in arms meant just that: brothers. Pat often thought about the two bullets Chris had taken to save him from a sniper's ambush in 'Nam. One to the right shoulder and the other in the ass. Over the years there had been a million jokes about the second shot. They always started the same. "Did you hear the one about the guy who goes to see his proctologist and—" "Yeah, twice," came the stock reply from Chris. How Chris, himself wounded, had pulled Pat from that chaos was a miracle. On that night of burning pain and fear, two young men formed a bond that all the minions of hell would be unable to break. Through the hard rain of booze, guilt, and rage, the grind of skeletal economics, and the baptism of one daughter and the funeral of another, their friendship had been well tested. Pat took one look at his friend and suspected that hard times were about to come prancin' down the road again.

"You look like shit, Moon."

"Yeah, and you look like hell." The same opening line for almost twenty-two years. *Thank God for that beat-up mug and those warm baby blues*, Chris thought.

"Sit on it."

"That's getting pretty old."

"So are you. Well? What is it? Carroll up your ass again?"

"Firmly. He's built a condo and moved his family in. Not that I can blame him. Ivanelli's screaming so fucking loud he's wakin' up babies in China. I wish there was something I could give the son-of-a-bitch, but this piece a shit ain't left clue one that's useful. Nothin'! Nobody's that smart. Well, at least nobody who's this sick. He slits their throats and has time to carve them up. All without a god damn trace. What the fuck is he? A ghost."

"No. A ghoul."

"Tell the truth."

"Be patient, you'll turn up something. The point man always breaks open the shit. You know that. Just keep watching. Somethin'll break, just a matter or time."

"Time we don't have."

That's true. "Hey, Lindy's been asking how you're doing. She missed your sorry ass Christmas Day. I think she's got a new friend for you to meet."

"I ain't recovered from the last one. Where the hell did she dig her up from, anyway? How about some help on this?"

"Fuck you. You're on your own."

Damn straight. Out here, waiting for the shitstorm to hit and no help in sight. It's not like the 'Nam. "Hey, when are you going to fix the jukebox? A man can't digest this slop properly without a little music. I could do with the Rascals about now."

His frustration ratcheted up a few notches, and the low-level headache that had been fingering his temples explosively blossomed. The snippet of "Groovin'" that had barely begun was banished by sharp stabs of pressure as Julie Driscoll's disturbing reading of the chorus of Dylan's "This Wheel's on Fire" whirled about his thoughts like a mocking carnival melody.

"Just as soon as you start payin' for lunch."

"The hell, you say."

"Okay. Be right there. Sorry bro', gotsta run. The money's talkin'. Stop for a brew later. By the look of it, you could stand a little R&R. Later, Moon. Gotta take care of the payin' customers."

If I could just get a clue—just one. "Huh? Yeah, later," Chris said as he reached over the counter for the aspirin bottle. *Better take a couple extras for later. It's gonna be a long day.*

* * * * *

The *Zhou Texts* sat before Gregory Bradshaw Marsh, on a lectern of black marble and oiled wormwood, surrounded and illuminated by seven tall black candles, positioned to form two sides of a triangle. A nest of seething expectations drove him to the ancient tome. He placed his trembling hands upon it. His fingers had been dipped in blood, and then dried—one could not touch the blessed tome with impure hands. All the answers he'd longed after and desperately searched to find, for over two pain-filled decades, were finally at his fingertips. It had taken years for the messages in his head to clear, but he'd finally fine-tuned the voice and deciphered the communication. Thanks to this syllabus all the instructions in his head were now intricately detailed.

He'd spent a small fortune for this treasure. Seventy-five thousand U.S. dollars, plus expenses, had ultimately persuaded a collector of antiquities in Thailand to part with the *Texts*. The fool hadn't the sense to take the offer, but, after being repeatedly rebuffed, Marsh found it relatively easy to employ the talents of a cadre of highly trained craftsmen in southeast Asia to acquire it for him. Along with the holy texts, a small bronze sculpture had arrived. The soldier of fortune who had organized the acquisition had believed it had something to do with the tome and had sent it along, hoping for additional compensation. His bones were now rotting in some jungle. Marsh felt he'd been greedy, hence his additional compensation.

The sculpture indeed had something to do with the texts. It was a painstakingly crafted representation of Kassogtha's magnificence. In certain occult antiquities markets either of these items were priceless. Marsh believed both to have originated in the Zhou dynasty, ca. 1100 B.C.

Marsh encountered more difficulty, although less expense, in having the text translated. Once translated, however, he discovered revelation upon revelation. The tome was almost complete; portions of the beginning were missing, a mere four pages, and a small section near the end was unintelligible. Everything alluded to in *Las Reglas de Ruina*, written in 1520 by Philip of Navarre about Kassogtha and the *Zhou Texts*, had proven to be true.

The cattle had an expression: "The truth will set you free." For once they were right. The means to shatter her prison and open the

gateway were illustrated in the text, and with these truths he would
soon release her truth upon them: the ultimate truth—death.

* * * * *

At eight years of age Chris Stewart had entertained a wide-eyed
world of smile-inducing dreams and magical illusions. Baseball and
Sky King. Owning a big black dog and a fast red bike—with a pair
of baskets for hauling all manner of goodies. A secret tree house out
back, near the top of the old oak—close to the sky, and the stars.
Fishing on sunny Saturday mornings with his dad. Cowboys—he
wanted a pinto just like Little Joe's, candy, and comics—his father
had painstakingly painted an old garbage can lid, transforming it
into Captain America's shield. But the loss of his father in a hunting
accident in 1963 scared more than a few of his dreams permanently
back to Never Never Land. In fits and starts, Chris shed his childhood while rubbing against adolescence. A few more dead. Ten years
later his mother's slow death from cancer and the horrors of 'Nam
damn near finished the rest.

At thirty-two he had still clung to a tattered last few despite the
tragic death of his wife and daughter in an automobile accident.
Thirty-two somehow became forty-three as he watched the years
pass—some in the bottle, all in pain—leaving few dreams and no
illusions. Now the files and photos spread across the desk in his den
were fast removing what little remained of his battered belief in
human decency.

Murder he'd seen plenty of, but these atrocities were too savage
to be termed murder.

Alone in his guilt-haunted den, trying not to look at a bottle of
Scotch within arm's reach, he was praying to God to restore his faith.
He was going to need something to bring him through his time of need.

What could do this? he asked God and himself.

Chris found it hard to believe that the butchery the photographs
contained could be caused by a human being, but the still images didn't
lie. He had seen or had been a part of a great deal of death in his life
and was always sickened by it, but now he yearned for one more death.
Pulling the silver crucifix that hung around his neck from under his
shirt he pressed it to his lips and with his eyes clamped shut asked God
to be allowed to bring this rabid monster down.

Chris Stewart believed in an eye for an eye. He believed in justice: justice unencumbered by the courts and liberal cries for moderation and understanding. When called for, he was all for the justice of a hollow point, or the electric chair.

"Damn Cuomo! He's one of the last few decent ones. Why can't he understand why we need the death penalty?"

At 11:43 p.m. Chris finished his third Coors as he watched a television commercial for the Clapper. One, two. Clap off. *Bang! Bang! You're dead, you son-of-a-bitch! Soon, real fuckin' soon.*

❦ Chapter Two ❦

For Chris, Tuesday arrived after only four and a half short hours of fitful sleep. By 6:30 a.m. he was sitting at his desk, currently stationed in a large conference room that had been commandeered as a command center for the newly formed task force, vaporizing mental cobwebs with the steam rising from his tea mug. The gunmetal gray room, adorned with little more than stark crime scene photographs, oversized desks covered by papers, phones, and coffee stains, and cork boards crowded with the facts and faces of the dead, was located in the rear of the second floor of the Schenectady Police Department.

Chris stared at the latest and youngest victim, a sixteen-year-old girl who had undergone both the blades of the M.E. and of the butcher who had taken her life. In a few hours she'd be buried. Chris hoped she'd finally find peace.

Three days had passed since Angela Shire was murdered on New Year's Day and so far nothing new had been uncovered. There was surprisingly little evidence after seven deaths which could be used to apprehend the murderer. The police were in possession of a great deal of physical evidence that would eventually convict whomever they caught, but they had no leads to the who, let alone the *why*. Like the piercing talons of a migraine, Chris couldn't shake the why.

He looked across the room at photos of the pained death masks pinned to a large cork memo board. *Some of them were really pretty*, he thought. Sipping his cooling tea, he wished for a break. He'd take anything. Anything at all.

"Morning, Chris. Don't suppose there's anything new?" Rolly Hawkins asked. Investigator Roland "Rolly" Hawkins was Stewart's partner. For the last four and a half years they had had a 79 percent arrest and conviction record, the highest in the city, until this killer had surfaced.

Chris shook his head. "One bit of good news: Matthews is coming back today. So I can get my ass out of this damn chair and maybe, just maybe, catch this bastard."

"Don't let it kill you. We'll nail this psycho. Then he'll get some fancy-ass vampire with a forked tongue who'll stand before God and the judge and claim mental defect on a stack of shrinks. Hell, you know the program. Creep will wind up upstate, with a scenic view of the Adirondacks we'd kill for."

"The only view he's gonna have is complete darkness," Chris spat.

"Easy, partner. Something's got to break. This guy likes the taste too much to stop now."

"That's what scares me. Let's run over this stuff again."

"Shoot," Rolly said with a smile, pointing his finger at Chris as if it were a pistol.

Over cold coffee and hot curses they spent the next two hours reexamining facts they already knew added up to nothing: victims' names and ages; murder site layouts; the perp's footprint size and depth; DNA analysis of hair and fiber—

"And then there's this asshole's sperm. That's what really bugs me. This asshole's got time to jerk off on these girls and no one has seen anything. Don't these girls even scream?"

Chris rubbed his temples. His head was pounding again. *Jesus! These things are becoming so frequent. Can't remember when I didn't have one. Gotta be from stress.*

"Look at this last one. Two sets of footprints walk into the alley, side by side, then the cowboy boots go around to the back; he's behind her. There's no sign of struggle. He walks or drives up to them and starts talking. They deal, and then he nails 'er. No rape, no sodomy. Every vic's been found with her panties intact and no signs of oral penetration."

"Right. M.E. says he cuts their throats from behind. He's standing behind them. Let's say fondling their breasts. We know they have their shirts open from the splatter patterns of the blood. He's right-handed; the slashes to their throats are from left to right. After he cuts them, he pushes them away and just lets them bleed to death. Then he severs the breasts. Why both? Why not a nipple? Be easier to walk away with a nipple. Wouldn't one trophy suffice? Does that mean anything, taking both? Then he beats off and splits. Christ! What a spooky bastard."

"Agreed. I'm going to head over to the lab and see if I can hurry the test results on those fibers with a personal ASAP. I'll call as soon I get them."

"Great. More paper that probably won't tell us a damn thing. The murder books on this are going to weigh more than a set of encyclopedias with a small elephant sitting on them. Hey! Be a sweetheart and don't bring me anything but good news, huh."

"You want good news this year?" Rolly asked.

"If you want a vacation . . . ."

"Consider it done."

* * * * *

Gregory Bradshaw Marsh licked the flap of the envelope and smiled. He'd spent hours painstakingly preparing the letter he was about to mail to the detail-starved media. Beside his right foot a pile of crumpled and shredded papers, many shy of the wastepaper basket, demonstrated the energy he had poured into composing the right message, an acidic defoliant that would strip all feelings of security from the city's populace. It was his belief that after receiving the letter he'd control the press. Marsh was positive journalists like Jack Beckett would fuel the fires of terror he had generated once he dangled his declarative morsel before them.

It was time to stir up the cattle. Their anxiety and fear were important elements; he required a great deal of energy to open the portal. High levels of fear and stress in the herd were vital if the ceremony was to be successful. Without them, there wouldn't be enough psychic energy to release his exalted queen from her prison. To the cattle, he was just another Gacy or Dahmer, a malignancy they hoped would soon be cut away. Their fears needed a push, a big one. The cattle were far too content at this point. They were certainly disgusted, loudly voicing their concerns, but they really weren't afraid, let alone terrified. He was, after all, only preying on whores. Once they were made aware of his divine mission, and their own impending doom, their sense of security would quickly flee. His message would ring throughout the newspapers and the airwaves. When the level of fear was properly heightened, he would toss his burning match into the accelerant.

His next victim wouldn't be a prostitute. They were becoming too wary, and the increased police activity on the streets was making his hunting increasingly difficult. Taking a female from outside the community of prostitutes would send giant shock waves through the populace. Fear and panic would spread like wildfire.

Sitting comfortably for the moment, he felt everything was working out brilliantly.

Yesterday Roaker's packages from Arizona had arrived. Marsh had flown into a blind rage when Roaker's hirelings had called saying they were lost. Somehow the dolts had found their way onto 787 and into Albany, instead of just following 87 north.

"Can't anyone follow simple directions?" he'd screamed into the phone. At the proper time they would have to be disciplined, and Marsh knew just what form that discipline would take.

An hour later they had pulled into the driveway with his delivery. Suddenly overjoyed, Marsh closeted his anger.

Secured within the metal-banded crates were three of the coming ceremony's required nine candlesticks, each a different size, shape, color, and weight. Quickly dismissing the underlings, Marsh went to work opening the heavy crates. Sweat and aspiration lubricated his labors.

"Finally open," he said, the date of the ceremony now almost a solid presence standing beside him.

His eyes reveled as they slid across contours. As he stood reverentially admiring the inspired craftsmanship, Marsh found them to be even more wondrous than he'd originally envisioned. Roaker's descriptions, although tantalizing, didn't do them justice. The three candlesticks had been carved, or sculpted, to represent certain Holy Ones, deities directly linked to his exalted goddess.

The first to demand his attention, Lord Cthulhu, ruler of the deep ones, was depicted as a sprawling octopoid monstrosity, sculpted from deep green jade which felt oddly moist to the touch, although it was absolutely dry. Marsh's breath stilled before the magnificent piece of statuary.

To Cthulhu's right, carved from the bleached bones of human remains and walrus ivory, was a stark likeness of Ithaqua, the Thing That Walks on the Wind. It was difficult to determine its age, yet the work appeared to be ancient, and of a style associated with the Inuit. Marsh had to wear heavy mittens as he unpacked the Wind Walker's candlestick, as it seemed frigid to the touch, as are the frozen Arctic wastes Ithaqua roams.

The last candlestick that he unpacked was larger than the two others. A squat, black (basalt, he thought) sculpture that represent-

ed Hastur, He Who Is Not to Be Named, exiled to a dying orb near
the star Aldebaran. Marsh left on the stiff Tcho-Tcho ritual mittens
while handling Hastur's candlestick. When the image of the
Unspeakable One was in position he thanked his goddess, after noticing the faint scorch marks on the thick mittens.

Referring to the exacting instructions in an ancient manual, he
spent a great deal of time configuring the arrangement of the ceremonial candlesticks. When all nine were properly positioned around
Kassogtha's altar, he would be ready for the final steps to begin.

There would be no margin for error—no second chance.
Everything must be right for the ceremony; the stars would not reach
the exact degree of influence again for fifty-one years. At forty-two
years of age, Marsh couldn't wait until 2045 to hold a second ritual
of deliverance.

Centered in a triangle within a circle within a square,
Kassogtha's altar was hewn from a gigantic piece of gray-blue marble, nearly seven feet long and almost four feet wide. Varying in
height from 34 to 39 inches, it rose from the poured concrete floor
to command the center of Marsh's underground shrine. Shaped like
a deformed, snakelike apparition, coils intertwined into an unsolv-
able knot, it was the heart of his temple.

Marsh often marveled at the workmanship that had gone into
creating the sculpture. Devoid of head or tail, the twisted shape
resembled an alien construction of fluid angles. Its outer walls were
partially covered with small, uneven, vagina-like orifices, each surrounded by tentacles of varying lengths.

Placing Cthulhu's candlestick on the western side of the shrine
facing east toward her altar, Marsh smiled. "Soon you will do more
than just gaze on your beloved queen."

Ithaqua's candlestick, the second to be stationed, was closer,
northeast of Cthulhu's, almost facing due south. Hastur's was set in
the southeastern quadrant of the shrine, facing in a northwesterly
direction. With luck the next three, if everything remained on schedule, would arrive in three days, on Friday the 7th. That would give
him sufficient time to place them before Sunday night's hunt.

He had already chosen his next victim. In five days he would take
her. A cautious and precise hunter, he'd been shadowing her activities
for weeks. The "cow" he'd been stalking was completely unaware of

his nighttime surveillance. Donnalee O'Donnell was going to be one of his easiest kills. Her precise schedule marched forward like clockwork. As far as he could ascertain, after weeks of following her, there was little, if any, likelihood of change in her daily routine.

This mindless bitch must have the most boring existence, he thought while reviewing his notes on her.

Leaving St. Clare's Hospital after her shift at 11:25 p.m., she'd walk to her car and quickly jump in. Once out of the cold arms of the wind, she'd light a cigarette and shove a tape into the car's cassette player. Allowing the car to warm up for five minutes, she would then drive two blocks to the Price Chopper supermarket on the corner of Eastern Parkway and McClellan Street to purchase premade salads and lunch meats for dinner. Dinner covered, she would drive her gray '87 Dodge Colt thirteen blocks home.

It was there at her home, the only currently occupied house on a quiet cul-de-sac near the densely wooded acreage of the northeastern edge of Central Park, that he planned to take her. As she got out of the automobile, he would rise from the thick pine and evergreen wall that crowded the left side of her driveway. One slash and the prize would be his. Quick, simple, and sweet.

An idea suddenly took him, a momentary flash of brilliance. He'd take a second victim Sunday night, just to toy with the cattle's fears. It was such a simple idea, he amazed himself. The night's first victim would be a nurse. A nice, quiet, single woman, seemingly pure and sweet. The shock waves created by her death would be gigantic. Then swiftly, filled with the invigorating pleasure-rush of bloodletting, he would take one of the many willing young men who came and went nightly from Spree's, a gay nightclub on the other side of town. He'd observed them prowling and flirting outside the dance club on three of his scouting forays. They would be easy prey.

Kassogtha, they're disgusting! Outside kissing and running off to cars to spend a few minutes of depravity away from the eyes of the night. It's almost too perfect.

The following day's newspapers would carry banner headlines: TWO BUTCHERED IN ONE NIGHT. A young single female who wasn't a hooker and a young gay male. No one would be expecting him to begin preying outside the pool of prostitutes he'd been ravening. They had no reason to suspect he would change his hunting patterns, not after the deaths of the seven prostitutes.

Then would come his crowning deathblow to their ill-perceived security—a child.

Sometime after his second letter had been received by the *Times-Herald* he'd take a child, a young one; a female would be best, he thought, six, maybe seven years old. The levels of fear would increase one-hundredfold if he butchered one of their children. Marsh laughed, thinking it would be easy: a quick grab off the street on its way to school. He liked the idea of a child; it would make his terror campaign complete.

* * * * *

At 11:15 Chris' beeper went off. Walking over to the reference desk of the library he asked to use the phone. Laurinda Sanders, the head reference librarian of the public library's main branch, smiled as she gently pushed it toward him.

"Remember we made a deal. Only good news, Rolly," Chris said.

"Sorry. The fibers came from a fifty-fifty cotton-polyester blend. Probably a shirt. Lab said it's cheap material. Smart money says it's something anyone can pick up at any K-Mart or Wal-Mart for under ten bucks. One other thing, the fibers were clean: no colognes, no hair, no—"

"Shit. Okay. I'll see you later. Beep me if anything comes up."

"More bad news about the murders? I wish there was something I could do to help," Laurinda said. Twenty-odd years, a war, prejudice, and a brutal marriage that had ended with her lying in St. Clare's emergency room hadn't dimmed her feelings for Chris. They were the best of friends and almost something more. "How about dinner later? I haven't seen you in over a week. I'm sure you could use a break from all this . . . . Look at yourself, you make Oscar Madison look well kept, and I'd be willing to bet next week's salary you're not eating or sleeping."

"Dinner'd be great, but—"

"No buts, Mr. Stewart. If it's late, we'll order a pizza from Chet's."

"Okay. See you later then."

Chris found her wide smile and shining eyes almost impossible to resist. *Maybe someday*, he thought. *No, that would just ruin a great friendship.*

Watching Chris leave, Laurinda's thoughts drifted back to a spring afternoon in eleventh grade when their lips had met for the first and only time.

* * * * *

The sixth day of January hit town on bitterly cold northerly winds. By mid-morning the temperature had shed eighteen degrees.

Jack Beckett sat at his desk trying to find a new slant on the murders. It had been days since the last murder and the story was going cold without new information to pump into it. Beckett could tolerate cold coffee, but not a cold story.

Beckett's contacts at police headquarters had nothing new to offer. There were no new leads. The police were waiting for the next slaying and hoped the killer would make an error that would lead to his identity.

Beckett had no idea that he would provide the next lead.

He decided to skip going through his mail until he returned from lunch. Gallo's had minestra as today's lunch special, and Jack couldn't conceive of missing Mrs. Gallo's minestra. While pushing his chair away from his desk his eye caught the letter. A black envelope. Beckett had never seen a black envelope come across his desk before. *From some weirdo*, he thought. *Just this one, then off to the beans and greens.* Beckett opened it. "Christ, this has got to be a hoax."

The letter, on cheap 20 lb. paper, was handwritten in black ink with a soft-tipped marking pen.

beckett—
DELIVER MY HOLY DECREE!
HEAR ME, cattle.
THE FIRST SEVEN STEPS HAVE BEEN TRODDEN.
THE BLACK MAW CLOSES ABOUT YOU
AND DEATH WALKS.
YOUR WHORES HAVE BEEN FED TO HER GLORY.
NOW THEY SUCKLE ON THE BLOATED TEATS OF INFAMY.
SOON, THE STARS WILL ALIGN
AND SHE WILL COME TO REASCEND HER HOLY THRONE.

OUT OF DARKNESS A HAND WILL REACH AND ANOTHER WILL BE
TAKEN.
IÄ! KASSOGTHA! HPTUGH! G'GCHNA NI'ZOS I'GAQ! THAT IS NOT
DEAD WHICH CAN ETERNAL LIE,
AND WITH STRANGE AEONS EVEN DEATH MAY DIE.
IÄ! KASSOGTHA,
QUEEN OF THE GREAT AND HOLY ONES,
MOTHER OF INCESTUOUS DEBAUCHERY,
THIS WORLD BECOMES A GARDEN
FOR YOUR GHOULISH FEAST.
IÄ! KASSOGTHA!
WITH THEIR DEATHS,
I BREAK THE LOCKS OF YOUR PRISON.

KNOW ME BY MY MARK.

"Oh my God!" *It's him! It's him, I know it.*

Jack Beckett was a good journalist; more importantly, he was a good newspaperman. He often flew by the seat of his pants, letting his instincts be his radar. Beckett knew his radar had found something; it was beeping wildly.

I've hit the mother lode. He's chosen me to talk to. I'll win a Pulitzer and write my own ticket. Lordy, Lordy, Lord. I'm rich, Beckett thought, picking up the phone on his desk. "Al, me. You better drop everything and get down here. I've got the biggest fucking story this paper's ever seen, right here in my hand. Hurry. You won't believe this."

It took Al Jankowski two and a half minutes to burst through Beckett's door.

"Beckett! This—"

"Don't say a word. Just read," Beckett said, handing Al Jankowski, the *Times-Herald's* managing editor, the letter.

"You don't think this is real . . . . C'mon Jack. Some wacko out there is just trying to see his twisted prank make the headlines."

"No. It feels right. I'm not sure why, but I know it. I'll bet on it. Look, it makes sense. This freak has been invisible, and it's been over a year since the first hooker was killed. By now, he must be starved for some recognition. Something big is about to happen and he wants us to know it."

Jankowski scowled, thinking Beckett was a jackass for buying into this hoax. "Christ, Jack."

"Read the thing! He's a twisted fanatic who craves power. Power that's fueled by fear. And how do you create the kind of fear he hungers? Feed the media some juicy tidbit, like this, and hope they'll spread it far and wide. Read it again, feel it. It's all there, the dead hookers, the reference to breasts, cattle, Queen of the Great and Holy Ones—what the hell are they? Some kind of Gods? It's him, and we've got him talking to us. We own this story."

Beckett started to whistle "We're in the Money", as Al Jankowski started thinking about the request to withhold the letter from print the police were going to ask for and receive.

* * * * *

At 3:30 p.m., forensics was busy testing the letter, the ink, and the envelope. A homicide investigator was busy working with the postal service trying to track the letter's delivery route by the postmark. All parties involved hoped they'd found a lead that would finally point toward a suspect.

Chris sat rereading the letter for the twentieth time in almost four hours. Edgy and frustrated from being temporarily forced to command the task force for the last five days, while Lieutenant Marlin A. Matthews underwent an emergency appendectomy, he wanted to be on the street. Being a good cop, Chris knew cases are solved by careful review of evidence, but he also knew he wasn't going to uncover any new evidence sitting in Matthews' chair directing traffic.

Please let me figure this damn thing out. That's it! Lauri. This shit doesn't mean anything to me, but I got my degree courtesy of the Corps from Chu Lai U, she's got a real lambskin from Tulane with honors in literature. He reached for the phone.

"Hi. I'm afraid dinner's off. We've got a lead. Our demon sent us a note via the press. I was heading over to see you in a few minutes. I'm hoping that with your knowledge, not to mention your research skills, you might be able to translate part of the note. I think a couple of the words he uses in the note might shed some light on things. Think you could you spend a couple of hours doing some digging for me?"

"Sure. Whatever I can do to help. You know that. Besides, it seems my plans for dinner have been canceled. So I guess I'm free. Do you really think it's from him?"

"I'm not sure, but it's too risky not to assume it's real for now."

"Give me the words and I'll start looking."

"First one's a name, I think. The way the note reads, it's some kind of deity. We've been checking that, but so far we ain't found a damn thing. Kass-og-tha." He spelled the name. "Ring any bells? And a word. *Iä*. No idea what language. We know it's not Italian or Spanish. Any ideas, off the top of your head?"

"Nothing comes to mind, but I'll start looking. Hopefully I'll have something when you arrive. I'll see you shortly. Bye."

Laurinda Sanders looked at the two words she'd written. Neither appeared the least bit familiar. *Where should I begin looking? Kassogtha? Eurasia, or maybe the Asian subcontinent? This "Iä" might be easier to find. Guess I'll start with that.*

For the next hour, she pored through well over a dozen foreign language dictionaries, yielding nothing. Simultaneously she searched through the library's computer: again nothing. She continued for the next twenty minutes, repeatedly coming up empty, until Chris came in with two sodas, a box containing four dogs with the works from Pat's Boulevard Grill, and a weak smile.

"Hope these are still warm. Pat double-wrapped them for me. Plenty of onions, too. Hope you weren't planning on any heavy necking later."

"Very funny, Mr. Stewart. I couldn't get a date if I wanted to. Everyone's afraid to ask me out, once they get wind of the fact that my best friend is a cop." *Who happens to look rattier than Columbo on a bad day*, she thought. *God, you need some rest. Your eyes look like you've gone a few rounds with Mike Tyson.* "Besides, you know full well my height intimidates most men," added the six-foot-one beauty.

"That's my plan. To keep you all to myself . . . . Don't suppose you've had any luck so far?"

"Sorry, I haven't. Maybe the note will help. Seeing the words in context may give me some clue."

"I hope so."

Chris handed her a photocopy of the note as he slid two hot dogs in front of her. She began to read as she devoured the first.

"This is sick. Cattle? Your killer has a real power problem. There are religious overtones here. It's part royal proclamation and part prayer . . . . This section seems in some way vaguely familiar. It's almost as if I've seen or read it before," she said, pointing to the couplet, *That is not dead which can eternal lie, and with strange aeons even death may die.* "I'm not sure—maybe I've just seen or read something similar. It seems we have three things to search for. These two words and this couplet."

Couplet? "You think those two lines are from a poem?"

"Maybe. We have some CD-ROM's that contain thousands of poems. I'll have the computer search for the couplet. Hopefully we'll get lucky. While the computer's searching, we'll continue looking for these words. You take the name, while I look for the word. I've pulled all the library's books on myth and legend from the stacks. I also pulled geography and religion. They're over there on the table. I'll continue looking for *Iä.*"

The library was busy for a Thursday night, but quiet. For the next two hours they continued to search, finding nothing and talking little.

"I'm not having any luck. This word may be from an ancient language. Possibly Arabic or Sumerian, or some other Mid-Eastern language. Unfortunately the library has few books on the subject. I have a friend, Eva, I think you've met her, her husband chairs the language department at Union. He probably could help us, his expertise is ancient Mid-Eastern languages. Unfortunately they're away until Monday . . . . Maybe we should take a break. You could use some sleep. We can come back and try tomorrow if you like. I have some books on mythology at home that the library doesn't own. Maybe we can find 'Kassogtha' in one of them."

"Damn. I hate to give up on this. I'm certain there's something here. It's just—hell—okay, sounds like a plan to me. I guess we're not gonna turn up anything tonight. I could go for a beer anyway, and I have a craving for a Mounds bar. C'mon, I'll buy." With a halfhearted smile he handed her the last book to set in the nothing-here pile.

I have a craving too, she thought, *and tonight I believe I'll satisfy it.*

Unable to find anything, they closed the last of Laurinda's books on myth and legends at 10:15. Four empty Coors cans sat on the coffee table, along with a full ashtray and a blank note pad. Weary eyes and frustrated hearts tried to console each other.

"Guess I'll pack it in for tonight." Chris reached across the sofa and took her hand in a gesture of thanks. "Thanks for the help. Guess it's time to head home."

Laurinda moved across the sofa, closer to him. Her left hand reached up gently to touch his rough face. "Not tonight . . . I want you to stay," she said before she kissed him for the second time in her life.

He closed his eyes as she filled his nostrils, and let it all go, the hesitation, the doubts, the fear.

❦ Chapter Three ❦

"Again! Can't you do anything to silence that incessant wailing?" Herbert Walters demanded from behind his wall of newsprint. Walters, owner and president of Walters Bakery, which ruled the northern and central regions of New York State with an iron economic fist, wanted his home to run the way his business did: without problems, or, more importantly, questions. "All I ask is one hour of quiet after a long day. Do you think that's too much to ask for in my own home? Well? Do you?"

"He's only a child," his wife Sonia said in a tone she hoped might soothe. One underscored by fear. "He can't help himself. You know very well what the doctors have said about his headaches. We must be patient."

"My patience ended weeks ago. See to that noise or I will."

"Yes, Herbert." she said, hurrying off to quiet the child before one of her husband's rages began. *If only he could control his temper*, she thought. Despite her fears, she felt it was better here than in the horrible place she'd been raised. Both she and the child were safer here than they would be under her father's roof.

The thought of her father made Sonia shudder. The memory of his face was a vision of hell. She'd endure the barbaric brutality of her husband's rages, the abhorrent child's suffering, a life of flight, and living in shabby rooms to be sure she was forever free of her father and family. She'd die first if she had to.

* * * * *

His parents smiled out at him from under the summer garden's rose trellis as Gregory Bradshaw Marsh walked past their photograph on the hall table. Angered, he almost reached out and threw it against the wall.

"You weak bitch," he spat, expelling soul-deep emotions with the furious immediacy of a thunderclap. *For eighteen years you deprived me of my birthright. All the pain I endured would have been needless if I had only known. All those nights when my head was on fire, suffering your lies. Wherever you are now, I hope you're aware of your defeat. All those years you tried to keep me from my destiny were for nothing. Soon your father's demons will reign. I only wish you were here so I could feed you to them.* "Suffer, you bitch."

He jammed the photograph in the table's drawer.

* * * * *

Marsh had dismissed the servants a month ago, informing them he'd be abroad for a year or more. To stifle questions and the possibility of rumor he gave each a year's severance pay and a glowing recommendation. As the time of her coming drew near there would be far too much questionable activity going on in the mansion for him to have curious eyes about.

He knew he should have let them go sooner, but he had been too excited by the arrival of Roaker's packages to have his accountants prepare the checks earlier. His accountants were also informed of his coming trip and had accounts set up in eight foreign banks.

Everything must look right, he thought. *In a few more weeks the Holy Ones will be here and these ruses will be unnecessary.*

All smiles and hot excitement, he sat in the library going over his plans for Sunday evening. In sixty hours, Donnalee O'Donnell would dance at the end of his string. In two or three days, his unwilling pawn, Beckett, would receive his second declaration. This time with irrefutable proof.

Hair samples? No, blood samples. Blood's perfect.

His concerto of fear was building nicely.

Standing in front of a shelf which had formerly housed oversized art books when this was his stepfather's library, Marsh's eyes caught the spine of an LP he had not played in years, the Black Abyss' *Dark Garden.* This was surely a sign that all his labors would soon ripen into sweet fruit. He'd heard of the recording in 1968, when a fan of Philips' recording artists H. P. Lovecraft had mentioned the Black Abyss' new LP before a Halloween concert. The concert, at Union College's Memorial Rink, had featured both bands. It had taken him three years to find their recordings, finally coming across them in the cutout bins of J. M. Fields department store on Eastern Parkway.

Marsh basked in the sweetness of irony, rolling in the emotional waves like a playful otter: Donnalee O'Donnell stopped in the Price Chopper supermarket every night after her shift, the same building which, some twenty-three years earlier, had housed J. M. Fields.

Marsh pulled the LP from the shelf, letting his finger outline the shapes on the painted cover that had gripped him so many years ago. Perched in a gray-husked, barren tree under leaden skies were black objects. Crows, but not crows. Something more. He knew death's black angels had been feasting on the pair of corpses (Marsh liked to believe they were his parents) that were hung from nooses tied to the gnarled tree. Below the tree, which was surrounded by waving long brown grass, lay piles of human bones. Turning the jacket over he read the dedication.

> *To the mad poet Justin Geoffrey, who by his own hand*
> *extinguished the hellish fires that raged within his soul.*
> *Blinded by visions of hellish nightmare,*
> *he gave you his warnings,*
> *though his words fell on deaf ears.*
> *Children of today, I caution you.*
> *Do not make the same mistakes! Nightmares reign!*
> *Hold the light of your hearts up against it.*

Bah! Nothing but the words of fools, Marsh mentally spat as he began to laugh quietly.

Walking to the Technics turntable, he placed the record on the platter and pushed the power buttons on his Macintosh amplifier and preamp, watching the power indicators glow red, like the eyes of some demonic beast. With controlled precision he placed the tone-arm on the record and adjusted the volume control knob to twelve o'clock. Like an unexpected sound cutting through darkness the room filled with hellish chords of terror.

"'Fear runs rampant, as he comes. Feet falter, as he draws near. Dreams crumble, you're on your knees. Nightmares here! Nightmares here,'" Marsh awkwardly croaked, trying to sing along with his favorite Black Abyss song. It was called "In Nightmares": four minutes and fifty-three seconds of distorted guitars swirling and slashing under coarse broken vocals. No drums. No bass. Just razor chords of jarring dissonance in a feeding frenzy.

"'Nightmares here! Nightmares here! Rending teeth, that cut and slash, they've returned, from the past. Rising from the oceans, falling from the stars. Angry! Hungry! NEAR! No savior to stand behind, no release for your mind. Nightmares here! Nightmares here!'"

As he sang along, he envisioned the ragged panic of the human herds trying to flee the horrors that would soon reign over them. He could see them, bleating and self-obsessed, stomping over one another as they tried to claw their escape from the extensive clutches of the Holy Ones.

The song ended as he reclined in his stepfather's black leather armchair, drained from his orgasmic visions of horrific destruction. Slowly, a brooding organ began to fill his ears as "That Which Is Not Dead (Cthulhu's Song)" roared from the speakers like some rancorous communication from the edges of sanity.

Overjoyed, he pondered coming events. In less than a month, Lord Cthulhu would rise from his prison, the sunken depths of R'lyeh, to wed his bride, his sister Kassogtha. Together, as king and queen, as god and goddess, they would spread hellish destruction from Polynesia to the Labrador Sea.

* * * * *

In the waning light of late afternoon Marsh saw the delivery truck come up his driveway; his shipment from Europe had arrived. Motohiko Yano had delivered as agreed. If everything was as promised, Yano's place at the ceremony would be secured.

The driver and his helper put the heavy crates in the basement. After they'd left, Marsh unlocked the door to his shrine and with a dolly brought the long-anticipated treasures inside.

Minutes later they sat before him uncrated. Shudde M'ell, the Burrower Beneath, M'nagalah, the once and soon to be again, Master of Tethys, and Cyaegha, the One Who Slumbers in Eternal Darkness.

Hellish laughter filled the shrine as Marsh reeled, taking delight in the fact that Cyaegha's candlestick was made from black plastic.

"Technology cast in the image of one of its coming destroyers." Marsh wished he knew who had crafted this work. *These cattle only get what they deserve.* "They'll do anything for their meager coinage; just look at their whores and their self-promoting leaders."

Picking up the lightweight object he walked four steps due east from the altar and placed Cyaegha, a swirling black mass that seemed all tentacles and claws, facing west toward the queen of damnation. Using the dolly he moved the limestone carving of Shudde M'ell, the wormish-bodied, squid-beast king of the chthonians, to its appointed position facing the queen. Following a great deal of grunting and straining, the now sweat-covered Marsh managed to get the black stone carving of M'nagalah in place.

For a brief moment he envied Roaker, the self-appointed high priest of this bloated, multi-eyed mass of raw-appearing tentacles. Truly M'nagalah was wondrous to behold. Marsh fantasized as to what the spawn of Kassogtha and M'nagalah might look like. "Seraphic." *My dreams begin to manifest themselves*, he thought, his muscles sweetly aching from his labors.

* * * * *

Chris awoke, for the second time since Friday morning, to sunshine and the scent of tea wafting into the bedroom. For a few moments he basked in the warmth of the sun's rays and the memory of Laurinda's arms, until a cloud drifted across the sun's path. In the diminished light, the frustration and anger of the case resurfaced.

Damn. Can't I get a break anywhere? he wondered.

Outside the bedroom doorway he could hear Laurinda's smoky alto singing Anita Baker's "Sweet Love" as she rustled through the pages of the Sunday paper.

This Sunday morning had been coming for years, and now that it had arrived he was angered that he wouldn't be able to lie here and just quietly reflect on last night's passions, passions he'd spent years longing for.

"Hi there, sleepy." Laurinda beamed as she entered the room and bent down to kiss him. "I've made a pot of tea, if you're interested."

Interested. I've been interested since the first day I got up the nerve to talk to you in eleventh grade. I wonder what would have happened if your brothers hadn't beaten the hell out of me when they learned about us. "Interested? I sure am. Look, I—"

"Not now. We'll talk about that later, okay?"

"Okay."

Chris watched her leave the room. Even in a baggy, triple-X, gray cotton work shirt and rag socks, her dark mahogany form moved through the fingers of sunlight with regal bearing. *She can have any man she wants. Why did she pick me?* His thoughts drifted back to the fall of 1970, when he was on R&R toward the end of his second tour in Vietnam. It was there that he had first seen Mati

Klarwein's painting, *Annunciation*, on the album cover of Santana's
Abraxas LP and thought she'd posed for it. He'd returned to the bush
singing "Black Magic Woman."

How many nights, fighting for his sanity in that overgrow hell,
had he clung to fantasies of making love to her? Over the years he
often felt the single reason he'd survived that diseased war was the
redemption he knew he'd find in her arms. Yes, indeed, a magic
woman. The song's rhythms tattooed in his head.

After showering—singing parts of "Black Magic Woman" and
twice getting a mouthful of water for his off-key efforts—he sat
down to cinnamon donuts and tea. Guilt hit him. He'd been up nearly an hour and had barely given the case a thought.

"I should check in. Make a few calls. Maybe around one or two
we could go back to the library—see if we overlooked anything."

"That sounds fine." Moments later the doorbell rang. "Oh, dear.
I've completely forgotten about Sarah coming to pick me up for
church. What should I tell her?"

Sarah Andreyo and Laurinda had been attending Sunday services
together at the First Baptist Church of Christ for the last fifteen
years. Neither had missed more than a handful of services.

"Tell her the truth. I stopped in for breakfast."

"Christopher James Stewart, you're shameless!" she reprimanded
him as she went to the door. "Hi, Sarah. Chris is here and I was
thinking of skipping services today."

"So was I. Is everything all right? I was going to ask if you could
take Michael to church with you. Mom's still in St. Clares and I
thought I might go up and see her early. That way I'd have time to
take Michael shopping later. Do you think he could stay here for a
little while? I hate to have to run him all the way home. I won't be
more than a couple of hours," Sarah said.

"I don't see why he can't stay."

"Thanks. I'll pick him up around noon. You could come with us
if you like."

"I'd love to, but I can't today. I have to go into work later to
check on some things for Chris. Another time?"

"Okay. See you in a bit. Behave, Michael. See you later."

"Bye. Well, it seems you'll be missing church this morning,
Mike. Would you like something to eat?" Laurinda asked.

"Nah, had breakfast, thanks. Maybe I'll watch MTV. Hey, Chris! What's up with the murders down at the cop shop?" Mike Andreyo asked.

"Not much. What's shakin' with you?"

"Nothin'," the sixteen-year-old replied as he went into the living room to watch MTV. Mike enjoyed two things in life: MTV and horror stories. Two minutes later he returned to the dining room. "Hey. What's with the Lovecraft stuff?"

His hand held a single sheet of notebook paper, which he'd discovered in the living room. There were two words and a line of text written on it.

Chris almost jumped as he recognized the sheet of paper. "You recognize those words?"

"Yeah. It's Lovecraft. Somebody reading his stuff?"

"I will be as soon as you tell me who he is." Turning to Laurinda, he asked. "Do you know this Lovecraft?"

"Of him, yes, but I've never read his work. Early 20th century horror, I believe. I'm sure the library has some of his books."

"Mike, this is important. I need to know everything you know about Lovecraft and his work. Especially those words."

"This got something to do with the murders?"

Chris nodded.

"Wow! Let's see, un, this word and these two lines are about Cthulhu."

"Who?" Chris asked.

"Cthulhu. He's sorta like the king of the Great Old Ones. You know, the biggest and the baddest."

"Great Old Ones?" Great and holy ones. "Wait, let me write this down and spell any names, like this Cat-two-lou. How do you say it?" Chris asked, trying to remain calm. *Maybe we finally have a real lead. Damn! It's about time.*

Mike spelled it. "You pronounce it kuh-THOO-loo. He's an alien, like a god. Came to Earth before man evolved. He ruled Earth. See, there was this war and he was defeated and imprisoned in *R'lyeh*. It's a city at the bottom of Pacific."

Ril-Yay. Kuh-THOO-loo. "A little slower, Mike. And remember I don't know anything about this. So explain it simply," Chris said.

"Got ya. I don't know much about Lovecraft. I've only read a few Mythos books. That's what they call it. The Cthulhu Mythos. They're okay, but they're not as good as Anne Rice's vampires. Man, she's the best. Lestat kicks ass. I'd do my homework for a whole year if she'd do a werewolf book."

"Lestat? Is he one of these Great Old Ones?"

"No. He's a vampire."

"Skip the vampires. Tell me about Lovecraft?"

"He wrote horror stories back in the twenties, I think. Maybe it was the thirties. These words come from his stories about the Mythos. There are stories by Lovecraft, and by other writers too. See, in the Mythos the universe is ruled by the Outer Gods, they're evil. There's six or seven, maybe more. Do you want their names? I know a couple. I wish we were at my house. Cause I've got some Mythos books."

"We'll get them later. First give me the basics. We'll fill in the holes later."

"Sure. So we got these evil gods who don't have much to do with people. Then there's the Great Old Ones."

"Are they ever called the Great and Holy Ones?"

"Not that I know of, but they could be. Most of the stories are about 'em. They're not really gods, they're more like super evil aliens, although they're worshiped as gods by evil, weirdo cults all over the world. The Great Old Ones are at war with everybody. They want to rule the universe, but they're held in prisons, outside this dimension or in other galaxies. Some are imprisoned here, under the earth or beneath the ocean. They can be called from their prisons with evil rites and spells. Their priests get their spells from old books. So, like I said, Cthulhu is the most powerful Great Old One. He's like the king.

"These things came here before man was created. I think it was in the Jurassic period, you know, when the dinosaurs walked the earth. I'm not sure how many Great Old Ones there are, at least twenty, maybe fifty. Could be more. They have names like Tsathoggua, I don't know how to spell that one. Yig, he's the Father of Serpents and my favorite, Miivls the Black Madness, and Vn'vlot the Annihilation of Light. They warred against each other for possession of the southwestern side of the tip of Gondwanaland. That's some old continent. They're imprisoned together in the Great Nebula of Orion. The two warriors were condemned to fight an eternal war against each other.

"See, all these monsters are stuck in prisons waiting to be released. So, there's these goofed-out cults that want to let them loose, but they have to wait until the stars line up right. You know, some kind of evil take on astrology."

When the stars align! That what this demon believes. He thinks these things are real.

"Then the Great Old Ones can return and rule again. That's about all I know. Except in Lovecraft's books most of the cults and worshiping takes place in Massachusetts, in places called Arkham and Dunwich. A lot of the stories take place in England too. Remember I don' know it all. Just parts. One other thing, Chris, there's an expert right here in the city. He owns a bookstore downtown, and he's writing an encyclopedia on it. Man, he's a Lovecraft nut. He's got bookcases filled with this stuff. And if you ask him a question he'll spend an hour giving you an answer."

"An expert here?" *Him, I've got to talk to.*

Chris and Laurinda had sat quietly listening to Mike explain the Mythos. They had a million questions.

Chris was hooked on two words, *cult* and *worship*. Like a neon sign flashing in the desert night sky a third word kept recurring—*sacrifice.*

This freak believes in this stuff and he wants to free these things. Is he working with a timetable? God help us, he might be a they. But how could that be possible? The DNA tests on all the sperm and hair samples match—only one killer. Still, that doesn't mean he's not a part of some group. "That's great, Mike, but what about these words? What do they mean?"

"The two lines refer to Cthulhu. See, he's imprisoned. He's like dead, but not dead. It's not like vampires, it's more like he's sleeping, waiting to be released. This one here, Iä, it's like, ah, *Hail*! It starts spells or rites in the stories, you know? Hail Cthulhu, something like that. Kassogtha?—that one I don't know, could be a Great Old One. Sounds like one of their names. Bet Cosmo knows who it is," Mike said.

"Cosmo? Who's that?" Laurinda asked.

"He's one of the owners of The Horror Corner. The bookstore I told you about. It's on Nott Terrace, by Vale Cemetery. Used to be a pizza place."

"I know the place. The church across the street complained about gory posters in the windows," Chris said.

"I've been in there," Lauri said. "Mike, do you remember those autographed vampire books I gave you for your last birthday? They came from there. The place was a bit creepy. I remember the owners. One was very thin, quite pale and tall. The other was short and a little heavy. Hirsute. But they didn't seem the least bit scary. Odd perhaps, but very pleasant and helpful."

"Just how well do you know these guys, Mike?" Chris asked.

Mike shrugged. "I go in every couple of weeks and hang awhile. You know, a couple hours on Saturday. They know me. Sometimes they knock down the price of things I want because I don't have enough money. They're pretty cool. Mostly I talk to the Wizard about music. He plays his guitar in the store a lot. Man, he can play. Just name a song and he'll rip into it. They've got this band called the Hellhounds. You know what else is cool? They live over the store."

"I've seen the Hellhounds at the Ramada and you're right, he can play. Since you know these guys, I think you and I should go pay them a visit. I've got a lot of questions I need answers for."

"Cool."

❦ Chapter Four ❦

On September 17, 1979 Cosmo Renaldi's father died of a massive coronary, leaving behind the family home on Michigan Avenue and an old three-story building whose bottom floor had been used as a gas station and later as a pizza parlor. He also left a small life insurance policy. The money from the insurance policy paid for the funeral services and burial, leaving Cosmo with $643 and an empty building.

For the next month Cosmo walked around trying to decide what to do with the building. What he knew about making pizza was what he liked on them, and what he knew about repairing cars could be written on the head of a common pin by a preschooler with a fat, black magic marker.

Three months later, the $643 had vanished and the FOR SALE sign still remained in the former gas station/pizza shop's front window.

"'Help me, Mr. Wizard'," Cosmo quoted from a favorite cartoon of his youth.

Sitting at a picnic table which was used by the club he was performing in as seating for its clientele, Cosmo was currently working on his third beer. Seated across the table from him was his partner in crime, the Wizard, Cosmo's senior by three years.

The Wizard was 6'4" and weighed 140 lbs. It was doubtful his skin had ever seen the sun's light. This skeleton, whose skin tone could have well descended from Elric of Melniboné, and his bulky compadre had been fronting some type of band since high school.

In '71 they'd formed a hard rock outfit called Iron Maiden, inspired by Iron Butterfly and Platinum, the female member of DC Comics' The Metal Men. By '73, the rock-this-joint heaviness had metamorphosed into a six-piece art rock/post-*Bitches Brew* ensemble of rubber bass and space-bound guitar freakouts, which they called Galactus (at Cosmo's insistence). Later, as punk raged, they soared playing white noise versions of pop standards as Diet of Worms. This incarnation of their continuing musical metamorphosis was a blues band called The Hellhounds.

"What am I going to do with the building if it doesn't sell?" Cosmo asked his best friend for the hundredth time.

This time the Wizard had an answer. "What if you don't sell it? What if we both sold the old homesteads? Face it, neither one of us needs the size houses we own. We'd take the money and start our own business. We could both live upstairs, either together or on separate floors. Think of all the room we'd have for band rehearsals. We could probably change the lower floor into a store pretty cheap, and still have a bunch of cash left to stock it with."

"What kind of store?"

"We'd own Schenectady's first horror shop. We could sell new and used books, magazines, models. We could make VHS copies of movies we have and sell them. Look at the size of our collections. Hell, we've got enough stuff between us to start out. The overhead would be low, and the band could keep us in cigarettes and beer."

"You're a genius! Why didn't you say something weeks ago? The location is perfect. The college is two blocks away and don't forget the cemetery next door—make a nice piece of atmosphere. Let's do it."

Four months later, the houses they'd inherited from their deceased parents sold, The Horror Corner opened for business. It hardly brought in a dime, but it didn't matter. The Hellhounds paid the bills by gigging on weekends.

* * * * *

Gregory Bradshaw Marsh returned home from the convenience store, enraged. For the last three days he had purchased the newspaper, waiting to see Jack Beckett deliver his proclamation.

"Nothing!" he'd screamed three times on the drive home.

Again today, the Sunday *Times-Herald* had ignored him. He'd mailed his encyclical Tuesday, five days ago. Surely Beckett had received it by now. It had been placed in a busy mailbox with the right postage affixed, and he'd sat there until 1:15 p.m., when it had been picked up along with the other contents of the mailbox. Perhaps that pig Beckett had not seen his mail. Perhaps he thought it was a hoax. *Yes, that's it,* Marsh thought. Beckett didn't think the letter was real. In a blind rage Marsh swept everything off the desk top. He would make that pig Beckett believe. He knew exactly how to make him believe.

* * * * *

Chris pulled his slightly beat-up '89 Ford Taurus into the parking lot of The Horror Corner. He'd driven by a thousand times on his way to work without ever really noticing the place.

"Christ almighty. Don't you think this is a little spooky? Right next to a cemetery."

"It's cool. That's the Wizard's van. Guess they're home, but I bet they're sleeping. Don't forget it's Sunday and these guys are musicians."

"Sleeping," Chris said as he closed the Ford's door. "I doubt any-one could sleep with *that* playing."

"Sounds great to me," Mike said, the sound of the guitar inside the store momentarily ebbing.

Right. "Let's see if we can get their attention."

Chris walked to the front door. He held his head to the glass and peered in.

Inside, a guitarist was perched on a stool toward the rear of the store, a custom-color, black '55 Fender Stratocaster in hand. When there was a pause in the burning chords of musical lightning, Chris banged on the door's glass.

The Wizard looked up. Shaking his head, he yelled, "Closed!" Before he could return to his playing, Chris held up his shield. Chris didn't need to read lips to know that the Wizard uttered only one word. *"Shit!"*

Walking to the door, the flashing badge still shining in his eyes, The Mothers of Invention's "Who Are the Brain Police" began rum-bling through the Wizard's mind.

The door, with its CLOSED warning, was opened by a lanky fig-ure in worn black jeans and a loose black tank top. His expression, accented by salt and pepper stubble, a small diamond stud in his left ear, and a black Pittsburgh Pirates cap, was hostile. Embedded in the flesh of his right biceps was the face of a horned, milky-eyed Medusa, reminiscent of an H. R. Giger painting. In a soft voice of even tone he said, "Look, officer. I just got a bit carried away. I'll hold it down."

Chris smiled. "I'm not here about a complaint. I'd appreciate your help in a police matter."

A short bulky figure, a biker Buddha, wearing a deeply faded yellow sleeveless T-shirt (revealing tattoos of Odin's ravens, Hugin on his right biceps and Munin on his left) with a tie-dyed condom and

the slogan *Be Grateful NOT Dead* on the front, walked from behind a
desk in the rear of the store and stood beside the Wizard.

This must be Cosmo. The Wizard and the Warrior, Chris thought
looking at the hairy, heavily muscled figure.

"How may we help you?" the compact hulk with a Buddha belly
sporting a Diet of Worms *Earthly Delights* banana-colored do-rag
asked. "Hi, Mike. I take it you're with him? A friend?" Cosmo looked
Chris squarely in the eyes as he addressed him. "Hi. Name's Cosmo.
C'mon in. It's cold and the Wizard here detests cold. Snaaaake lover,
you know." The hissed last phrase was gleefully whispered just loud
enough for the Wizard to hear.

Chris entered the over-warm store and looked around. *Yaow!
What have I gotten myself into?* Even though Laurinda had briefly
described the shop to him, seeing it was something else entirely.

The horror emporium consumed the entirety of the first floor.
Ninety feet wide and sixty-four feet deep, The Horror Corner was the
delight of every horror fan for fifty miles with its array of locally
made resin skulls (werewolf, human, and the *Alien* creature were currently the best sellers) and wild grass-filled voodoo dolls imported
from New Orleans. One could purchase Godzilla as a model kit or a
toy figurine, eight-inch tall statuettes of Anubis, or a likeness of
Kulthus. Three ninety-five would get a collector goblin, ghoul, or
gargoyle claws made of resin. In addition to the expansive selection
of vendibles, prized one-of-a-kinds lurked everywhere: two beautifully humored Gahan Wilson renderings of Yog-Sothery hung by
autographed photos of Carter, Lumley, and Bloch, a Karloff signed
copy of *The Grinch That Stole Christmas* laughed at smoke and dust
from its glass armor, a framed and signed Alice Cooper *Killer* gate-
fold calendar still announced days two decades past, and an antique
pint bottle of reddish fluid labeled Dippel's Oil promised the promise
of a thousand snake oils and more.

Before completing his panoramic scan, Chris' gaze encountered
the store's mascot. Housed in an eight-foot by six-foot by six-foot
glass environment was a seven-foot-long albino king snake ominous-
ly dangling from a knotted tree limb. Affixed to the glass was a
plaque which read "Darkness, the Melancholy King." Chris shivered.
Excepting Bugs and the Easter Bunnys, he decidedly didn't like
rodents, wasn't much for insects, and he hated snakes.

To the left was a counter predominantly covered with models of monsters, most of which Chris didn't recognize, one of which had a hairless head that was completely covered with pins sticking from it. *Christ, he's a creepy looking bastard*, Chris thought as his revulsion turned to delight seeing two models of the creature from the film *Alien. Well, at least there's something here I recognize.*

Inside the glass counter were a myriad of vinyl masks of horrors Chris couldn't name, serial killer collectors' cards, and small, die-cast metal figurines of assorted monsters. Behind it on the wall were horror writers' autographs and handwritten pages from letters in frames. Many had price tags affixed; some of the prices were horrifying.

Covering a large section of the wall beyond the counter was a waterfall style magazine rack, filled to capacity with current and back issues of *Bone Saw, Grue, Necrofile, LORE, Midnight Shambler, Eldritch Tales*, and a dozen other horror magazines, none of which Chris had heard of. Beside them sat five sealed copies of the *1994 H. R. Giger Calendar*, the cover's bold red larvae lips bursting through fiery mists. Astride the sensual lips adorning the Giger calendar sat a few copies of the sexy, mock-horror Elvira calendar, as well as calendars filled with gargoyles, a Randall Marsden calendar called *Topology of Nightmare*, a few copies of the Psychotronic calendar, and a variety of other booklets, newsletters, and fanzines.

In the next rack fluorescent green copies of the annotated *The Shadow over Innsmouth* clashed with coral-toned copies of the second printing of Joan C. Stanley's *Ex Libris Miskatonici*, and a pink, seventh printing of the *History of the* Necronomicon. Beside the small press-issued material, horrified and horrific faces glared and shrieked at him from the glossy covers of *Fangoria, Deathrealm, Cinefantastique, Gorezone,* and *Deep Red. What the fuck are they doing to that girl?* Chris winced looking at one particular cover. *Jesus, Mary, and Joseph!*

A floor to ceiling bookcase ran the entire length of the store's front wall. One shelf held an array of various Poe treasuries and over three dozen books on or about Frankenstein. Another held collections and anthologies. There were sections labeled ghosts/hauntings, witches, werewolves, zombies/cannibals, and vampires, as well as gothic, modern, splatter, erotic, and serial killers. Stephen King and Anne Rice were libraries unto themselves.

Chris shook his head from side to side as he read titles like *The Throne of Bones, The House of the Worm, The Hastur Cycle, Satan's Lovechild,* and *Ghoul.* Another section of shelves, half a wall in length, housed videotapes. Chris scanned spines bearing titles similar to the books. *Cold Banquets, Halloween, Feast of the Undead,* and *Godzilla vs. Cthulhu. Bingo! I'm in the right place,* he thought. *The Holy Virgin Versus the Evil Dead, Busty Biker Babes vs. the Flesh Eating Zombie Clowns From Pluto. Biker Babes? Think I'll stick with Bruce Willis thrillers,* he thought. *Christ, this is Sunday, not Halloween. I ought to be at Mass, not in Schenectady's version of the American Museum of Horror.*

Standing at the edge of a matted brown carpet remnant where band equipment was set up, Chris recalled his friend Freddie's garage, doors open to the summer sunshine, where Saturday afternoons were spent in pleasure-filled attempts by the Blue-Tones at "Turn Down Day" and "Hanky Panky." As he slowly scanned the instruments he wondered if Freddie would have pursued music if he'd returned from 'Nam.

"Interested in music?" the Wizard asked.

"I'm not a nut about it, but I like music. Mostly the oldies. You guys have a lot of instruments."

"This is just the practice equipment."

All that to rehearse? Chris thought as his gaze scanned the assemblage a second time.

There stood the Wizard's now silent black Strat, perched above a fuzz box and a Vox Cry Baby wah-wah pedal, holding court in the center of the carpeting with a Martin D-28. To the right an old set of Rogers 360's with double basses, adorned in airbrushed peacock feathers, sat under six golden Sabian cymbals. Partially ringing the carpet like a great, uneven wall were six Fender amps, a Sunn bass amp, and the Wizard's irreplaceable Sears Silvertone. Mike stands, cradling three Beyerdynamic SEM 81's, stood like dead trees above a gnarled web of black wiring covering the cheap carpet. Face to face with the Strat, seemingly on guard, a sturdy wooden cross with a scarecrow's head was armed with an array of harmonicas, a ratchet, sleigh bells, a cabaca, and a leather quiver of drumsticks. Beside the wooden sentinel stood a headless metal form whose iron ribs held Cosmo's assorted musical weaponry—tambourines, maracas, wood blocks, and four large cowbells. Two feet away a pair of eighteen-inch-long rain sticks rested atop two scarlet-smeared conga drums. Each drum bore the black outline of a large eye, reminiscent of Alice Cooper's *Killer*-era eye makeup, and although Chris thought they were crudely painted, perhaps by the innocent hand of a child, something about their wide-eyed stare deeply bothered him. On the left sat a Fender Rhodes and a fifteen-year-old Oberheim Polyphonic synthesizer, and behind them a large black gong deeply inscribed with five primitively shaped runes of brilliant yellow. Chris thought they bore some resemblance to scorpions.

Horror and rock—in bed together? Chris almost laughed, thinking about a tune he'd heard in the '70's called "God Gave Rock 'n Roll to You." *Old Scratch might have something to do with this stuff—but God?* He turned to view another section of the shrine.

Behind a braided red rope barrier stood a video release, cardboard stand-up of Leatherface from *Texas Chainsaw Massacre Part 2*. Above it, in a bold crimson frame, was a large film poster of Dario Argento's *L'oiseau au plumage de cristal*. Bookending the vivid film poster was a slightly battered print of Frank Frazetta's *The Death Dealer*, and, to the right, two H. R. Giger posters—a framed 40" x 22" print of *Spell II*, and a framed and hand signed print of *Necronom IV*.

A bit beyond Giger's posters Chris paused to look at a custom-framed Randall Marsden original. Like Giger, the expatriated American surrealist Marsden, a self-proclaimed Giger admirer, merged biology with technology. Mutated women with ornately patterned scales or surreally shaped feathers occupied half-light worlds of claustrophobic fears and tormented grace. The arduous struggles of races not yet born raged on Marsden's canvases.

There was something about the painting Chris didn't like: Maybe it was the way the deep purple shadows gripped the woman's breasts, or perhaps it was the fact that Chris couldn't stand the color purple—it was oppressive to him, authoritative and cruel. Haunted and sorrowful, those were the words Chris thought of as he looked at Marsden's *Annabell's Ordeal in Shadow*. He felt drawn to the airy beauty's struggle for grace in the encroaching deep shadows cast by a landscape of outré technology. There was something in her soft frightened eyes. As her eyes held his, Chris knew she was intimate with grievous loss and the tortures endured by a gentle soul trapped in a world of madness.

It's as if I can touch her torment, he thought. *Guess if anybody's gonna know about this guy Lovecraft and his horrors, it'll be these two. Everything here is death, horror, and torment. This must be the right place.*

"She's a beauty, ain't she? Annabell, the model in all of his work, was his wife. He lost her in childbirth. Baby died too." Cosmo added in a near whisper.

More death. Does everyone suffer these nightmares? "Is this one the same painter?" Chris asked quickly stepping away from the painting to a poster apparently created by the same hand.

"Marsden, yeah. Called *A Thousand Blades in a Poet's Tear*. He died last year. Murdered in his London studio."

Chris could see the pained rage and horror contained in the single mauve teardrop. It was as if the apocalypse had been given a tiny world of its own to war upon.

Whoever this Marsden is, was, his visions speak a truth I know too well, he thought, trying to shift his gaze to some neutral spot. He found none.

". . . belonged to the Biomechanical school of surrealism created by H. R. Giger. A few years back Marsden painted two series of works based on Lovecraft."

Lovecraft. The word hooked Chris. *Please let this guy give me some answers. Maybe this is my lucky day.*

"One series was Cthulhuvian entities, unfortunately I don't own one of those, and the other series was what he called his Xothic Environments. After his wife died he lost interest in Lovecraft's monsters. One of his non-Lovecraftian paintings, *The Breeze in the Nursery*, is almost famous. You might have seen it in magazines. Two years ago it was used in a national ad campaign against child abuse. It's a mauve and dark purple painting—all his paintings are done in purplish colors. Like I was saying, it's of open French doors and an infant sleeping in a crib. Vapors are floating through the doorway, starting to form some horrific apparition. The slogan reads "Don't Let Nightmares Steal Our Children's Dreams'."

Chris tensed as Cosmo's words brought back depraved images—tiny broken necks and bloodied cherubic faces. In recent years Chris had investigated the homicide of four infants. Disgust and anger welled in him.

Above Chris' head, dangling from the ceiling like gallows victims separated from their bodies, raged a storm cloud of shrunken heads, harsh flat faces under once shiny black hair soiled by smoke and dust. Stark visages faded brown and bleached white, like bones; desert bones. *Pained, forever-tortured souls*, Chris thought, while staring at the distorted, desiccated faces; eyes and lips forever sewn together with thin, dried rawhide strips, or strands of their own hair. Focusing on one small face he was certain could have been a beautiful child in life, Chris wondered why there were so many.

God, there must be hundreds.

As he continued staring, the many blurred. He momentarily lost his mental balance as the foaming pool of twisted faces melted and meshed together forming a scared chaos, a freak show of withered masks, each straining to open its stitched shut lids. His throat tighten and his stomach soured. Something from his childhood rose, an unsettling feeling of dread. In the space of a single heartbeat, Chris wished his mother's voice would call him away from this tableau of grotesqueries. Somehow, he was certain, these eyeless beings could see him. Almost physically shaking himself loose from their ocular grip, he mentally grasped the thin lifeline of rationality.

C'mon, damn it! You know they're not real. Man oh man, this is some place. Guess I'm not in Kansas anymore. At least Rod Serling didn't greet me at the door.

Cosmo and the Wizard had been chatting with Mike about a new werewolf anthology, letting Chris take in the sights. Twice they exchanged humored, knowing glances as they observed Chris' reactions to the store's decor; they'd seen similar reactions before.

"Sorry," Chris said, realizing a couple of minutes had passed while he was woolgathering. "My name is Stewart. Schenectady PD. Homicide division. Well, you saw the badge. I assume you're aware of the prostitutes that have been murdered recently? I was hoping you could answer a few questions. I've been informed, by Mike here, that you guys could provide me with some information on H. P. Lovecraft and the Katola—"

"Kuh-THOO-loo, Chris," Mike corrected.

"Right. Katooloo Mythos. Mike has begun to give me some, ah, details. General background. He said you'd be much more knowledgeable on the subject."

"Wait a minute. You think that the Mastectomy Murders have something to do with Grandpa Theobald's myth cycle?"

"Who?"

"H. P. Lovecraft. He often called himself Grandpa Theobald. I don't mean to be rude, but this *is* a joke, right?" Cosmo asked.

"No joke. And we do think this psycho believes in this mythology. I was hoping you could help me. I've got a couple of words here—stuff from Lovecraft, and I really need to know what they mean."

"Superstitious phantasmagorical nonsense! Nothing more than horror by weak and far too vague implication. Lovecraft was merely a toothless shark. Not my cup of tea. Give me the master of ghouls, Brian McNaughton, and Barker, Slade, and Brite. Now there's the four horsemen I like to ride along with as they journey across the mindscapes of the human, and on many occasions inhuman, soul," the Wizard soliloquized. "And while you're at it, throw in McCammon, Koja, and Simmons, to make it the magnificent seven. Now there's a number. Holy, mystical, lucky. Seven days, seven seals, seven plagues, seven—"

"You'll have to forgive him. He prefers his horror a bit on the raw side. Often poetic, but always bloody. He believes the Mythos is much like the music of John Cage, entertaining ideas, no substance."

"John Cage?" Chris asked.

"20th century classical composer—member of the avant-garde. He has a work which is four minutes and thirty-three seconds of silence, and another piece entitled $0'-0''$, which allows any number of musicians to play anything they wish," Cosmo explained.

"It's the only classical work I perform," the Wizard jokingly added.

"I think I get it," Chris said.

"Can we take your coats? How about a drink? Soda or tea perhaps. Sorry we don't drink coffee," Cosmo said, trying to compose himself after Chris' revelation about the demon who had been butchering the city's prostitutes.

"Mike? Soda? I don't suppose you have any Earl Grey?" Chris asked.

"I'm sure we have some," the Wizard answered. "The Earl for you, too, Cos?"

Chris was stunned. Tea drinkers and they might have some Earl Grey sitting around. *This is my lucky day.*

"Please, on ice, thanks. You said you had words you needed defined? Can I see them? Why don't you c'mon back to my office. We'll be a little more comfortable. Besides, all my research is there," Cosmo said as he led them back to his desk.

The store's right rear corner had been turned into a makeshift office, complete with a new computer sitting atop an oversized, battleship-gray, metal desk, the sides of which were plastered with rock and roll bumper stickers.

Flanking the purring PC perched two sinister-faced gargoyles, one flat black, speckled with gray, one yellowed white. Fangs bared, wings folded, they surveyed the store like posted sentries.

"I hate to mention this, but it's important that our talk stays confidential. This is a police matter."

"Our lips are sealed tighter than Cthulhu's sunken tomb," Cosmo promised with a smile.

"Just as tightly as that little guy," the Wizard said, pointing to a brutally shriveled red face directly over Chris' head.

There's something about these two, Chris thought. They weren't what he'd expected, and they didn't seem all that strange. In fact, he was beginning to like them.

On the opposite end of the desk, between two small mahogany Buddhas (both sitting with huge bellies and glowing smiles), stood a tastefully framed photograph of a stunning young brunette, which had been signed, *Mr. Beeeeeer—Betcha By Golly, Wow, X O X O, Virve.*

Chris recognized her. He'd busted her two or three times about seven years ago, while he was working vice. Seemed like a nice kid. Working as an exotic dancer to pay for tuition at SUNY Albany, he recalled. Too bad she got caught in the mayor's political morality war. *Wish I wasn't stuck in Vice when that asshole was trying to close anything that even hinted at adult.*

Cosmo noticed Chris' gaze as the Wizard set down their drinks. "Sugar? Milk? That's Virve. She's beautiful, huh? Couldn't stand the cold here. Split for the coast two years ago," Cosmo murmured as Chris handed him a copy of the letter that had been sent to Jack Beckett. "Hmm . . . holy shit! It's one thing to read this stuff for fun, but this—it's sick. Yo, Wizard! I think you'll want to see this. It's got teeth and then some. This fucker really believes in this shit. Christ, we're all in trouble. What do you want to know?"

"Mike says you're an authority on this myth thing."

"Mythos. The Cthulhu Mythos. And I'm just a half-rabid fan with some knowledge and a few contacts."

"He told me you're writing an encyclopedia on the subject?"

"Well, I'm trying, but I'm not the only one who's had the idea. And I wouldn't call it writing, let's say compiling. Mostly it's just tinkering."

"Got it. First, I'd like background on the Mythos and this note. Whatever you can tell me. Word by word. Line by line. I'm hoping this contains something that will give us a real lead." *Or better yet, a miracle.* Chris hadn't attended church since his wife and daughter's funeral seven and a half years ago. Now here he was, sitting with this most unlikely congregation, in the most unlikely church, on a Sunday morning, praying for a miracle.

Cosmo never turned down a chance to talk Lovecraft; he hit the ground running. "First off, the Cthulhu Mythos is the literary creation of Howard Phillips Lovecraft. Very simply, the Mythos is a very large body of stories, novels, and poems, tied together by common elements: names, like Cthulhu and Nyarlathotep, dates, places, and at the core an idea, or theme, which we'll get to. These elements all occupy the same, or relatively the same, fictional universe, much like role-playing games and comics do. Beyond that, even Mythos experts and scholars can't really define Lovecraft's creation. The damn thing's evasive. And when they do get a handle on the myth cycle, someone seems to come along with a new slant and change their minds."

Chris sipped his tea and took notes while Cosmo, engrossed in his erudite rhapsody, recovered much of the ground Mike had mapped for him less than an hour earlier.

"HPL borrows a few odd elements from various mythologies and uses them, as well as his own ideas, to create his new myth cycle. From Christian mythology he takes the *Bible*, or the idea of it, and turns it into the *Necronomicon*. The *Necronomicon* is an eldritch tome of blasphemy which his characters use to invoke their dark gods. God, who represents light or good, becomes the Elder Gods in Lovecraft's myth cycle, at least in the opinion of some. I happen to be one of the some. Remember I said these are my opinions.

Lovecraft transforms Satan into the Outer Gods and the Great Old Ones, his evil deities. Paralleling the Christian God's need for man's worship, the GOO also need man as a means of escaping their prisons. They also need us for sustenance.

"Then HPL turns a version of the Apocalypse into the GOO returning to reclaim the Earth. *Voilà*, the Cthulhu Mythos. There's no equivalent of heaven and hell in the Mythos, although I guess R'lyeh could be construed as a kind of Olympus, a holy city of the gods inaccessible to man, except R'lyeh houses only Cthulhu. In creating his pseudomythology HPL borrowed names and elements from other writers. He took Hastur and Carcosa from Ambrose Bierce, and The King in Yellow from Robert Chambers. HPL had fallen under the spell of Irish fantasist Lord Dunsany, and Dunsany's cosmicism and his Peganian gods exerted great influence. Lovecraft also shares H. G. Wells' idea that life out among the stars would not be friendly or sympathetic to humanity. I view HPL much like a sparrow who gathers leaves, grass, and twigs to build his nest—Lovecraft takes a thread from here and another from there and with his found treasures and his own imagination weaves a finely wrought tapestry."

"Could you slow down a bit? I'd never make it as a secretary."

"No problem." Cosmo paused, filling his lungs with mentholated smoke as he tried to decide how to proceed. *Should I mention Lovecraftian criticism?—Ladieees and gentlemen! In this corner. The Deconstructionists. A bunch of idiotic yaps, claiming there's no Mythos. Christ! How the hell can anyone claim there's no Mythos at this point in its history? Then there's us Derlethians. Our goal is to completely detail the Mythos, often with scientific precision. Forget it. We'll travel the halls of academia later.*

"Lovecraft's myth cycle has existed since the '20's, and over the years many writers have contributed to its evolution, so the Mythos can be approached in a number of different ways. Some view it from a strictly historical perspective; others, like myself, see it in a more religious light. Your killer and I seem to have based our viewpoints on the same religious, good-versus-evil approach outlined by August Derleth. Lovecraft's pantheon of deities, like many other mythological pantheons, is tiered, although not in a strict sense, with Cthulhu just about in the middle of the whole shebang. Remind me to give you a copy of Reverend Robert M. Price's 'Theogony of the Old Ones'."

"What's that?" Chris asked.

"A genealogical account of the gods. A family tree."

"Gotcha." *Christ, I'm going to put a fictional family tree of some weirdo horror story gods in the murder book; somebody is gonna think I'm the nut.*

"The Outer Gods occupy the first tier. Like the Olympian gods, Lovecraft's gods didn't create the universe, they were created by it. By making them creatures of an evolutionary universe HPL makes them more believable, but no less incomprehensible to 20th century readers. Yet the Cthulhuvian deities retain their godly status by being for the most part unattainable to lowly man. Another factor you have to take into account is their physical appearance. Many of them resemble gigantic, horrifically mutated marine creatures, in other words, incomprehensibly alien. Other factors also contribute to their godly, or godlike status. Things like their age, which borders immortality, we know these entities are millions, possibly billions, of years old. Their powers, which are beyond our comprehension and most of the time beyond physical law. These cosmic beings stir our curiosity and our fears much like the gods of other ancient myth cycles. By the way, HPL hated seafood and was afraid of the sea—that's how Cthulhu and his aquatic minions were chosen as the bad guys."

"You mean they all look like fish?" Chris asked.

"No, but many have marine aspects, like tentacles or gills. The majority resemble reptilian-based beings. Two of the GOO are even capable of limb regeneration. A bunch look like insectoid life forms, and then others appear as strange mammalian mutations. Gnoph-Keh looks like a bearish rat with a unicorn horn. Others take on odd, or maybe I should call it monsterish, humanoid or wormish forms. Many of the GOO have wings. One of the GOO, Cthugha, looks like a cloud of living fire. A few are amorphous. There's really no rules. Here's a few pictures that will give you the general idea, if there is one. Mythos entities are almost as diverse as, let's say, life here is."

"I hardly think biodiveristy is as widespread among the Great Old Ones as it is here on Earth," the Wizard commented.

"Thank you, Mr. Darwin. Now, as I was about to say, Lovecraft wrote fourteen Mythos stories between 1921 and 1935. Almost all of them appeared in a pulp magazine called *Weird Tales*. Let me add another thing before we go on—the Mythos in HPL's stories isn't as clear-cut as, say, Greek mythology. Lovecraft felt real mythologies bear inconsistencies, and if his myth cycle were real there'd be variants between written and oral histories, as well as variants and possibly conflicts caused by differences in cultural perception. There'd also be variants caused by people from different eras. A 5th-century Chinese monk would see things in a distinctly different light, than say a 18th-century British metaphysician, or a late 20th-century American cosmologist. Over the decades many Mythos writers have tried to iron out the wrinkles and make the Mythos a bit more cohesive."

"Does this thing get less convoluted as we go along?" Chris asked.

"No. We're not talking about Conan or Burroughs' Martian stories. And while we're mentioning Conan, let's move along to other writers who contributed to the Mythos. Lovecraft encouraged, or at least didn't discourage, other writers from adding to or expanding upon his, as he called it, pseudomythology. So other authors like Frank Belknap Long, Henry Kuttner, and Robert E. Howard, who created Conan the Barbarian, and August Derleth, a rabid Lovecraft devotee, did just that. By the way, Derleth's opinions and contributions to the Mythos are vital to its development and we'll explore them in depth later. Robert Bloch, the author of *Psycho*, I'm sure you've seen Hitchcock's film, was also a notable contributor. These people and others added deities, there's over seventy of the GOO at this point."

"Goo?" Chris asked, wondering for the fifth time what "goo" meant.

"That's what I call the Great Old Ones. G-O-O. GOO."

"GOO. Okay."

"As things went along these writers added new places, people, and forbidden books. Old, evil grimoires or sorcerers' handbooks, which contain spells, histories, descriptions, legends, and warnings about the horrors of the Mythos. There are currently over sixty of these dark books of knowledge in the Mythos. I can give you a list if you like."

"Thanks. It might be helpful."

"In the sixties and seventies a new generation of, if you'll pardon the expression, disciples came along to further expand the Mythos. Ramsey Campbell and Brian Lumley are two of the better known of these disciples. As we speak, the Lovecraft circle continues to expand with writers like Brian McNaughton, T. E. D. Klein, Stephen Mark Rainey, Thomas Ligotti—who creates more atmosphere and tension in a single sentence than most create in an entire novel—Will Murray, Don Burleson, and my dear friend, mentor, and head Mythos informant, the madcap Mr. Thomas Hartwell Desmond. You might have read his recent bestseller *Eyes of Stone Tears of Rage*."

"I haven't read it, but I've seen it. My friend Lauri read it. Was it a Mythos book?"

"No, but it does make two small references to the Mythos. It's about the murder of a young homeless woman and a vengeance-seeking gargoyle who loved her from afar. It's part adult fairy tale/love story, sorta a *Beauty and the Beast*, and part murder mystery. Whole thing's really a lengthy metaphor. Takes place here in Schenectady. The gargoyle lives atop that white office building on the corner of State and Ferry. It was inspired by these two," Cosmo said, pointing to a pair of large gargoyles, made by Distortions Unlimited, perched on his desk. "This one's Ignatius, means fiery in Latin, and this is Cornelius, he's named for the Wizard's previous lampropeltis."

"Lampro what?"

"King snake. I'm a big gargoyle nut. It all started with the Grey Gargoyle in *Journey into Mystery*; Thor's comic. Then when I saw the made-for-TV movie in '72; well, Jennifer Salt in that white halter top, talk about lust at first sight, and Bernie Casey as the gargoyle. I was a big Rams fan at the time."

"I'll say he's nutty about gargoyles. Has three backup copies of the movie upstairs just in case something happens to his primary. Probably has about twenty more of these upstairs," the Wizard said while pointing at the pair of gargoyles. "Somewhat smaller though. He's been planning to put a couple up on the roof for years now. Says it'll keep the demons away," he added with a chuckle.

"With this nut walking around we could use 'em," Cosmo said.

"I doubt he's going to show up looking for us," came the Wizard's retort.

"Gargoyles, huh. Maybe they'll be tied to my next case," Chris said in an attempt to bring Cosmo back to the subject of Lovecraft.

"Right. Sorry, I sorta ramble. Another member of the new Lovecraft circle is the brilliant and beautiful Maria Paulina Houdon. She writes poetic, tortured historical romances of betrayal, madness, and death, set within the confines of the Mythos. She's also an accomplished poet, with two intricate volumes of Mythos poetry. The first volume is in the form of Shakespearean sonnets, and the second, which I prefer, is in the French form, the *villanelle*. And there's other poets contributing, Mollie Burrleson and Ann Schwader. These are some of the current torchbearers of Lovecraft's legacy. Just about all modern horror writers owe a debt to Lovecraft, and many have contributed to the Mythos. Even Stephen King has contributed a couple of stories to the Mythos. All the books and magazines in these bookcases deal with the Mythos," Cosmo said, pointing to the bookcases lining the wall near his desk. "The books in this other one are reference books about Lovecraft's work and life. As you can see, there are quite a few. We've got L. Sprague de Camp's biography of Lovecraft, and Robert M. Price's wonderful *H. P. Lovecraft and the Cthulhu Mythos*. Tierney's *The Derleth Mythos*, Lévy's *Lovecraft: A Study in the Fantastic*, Mallard Sharpe's *Cthulhu: Alien or God*, Peter Cannon's *Sunset Terrace Imagery in Lovecraft*, and Tyler Sinclair's *Grandpa Theobald*. This one here is very interesting. It's supposed to be the *Necronomicon* itself. That's Lovecraft's black bible I mentioned. Did Mike tell you about it?"

"No. I don't think so," Chris said as he leafed through his notes.

"Sorry, I forgot about it," Mike said.

"It's okay. You're not an expert, remember?" Chris said.

"So, let's see, the mad Arab, Abdul Alhazred, was butchered by invisible claws and devoured during broad daylight in Beled el Djinn, the city of devils. Alhazred wrote his book in the 8th-century A. D. The most often quoted line from the book is, 'That is not dead that can eternal lie, and with strange aeons even death may die.' That's your couplet. It refers to Cthulhu himself, who lies dreaming of reconquering the world while in a city sunken under the Pacific. The *Necronomicon* is about a thousand pages long. Of all the forbidden books in the Mythos it is the most complete. It contains histories, spells, prophecies, etc. Just about every author who has contributed to Lovecraft's demon-filled genealogy has quoted from it once or twice."

"Can I read that?" Chris asked, pointing to the paperback Cosmo was holding.

"It's fake. As far as I'm concerned this *Necronomicon* has nothing to do with the Mythos. This is little more than a joke," Cosmo said with a wide smile which seemed ready to burst into boisterous mirth. "No one has yet attempted to write the fictional work. Many fans, including myself, feel it would be impossible to write the book and do it justice. Most writers just quote a line or two. Sometimes they'll describe the contents of a chapter, but that's about it, except for this book here. It came out in nineteen-eighty and according to the editor, someone named Simon, this is the real McCoy, although it doesn't read like I envision Alhazred's horrific tome would. Most fans and critics just disregard it. Now the interesting thing is that it was rumored that a cult in Arizona has actually tried to invoke some of the GOO with the incantations and spells contained in this book. Crazy, really crazy. Weirdos out there thinking the Mythos is real. This is entertainment, just a seventy-year-old literary parlor game. Sorry, I guess I got off track. It's just that I love this stuff so much. I can't believe that some wacko out there thinks this is real. I mean here in Schenectady, of all the places."

"Nobody ever thinks these things happen where they live," the Wizard said.

"Thank you, Mr. Zappa. Still, it's *bizarre*," Cosmo said. "Especially in this cultural tuna sandwich. Sorry, where was I? Oh yeah, your letter. Are you sure this is from the Mastectomist?"

"We're fairly certain it's him," Chris replied. *The letter's clean. No fingerprints, and the stamp was moistened with water, not saliva. It's him. He's finally crawled out of his hole looking for recognition.*

"Unbelievable. Kassogtha. Hot-damn! I can't believe I'm seeing her name. Of all the GOO to choose from—he picks *her*. Man, she's a Mythos deity that's not very well known. Only the most devout reader, and a lucky one at that, or someone who just happened upon her by accident, would know of her. As far as I know she's the rarest Mythos deity."

Chris almost asked why, but checked his question. He was starting to get a feel for Cosmo's rambling presentation and knew his anecdotal cul-de-sacs would eventually lead to an answer.

"The first story she appears in is W. Shorter's 'Kassogtha's Song.' It was published by Morning Lake Press, Boston, Mass. In an anthology called *The Black All-Seeing Eyes of Night*, edited by Dom Vitous. I have a copy here," he said, removing the book from a sealed plastic bag. "Copyright 1971. This is rare. Only a couple hundred copies were printed, probably all sold in the Boston area. Over the years I've only met six or seven guys, all writers by the way, who have ever read or even heard of this story. In the story she's described as being a hollow, snakelike being, devoid of head or tail; one end filled with horny or clawish looking teeth, something like the mouth of a lamprey. Imagine a nest of snakes shaped like a gigantic heart, then imagine that mass is a single entity. Shorter's snake-goddess is covered with doorway-sized, vagina-like orifices, which ooze some form of putrid smelling, slimy substance. These orifices are surrounded by small phallic-like tentacles, nine or ten feet long. Overall, this monstrosity appears as a large mass of writhing snakes, which have, let's say, knotted themselves together. Although it's not stated, it's implied that if this entity was untangled, it would be a mile, or perhaps miles, long and probably wide enough to drive a car through.

"Shorter's story is about a rock band that rents a house in the mountains, somewhere in Vermont or New Hampshire, I forget which, to compose songs for their sophomore album. Shorter took the idea from The Band and *Big Pink*. While there, the band meets a large group of beautiful women, who are members of a cult that worships Kassogtha. Using sex as inducement these women try to lure the band into a ceremony where they will be sacrificed to Kassogtha. When the last band member is killed, Kassogtha will reenter this world to rule. At the end of the story a gateway partially opens and Kassogtha takes the band members before the gateway suddenly closes. One band member escapes. As the story closes, we find him a patient in a mental institution, stark raving mad."

"How the hell do you remember all that?" the Wizard asked.

"It just moves in and roots itself I guess. Now, there are only three other references to Kassogtha that I'm aware of. The first one is by Lin Carter, one of the most undervalued heirs of Lovecraft, at least as far as I'm concerned. His 'Zoth-Ommog', in *The Disciples of Cthulhu* is essential. There's a German record company named after Zoth-Ommog. They put out industrial dance music. You know, fast, noisy, hundreds of beats per minute. The kind of stuff they play at raves. I never paid any attention to it, except they put out a record by someone named Mentallo and The Fixer I was always going to buy just because of the name."

"Comic book bad guys, right? Nick Fury, I think," Chris said.

"Yeah! Hey, that's great. You read comics?" Cosmo asked.

"Way back. A few, The Avengers and Thor. The Fantastic Four and Captain America were my favorites," Chris replied.

"Man, I loved Thor, and Spider-Man. And I think Cos' love of the occult was born in the pages of *Strange Tales*," the Wizard said.

"It was indeed, but the Thing was my idol," Cosmo said.

"I liked Ben Grimm too, but we were talking about Lin Carter and his connection to the Mythos."

"Sorry. He also wrote a wonderful reference book on the Mythos. Here it is! *Lovecraft: A Look behind the Cthulhu Mythos*. She's not in this, Lin wrote this before he wrote the story that mentions her. Lin, I'm very sorry to say, left us in '88. Cancer. Damn, I miss him. Nice guy, and he wrote a bunch of wonderful stories, not just Mythos stories either. There's the Callisto series and the Thongor books. Lin was a damn fine editor as well. He's responsible, in part anyway, for my interest in Lovecraft. And he certainly livened up a convention or two. I remember him and the Wizard at one convention, hell, they must have spent close to three hours in a discussion of Burroughs this and Howard that. It was Barsoom versus Callisto, and Verne's core or Pellucidar. Man, they were like two kids."

"I don't mean to be rude, but what do Burroughs' Martian stories or Jules Verne have to do with Lovecraft? Could we get back to the Mythos?" Chris asked.

"Sorry. Carter mentions Kassogtha in his story 'Nctosa and Nctolhu', which appeared in *Mysterious Travelers Volume II*, published by Vertical Invader Press. Another very rare book. Nctosa and Nctolhu are Kassogtha's twin daughters, sired by her brother, Cthulhu. They're imprisoned on Jupiter, in a hurricane three times the size of Earth, called the Great Red Spot of Jupiter. Story's from '75. In the story, Lin states that Kassogtha is their mother and Cthulhu's their sire, that's it. Basically it's one line. See, Kassogtha is/was, whichever . . . . She was Cthulhu's third mate. His first was Idh-yaa, then there was Sk'tai, who he murdered. Kassogtha's next appearance is much like the one in Lin's story . . . Inger Lise Aasterud writes Cthulhuvian tales involving the 9th century Norwegian mage and warrior Turgeis Herjulfsson. Her novel *Black Tales beyond the Northern Ice* is the story of Herjulfsson's first deranging journey into Mythos country, which takes him four years by the way. Ms. Aasterud writes of Turgeis' adventures in the lost ice city of

Kmorheim, his imprisonment in Imbelinn, and his discoveries in the great hall in Tyryar. In Tyryar he confronts the Great Old One Rynvik, who lives partially submerged in a crimson pool with his harem. Held prisoner and roughly tutored by Rynvik's eldest son, Ult, who wants Herjulfsson to find the means to free his father, the black-hearted adventurer learns that Rynvik's three sons' mother is the dreaming king's snake-goddess. One can only assume the dreaming king is Cthulhu, and the snake-goddess, Kassogtha. Again, it's basically one sentence about Kassogtha."

"Christ. All that, for that one little tidbit? Cos, ever heard the phrase, get to the point?" the Wizard asked.

"Yeah. The last story Kassogtha's in, is mine. It sits locked in this drawer. Unpublished and virtually unread. And I might add, never discussed, except with my bro' here. Now, my little story here is called 'The Hand of Zwnul.' It's about a priest driven by avarice and lust, who loses his hand, his sanity, and ultimately his life by trying to obtain a jewel and an arcane book of demonology that would open the doorway of Kassogtha's prison. Again let me emphasize, no one but the Wizard and I know anything about this story. Sorry it took so long to get here. I know I ramble too much, but if this killer knows of Kassogtha he's got some deep knowledge on this subject. I mean *very* deep. So unless your killer is Bob Price, Don Burleson, or Steven Mariconda, they're a few notable Lovecraft scholars, he's got a lot of time and money to seek out and absorb this stuff."

"Shit," Chris muttered. "I'm going to have to deputize you guys. I hope your consulting fees are reasonable?"

"We drink Pabst. Preferably tall boys," the Wizard said. At twelve a rabid Sherlock Holmes junkie, and now, in addition to horror, a devout fan of Raymond Chandler, Andrew Vachss, and Michael Slade, he was delighted to be involved in solving a real-life murder mystery.

"Okay. First you've got a ton of reading to do, if you're going to understand what this butcher believes in. Stories about the Mythos have appeared in novels, anthologies, and the small press—houses like Necronomicon Press, Fedogan & Bremer, and Arkham House. And then there's the fanzines and the small circulation magazines like *Crypt of Cthulhu, LORE, Cemetery Dance,* and *Midnight Shambler.* There are numerous reference books, in addition to Carter's, on the

subject of Lovecraft and his work. Even today the Mythos grows at a
rate that I find hard to keep up with. Good thing we've got a spare
room. But don't worry, rent's cheap."

*I've got to spend time here, with all this stuff? Christ, I don't even like
horror.*

"Now, to your letter. Cattle. The Mythos deities consider
humans prey. We're food, plain and simple. Imagine the universe as
a great ocean dotted with islands. Islands which bear spices or
wealth. Not unlike, let's say Columbus, the GOO are looking for
new worlds, worlds filled with riches. In this case the riches happen
to be food and the Earth is a rich island.

"In the next line, I assume the seven steps refer to the dead prostitutes. Seven down and we've no idea what he's using them for or
how many he needs for his ritual. But he's not finished. He says so
right here. Next. The alignment of the stars. That appears in a lot of
Mythos stories. See, these beings or gods are *outside*, imprisoned,
waiting to come back and reclaim the Earth. In the stories, someone
or some cult is waiting for when the time is right to hold a rite of passage. This would allow the GOO to reenter this world. Your freak
here is ready to conduct one of these ceremonies. Oh shit! How did
I forget this? There was a second cult that bought into this myth
cycle. Back in the late seventies there was a cult, twenty or so members strong, which worshiped Cthulhu—no, Hastur. Anyway, they
were based out in Oregon somewhere. I'm certain they were linked
to two or three deaths; sacrificial murders. Two young women and a
child as I recall. Some of the members went to jail. They're doing life.
I think it was around '76, '77."

"You're shittin' me, right?" Chris asked while writing notes to
check with police agencies in Arizona, Oregon, and the FBI regarding cult activity.

"No. This is the straight-up skinny. Dark ceremonies and human
sacrifices. I remember someone at a con telling me about it. Later, I
saw it mentioned in the press, somewhere. Maybe in a magazine.
Scary shit. You take me and the Wiz here. This is our business. It's
fun. Just two big kids playing with ghost stories, but we don't believe
in any of this crap. Fuck that noise. Vampires, werewolves, monsters.
It's all a game to us. But your psycho, he's real and he's not playing a
game. The next part of his letter, here, the one that begins, *Iä, Iä,*

Kassogtha. Translates to 'I hunger, I hunger, Kassogtha.' *Iä* starts most spells and rites in the Mythos. Your couplet comes directly from Lovecraft's writing, it's in 'The Call of Cthulhu', and it pertains to Cthulhu himself. Remember I mentioned, 'That is not dead'?"

"Yes. The mad Arab's bible."

"Right. This rune, or mark, presumably his signature, baffles me. It might be an eye, or maybe these marks here are fangs. Maybe the circle is the universe? I really have no idea. I'll look around, it might come from something, but I don't think so."

"Are there any local Lovecraft fan clubs this butcher might be involved in?" Chris asked.

"Fan clubs no, but there is role-playing."

"Never heard of it."

"It's a type of gaming where the players try to resolve a story line or adventure by becoming or controlling one or more characters. Have you ever heard of *Dungeons and Dragons?*"

"Yeah, I recall Mike playing it."

"Not for a while. Got bored with it."

"Okay. There's a chance, a small one mind you, that this guy might have been involved with role-playing at some point. Maybe he still is, but I doubt it. There's a company in Oakland, California called Chaosium. They produce a role-playing game called *Call of Cthulhu*. Naturally it's based on the Cthulhu Mythos. Okay, you've got two possibilities here. One, out on Central Avenue there's a place called Imagination Comics, they carry the game and the figures that go with it. This is one of the figures. It's an Elder Thing, and this one is Cthulhu; cost me fifty bucks. Fantaco in Albany also carries most of the stuff. Either place might help. Maybe they know of some rabid player. Hmmmm . . . I don't know, but there might be some kind of connection. See, Chaosium makes almost sixty reference and scenarios books for the original game. They also make Miskatonic University T-shirts, Mythos posters, and Cthulhu for President bumper stickers, as well as imitation Miskatonic University degrees. As you might expect I have all three," Cosmo said, pointing to three framed Miskatonic U. degrees (a bachelor's, a master's, and a doctorate, all in scholarly-looking Latin).

"They also produce a series of books, Call of Cthulhu fiction. Here's my point. Chaosium has a subscription service. Every time a new book or game scenario comes out, it's automatically sent to you if you're on the list. If your killer is into this stuff, maybe they've got his name and address on file. He might have purchased a degree or two, or maybe some of the books. Here's their address and phone number, but they're not open on Sunday. Talk to Lynn or Charlie. They're both very knowledgeable cats. They're in Oakland. Number's 510-555-7681."

Might be a good lead. "Is there any part of or story in this Mythos that mentions severing women's breasts as part of some sacrifice, or something to that effect? I'm trying to figure out what he's doing with the breasts he's harvesting."

"If you ask me, he's either eating them or playing with them," the Wizard interjected.

Chris involuntarily shuddered at the thought of cannibalism.

"Sacrifices in the Mythos are almost always human, but they usually involve killing the victim, not taking pieces of them as trophies. Although sometimes the brains or heart are taken or eaten. Taking breasts is a new one. The Wizard might be right about this guy eating them. More than a few of these animals are cannibals."

How the hell did we breed one of these horrors here? "Would you guys mind if we took a break? I need to fill my partner in. Could I use your phone? One other thing, could you two teach a crash course on the Mythos to six cops? Today if possible. You guys interested?"

"Bring 'em on," the Wizard said. A serial killer/horror fiction fan—he was hooked. Walking away, he began singing a line from an old Human League song about being both vengeance and the law.

"Look, Chris," Cosmo said, "We haven't even started to scratch the surface yet. I've been a Mythos buff since 1970 and I don't know anywhere near it all. The only thing I know is you've got a shitload of research to do if you're going to catch this freak."

"Shit." Chris lit the first cigarette from the day's second pack.

"Something else occurs to me. Schenectady has a direct connection to one of Lovecraft's non-Mythos stories. There's an old house in the Stockade on Green Street. I forget the number, but it's right where the houses on the street change from wood constructions to brick. It was built on a site that was a Dutch graveyard which was moved as the city grew. The house provided partial inspiration for HPL's 'The Shunned House.' Lovecraft was attracted to

Schenectady's shunned house by a legend that says there was a 'whitish pattern on the dirt floor' of the cellar which looked like the silhouette of a human, and no matter what was tried, the disquieting shape couldn't be removed. It was rumored to be the grave of a vampire impaled to the spot by a spell. Which is fascinating as it's the only tale of vampirism in New York State history. Both Schreffler in *The H. P. Lovecraft Companion* and de Camp in his biography mention the legend. Lovecraft discovered the details in Charles Skinnner's *Myths and Legends of Our Own Land*. The main branch of the library has a copy. It's old and rare, so you can't check it out, but you can read it. Ten years ago you had to sign to examine the library's rare editions, but they did away with that requirement years ago. It's too bad too, because if they still kept records, it might have provided you with a list of names to check out. I'll bet if this monster is a native Schenectadian he looked at the book sometime. Every local Lovecraft buff I know has. Me included."

At three p.m., five homicide investigators armed with pens and notebooks filed into The Horror Corner for class. The remaining two members of the task force were not present. They were a few short blocks away, manning telephones.

❦ Chapter Five ❦

Gregory Bradshaw Marsh spent many nights of his youth cowering in a corner of his darkened bedroom. When the agony gripped him, he desperately tried not to scream, knowing exactly what horrors his pained cries and moans would summon. The headaches he had suffered since shortly after his sixth birthday were agonizing. Yet the beatings he underwent at the hands of his stepfather were far worse.

Sometime shortly after dinner, which was served promptly at six-fifteen or else, the J&B that Herbert Walters had begun drinking at five-thirty kicked in. Usually he put away three or four doubles before dinner. If dinner went well and the house remained quiet he would retire to the library after dessert and settle in with his paper and the remainder of the bottle. Most evenings he was asleep in his armchair by nine.

These were the nights that Sonia Arnold Walters spent each afternoon praying for. If all went well he wouldn't beat her or the child that she had never wanted, the child she loathed. Sonia Walters lived in hell. Either she had to endure his beatings, or sometimes, even worse, his lusts. First the horror at her father's hands, now her husband's. Worse yet were the nights she had to try to comfort the child she still wished had died in her womb. If Gregory did not suffer those headaches, if he could remain quiet and unnoticed, she felt the beatings would stop. But the beatings went on, and while she tried her best to silence the child, holding him close to her ample bosom, speaking to him in soft tones, she found all her attempts barren. Nothing would quiet him.

Herbert Walters had spent a small fortune on doctors trying to cure his stepson's headaches. As yet, the doctors had been unable to accomplish anything. They had no explanation for them. Sonia knew all too well why the boy suffered.

All male children descended from her great-great-grandfather, Captain Obed Marsh, patriarch of the Innsmouth Marshes (and rumored sire of many of the Newburyport Marshes), had suffered these headaches. They were passed from father to son, and she was well aware they were incurable. They were locked into bloodlines.

Bloodlines which began when Ida Louise Marsh bore a son sired by her father Captain Obed Marsh.

At seventeen, Sonia fled Innsmouth. To escape the nightmares suffered at the hands of father, she took the only bus—an antiquated machine which periodically backfired and belched black smoke—for Arkham, where she boarded a train for Boston and freedom. Standing in the train station in Boston, she learned that her funds were insufficient to take her to Chicago or Philadelphia. She was informed that Albany, New York was as far as she would be able to go. *That will do for now*, she told herself.

Two years later, she was living in a simple but nice flat in Schenectady, New York, with her infant son. Sonia had found employment as an accounting clerk at the Walters Baking Company. Things were going well. The following year she moved to Clifton Park as Herbert Walters' wife. She had entered into marriage with Herbert Walters feeling his wealth and power might protect her from the cruelly authoritarian and abhorrent grasp of her father. For almost three years she had lived in fear that her loathsome father, or one of his minions, would come to reclaim his prize. Little did she understand, on her wedding day, that she had exchanged one kind of monster for another.

Shortly after Gregory turned nine, he started believing his headaches were communications from some place or thing he could not yet understand. He found what he thought was his first clue in a comic book he purchased at Baum's newsstand one Saturday morning, while shopping with his mother. The comic told the tale of an astronaut stranded on Mars, who was being driven insane by Martians (they were sending painful noises into his space helmet). The Martians feared if he returned to Earth with the gemological information he'd acquired, Mars would be overrun by earthlings.

Young Marsh was now certain that his painful headaches were caused by his inability to interpret the messages he was receiving. He knew the messages weren't intended to harm him. The pain arose because he failed to reply. Once he could understand and respond, his pain would disappear. On that Saturday he began his silent search for the key to understanding these encoded messages.

Marsh was an intelligent child. He was also an excellent student, when the headaches didn't interfere with his studies. Now that he had discovered the cause of his agony, he plunged into his studies with a zealot's vigor. Somewhere in the books of his stepfather's library he was certain the knowledge existed that he needed to end his suffering. Over the next four years he searched in vain. One sunny August afternoon in 1965 he thought he heard elements of the messages coming from a radio.

Gregory, hurried along by his mother, had come out of Proctor's arcade in downtown Schenectady. When his mother stopped to check her shopping list, he heard the sound coming from a small Motorola 9-volt transistor radio. He was mesmerized by the sound emanating from the tiny black box.

"What's that?" he asked, pointing to the radio in the older teenager's hand.

"A radio, kid," sneered the youth.

"Not the radio. I mean the song that's playing. Do you know its name?"

"Don't you know anything? It's the Rolling Stones, kid. The Rolling Stones. 'Satisfaction.' It's rock 'n roll. Rock 'n roll, kid," he said as he quickly walked away, leaving Marsh with his first clue.

Less than ten minutes later, Gregory and his mother were in Apex Music Korner, asking the proprietor, Larry, for the Rolling Stones' "Satisfaction." Into the bag went Marsh's first rock and roll recording.

An hour and a half later, he took the single from the yellow bag and placed it on the Zenith record player in his bedroom. From the speakers came the mesmerizing sound he'd heard earlier and for the next three minutes and forty-five seconds he was lost in it. Something was here, he could feel it. Something alive in the music, parts of the bass line, and of the lower frequency notes of the guitars, resembled elements of the noise that screamed in his head.

There was also a sheet of paper in the bag: the **WTRY BIG GREAT 98 SOUND SURVEY.** At number nineteen sat the Rolling Stones. Above it was Bob Dylan's "Like a Rolling Stone", and the Beatles' "Help", and one, listed below it, at number twenty-five, he knew he would have to obtain. It was called "We Gotta Get Out of This Place", by the Animals. Gregory Bradshaw Marsh was certain some of the other songs on this list might help him to understand the noises in his head. Here, in this music that the teenager with the radio had called rock and roll, was the means of unscrambling the messages he was unable to stop or understand.

Over the next four years he pursued this music called rock and roll with a boundless lust, continuously searching for the key that would decode the messages in his head. He spent countless hours in Apex Music Korner, playing the B sides of singles on the three turntables at the side of the store, listening for answers. But only small pieces came to him.

Pieces of his answer came from Iron Butterfly, in "Iron Butterfly Theme", and Blue Cheer's "Out of Focus." Glimmerings were everywhere. He discerned elements in Hendrix's elaborate leads, in the sounds that came from the lugubrious organ on Vanilla Fudge's albums, in the twin screaming guitars of the MC5. Slowly, he began to understand Morrison's howls and *Tommy*'s mania. If only he could put the sound fragments together, he'd have the message.

Bag upon bag of singles and LP's were purchased. Almost every Saturday brought some new recording: Steppenwolf's explosive *heavy metal thunder* or the Grateful Dead's cosmic "Dark Star." CCR's "Bad Moon Rising" fought for playing time against Grand Funk's "Paranoia." Can's *Monster Movie* played in his head, while Zappa's Mothers freaked out, and the Stooges blazed through "1969". Platter after platter spun on his turntable as he continued searching for a rawer, louder sound, the twin of the harsh, blurred resonance that reverberated within his mind.

It was during the fall of '68 that he attended his first concert. While getting a book from his locker he overheard two of his fellow high school students talking about one of the bands, the Black Abyss, which was to perform at the concert. "My brother says they play these long, rambling psychedelic nightmares. Imagine if Hendrix was into witchcraft and space travel," young Marsh heard them say.

For a reason he couldn't explain, he felt he had to see this show. And see it he did. The multicolored lights flashed. The thunderous vibration of an amplified bass. Dissonance reigned. Guitars screamed. He was so overwhelmed by the opening act, the Black Abyss, that he didn't stay to see the show's headliner, H. P. Lovecraft. He was saddened, even angered, the following Saturday, when he was informed by Larry, at Apex Music Korner, that the Black Abyss had no recording available.

After the concert the frequency and the intensity of the headaches increased. They now exercised their crushing influence at least once a week. Marsh would not discover the cause for another three years.

In 1969 he purchased a recording by an up and coming "eclectically arty" British band solely for its cover. Marsh couldn't explain why, yet he felt a distinct connection to the starkly painted cover where washed-out red tones permeated the face of a black-toothed crone contorted by fear. Strangely engrossed in the palpable terror in her eyes, he thought, perhaps, she was a witch about to be burned for her blasphemous transgressions. Yes, he was certain, more certain with every stimulating second his gaze remained fixed, that the reddish cast of the pain-distorted face was caused by fire.

Marsh delighted in the severe image. Closing his eyes, he heard the anguished scream of the woman, her lips peeled back in terror as her frantic bulging eyes were riveted to . . . what? Were the tips of the fagots surrounding her aflame? He stared at her flared nostrils. Could she smell the burning wood? He looked again at the panic that had seized her eyes. Were the bundles of fagots dry? Or perhaps they were just cut—green. He smiled at the idea of a quieter fire dispensing a slower, more painful death.

The minutes passed as he considered the cover. At the end, what did the screaming eyes behold? What vision raped her soul?, he wondered, hoping his answer lay under the shrinkwrapped cover. It didn't.

Most of the eight songs on Knights Templars' *Seen Through the Lens of Distortion* were a disappointment with their pretentious classical pastiches and attempted jazz interludes, but the opening song, "Mankind, Unclean", held him. He repeatedly returned the song, letting Hugh Knight's searing guitar work, bonded atop piercing horns, burn into his brain. And then there were the lyrics. Fragments. Some of them would not leave him. " . . . In the brutal claws of exile . . . screams for freedom . . . behind the prison doors . . . blood-racked pain . . . unjust tormenters . . . ten-thousand agonies bleed."

Poetic fragments from some of the other songs spoke to him as well: " . . . behind the black gates . . . veined with cracks . . . implements of death . . . when all men are torn apart by nightmares forming . . . truth is a deadly friend . . . the fate of mankind is at last revealed . . . the corroded chains of prison gates are shattered . . . I walk strange roads blown by shifting winds . . . in a long forgotten tongue . . . the once silent voices will sing . . . to summon back . . . I strive to grasp the prophesy . . . the faithful will pull the strings."

Somewhere in these snippets of lyrics, in the muted musique concrete layered beneath the quintet's rock and roll fire, there was something. Now more than ever he was certain the noise in his head was a message. Marsh began to feel he was getting close to finally understanding the puzzle.

Hours were spent pouring through countless books. Science fiction. Poetry. History and mythology. Growing, learning, searching. Always keeping his radio on. Listening. Always listening, waiting for that one new song that would unlock the door that held his answer prisoner.

As he developed, shedding the confinement of his adolescence, the beatings became less frequent. Gregory had grown into a tall, powerful man. He now towered over his slim stepfather. Soon he would be free.

September of 1969 also brought college. At the age of seventeen, he had enrolled at Union College as a history major. Knowledge was now at his fingertips. The first time he entered the library of Union College's campus he felt it. The air was alive with it. There was an answer here. Somewhere in these stacks it was waiting. Now, all he had to do was uncover it.

Two years passed, but still no answers became apparent. Strengthened by the draught, he shook off disappointment. He knew they would come.

Two years later, in September of 1971, while returning home from a trip to New York City, his parents died in an automobile accident on the New York State Thruway. Gregory Bradshaw Marsh had been nineteen for almost a year. He had no siblings and his stepfather had no living relatives. Gregory Bradshaw Marsh inherited his stepfather's fortune. His time was at hand.

At 11:35 a.m., on October 17, 1971, Marsh left the offices of his stepfather's lawyers. All the papers that would turn the family fortune over to him had been signed. Freedom had arrived in the form of seventeen million dollars. To celebrate, he decided to walk the five blocks downtown and buy some records or perhaps a few books. On his way downtown he decided to skip the record stores. Later he'd drive uptown and browse through the cutout bins at J. M. Fields department store for albums. First he was off to the Union Book Company.

Scanning the books for twenty minutes, he began to feel he was wasting his time. He hadn't found a thing in the history or reference sections. Frustrated, he decided to look at the science fiction paperbacks before leaving the store.

There they sat, four Ballantine Books paperbacks, with those covers.

Four faces of nightmare glared out at him. The first held a skull, the upper three quarters devoid of flesh, its brains shooting through three jagged holes in its top. Beside the first, the face of a fanged man, the lower half made of fleshy bricks, the top riddled by worms burrowing into its brain. To the right of the second, a balding, bulging-eyed face of dissolving clouds. And the final cover. The sunken-cheeked face of horror itself. Pressure pushed its eyes from their sockets and the skull was split open, from crest to chin. From the fissure, red bats were fleeing. The only reason the skull had not completely split apart was a band of metal, affixed like a sweatband across the forehead, holding the two halves together. Attached to the iron band, where nose and mouth should have been, was a large padlock. The cover reflected his frustration; his answers were desperately trying to shatter the walls of their prison. He had to own it.

The book was entitled *The Tomb and Other Tales*, by H. P. Lovecraft. Where had he seen this name before? Yes. The rock band, he'd seen their records. They had played at the concert he'd left early.

What a fool I've been!

Without examining the contents of the books he held tightly in his hands, he took his finds to the front counter and purchased them. He hurriedly walked the few short blocks to Apex Music Korner, where he was informed that H. P. Lovecraft's albums were currently out of print.

Twenty-five minutes later Gregory Bradshaw Marsh was looking through the cutout bins of J. M. Fields, where he found two recordings by the rock band H. P. Lovecraft and the Black Abyss' *Dark Garden*. The latter he had been searching for these last three years. On fire with expectation, he flew home with his newfound treasures, and spent two hours immersed in the three albums he'd purchased. Pouring over the covers, reading and rereading the liner notes. Memorizing lyrics.

Seven years of buying and listening to rock and roll records, hoping to find the key, and now he felt it was in his hands. Yet he still couldn't grasp it. Suddenly his thoughts went back to the books. That was it. The books held the key to deciphering the sounds on the records.

Marsh took the books from the bag and reexamined them. The faces on the covers reasserted their hold over him, like a snake holds a bird, frozen in a dance of death. Death—the ultimate prison. Prisoner, he thought, mentally holding the word up for inspection. The word awakened something within him. It was part of the message. He was certain that even the covers themselves were part of the message. Yes, the pain was caused by the writhing thoughts in his head trying to burst through. Marsh opened the books to see who had painted these visions. John Holmes. Surely Holmes was in communication with, what? Across from the page that held the artist's name, he saw the name. Cthulhu.

It was also on the cover. *Tales of the Cthulhu Mythos Volume 1.* Cthulhu? He knew he was close. Marsh read the book's introduction. It was there. A race of gods held prisoner, outside the boundaries of earth, below its seas and crust. Mastery of the planet had been torn from their grasp. Now they were trying to get back in. He swiftly read on, consuming the words, sometimes entire paragraphs of them, in chunks. Like a ravening animal he slaked his hunger, missing more than a few details in his gluttonous haste.

Hours later, he set down the book, his head pounding. The pain was more intense than it had ever been.

"Why?"

He was beginning to understand, wasn't he? The pain should have diminished, but it didn't. Almost every page held new elements of the message. On page 38 he discovered the worm-eaten tome of blasphemous, forbidden knowledge, the *Necronomicon*. Reading of Abdul Alhazred's black bible, written in Damascus in A. D. 730 and translated into Latin by Olaus Wormius, he knew he was a step closer. On he ventured, discovering other books of arcane lore: von Junzt's *Unaussprechlichen Kulten*, *Cultes des Goules* by the Comte d'Erlette. Among his discoveries were words, *Ph'nglui mglw'nafh Cthulhu R'lyeh wgah'nagl fhtagn*, and names, the Tcho-Tcho people, Shub-Niggurath, Yog-Sothoth, Nyarlathotep. Further on he encountered places, Dunwich, near the banks of the Miskatonic River that ran through eastern Massachusetts, the plateau of Leng, sunken R'lyeh, witch-haunted Arkham, Massachusetts and Innsmouth, its shadowy sister city to the north. Suddenly his headache stopped.

Innsmouth was the key.

Where had he heard that name before?

It took him two days to recall where he'd encountered the word Innsmouth before. He found it on his birth certificate. There in black and white was the name. Mother's place of birth: Innsmouth, Massachusetts. Mother's name: Marsh. Father's name: unknown. He also found Innsmouth mentioned in one of the other books illustrated by Holmes, *The Lurking Fear and Other Stories*. Mesmerized by realization he reread Lovecraft's "The Shadow over Innsmouth." He was a Marsh, an Innsmouth Marsh.

There in the home of his ancestors lay his answers.

❦ Chapter Six ❦

"Let me show you a map of Lovecraft's Massachusetts. I think you'll find it interesting, maybe useful. You may also want to check with the cops to see if anything similar to these murders has happened there. I'd bet your killer has been there, at least for a visit. It's so close, I don't think he'd be able to resist seeing Lovecraft country," Cosmo told Chris, pulling a map from a drawer.

"Wait a minute! I thought the Mythos was fiction. These are just horror stories, right? You're not telling me any of this nonsense is real?"

"The stories, the GOO, no. But some of the places in the stories exist. Miskatonic U. and Arkham, Newburyport, Innsmouth, Dunwich, they're real places. Here," he said, pointing to the map he had placed on his desk, "in eastern Massachusetts. They were small decaying towns, but they're not all the corrupted antiquated villages and small municipalities that Lovecraft describes. Innsmouth, which Lovecraft described as being on the verge of extinction, is currently a tourist trap. In fact, there's a few bucks to be made off of HPL these days. Last year at Gorged, that's a big horror convention held in New York, Tony Ottaviano, who runs a store like ours in Arkham, told me the town fathers estimated over seventy-five hundred tourists visited Arkham last year. That's a huge chunk of change to a small college town. I've been there myself, took the bus trip from Arkham up to Innsmouth. Didn't think the bus was gonna make it a couple of times. Rickety old thing, belched black smoke and bucked like a snake-bit bronco.

"We stayed in the Gilman House, like in Lovecraft's story. Only hotel in town, and creepy as hell, stark, almost seedy, but fun. Me and the Wiz took the harbor cruise. Man, there we were out on this modern two-deck party boat. Had a great dinner with mountains of steamers and lobster, which the Wizard wouldn't touch on threat of death, but he did okay with the salads and free beer. The boat was called the *Hetty*, after one of Captain Marsh's ships, took us out to Devil's Reef. There we were, out floatin' on the reef on this floating party by moonlight. The Wizard even got a kick out of it. We sat in with the band."

"This just keeps getting weirder. Horror stories coming to life." *Shit. I need a beer.* "You know, Cos, when this is all over I'm gonna sit in my backyard with a couple of brews, play horseshoes, and watch my cukes grow for about six months," Chris said as he shook his head in disbelief.

"Horseshoes!" the Wizard exclaimed. "I love horseshoes."

"Six months, huh? That's July. Me and the Wiz will bring the beer."

* * * * *

Investigator Willie Stanton handed the report to Rolly Hawkins. "You're gonna find this interesting. Computer spit out three possibles. Different MO's, but I've got a bad feeling about this."

Rolly Hawkins read the information on the first murder victim—twenty-year-old Caucasian female, found with her throat slashed and missing her right nipple, off King's Road in the Pine Bush in '75. The other two homicides had been committed in Essex County, Massachusetts. There had been two campers murdered in the summer of '72. Both had had their throats slashed and their breasts mutilated. One was victim missing her left nipple. The Essex County victims were both Caucasian females in their early twenties on a camping trip. Their unclothed bodies were found floating in Innsmouth harbor, two weeks after their reported disappearance. All three murders remained unsolved.

Rolly shuddered at the thought of floaters. *Glad I've never had to deal with bodies in that condition.* "Chris is not going to want to hear this," Rolly said, wondering where else their psycho had been in the last twenty years.

* * * * *

Gregory Bradshaw Marsh sat down at his desk and picked up a black soft-tipped marking pen and began to write.

beckett
YOU HAVE CHOSEN TO IGNORE MY WARNING.
DO NOT DO SO AGAIN!
DELIVER MY WORDS OR FACE MY WRATH!
THE DAWN OF DARKNESS AND DESPAIR IS AT HAND.
cattle, LOOK UPON THE FACE OF FEAR.
SHE COMES TO SHARPEN HER TEETH ON YOUR FLESH.

IÄ! KASSOGTHA! HPTUGH! G'GCHNA NI'ZOS I'GAQ!
I OFFER THEIR WORTHLESS DREAMS,
TO FEED YOUR AGONY.
IÄ! KASSOGTHA! HPTUGH! G'GCHNA NI'ZOS I'GAQ!
THAT IS NOT DEAD WHICH CAN ETERNAL LIE,
AND WITH STRANGE AEONS EVEN DEATH MAY DIE.
THE STARS ALIGN. RISE FROM YOUR DEATH!
QUEEN OF KASHKASH, CONSORT OF CTHULHU.
RIP LIGHT FROM THE WORLD WITH YOUR BLACK GLORY.
cattle, TERROR COMES!
FEAR THE HAND OF HER DISCIPLE.
IÄ! KASSOGTHA!

KNOW ME BY MY MARK.

CEL GOR'RU GR'XUM FNG'I

Marsh looked at the message he'd written. This one had to be right. Time was growing short and the cattle's fear had to be properly groomed. Beckett must spread the word. He must be made to believe. Marsh placed a small piece of flesh from a breast in a zipper lock sandwich bag, carefully expelling the excess air. The message and the sandwich bag went into an envelope bearing Beckett's name. "Now the pig has no choice but to believe. The herd will now know fear."

Marsh sat back in his chair. Eyes closed, he envisioned blasted landscapes replacing the lush forests of Earth. Reveling in the destruction, he watched the great plains turn into deserts of infertile void. Mankind with its hollow banter of ecology had no reason to fear the Earth's destruction by its own hand. The Holy Ones would reshape the planet to their needs when they arrived. Terror would soon return to the collective heart of mankind as it was plunged back into darkness. Electricity and communications would be banished, as man would sit huddled in the shattered remains of his once-bustling, noisy hives, now cold crumbling crypts, alone, afraid, and uninformed.

The virulent flood of his dreams would leave human bellies as empty as despaired eyes were full. Screams became the sweetest of song as Marsh envisioned New York City blasted into a mountainous pile of rubble. The cattle would still inhabit it, but it would be nothing more than series of shallow canyons and caves crowded with the rank odors of excrement. Humans would scurry through what would amount to nothing more than one labyrinthine rathole.

The dark ages would return as life became little more than a desperate scavenger hunt. Nights would bring forth other worldly terrors to prey upon the massed packs that hid in basement cavities praying to their deaf deities, or trying to organize plots to free themselves from the smothering grip of the Holy Ones.

Laughter filled the room as he imagined the cancerous wars of pettiness that would arise over small scraps of food or safe shelters. He could see the bones of compassion trampled into the desolate ground as survival dictated the new constitution; pity not merely absent, but forgotten, as greed replaced law. Marsh savored visions of rape, robbery, and treachery human would savage on human. He could hear the voice of reason suffocate in its own blood, while symphonies of discord wailed unabated. In his mind he saw himself, lord, priest, cruel shepherd of his beloved queen Kassogtha's herds, governor of the lands surrounding Kashkash, the one seat of power, where she would hold court.

Winds heavy with the rank perfume of oppression warmed him as he stood on the upper balcony of her grand fortress. Its battlements would stand forever as monuments to savagery. Below him the sharp-pitched pipings coming from the rookery climbed to reach his ears; truly he was blessed.

* * * * *

"I hear that. Look, I'm gonna be here for a while, they're still filling me in . . . . Yeah, I'll be reading this stuff for days. At least two. Okay, later." Chris cradled the phone. Essex county, near Innsmouth. Damn it, three more victims. "Cosmo, I've just been informed we've got three more. Back in '72 there were two campers, young women, murdered in Essex County, Mass."

"Near Arkham?"

"Innsmouth—"

"Innsmouth? Fuck me."

"Guess you were right about him making a pilgrimage to the east. How many of these stories did you say I've got to read?"

"There's about forty novels, over a hundred and fifty poems that I know about, three plays. And short stories, hell, there must be a couple of thousand of Mythos-related pieces."

"Two thousand? Is this stuff that popular?"

"Remember, the Mythos has existed since the '20's. Besides, Lovecraft is an important writer when you examine the development of horror. Another thing, his work has spread into the occult."

"Huh?"

"The Satanist, Anton LaVey, has a section in his companion to *The Satanic Bible* entitled "The Metaphysics of Lovecraft." In two of his ceremonies he mentions Cthulhuvian deities by name. One ceremony is called "The Call to Cthulhu." You can guess what it's suppose to do . . . . I've heard a couple of people say it's a joke, but there's more than a few who think LaVey and other occultists aren't bullshitting. They've got Lovecraft in bed with Crowley."

"Christ, I've got to read horror and satanic crap too?"

"You don't need to read it all. I think the stories on this list will give you a good start, unless something changes," Cosmo replied.

Changes? Hell, that's about all we'll see from here out. This bastard's gonna freak any day now. Another couple of days without finding his letter in the paper and he'll blow. And if another prostitute shows up dead this thing's gonna hit the national press like a presidential sex scandal, Chris thought as he popped the tab of a Pepsi—regretting it wasn't a beer—and went back to his reading.

An hour later, Chris came across something. "Hey, Cos. Take a look at this?"

Cosmo walked over to the desk where Chris sat reading, and looked over his shoulder. "Shit. I must be gettin' old. I don't remember that. Sorry I didn't recall the words when I saw the letter."

Cosmo looked at the page from W. Shorter's "Kassogtha's Song" that Chris had been reading and at the letter. They were a perfect match. IÄ! KASSOGTHA HPTUGH! G'GCHNA NI'ZOS I'GAQ.

"Like I said, this book is very rare. No one who owns a copy would think of parting with it. It's one of the absolute rarest items associated with the Mythos. There's no doubt now, your killer has read this story. This guy probably knows as much as I do about the Mythos, maybe more," Cosmo said.

Chris wasn't the world's biggest reader and he wasn't a big horror fan. And he damn sure didn't want a degree in Lovecraftian literature or Satanism. His look said it all.

* * * * *

Laurinda was worried. Shortly after Chris and Mike left, she'd driven to work and taken out every book the library had by Lovecraft. For the last hour and a half she'd read story after story, searching for something, some clue, which might aid Chris in his hunt. At the pace Chris was driving himself, he'd kill himself if he didn't let up soon. Laurinda had waited far too long to be in his arms to let this beast take Chris from her now. She tried to dispel the frustration she felt by recalling how wonderful it had felt to lie in his arms, but her fantasies kept dissipating like clouds dissolved by the wind. She needed to cheer herself up.

"Grandma, hi. How are you?" Laurinda asked. Normally she called her grandmother every other Sunday evening, but this was different. She needed to hear her grandmother's voice.

"What is wrong, child? You never call during de day, and we just spoke last *dimanche*. Is there trouble?" Eighty-one years of life may have taken the edge off her body, but it hadn't touched her mind. "Do you need my help, child?"

"Grandma, now really. Can't a girl just call her grandmother to say hello?"

"Yes, she could. *Bon jour. Ça va?* . . . Now tell me de trouble that has found you. I can hear it in your voice, child. He has not returned, has he?"

After all these years the thought of her ex-husband's pummeling fists sent waves of fear rippling across her skin and her psyche. "No. It has nothing to do with him, thank God."

"I give thanks to de loas. Is your mother then spitting in de pot again? *La coeur de cette femme est une pierre.*"

"You know it's not her. Why would you think that? You know she won't even speak to me."

"Child, you well know my daughter's darkened heart. In her eyes you are nothing but un white man's *pute*, and I am nothing more than Hoodoo's old *sorcière*. We are *sale* stains on her pride. Is there trouble for the fair one?"

"Yes. It's these killings. They stir up old demons. He's driving himself too hard. It's like he's possessed."

"We have spoken of this before. Child, you must now heed my warnings. The loas have seen de signs. Beware the gate of *ombres*. De *bête* who de fair one hunts works for darkness. He dreams of crushing all light. Do not be drawn into de black. I will send a charm to you, *Le Pierre du gardien du ciel*, de star of light. Hold it well, child. It will help you. Give de second charm to de fair one. Tell him to keep it with him every moment. De powers of darkness desire his bones. De same goes for you, child. Do not let de star be parted from you at any time. Wear de stars around your necks when they come, and leave them there! *Comprends-toi?*" commanded Laurinda's grandmother, the high mambo of one of New Orleans' oldest voodoo *hounfors*.

"Grandma. You know I don't believe in loas or voodoo."

"*Non?* There was a time you did. *Vrai?* Oggun and Erzuli aided you. Did they not? You believed their aid helped to bring de fair one home from that jungle, safe. *Oui?* But now, too many books have turned your eyes. Beware your western thinkers who have forgotten de land. They seek to know what it's made of, not what it is. Think, child, the truth lives in your heart. You must keep de tradition. Remember, de soul is only sure when it sings. Have faith in de loas and they will provide. One other thing, *ma chère*, I am sending Henri to watch over you."

"Grandma, no. Please, I promise I'll wear your charm, but don't send Henri. There is no need for him to be here. Things—"

"Do not fret, *chère*. Think of your cousin's arrival as, what shall we call it? *Bon*. A vacation."

"Grandmother, please—"

"No. It is done. Please respect my wishes, I will speak with you soon. Do as I have said. I love you. *Au revoir*."

"Love you too. Bye-bye." *Damn. That was a mistake. I should have known better than to call her. Once she starts to worry, she's liable to do anything. Amulets of protection. What am I going to tell Chris? Her and her loas. Voodoo spirits and warnings from an old sorceress, he'll flip. Laurinda Allegra Sanders, just what have you gotten yourself into? And Henri. How am I going to explain Henri's sudden visit? Chris is not going to like this. Not one bit.*

* * * * *

Laurinda Allegra Sanders was born on a humid evening, at 6:09 p.m., July 7, 1951 to Deirdre Marie-Thèrese, a nurse, and George Moses Sanders, a lawyer, in St. Clare's Hospital. She had been named for her father's two sisters, Laura and Linda, and her mother's sister Allegra, a nun who had contracted malaria while doing missionary work and died in the Sudan in 1947. She was a healthy, cheerful baby who blossomed into a tall graceful young woman whom her parents adored. Until the spring of 1966.

Shortly after school, on the first Thursday in May 1966, Laurinda burst through the back door into the kitchen, in tears. Twenty minutes earlier her three older brothers had arrived home from school with an appalling tale. In a series of rapid exclamations they delivered the lurid details to their mother. Laurinda's mother sat at the table aghast. This was impossible. No, intolerable. Her own daughter had betrayed her and everything she believed in. She would deal with this problem swiftly.

"Do you have any idea what you've done? A *white* boy! How could you do this to your father and I? *Well?* What's wrong with you? You kissed a white boy? Dear Jesus, where did we go wrong? Well? What do you have to say for yourself? Have you no respect? Do you know how many blacks have suffered and died by the hands of the whites? This will kill your father. You will *never* see or speak to this boy again! Do you understand me?"

The appalling exposé stewed for two days. On the third afternoon, under a broiling sun, Chris received an intense beating. Laurinda's hulking brothers met Chris on his way home from school, where he was told in no uncertain terms that he was never to see or speak to their sister again. After that painful afternoon, their secret meetings and talks became impossible to arrange. The eyes and ears of her overvigilant brothers seemed to be everywhere.

During the next two years Laurinda and Chris exchanged occasional glances and smiles in math and english class. Cautious, they found only one opportunity to speak, to brush wanting fingers; yet they remained faithful. They were able to pass notes to each other five times without being discovered, quickly destroying them after they were read. Even thought they politely dated others, their feelings toward each other continued.

Someday. That was the word they exchanged in their notes and held in their thoughts. Someday.

The rift between Laurinda and her family deepened over the next two years. Laurinda continued to be an excellent student. She dated the appropriate young men in an effort to appease her parents, although she had no interest in dating anyone but Chris. She obeyed her parents and was always courteous, but she never forgave them. In her heart she knew that neither she nor Chris had done anything wrong. Her parents' bigotry became absolutely intolerable to her.

This was the sixties. Prejudice and racial hatred was stupid and immoral, as far as she was concerned. People were people. Some were tall, some were overweight, but they were still just people. Skin color wasn't any different than the color of one's eyes or hair. And it certainly didn't classify or define anyone. Laurinda couldn't wait to leave home and attend college.

Three months after her graduation from Mont Pleasant High School she left to attend Tulane University and never returned home. Her deepest regret that summer was that she was unable to see or speak to Chris. Laurinda had heard from a friend that in July he'd been drafted, and instead had chosen to enlist in the Marine Corps. Sadly she learned he would probably be sent to Vietnam by Christmas.

❧ Chapter Seven ❧

Gregory Bradshaw Marsh arrived in Innsmouth on April 23, 1972 and checked into the Gilman House with one suitcase, a copy of Fall's *Historical Atlas of Massachusetts,* months' worth of hope, and a mind swirling with dark questions. *Is this where I belong?* he asked himself as he looked out the window of room 301 onto New Town Square and the offices of the Marsh Refining Company.

Was he aware that a large number of Marshes lived in Innsmouth? He was asked by a sheepish desk clerk with frightened eyes. Was he a relative?

"Yes. My mother was born here," he replied, waiting for a reaction behind a feigned smile. "Her name was Sonia, Sonia Arnold Marsh. Did you, by any chance, know her?" an amused Gregory Bradshaw Marsh asked as he watched the proprietor take an involuntary half step backwards.

"Don't think so," came the lie with the key.

Marsh spent his first evening excited and nervous, inquisitively strolling the deserted, poorly lit streets. As he walked, north on Federal, over the falls, with no particular destination in mind, he reeled in the salty air. The brisk, heavy air fit him like a comforting old coat. *Home at last?* he wondered, while standing on the New Church Green, before the old Masonic temple that had been transformed by the Order of Dagon. *Yes. I'm close, very close.* He was quite certain that by this time tomorrow the appropriate people in town would be aware of his arrival.

The following morning, after a short walk to the old shipyard and out on Water Street to the lighthouse, where he lost himself gazing east to the reef, and back (turning on Southwick and then again on Federal), he began to wonder when, or if, he would be contacted. Surely he must have some living relatives here. The certainty that his ancestors held the necessary information for him to finish unraveling the communiqué that plagued his every waking thought held him firmly in its grip. The anticipation of finding answers was difficult to quell, but he felt it would be better if he allowed his relatives to initiate contact.

At 12:45 p.m. he sat down to a lunch of chowder and baked scrod in the dining room of the Gilman House. *I should just walk up to Washington and Church, ring the bell and introduce myself,* he thought. *Why didn't you see if the house is still there? After lunch, I'll do just that.*

Having made his decision, he was about to begin the lemon-perfumed scrod when a slim youthful figure in an expensive dark suit approached his table and asked if he might be the Mr. Marsh who had registered yesterday? The Mr. Marsh whose mother was Sonia Arnold Marsh? Yes, Sonia had indeed been his mother, he replied. Might he inquire as to who might be asking? Mr. Ethan Elihu Marsh, his mother's nephew and his grandfather Ernest's lawyer, came the reply.

"It's remarkable how much you resemble your maternal grandfather Ernest," noted Ethan Marsh. "If you wouldn't be too offended, I was wondering if you might have some documentation to prove that you are who you say you are?"

"I have my mother's birth certificate, her marriage license, and my birth certificate. I trust you'll find them sufficient?" Gregory replied, handing his cousin his bona fides. "And for whatever credence you care to apply to it, I can feel things about this place. Call it déjà vu perhaps."

"Yes, everything appears quite in order," his cousin commented, scanning the documents that had passed between them. Ethan Marsh smiled to himself as he read the birth certificate of the man sitting across the table. One line in particular brought a smile to his face. Father's name: unknown. "I hope you will accept my apologies on behalf of Grandfather. I'm sure he will be very disappointed he was unable to personally greet you. Unfortunately he is away at the moment tending personal affairs."

Following a brief conversation, Marsh (who had wolfed down the scrod as his cousin eyed the trio of papers) and his newly acquired relative collected Gregory's belongings and promptly checked him out of the Gilman House. As they left the lobby, the proprietor crossed himself and began to worry what new horrors might be looming on the horizon with yet another Marsh returned to the fold.

A short silent drive brought them to the home of his cousin. Gregory was taken aback. Before him it stood, white against the picturesque blue sky. Painted, proud, radiant. The air surrounding it was alive with fragrance. Marsh was shocked to find the mansion in this condition. Shouldn't the house and its grounds be in near shambles? According to Lovecraft, this was nothing less than the cancer-filled house of Usher. Perhaps its lush gardens and the bright crocuses dotting the utopian green lawns made it more puzzling. For behind the facade, Marsh hoped, lay the seed of a demonic plague which would nullify the bright dreams of mankind. Somewhere, perhaps buried in a sepulcher under the mansion, lay the true image of this architectural Dorian Gray.

Inside, the mansion continued to offer affluent, immaculate splendor. Finely framed portraits adorned brightly painted walls. Expensive-looking antiques presented an air of refined taste and old money.

Marsh was shown to a good-sized, second-story bedroom which he would be occupying while staying with the family. Ethan informed him that the family would gather for introductions and drinks at four. Dinner would be at five-thirty, if that were acceptable. If there were anything that he might require before then, he should simply ask. Ethan hoped the room was suitable and, should he so choose, he could explore. Gregory was to feel free to treat the house as if it were his own. Ethan also informed him that the family's library downstairs was one of the finest in the region, if he were interested.

Shortly after unpacking, Gregory turned to find a young woman framed in the doorway. Through full, pouty lips came a smile that he felt could only be described as carnivorous. Her heavy-lidded, dark eyes seemed to have sized him up and found him adequate. But for what, he wondered.

"Ahhh . . . you must be the cousin that Ethan mentioned," the bewitching young woman said as she entered the room. "I am Ida. Ida Louise Marsh, Ethan's sister. And you must be poor, long-lost Sonia's son," she said while extending a pallid, long-fingered hand. "I'm very pleased to meet you. I hope we shall find some time to spend together, getting acquainted. I would like that very much. Very much indeed." Her words flowed slowly as her slender hand lingered in his.

Without removing his hand from hers, he replied. "I'm certain that we shall be able to find time to become acquainted."

* * * * *

Chris put down the book he'd been reading and rubbed his eyes. As he lit a cigarette his thoughts coiled, mimicking the smoke. *We're making headway, but are we getting anywhere?* Momentarily, his mind began to drift along with the ethereal atmospherics WRPI was playing. *Sometime in another life I owned this.* Chris butted out the cigarette in frustration. *What the hell is the name of this song?* he asked himself, half delighted to be distracted from the story he decidedly didn't like.

"Hey, Cos. Do you know what this is called? I know I know it, but I can't recall the title."

Cosmo listened a moment. *Fripp. Eno?* "Yeah, it's one of those Fripp & Eno compositions. Something like 'Wind on Water' or 'Wind on Wind.' Maybe, 'Wind on Light.' Wind on something. But I don't remember what."

"Right! The record was . . . *Evening Star*, I think. I owned it in my younger days." Chris recalled those first couple of years after 'Nam. Readjustment, they called it. *Yeah. It sure took some readjusting all right*, he thought, as images of Tet, Chu Lai, and Echo company ran roughshod across his consciousness. *Could use a beer*, he thought, his hand rising to massage the physically healed wound on his left shoulder. *Eh, ain't got time for that shit now. Stay on track, Stewart! Focus.*

An hour later, thankfully leaving the gore and gloom of The Horror Corner behind, Chris set a stack of books on the dining room table in Laurinda's apartment and was greeted with a warm hug and a tender kiss. Twenty minutes and two beers later, the shit hit the fan.

"What? You're joking, right? She's sending us some voodoo jewelry to wear. Look, I know you think she's a sweet old lady and all, but this? I don't know. This case has nothing to do with voodoo. Christ, we're after a psycho who reads books about alien demon-gods. He doesn't practice voodoo. I've no doubt this animal is a ghoul. Hell, he might even be a cannibal, but he's not a god damn zombie," Chris said, instantly regretting his sarcastic tone.

"There's one other thing."

"No," he said, holding up his hand. "Let me guess. We've got to sacrifice a chicken—" His humor was short-lived.

"Christopher James Stewart! Don't be ridiculous. You know full well that my grandmother doesn't practice *that* kind of voodoo. Her sacrifices are *mange sec*, without blood. Grandmother's also sending cousin Henri here to protect me."

All the devil's bats fled hell.

"Just what the hell am I? Christ almighty! I'm a cop. I patrolled the Hill for two years and worked Narco/Vice. And let's not forget I walked 'Nam and managed to keep my ass alive. Hell, I've even got a license for this!" His hand went to the pistol, strapped to the left of his heart. "Just what in the hell is he coming here to protect you from?"

"Chris." The word came soft and slow, like honey. "Just listen for a minute. Please?"

* * * * *

The 18th-century grandfather clock in the library softly chimed eight times. Gregory Bradshaw Marsh turned and took note of the time. Rising from the armchair he walked across the room, his shadow blotting out some of the white marble tiles of the floor's chessboard pattern. Pleased, he paused and smiled at the distorted silhouette lying before him. *The legacy of Innsmouth does indeed run through your veins*, he thought, mentally embellishing the shadow until it resembled a deep one.

From the watch pocket of his jeans he removed a wellworn key and unlocked the top drawer of an imposing oak desk which had once belonged to his stepfather. In front of him lay his surveillance file on Donnalee O'Donnell. Removing the file before he closed and locked the drawer, he again took note of the time. As anxious to be about his craft as a ballet critic on opening night, he wondered how well his ballerina would dance for him. He envisioned her fearful pirouette, the graceful leap of the blade, heard the bravos of his heated breath. Certain of a splendid performance, he tucked the file under his arm and went upstairs to change.

Marsh removed his jeans and shirt and put on thermal underclothing to ward off the cold. "This should do it," he told the image in the mirror before putting his black jeans and deep green flannel shirt back on. After he'd finished tying his ten-inch hiking boots and admiring himself a second time in the floor-length mirror, he took the file and his keys from where they lay on the bed and went to the basement to finish his preparations.

Sitting at the work table in his basement shrine, Marsh wondered how early he should arrive at her home. He needed to be early enough to conceal himself, but he didn't relish the idea of crouching in the bushes for very long; temperatures were predicted to be dropping into the single digits. Adding the wind chill factor to his mental calculations, he realized the temperature would drop well below zero. Deciding that if he arrived at eleven-thirty he wouldn't have more than a half-hour's wait, he closed the file he'd been reviewing.

As Chris lay quietly in Laurinda's arms, Gregory Bradshaw Marsh settled into the evergreens bordering Donnalee O'Donnell's driveway to await her arrival. It was 11:31 p.m. Marsh, ensconced in a stand of evergreens, thanked Ithaqua, lord of the Arctic wastes, for the winds that were howling tonight. They would cover the sounds of his movements when he took her.

* * * * *

Donnalee O'Donnell sat in her car while it warmed up, trying to decide what she was going to do for the next two days. She had switched days off with Kathleen Campbell and found herself with Monday and Tuesday free. "Free to do what?" She'd done her marketing yesterday and the pantry was well stocked. There was no cleaning to perform and her calendar was distressingly free.

"I've got a mammogram scheduled for a week from Friday and my teeth get cleaned two weeks from Tuesday . . . some social life you've got, D." *If that lying bastard Dan hadn't ruined everything by screwing around with everyone who'd have him, I'd at least have someone to spend my evenings with. I can't believe he slept with that air-headed little slut in the ER.* "The whole friggin' hospital knows she's a disease factory wiggling around on two legs," she said, pushing a homemade Eric Clapton compilation into the cassette player.

It had been two months since the embittered split and she still found herself livid every time she thought of his zipless entanglements. Expelling the venomous image of him coupled with some eager young tart, she toyed with the idea of doing some shopping tomorrow—she needed some kind of diversion (anything was better than this empty hell of anger), but there wasn't anything she really needed. Besides, she detested window shopping.

What's the point of looking at something you're dying to own and can't afford? she wondered. *Maybe I'll curl up with that new John Sandford serial killer novel I got yesterday. I'll spend the next couple of wintry nights reading—what's it called?*—Winter Prey. *Yeah, perfect. There's a ton of snow covering the park and the winds are blowing like mad; setting's perfect. I hope it's as good as his last few.*

As Alan Clark's keys underscored and accented EC's stinging guitar lines, Donnalee, now armed with a pleasurable way to spend an evening or two, smiled as her soft yet spirited soprano twinned Clapton's statement about post-witching hour activities. She dropped the car into gear as Clapton's version of "After Midnight" faded and "Better Make It through Today" began crying.

* * * * *

Marsh checked his watch. *Where's the bitch? She should be here by now. Snow must be keeping her.* He'd been crouched in the bushes for almost thirty minutes and the cold was beginning to annoy him. *Patience*, he thought. *She'll be here soon.*

To warm himself he sought strength in prayer. Within moments the tight grimace frozen across his bird of prey features melted into a carnivorous smile. He shifted the steel talon from hand to hand as if it were a nervous twitch. He was ready for the dance; more than ready.

Moments later his prayers were answered as an automobile's headlamps appeared down the street. He mentally flexed as the unshoveled snow in the driveway glistened in the light. Donnalee O'Donnell turned off the engine and got out of her car. As she closed the car door, Marsh quickly rose from behind the bushes, scalpel in hand. Reaching out, his left hand snared a fistful of long blonde hair. Holding tightly he yanked her head backward, while his steel talon ripped across the delicate, pale flesh of her throat. With a vampiric bloodlust he carved a wide bloody gorge. Pushing her down and away from him, so he'd avoid blood stains on his clothing, he watched her flop on the driveway. Her hands clung about her throat, trying desperately to close the wound as she bled to death.

Number eight, he thought as he cut away her jacket, sweater, and bra. "Marvelous. They're larger than I thought," he said, watching her breasts jiggle. Removing his glove, he let his finger play with her dark left nipple for a moment before the scalpel began to sever her ample breasts.

"Iä! Kassogtha! Infinite doorway of pain, whore of abominations, mate and sister of our sleeping lord, Cthulhu. I offer another bitch to feed your torment," Marsh hissed into the raging winter winds, as he ejaculated on her maimed corpse. No longer did he feel the biting pain of January's winds. The blood-sperm mixture on his hand and his prayers warmed him.

Placing the steaming breasts in two large plastic zipper-lock freezer bags, he walked the block and a half to his parked car and placed them in its trunk under an old blanket in a cardboard box. With his prizes safely tucked away, he thought, *One down, one to go.* Driving away, he allowed himself a smile.

Marsh was in his own version of heaven as he drove south on Erie Boulevard toward Argyle Place and Spree's to find his second victim.

"I'm out on a spree," he said. "A killing spree."

Harsh laughter filled the car as it picked up speed. He felt vast. Untouchable and perfect.

Marsh pulled his car into an out-of-the-way parking lot on Railroad Street that was only used during the daylight hours by a few small local businesses. The lot had been plowed earlier and the plows had created sheer canyon walls of soiled snow along its borders. They would provide perfect cover for taking the night's second victim. Before leaving the lot, he changed his coat, feeling his heavily lined denim work coat wouldn't be very appealing to any of the young men in the club. From the car's trunk, he removed a bright red ski jacket trimmed in yellow.

Not bad. Hair's good, jeans seem tight enough to do the job. I should attract something quickly. His face, moments before callous hauteur, now beamed with a friendly, promising smile. High on confidence and adrenalin, Marsh walked the half block to Spree's.

At the door, while being sized up by the bouncer, he tendered the five-dollar cover charge. Immediately buffeted by throbbing rhythms of overwhelming volume and swirling, flashing, multi-colored lights he entered the club and paused.

The curtain has risen. Act two begins. Remember to smile. Act willing, but hesitant, and say as little as possible. Such filth!

At the bar he ordered a Heineken and was quickly served by a winking male bartender. *Subhuman vermin,* he thought, wishing he could outwardly display his disgust.

Noticing an empty table in a darkened corner near the back he decided to assess possible targets from its shadowy security. In and out of pockets of light, skirting glances and offers, he slowly walked around the edge of the dance floor toward the table, allowing the club's patrons to look him over. Hopeful smiles, elbowing their way through two or three winks, a blown kiss, and a loud, musical wolf whistle sailed his way. In the dim corner Marsh sat down with his beer and began surveying the herd.

Quicksilver fools, painted and parading. Ready to tumble for a smile. This is going to be easier than I thought. Marsh took a pull off the beer bottle. His hooded eyes smiled.

Marsh found it difficult to keep his eyes off the DJ, an overweight redhead endowed with pendulous breasts and an excessive amount of make-up. Eyes closed, head back, she swayed to the fast paced, beat-heavy music she was mixing. Marsh briefly watched her lip-synching the prayer-like lyrics, something about sweet obsessions and only being guilty of love.

Guilty of being alive is more like it, he thought as he continued staring at the redhead. *It's too bad I can't take that fat cow. She'd be perfect,* he thought. *Her tits would work well and I'd be under less pressure next week.* With his eyes fixed on her swaying breasts he began to formulate a plan to kill her instead of one of the young men. Before anything of substance could be developed, a sandy-haired man-boy walked up to his table.

"Hi. I'm James. My friends call me Jazz. Mind if I sit down?" the thin young man with an expensively perfect, inviting smile asked.

Marsh patted the seat of the chair next to his and returned the smile. "I'm Brad. Could I buy you a drink?"

"Sure. I don't think I've seen you here before. New in town?" James asked as his daring hand found its way to Marsh's thigh.

Control yourself! Vermin filth, he thought, shaking a bit from rage.

James turned up his smile, erroneously interpreting Marsh's shiver of revulsion as excited willingness.

"Yes. It's been two, no, three months now. This is the first time I've stopped in." *And the last, you stupid faggot.* "It appears to be a live-ly spot. I think I'll like it here." *Scum, by the holy vaginas of Kassogtha, you will pay for your debased trespasses. It's going to be fun to watch you bleed to death.*

After a drink and some small talk James asked if he'd like to dance. Maybe later, came the reply. First Marsh had another idea, if James was agreeable.

"I'm up for almost anything," the laughing young man answered.

They quickly decided to meet in ten minutes, near Marsh's parked car. Marsh explained that he was a bit shy and would feel more comfortable if they left separately. James eagerly agreed, certain this was going to be a luscious little rendezvous. Nursing his beer and watching the clock, James toyed with fantasies he thought they might indulge in away from the city's bright lights in a deserted parking lot at midnight.

James found Marsh just where he said he'd be. Marsh, in a well delivered nervous whisper, told James this was his first time and asked if James would accommodate his fantasies by allowing him to set the pace. Marsh asked the young man if he would turn around and unbutton his shirt, because he wanted to rub his hands on James' chest and stomach while rubbing up against his ass. "I'd just like to . . . shall we say, ease in slow."

"Sounds yummy," James huskily breathed, excited by the idea that this older man was cherry. His fantasies disappeared as Marsh's reared up with savage teeth.

After James ceased writhing, Marsh removed both nipples with the bloodied scalpel. A victorious smile came to his face as he stuffed the nipples into the young man's mouth. The kill's pleasure rush and religious fervor sexually energizing him, Marsh masturbated above the man-boy's chest.

That should obliterate your sense of security, he emphatically hissed at the near-sleeping city. *Two in one night! They'll be screaming in terror for weeks.*

Less than thirty minutes later he embraced the safety of his mansion with an intense feeling of elation and his two fleshy prizes in their zipper-lock bags.

Chapter Eight

Chris awoke at 5:02 a.m. Muscles aching and groggy from too lit-tle sleep, he stumbled out of bed and into the bathroom, leaving Laurinda quietly dreaming.

What a stupid shit I am, he thought, realizing his anger over her cousin's arrival was caused by his fear of Henri's possible interference with their new relationship, not because he was coming here to pro-tect her. *Stewart, sometimes you're a prize ass.* Cursing his insecurities and his stupidity he went into the kitchen to make a pot of tea. *Stop being greedy. You've waited twenty-some years for this; you can wait a few more days.*

As the tea sat steeping, he showered and shaved. Buttoning his shirt he tried to recall the title of a particular Roy Schieder film. "What was the name of it?" *Damn . . . .* "I can't seem to remember anything these days." *Well, whatever.* "It's almost showtime," he said to the frowning face in the mirror.

Back in the kitchen, Chris sat and stroked Laurinda's cat, an eighteen-pound orange tiger named Plato, while he smoked the day's first cigarette between coughs. "Once this case is over and the pres-sure's off, I'm going to quit these damn things," he told the purring giant. Chris laughed to himself at the thought of this case ever going away. Stirred by Chris' laugh, Plato rolled over in Chris' lap and offered his belly to be rubbed. After feeding the cat and finishing his tea, he left Laurinda an apologetic note (which he signed *Please forgive this very sorry idiot. Love, Chris*) and went out to his car wondering what, if anything, the morning would drop in his lap.

His beeper went off as he pulled into the police department parking lot. "Shit! This early." *Hope they haven't found another body.* Two minutes later, as he entered the task force's command center, which seemed busier than the Pentagon at the height of the Tet offensive, he realized today might not be a good day to buy a lotto ticket. "Rolly?"

"You're not going to believe this. It's sick, really sick. He butchered a man this time," Rolly said.

"What? A gay prostitute?"

"Gay, probably. A hooker? Don't think so. Found him off Railroad Street, in a parking lot near Spree's. Kramer's there now. The owner of the Schenectady Athletic Center on Church Street called it in about twenty minutes ago. He couldn't sleep, so he went in early to catch up on some paperwork. He found the corpse in the lot."

Why kill a guy? This butcher isn't gay. "Kramer really think it's our boy?"

"Yeah. Vic's throat was slashed from behind and his nipples were severed, and, get this, they were stuffed into the guy's mouth. Chris, this freak's gotta be taken down hard! Know what I mean? Who else would jerk off on a corpse? And why do a guy? I can't figure it. Makes no goddamn sense. I think he's gone off the deep end. I thought he was nuts before, but this?"

"Fear!" Chris half-yelled, a half dozen heads turning to look at him. "This demonic bastard wants everyone afraid. This is a terror campaign. Remember the letter he sent to Beckett. Well, I think he's really pissed off because he hasn't received any notoriety from the prostitutes, so he's decided to up the ante." *Shit! I should have thought of this before.* "Rolly, I think the lid just blew off hell and the heat's gonna fry everyone. Anyone call Matthews yet?" Chris asked, wondering how many aspirins he would ingest today.

"Yeah, right after Kramer described the condition of corpse. He's on his way there now. Screaming ten shades of blue murder. Told me to wake up Carroll and Ivanelli. Maybe you should handle that."

"Great, just great. Do you think I did something bad in a past life? Look, after I call the mayor and Carroll I think you and I should go take a look at the body. I've got an angle I want to throw at Matthews. We've run out of time to fuck with this bastard. It's time to reel him in," Chris said as he dialed a presumably sleeping Carroll at home.

* * * * *

Laurinda rose at 7:21 a.m. Brewing a pot of coffee, she noticed Chris' note. *He's taking it better than I'd anticipated.* "Hi, Plato. Was he in a good mood this morning?" A simple meow as he rubbed against her ankle was the only reply. "Looks like we've got some work to do around here. Cousin Henri's coming, and while he's visiting I want you to behave. Don't you take advantage of his good nature or his love of cats. Remember, Henri is our guest. Come on, it's time to tidy up before he arrives."

* * * * *

"Jack, there's another body."

"WHAT! When? I'll be right there."

Al Jankowski's hand was raised, as if to say wait a minute, while he finished on the phone. "Here's what I got. Carol Whittam's on the scene now. Not quite an hour ago, the police got a phone call. All we know so far is it's a white male, maybe twenty. They found him in a parking lot on Railroad Street, near Spree's. A cop she used to date says they think he was gay."

"So? Our freak kills hookers, not fags."

"Oh yeah? Then try this out. The dead man's throat was cut, and he's eating both his nipples. And someone left their sperm on his chest."

"That's him, godammit! What's he up to? Do they have any leads yet? How well does she know this cop?"

"Slow down. We've got to figure out our next move. I want you to call Carol and get all the details. Have her take this cop to lunch and pump him. Then try Stewart and see what he's got. Bug him about the letter. This is about to blow, so maybe they've softened. Work out the angle for this, and be back here in an hour with our lead story."

"Yeah. Yeah," Beckett replied as he left Jankowski's office with half a dozen angles all vying for position.

* * * * *

Laurinda's doorbell rang at 10:45. Standing on her porch was a finely tailored giant that would have made Conan himself stop and take notice. Henri St. John de Baptiste Freniere tipped the scales at over three hundred and fifty pounds of rock solid muscle which familial genetics had stacked over six and a half feet tall.

"*Bon jour, chère.* You look well." His warm tone was accented by a radiant smile.

"Henri, you lovable monster. Why didn't you call me from the airport? I was going to pick you up. Gran said you wouldn't be arriving until three. Come in," she said, rising on tippy-toes to kiss his cheek. Two years had passed since his last visit, and despite the circumstances surrounding this trip she was glad to see him.

Laurinda fondly recalled the summers in New Orleans, playing nanny to the then tiny, ever-laughing boy who had told her when he became a man he would make her the queen of New Orleans. How well she remembered laughing and fishing in the Pontchartrain on sunny summer afternoons with him. And the Mardi Gras of '72, with the two of them moving through the crowds, as if they were indeed king and queen, on the arms of her grandmother and her uncle, reeling in the wondrous sights and sounds—the floating papier-mâché smiles and the shining beads, stepping free and quick to the hot-blooded music and laughter, which rang through the streets like the inspiring poetry of summer sunshine.

In ways, Henri reminded her of Chris, and even more so of Pat Price. Henri and Pat were two pure souls who shone like bright suns on an often gray world. Their faces radiated love and laughter. Darkness could not choke their worlds. They simply would not allow it.

"It's so wonderful to see you."

"*Chère*, with every year you become more *belle*. I am so very sorry to arrive here under these circumstances. I hope you will forgive me, but *Grand-mère*, I've promised her. I'm sure you understand."

"I do. Please don't worry yourself over it, I know how Gran can be about these matters."

"Thank you." Without pause he removed a leather necklace case from the pocket of his jacket and held it out for her. "This is *Grand-mère's* charm. I've promised her I shall make certain that you will wear it. Please, would you be so kind as to put it on now?"

Laurinda took the case from his massive hand and opened it. Inside was a dark, five-pointed stone, slightly larger than a quarter and shaped like a star. It was quite lovely in a rough sort of way, although she could do without the rawhide thong that held it. Taking the stone from its case she felt its warmth. *Gran's magic? Nah. It's warm because it was in Henri's pocket. Still, it was inside a case. Don't be ridiculous, it's only body warmth. It has nothing to do with voodoo spells*, she told herself as she drew the thong over her head. As the soothing warmth of the stone fused with the warmth of her skin she was certain something had touched her, something pure. "There. Now you can relax a bit. Your promise to Gran is fulfilled."

"There is one more thing, *chère*. *Grand-mère* asks that you promise that no matter what occurs you will not take the stone from your neck. May I have your promise?"

"I promise on the grave of your beloved father that here," pointing to her neckline, "the stone shall stay. Although I think it's going to be very difficult to accessorize now," she said with a laughing smile.

"*Merveilleux*," he said, his smile mirroring hers. "Now, *chère*. When shall I meet the fair one?"

* * * * *

Cosmo entered the store to find his confederate lost in haunted slow blues. There were strains of "Hellhound on My Trail" in the improvisation that the Wizard was exploring, and there, a veiled reference to Bill Evans' "Turn Out the Stars", but the rest was hard to place. Cosmo hadn't heard his playing sound this lonely since the Wizard's mother had died from complications from a double mastectomy fifteen years ago. He was willing to bet that if he could see his friend's cheeks, they would be lined with tears. *Sometimes even in daylight we're forced to suffer our demons*, he thought. Cosmo knew his best friend's suffering had been brought on by this demonic butcher. *Christ, soon we'll have people accusing us of promoting this shit*, he thought, recalling past complaints. *I need to find a way to help Chris put this beast down.*

The Wizard paused to light a smoke. Coughing, he turned at the sound of Cosmo's creaking chair. "Didn't know you were here. Hope I wasn't bothering you. Tough sleeping, I guess."

"I don't think you could bother me if you tried. Man, that was beautiful. I haven't heard you play with such grace in a long time. This eating at you too?"

"I don't believe this shit. How the fuck can anyone do this to other people? And why? Look around at all this shit," he said, pointing toward an array of graphic merchandise. "This is a form of entertainment. It's not real. We don't encourage abhorrent behavior. Man, I'd love to have this reaver in the sights of my .30-.30. I'd show him the real meaning of horror. One excruciating shot at a time. Wonder how much he'd crave blood if it was his own?"

"Know what I love about you, you wiry old son-of-a-bitch? Inside you're the Easter bunny."

"Not today. Today, I'm a Komodo dragon who'd love to feast on that fuck's entrails. Cos, we've got to find someway to help bag this asshole."

"I'm am wit you my broda. Up for some reading?"

"Sure. What are we looking for?"

Cosmo stroked his thickly bearded chin and thought for a moment. He shrugged. "Seems we haven't got much time before this, what shall we call it? Mass arrival? Somewhere in here," he pointed to the bookcase behind him, "is an answer. And we've got to find it. I could really use your insights. Why don't you start with that pile of Des' books, and then, some of Lumley's?"

"Consider it done."

* * * * *

As Rolly parked the car on Railroad Street, Chris' ears were still ringing from the one-sided conversations he'd just undergone with the city's hardly beloved mayor and chief of police. Lighting a cigarette he tried to determine how many years he had left before he reached retirement age. "Too god damn many" is the answer that he came up with.

Chris approached homicide investigators Kramer and Tyner, both of whom already looked as if they hadn't slept in days. "Days seem to just get longer, huh?"

"Fucking-A, Chris," Kramer replied. "Hell, I'd even go on that damn cruise my wife keeps harping about if this shit would blow away."

Chris and Kramer had a friendly rivalry that went back ten years, but being tied as the primaries with three murders each didn't tickle either one.

Chris asked, "Found anything new, Rob?"

"Couple of things. Our boy wasn't wearing cowboy boots this time. He's walking around in a pair of hiking boots by the look of the footprints. The lab boys said the footprints look like they're from the same size shoes, though. They'll be positive later this morning. Why change MO's now? First he kills a guy, now different shoes. I don't get it. And why cut off the corpse's nipples and then leave 'em? I thought this monster—evil—takes his trophies home to play with. He sure had time to do whatever he wanted after he butchered this kid. Hell, he's gettin' his jollies off after he cuts them up. That requires time. Doesn't it? This is one sick fuck we're dealin' with."

"Sicker by the minute. Why different shoes? Traction maybe? In all this snow and ice the footing's a bitch. Nah. Doesn't make any sense. Hell, the alley the Shire girl was murdered in was almost a complete sheet of ice. If he needed traction, it was sure there. Besides, there's been no evidence at the other murder sites that the boots were bloody. They should still be safe to wear in public. Maybe they just got ruined from the snow. Do you think this attack was spur of the moment?"

"No," Kramer replied.

"Where's Matthews?" Chris asked. "I've got an idea I want to run by him."

"Commissioner beeped him about five minutes before you guys showed up. His ass is gonna be engaged to a proctologist by the end of the day," Tyner said, attempting a joke and a tired smile.

Better him than me, Chris thought, although he didn't wish the chief or the mayor on anyone, not even Matthews. "Anything else here?" Chris asked.

"Couple of things. One, we've got a good set of tire impressions, but I don't think they'll help much. Probably gonna be five million sets sold over the years. And two, we traced his steps right to Spree's, at least to the area by the front door. I just hope someone saw something. We've got Tony waking up the owner now. We'll get a list of employees and start checking to see if anyone saw anything in the bar last night. Oh yeah, M.E. thinks he died about midnight," Kramer said.

"Anything you guys need?" Chris asked.

"Nah. We've got it covered pretty well, I think. If anything comes up, we'll yell," Tyner replied.

"Then we're going to hit the lab and see what they've got. And I've got to find Matthews. Later, guys." As Chris walked away, he lit another smoke and to no one in particular said, "Fuck me."

* * * * *

Gregory was still reeling from his introduction to his strangely alluring young cousin, Ida Louise Marsh. Despite the sexual revolution of the sixties, Marsh at nineteen years of age had yet to participate in any sexual encounter. Nor had he ever thought of women in any sexual context whatsoever. Sex was of no importance to Marsh. He was on an all-consuming mission, and until the moment that he'd seen her framed in the doorway he had been quite certain that nothing could or would divert him from his quest. The feelings this young woman inspired in him were both exciting and shocking.

The anniversary clock on the mantle chimed, announcing the half hour. Twenty minutes had elapsed as he sat on the edge of his bed wondering what it would be like to touch more than just her pale hand.

Shaking off his carnal thoughts and finding himself with time and permission to examine the house, he wandered the hallways and open rooms of the Federal mansion. In dark, ornate frames Gregory encountered some of the Marshes who had once filled these halls with their presences and their dark pleasures. Abel Marsh (1753-1791) scowled through a window down on the east lawn. Nestled in the second floor sitting room, Charles (1692-1736), Caleb (1774-1831), and Aaron (1713-1769) seemed to be smiling over some tantalizing secret only they shared. Descending the stairway, the round, dark Marsh eyes of Riverius (1655-1725), Zachariah (1734-1800), and John Austin (1794-1847) appeared to follow him.

My dear ancestors, I have come home to you. How many of you knew the answers I seek?

Gregory was quite taken with many of the pieces of bric-a-brac he came upon. One in particular, a finely detailed piece of scrimshaw bearing the likeness of a deep one, sat outside the study on a brilliantly polished claw-foot pedestal table. With reverential care he lifted the carving from its walnut base. *Such artistry*, he thought, *and such power.*

Entering the ballroom, he faced two formally dressed young wallflowers, Urania (1672-1722) and Miriam (1669-1713), who seemed to be soliciting an invitation to dance. Five steps away, shadowed from the direct light of the afternoon sun, shoulders regally covered with a deep purple fichu, Irvette's (1756-1803) flushed features seemed bound in salacious reverie. Continuing his easy paced exploration of the ground floor he strolled on like an impresario happily acknowledging his favored clientele, admiring aged portraits of Obadiah, Elihu, Walter, and Rachel, who shared one end of the room with a Bosendorfer Imperial Concert Grand piano.

At the other end of the room, above an antique vase adorned with two unclothed nymphs flirting with a muscular black bull, the portrait of Anne (1834-1866), a raven-haired beauty with dark eyes, caught his eye. Returning her smile, he asked, "Did you turn the young sailors' heads as you strolled through town?" Stopping near the window on the far wall, he faced a silver-haired woman he guessed to be in her eighties. "Isadora, would you care to dance with your long lost great-something-grandson?"

In the wainscoted hall outside the ballroom he dallied at the window watching fluffy white clouds pass to the east. Before taking the few remaining steps lying between him and the library Gregory paid his respects to Partridge Marsh and his eldest son, Obed.

Marsh's nostrils recoiled from the pungent stench of cigar smoke which, over the years, had ingrained itself into the room as if it were a few good coats of paint. Yet he entered; he'd endured worse in his search for answers. Ornamenting the deeply colored, paneled walls of the expansive library were five portraits and the sculpted likeness of a woman.

Prominently mounted above the large marble fireplace, a foreboding cavern of darkness which lay quiet this warm spring afternoon, a strange ominous woman carved from coconut palm wood held court over the room. This apparently Polynesian woman with ichthyic features and scaly breasts had adorned the prow of Obed's ship, the *Sumatry Queen*. Age and fading paint heightened the disquieting nature of her weathered countenance. Family legend stated the figurehead's model was Obed's second wife. It had been given to the captain by the Polynesian chief Walakea to commemorate Obed's marriage.

To the left, finely detailed oil paintings of the *Hetty* and the *Sumatry Queen*, two of the old captain's ships, managed tempestuous seas. Between the floor-to-ceiling bookcases lining the wall to the right of the figurehead, along with the rudder wheel of the *Columby*, Obed's flagship, was a striking painting of the brigantine cutting through a raging storm.

Immediately to Gregory's right was a portrait of an odd-looking, yet strangely enticing, woman whose features he could not place. Asian? Polynesian perhaps? Still, there was something about the small flattish nose and hooded Marsh eyes that called to mind his mother's face. The longer he looked at the portrait, the more he was certain he could see his mother. At the bottom of the painting was a small gold plaque bearing the name "Ida Louise Marsh."

It can't be, he thought. He'd just left Ida, not more than forty minutes earlier. *An ancestor, yes, that's it.* He could see it now. There were resemblances. The hair color of the young beauty he had just left was blonde, not this deep, almost bluish black, and the lips— hers were full, pouty, not the thin slash of a mouth that stared out at him from the painting. The heavy-lidded, round Marsh eyes were present and delicate, flat nose was the same, as were the slightly weak chin and high cheeks, yet the hue of the woman's skin in the portrait was dark. Ida's was pale, almost alabaster. He recalled very well the skin of Ida's small moon-colored hand.

Laying aside his questions regarding familial facial traits, Marsh found himself drawn to a treasure he had some knowledge of. Occupying the center of the library, atop a deep green jade pedestal sculpted as a cyclone of rising fish, was a small glass jewel case. In it, on a bed of black velvet, was a golden tiara. The tiara held his gaze, and though he had never laid eyes on it before he recognized the mutated fish-frog-like creatures that were engraved on it. It was the head piece Lovecraft had written about in "The Shadow over Innsmouth." The marvel seemed too large for a human head. And something about the shape seemed wrong. It was elliptical as is the human cranium, yet there was a distortion present that made it seem alien in a way he couldn't define.

"Cousin Gregory. Excuse me. Yes, the tiara. I see you find it, shall we say, alluring. A marvelous piece of workmanship, wouldn't you say? It's a priceless family heirloom, lost for many years. How we suffered while it was apart from us. Family legend has it that a servant purloined it in 1873. We gave thanks when it was restored to its rightful home a decade ago. It is a source of great family pride. But I fear I ramble. Please accept my apologizes for boring you with old family tales," Ethan said.

"Hardly boring. I've been dreaming about this day for the last six months. As I have said, my mother never spoke of her former life, and when I came across her birth certificate, well, being alone, I thought, hoped, that perhaps I'd find relatives here in Innsmouth. And here you are. And Ida, of course."

"Of course," Ethan's flat words responded through a polite smile. "Now if you would excuse me I have some pressing business to attend to before the family arrives. Please continue to look around. You might find some of the family's books of interest. Until four, then."

"Yes. Until later. And thank you."

Ethan Marsh left the library and walked to a heavy oak door opposite the first-floor study. From his vest pocket he removed a large brass key, which he inserted into the much-used lock. Locking the door behind him, he paused, allowing his eyes to adjust to the diminished light. Down one hundred seventy well worn steps he descended into a voluminous cavern, the air thick with chilly damp and reeking of sulfur and salt. There, washed in yellowed torchlight, he found his sister working over a large obsidian altar. Sensing his presence, she turned from her bloody pleasure-taking. Drinking in her lithe, blood-splattered form, Ethan's dark smile widened and his arms went around her small waist.

"The library holds him as tightly as your eyes. Yes, my love. He is the one we have been waiting for," he whispered before his lips tasted the sweet skin of her neck.

Alone in the library, Gregory turned his attention to the books lining the shelves. Art, religion, history. Architecture (the grandeur of Byzantine domes and Gothic buttresses flanking the skeletal Bauhaus and surreal towers that dwarfed Babel) and poetry (Cynara stood broken in the shadow of "The Harlot's House" while the tormented, spurred by fiery souls, sang to "superhuman" hearts of "death in life and life in death"). Philosophy, some still unspoken in the lecture hall. Volumes on witchcraft and archaeology. Kafka, Wells, and Hugo. Proust. The names abounded. There were volumes in Greek, in Latin. Here was Baudelaire in French and Cervantes in Spanish. Nietzsche's Zarathustra spoke in German. Ford Madox Ford rested between Confucius and Camus. Rows of legends from countless countries.

At times his fingertips caressed a spine . . . a seemingly new copy of L. Sprague de Camp's *Lost Continents* and both volumes of Jacquetta Hawkes' *The World of the Past*, which were well worn. The Satanist Aleister Crowley's *Book of the Law* stood upside down between two seemingly human skulls. A mantle of fur-deep dust lay like a canopy on a trio of trilogies by Agrippa, Hay, and Grant. Half the titles lining the shelves Marsh had never heard of: *Annals of the*

Worms, H. R. Giger's *ARh+*, *Tractatus Magici et Astrologici*, Charles Bishop's *Les Diables Prosituées (A Historical Discourse on the All-Female Parisian Coven)*, and *Excommunicamus est anathematisamus*. Before him rested Joseph Glanvil's *Saducismus Triumphatus*. Was there another library in the state that owned a copy of this? he wondered. And here was another volume of the witch Crowley's writings, *Liber Aleph vel CXI*, resting against de Sade's *Philosophy in the Bedroom*, and an expensively bound edition of Pickman's ghoulish paintings pushing against a thick volume of Jackson Pollock reproductions.

Gregory Bradshaw Marsh felt that a good deal of the world's knowledge resided on these shelves, though he couldn't find that which he most hoped for. As suddenly as his hopes sprang from him, he turned and his eyes caught the spine of a tome bound in cracked leather; the spine bore the legend *Necronomicon*. Joy raced through him at the sight of the forbidden text. Almost without pause his eyes caught the title of the massive book next to it: *The Seven Cryptical Books of Hsan*, and next to it *De Vermiis Mysteriis* by Ludvig von Prinn, who had been burned at the stake for his writings. Marsh could hardly believe his eyes, there was Dr. Adrian Van Vliet's out-of-print *The Cthulhu Myth Cycle and Its Relevancy to 20th Century Man*. He remembered hearing of the rumored flight from Union's campus by the screaming archaeology professor in the early spring of '68, days before his reported suicide. Beside it sat *Monstres and Their Kynde*, and could that really be Justin Geoffrey's *People of the Monolith?* The last book on the shelf seemed to draw him, although he had not heard of it. *Las Reglas de Ruina*. Slowly he removed the brittle tome from the shelf and opened it. "The Laws of Ruin", written by a Spanish friar in the 16th century, Philip of Navarre, translated into English by Professors Theodore Hayward Gates and Pascal Chevillion in 1714.

His heart raced and his thoughts flew wilder than the storms that rape the Arctic landscape. He was now more certain than ever that his answers were here. Here in this room, here in this house, and here in these people. Like well disciplined soldiers his thoughts fell into formation.

Patience. Here!

Caution. Here!

Control. Here!

Gregory Bradshaw Marsh exhaled.

The storm that would bear his answers loomed on the horizon. He no longer felt bound by silent shadows. No longer was he a far cry from the truth. Ancient memories were placing their hands on doorknobs in the sealed rooms of his mind. Soon the doors would open and the truth would arrive.

As he read Navarre's words on the brittle pages before him, he envisioned the dark-skinned Spaniard as he sat before a heavy wooden table in a tiny bay of candlelight, praying to his god for strength as he recorded the blasphemous knowledge that Marsh now held in his trembling hands. Marsh knew the terrified Dominican brother's hands had also trembled, although for different reasons than his own, had while writing this arcane text. He could well imagine the horrors that clawed at the monk's psyche as he recounted this base knowledge. Hungrily, he read with great joy and immense hope, until on the seventeenth page he was struck by a thunderbolt.

> *She, the demon bride of Cthulhu, waits—*
> *beyond the black abyss to rip all hope from the earth.*
> *She yearns to gorge on the flesh of men.*
> *From her horrid wombs,*
> *she longs to birth her brother's monstrous spawn again.*
> *The headless gray snake, ever knotted,*
> *waits to grind the bones of man to dust.*
> *Sons of light!*
> *Fear the ever hungry thousand rending teeth of madness.*
> *Swords are nothing against her blasphemy.*
> *Protect the seals!*
> *Beware the foul cry.*
> *IÄ! KASSOGTHA! HPTUGH! G'GHNA NI'ZOS*
> *I'GAQ!'*

There was his answer. The word burned through his mind like scorching lava. *Kassogtha!* Quickly he read on. The words sang of the horrid she-beast who had coupled with her own brother to spawn blasphemies that would rip all light and hope from the slight grasp of mankind. His answer had arrived.

* * * * *

"Stewart, you're out of your fucking mind. By tomorrow morning this will be everywhere. Can't you count? We now have eight, count 'em, eight butchered corpses laying around the streets of this city! People are already going crazy and now you propose that we print this letter. No fucking way we're going proactive! I want the fucking lid nailed down. You got that?" task force Commander Marlin Matthews barked as one hand slapped his desk.

"Just wait a minute. This will work. Just listen another minute?" Chris asked.

"You just don't get it. This isn't about just hookers anymore. We've got a dead male. Gay maybe, but he wasn't a hooker. And—"

"God damn it, Marlin, that's what I'm trying to tell you. He's upped the ante. We're running out of time. The next one can be any-one. All bets are off. Can you hear what I'm saying? He's got almost seventy thousand people to choose from. Christ, you've got three teenage girls. Think about that! And you better not forget the mayor. He's got two grown daughters living in this city. You ever seen the chest on the younger one, Melanie? She could pose for one of those super-juggs mags. You better count on the fact that shit like that is running through Ivanelli's mind before you shut me out."

"You think I like any of this?"

"Than just listen. Gimme me five minutes."

"Okay. Not that it's going to get you anywhere. Well? Clock's ticking."

"Good. Now, this fuck's dying for headlines, right? You've read the letter he sent. He wants to see his name up in lights. Beckett's chompin' at the bit to run with this. So let's unleash him. And here's the thing, we keep Beckett tethered. He won't like it, but he'll still jump at the chance, and you know it. We feed Beckett and our boy's gonna come running. Did you read that report on the killer's beliefs? I've got an expert right here in the city and he's willing to help us on this. Just run it by Carroll, that's all I'm asking."

"I'll try. But I'm not pushing on this. If they buy it, they buy it. If not, well, like I said, I won't push. Understand?"

All too fucking well.

🐛 Chapter Nine 🐛

Tired and frustrated after four hours in the cold, Investigator Rob Kramer walked in and slumped down at the desk adjacent to Chris.

"Turn up anything?" Chris asked.

"A couple of things. I was right about the tires. Nothing. Good old Goodyears—ten billion served. The lab says they can match 'em when we find the car. Big fucking deal. So far, we've talked to two of the three bartenders who worked last night, and two of the waitresses. We've still got another waitress to talk to and we're getting a list together of people who were in the club last night. It's slow going. The vic's name was James Paul, went by the name Jimmy or sometimes Jazz. He was a hot little number, they tell me. Just about anybody, anytime, I guess. Last night he was just cruising. Seems there was one guy that he was sitting with for a while last night. They talked about ten minutes, had a drink, and young Jimmy left. Both left sometime after eleven. Not together, though. We've got a vague description of the guy. White male about six feet. Maybe two hundred pounds. Dark hair, maybe black. Eyes we don't know. Red ski jacket with yellow and bright blue trim across the back and on the sleeves. The one bartender said if the guy held out his arms like this," Rob Kramer extended his arms to form a T, "he'd look like a big neon T. Red stem with yellow and blue across the top. He was wearing new jeans. Tight. And get this—a nice ass. How the fuck do you put that in a description? And you're gonna like this, hiking boots."

"Sounds like a match," Chris said.

"I've got the lab boys working the table they sat at. They've got a good set of prints from what we hope is the perp's right hand. We're checking them now, and I'm hoping that there'll be a good dried boot print on the floor to match the prints in the lot. Maybe we'll get lucky?"

"That's a lot more than we had before," Chris said, thinking the beast had finally left more than fruitless traces of his passing.

The phone interrupted.

"They did? Okay. I'll call you after I get done with Beckett. Have a little faith. It can't hurt. Yeah." *A print and a lure. Now we're gettin' somewhere.*

"Beckett? What's he got to do with this? Thought we put a lid on him," Kramer said.

"We're going to let Beckett print the letter. Hopefully our boy will respond and Beckett will play him like a violin for us," Chris said, allowing a hopeful smile to light his face.

* * * * *

Chris, along with Rolly Hawkins, Cosmo, and the Wizard, sat in Al Jankowski's office at the *Times-Herald* waiting for Jack Beckett.

"When do we start? I've already written this article in my head a hundred times," Beckett said, storming into Jankowski's office.

"Not so fast," the managing editor said. "It's their way or no way. But we get the chance to have this guy all to ourselves. Whadaya think?"

"Done. Now give me the details," Beckett demanded.

"This is Cosmo Renaldi and his partner, the Wizard," Chris said.

"The what?" Beckett asked.

"The Wizard."

"Yeah. I heard you the first time. So what?"

"Look, Beckett, they're experts on the beliefs of this butcher."

"You're kidding? These two?" Beckett thought they looked like two rejects from one of those bands that the kids liked on MTV. "If you ask me—"

"I didn't. Now shut up and listen. They've got plenty to say," Chris commanded.

Beckett didn't care if it was Arnold Ziffel and Bozo the Clown sitting there, as long as they could provide him with more information on that weird letter, and the mind behind the hand that composed it. Beckett sat there chain-smoking and listening without interrupting for twenty minutes as Cosmo related the details, with the Wizard adding color commentary.

"Holy shit!" Beckett exclaimed. "This is for real, isn't it?"

"As hell. I brought you some reading material. Might be a good idea to start with this one," Cosmo said as he handed Beckett a copy of Maurice Lévy's *Lovecraft: A Study in the Fantastic*.

"What's this?" Beckett asked.

"It's the doctoral dissertation of a French professor, critic, and editor concerning HPL and his Mythos. It was published in '72, so

you won't find any references to Kassogtha. There weren't any stories written about her then, but it's a good overview of Lovecraft's
work," Cosmo explained, quickly deciding he didn't like this "asshole
one damn bit." "It's also a quick read."

"So, what's your story angle?" asked a very distrusting Chris.

"First I want to print the whole letter. He'll like that, but we
want him to respond, so we've got to have his letter contain an error
of some kind. Not too big, not too small. Cosmo, I might need a bit
of help on that. I want to read some of these books and you're going
to have to help me decide just what in this letter is important to this
freak. Call him a religious freak, some kind of fanatic. Maybe if I
compare him to Jim Jones, or Karesh in Waco? I know they're different, but that might bother him. He'd want to correct me. I'll bait
him with Lovecraft's mythology being taken way too far, and I'll say
something about this demon-goddess thing to suck him in. You guys
have a psychological profile on him yet?" Beckett asked.

"State police are revising now. We should have it later."

"Good. How about VICAP?"

Screw the Feds. "Nothing." *Does this ass think I'm stupid?*

"Okay. Way I figure it, by screwing up his little missive we'll be
forcing him to correct us. Then I'll try to mold my column to hopefully draw him into some type of a dialogue with me. Once he's talking to us we just have to see where it leads. Maybe I should change
his name, too? He didn't mention the one I already dropped on him,
so maybe I can stir him up a bit with a new one? Hmmm . . . religious, huh? Maybe 'Nightmare's Disciple.' Just a touch of religion.
Sound okay to you, Stewart?" asked the cocky reporter, who was once
again playing with the idea of his first Pulitzer. "There's one other
thing that I want to know. What if by talking to this freak he gets
pissed off at me? You guys gonna watch my back? I don't want to be
alone on this. I hope you guys are going to be close."

"Like flies on shit," Chris said, thinking that Beckett was literally a piece of shit. Chris could see what the reporter was thinking, and
Chris didn't think much of anyone who was in this for personal gain.

An hour and forty-nine minutes after Chris and company left the
meeting with Beckett and his editor, Jack Beckett returned with a finished article. Beckett had written the article Thursday afternoon when
he'd received the letter. It hadn't taken him long to rewrite it, fitting

in the information Cosmo had just given him. This would be a good opening move: Print the letter with a brief commentary by Beckett.

"Al, try this. I think this is good."

Jankowski looked up from the article on his desk. "Jack, do you remember what kids used to say when they played cowboys and Indians?"

Beckett shook his head from side to side in a negative response.

"Bang. Bang. You're dead." Jankowski held his hand out, thumb up and index finger pointed as if his hand were a pistol. "You've locked your sights on this creep and I do believe you've hit the bullseye."

"That's what I thought. If this doesn't bring him out, nothing will. Think the cops will go for it?"

"They have to. This nutbag isn't going to walk into headquarters and give himself up. Okay. Let's get this cleared and on the front page."

* * * * *

At 1:13 p.m. Marc Frisell, while delivering the mail on his route, discovered the body of Donnalee O'Donnell lying mutilated beside her car in her driveway on Londonderry Court. He promptly deposited his lunch near the body before he ran down the block screaming for someone to call the police. At 1:15 Michelle Erskin stopped watching her favorite soap opera, *Days of Our Lives*, to see just what in the world was going on outside her home. Before the second hand could strike twelve she dialed 911.

* * * * *

Chris had just dropped Cosmo and the Wizard off at The Horror Corner when the reported homicide came over the radio. White female, reportedly mutilated. "Fuck me. That's not even ten blocks from Lauri's." The two blocks between The Horror Corner and Eastern Parkway disappeared as if by magic when Chris floored the Taurus. In less than ten minutes Chris was turning on to Londonderry Court. *Two in one day. Dear God save us all.*

There were two patrol cars on the scene when Chris arrived. "This one sure ain't no hooker," patrolman Frank Koglmann said to Chris as he came around the cruiser blocking the driveway's entrance.

"Two in one day? We heard about the fag. An hour from now you guys are gonna think hell would be a nice spot to vacation in."

"I've thought that for sometime now, Frankie."

* * * * *

Forty minutes after Michelle Erskin placed the 911 call, she learned that the woman three houses down had been butchered by the monster she'd been reading about in the newspapers all winter. Michelle Erskine was horrified. She had been under the impression that the murderer only preyed on prostitutes. The mailman had quickly changed her perception on who was likely to become the butcher's next victim. As she walked back inside her home, she turned to look in the front hallway's mirror. "Thank God you guys never listened to me," she said as she looked at her underdeveloped breasts.

* * * * *

Chris spent the next two hours scrutinizing the crime scene: on his knees, looking at footprints and the body, walking the street trying to find matching boot prints, talking with the letter carrier. Twice he called Rolly. His time was spent directing, probing, and bitching. Chris walked around Donnalee O'Donnell's bungalow three times looking for boot prints and finding none. Three houses down the street he found four tracks that the wind had not obscured. The prints matched the one in the photo he had from the day's previous murder, confirming what he already knew. It was the same perp.

This one wasn't revealing much, except this woman wasn't a prostitute and this had happened at her own home. *Christ! This is a quiet residential street, not the Hill,* he told himself, thinking about the drug-infested streets of Schenectady's impoverished neighborhood. *The son-of-a-bitch stalked this woman. This was well planned and carried out. He didn't just happen upon her, but we never thought he just bumped into the others, either.*

As the M.E.'s team finished bagging the body and the forensics team moved stiffly in the cold, Chris squatted behind the bushes where Marsh had waited. Lighting a cigarette, he wondered about the newest victim. Where had his freak seen her? And other than for sheer terror, why was he now killing outside of the city's troop of prostitutes?

Think, damn it! Why is this fuck taking their breasts? Chris was aware of Thomas Harris' *The Silence of the Lambs*; he began to wonder if the killer had found some twisted inspiration from the novel's psychopath. *Can't make a girl suit out of just breasts, can you? You're approaching this thing wrong. Think in terms of the Mythos. He is.*

Think. This Kassogtha thing is some type of what? Fertility goddess? Or is she just some kind of sexual vessel? The whore of these things. That's still a fertility goddess, isn't it? Chris pulled a well worn photocopy of the letter from his pocket and read it again. *Breasts? Whores? Feeding whores to her? A whore for a whore? Okay. Breasts equal suckling? Full breasts, more milk? Maybe? Nah. None of the women were pregnant. You've got to be pregnant to have milk, don't you? It's something else. Are the breasts offerings? But why a male? He didn't have breasts. Forget the guy. Assume he's just to throw us off the scent. Whores? Breasts? No, it's not whores. This woman wasn't a whore. It's just the breasts. Yeah. Now what about them? Size? Shape? What do they call it? Cups. Are they all the same? I'll check with the M.E., but what about the color? Some are white and some are black.* Suddenly the thought of Laurinda rushed to the center of his consciousness. *Sweet mother of God! What if this fuck sees Lauri somewhere? She's only about nine blocks from here. Christ! I've got to find this fucker now.*

"Tucker! C'mere. Listen. I want everything you can find on this woman," Chris said, pointing to the blood-splattered snow angel O'Donnell's body had left in the white blanket of frozen ground. "And I want it *now*. I want to know her every movement for the last month. No. Three! I want work, shopping, friends, boyfriends, girlfriends. I mean everything. When you're done, I want you to know her better than your wife. I'm gonna look inside the house a bit, and then I want you to take it apart. I want photographs of the cracks the cockroaches live in. Got it? And I want the whole fuckin' block gone over, twice. Impound this car. Have it checked for prints, vacuumed. The works."

Chris removed the woman's keys from an evidence bag and went into her home. He was immediately greeted by a tiny, long-haired gray tiger kitten rubbing against his ankle. "Hi there, little one." Chris bent over and picked up the kitten, holding it gently while he stroked between its ears. "Yes . . . . Hi. And what's your name? Hungry? Let's see if we can find you some chow."

Chris sat at the kitchen table and watched the kitten eat. *Poor little guy. I hate to see you go to the shelter.* As he smoked a cigarette he

began whistling Erroll Garner and Johnny Burke's "Misty." *Yeah!*
Helpless. "Misty. Well, little one, it seems you've got a new name."
After feeding the no-longer-orphaned kitten which he had decided to
take home, he began looking through the slain woman's appealing
bungalow.

Clean and organized. Soft. Lots of blues and tans. *The sky and the*
earth, he thought. The comfortable looking furniture was a soft,
warm inviting blue. Someone interesting had lived here; he liked it.
It was homey.

Owls of almost every size and color imaginable perched nearly
everywhere he looked. Her living room contained shelf after shelf of
the nesting birds of prey.

Chris took note of the expensive-looking stereo system and what
must have amounted to hundreds of LP's. *Likes music, but no TV. Let's*
see what she liked. Rock. Box sets by Clapton, the Byrds, C, S, & N, the Bee
Gee's—didn't know they had one. I'll have to pick it up. Blach—Rod
Stewart. A disgrace to the name. Los Lobos, Billy Joel. Lot of Santana.
R.E.M., the Beatles, Lennon, and the Stones. Looks like she liked jazz too.
There's a bunch of it. Bill Evans, Sonny Rollins, Susannah McCorkle. Rolly
likes her—I think he said she's a hometown girl. Miles Davis. Lauri's got a
lot of his records. Brubeck and John Coltrane. Lauri has stuff by these guys too.
Hey. I've got this Pat Metheny record. A little rock for fun and some jazz to
mellow out with, just the way I like it. He made a mental note to have
her picture shown to all the local record stores. *Maybe our butcher saw*
her in a record shop? That fuckin' bastard. A nice-looking woman with some
taste and now she's dead. I don't know who you are, but you can bet your ass
I'll find you, and when I do you're going to pay for this.

Three large light oak bookcases occupied the opposite wall. Half
of the first was filled with books on quilt-making and crocheting.
Surprisingly to Chris, a large number of the remaining books were
horror; especially vampires.

Let's see what we've got. Seven by King. Ramsey Campbell. Wow. How
many we got? Eleven. Cos said this guy wrote Mythos stories. I wonder if any
of these others are about it. Foundations of Fear, Complete Stories and
Poems of Edgar Allen Poe, Prime Evil, The Year's Best Horror Stories
vol. 2 . . . 5, 6, 8, 10, 11, 12, 16. *Robert R. McCammon, four. Anne Rice,*
Anne Rice, Anne Rice, Anne Rice. And five more, I guess we liked her.
Ligotti? Think Cosmo mentioned him. Barker, Tanith Lee—Dark

Dance—*Don't know what yours is about, but this one ain't no waltz.*
Under the Fang, Anno-Dracula, Vamphyri! *Lumley—he's a famous
Mythos guy?* A Whisper of Blood, *and* Lost Souls . . . *by who? Poppy Z.
Brite! That's her name?*

Serial killer novels took up three entire shelves of the last book-
case. Charles Manson's photograph on the spine of former Fug Ed
Sanders' *The Family* caught Chris' eye. "They shoulda fragged his ass
but good," he told the shadowing kitten. *Shane Stevens,* By Reason of
Insanity—*good book. The Night of the Ripper.* "Three by Michael Slade.
I've read a couple of these. He's a little gory, but not bad." *Four of
Sandford's* Prey *series. We could sure use Lucas Davenport on this case.
Maybe he could have saved her.* The Silence of the Lambs *and* Red
Dragon, The Crosskiller. *"Shit!"* The Trail of Cthulhu, *she's even got a
Mythos book. Better check the bookstores.*

Chris went through the wastepaper basket. Near the bottom he
found a crumpled shopping list for kitten chow, pickles, butter, and
Lubriderm dry skin lotion, and two empty bags. One was from the
Up Your Alley record shop and the other from the Open Door bookstore on Jay Street. Both had sales slips inside them, dated within the
last four weeks.

*Did she shop downtown a lot? He's preying on hookers, working the
Hill. A guy off Erie, and a woman he might have seen on Jay. Maybe he
works downtown. What are we talkin', a fifteen-, twenty-block radius.*

Putting the bags back into the waste basket, he walked to the
coffee table. Sitting on the tidy surface was a clean ashtray, two
remote controls, and a red, metal twenty-fifth anniversary Schultz &
Dooley coaster. Next to the coaster sat a vampire bookmark which
said *"I vant to bite your book"* and an untouched paperback entitled
Winter Prey by John Sandford. Under different circumstances he
would have laughed.

❦ Chapter Ten ❦

It was Christmas 1968 and the VC were throwing a party in 'Nam' and everyone in Chu Lai had been invited.

Parris Island and the rigors of stateside training were now a long forgotten summer camp to PFC Christopher Stewart and the other marines in Echo Company. They were breathing the smoke and fire of hell now. Hot dogs, G.T.O.'s, and girls in tight, colorful sweaters were the legendary stuff of dreams.

A blanket of darkness settled on Hill 118, and the air was alive with mortar and small arms fire. Fireworks for Christmas. Chris would have loved it if he wasn't so damned scared.

The eighteen-year-olds back home were listening to Cream and Sly and the Family Stone, while Chris was embroiled in the call and response of M-14's and AK-47's. He'd been in country for all of two weeks, and was now knee-deep in the rising shit. This was his second firefight in less than a week. He'd barely had his cherry popped, yet he'd already seen enough death for two lifetimes.

"INCOMING!" screamed a quickly moving marine covered in mud.

Chris hit the bottom of the hole and pressed his head to the over-saturated earth. It would soon be muddy soup. His tears added to the moisture of the day's rain. Four numbered plastic bags had left by chopper today; one of the homeward-bound was in three pieces, one had no legs and half an arm, one no face—the luckiest just had two large holes in his chest.

Jesus, don't let me leave in one of those, he prayed, clutching the silver crucifix that hung about his neck.

He was already sick of this place.

During the day, he tried to walk tall, pretending he wasn't scared; at night, he lay in holes trying not to piss himself. Not that it really mattered, everything here was so fucking wet. He'd decided he was going to live in Arizona when he got back to the States. "No more of this damn rain." After an hour, the small arms chatter died away and Chris hunkered down in his poncho to try to sleep. When the sun rose, he thanked God. Day number fifteen began.

By the middle of February, Chris thought Lt. Col. Bull Fisher was God and the First Marine Brigade, Second Battalion Fourth Marines, were Bull's personal avenging angels. In his heart he believed that the 24th were indeed Magnificent Bastards. They took names, kicked asses, and let God sort out the bodies they left in their angry wake. Around his neck he wore the silver cross his mother had given him before his trip, his dog tags, and four ears that at one time had been attached to NVC soldiers. His tears had gone to live in a secret place in his heart. Often when he prayed now, his fingers clutched the ears instead of the cross. Hell had burned the veneer of civilization from him. He had learned to survive in the wastelands of nightmare.

There were four angels of death in Echo Company. If they were asked, they would have willingly battled the Four Horsemen of the Apocalypse with only coarse words. With their letters, the members of Echo Company sent their dreams home to the States for safekeeping, while they deprived demons of stealing their souls. Fear-conquering laughter and grief became the whetstone that sharpened them.

The fire team was the universe. Air, fire, earth, and water. PFC Patrick Michael Price—born Boston, Massachusetts, 1951. Air, the sun that shone through darkness. PFC Christopher James Stewart — born Schenectady, New York, 1951. Fire, the berserker who willed them on; always hoping home might lay beyond the next hill or paddy. Corporal Antonio Joseph Costansa—born Canton, Ohio, 1950. Earth, the foundation of dark truth on which they stood. PFC Thomas Edmund Gabriel—born Yaak, Montana, 1950. Water, who filled their hearts with abundant hope. Red, Hollywood, Connie, and Gabe. They knew each other better than the mothers at whose breasts they had suckled. Closer than lovers, they shared one body and one dream. They were warriors born of necessity. Let fear strike any man that crossed their path.

* * * * *

The doorbell of the Marsh mansion on Washington Street delivered its low-toned double dong at 3:40 p.m., announcing the arrival of the first guests. Gregory Bradshaw Marsh turned from his reading and stood dumbstruck as Judith Ann Marsh and her husband Thomas Waite entered the library. Ethan, taking note of Gregory's expression, instantly introduced them. Before a slack-jawed and wide-eyed Gregory stood his dead mother. Impossibility screamed as the reality before him offered its pale hand.

"My dear, dear Gregory. I am Judith Ann Waite, your mother's cousin, Ida's mother. I must tell you how delighted I was when Ethan phoned me earlier this afternoon. Thomas and I are so very pleased to meet you. Please allow me to express my deepest sympathies regarding the passing of your dear mother. We are all so glad that you've found your way home to us," the fifty-year-old woman standing before him said. As she released his hand her smile deepened. It was not a smile of joy, but the dark satisfaction that greed enjoys when it's counting the black coinage acquired by stealth and deception.

"Yes. It's nice to meet you as well," the off-balance guest said as his thoughts began to wonder about these Marsh women. The woman in the portrait, his mother, and now this cousin all bore a striking resemblance to one another. Gregory Bradshaw Marsh didn't know anything about genetics, yet his mind was turning toward questions regarding generations and the blood that flowed from one into the next. They could have been sisters. Two of them might have been twins. "Please pardon my stare. It's just you look so much like my mother. It's uncanny."

"Sonia and I were occasionally confused by the townsfolk. This similarity of features has always been a Marsh trait. At least among the Marsh women. But we shall have time to discuss that later. Ethan, if you would be so kind, I would like a sherry."

"Certainly, Mother," Ethan replied.

The other guests arrived and introductions were made. Gregory Bradshaw Marsh had returned to the bosom of his family, and what a dark heart that bosom contained.

The library was filled with pleasantries and smiles. Shaded polite smiles with cold voices. Marsh thought they sounded like crows trying to convince a dying squirrel they were vegetarians. He told himself to walk slowly in this newly found realm of shadows, and to keep his hand extended to avoid outcroppings posed by these laughing and drinking relatives.

Seated at the desk was eighty-three-year-old Warden, his cousin's great-uncle, who had yet to utter a word except a stunted, hoarse hello. Standing beside Judith and her husband were two petite thirtyish Marsh women—Seton and Norma, Judith's twin daughters. Again the resemblance to his mother was quite remarkable. Standing with Ethan and Gregory were Ethan's uncle Avery, his wife Millicent, and Avery's brother Merrick, with his wife Eunice on his arm.

Gregory Bradshaw Marsh carefully fielded their subtle inquiries as he tried to determine what they sought from him. He knew these people were truly delighted he was here, but he could feel their wariness, and as yet he could not determine their hidden agenda. They were waiting for something, but what he had yet to ascertain. Marsh realized his answers would be withheld until they observed the sign they awaited.

He'd been so completely engrossed by the others that he had forgotten Ida. Where was she? He thought to ask about her, but held his question. And there she was, tastefully attired in a simply cut black dress and a single pearl adorning her moon-colored neckline, poised in the doorway of the library. Every head turned to her and silence fell. She smiled and nodded, as if to grant permission to return to their conversations. She came to Gregory's side and placed her delicate hand upon his arm. For the next thirty minutes her hand never left his arm, and her eyes rarely looked away from his face. The queen had joined her consort, and all in the room seemed gladdened.

Gregory's blood ran wild at the sight of her. For a moment, shaking himself free from the magnet of her perfume, he tried to tell himself that this was his cousin, and they shared the same blood, and yet he could not rid his thoughts of Kassogtha coupling with her own brother, Cthulhu. Distorted by pressure and heat, his dynamic mental cinematics arrested him. Sweat blending with sweat, loins marrying loins, teeth raking nipples, screams melting into moans. Somehow he must find a way to have this creature who was clinging to his arm.

Dinner was served along with charming family stories and champagne. As dinner proceeded, perhaps due to the many magnums, the conversation softened and the laughter became warmer. There was much talk of the family's fishing fleet and last season's windfall profits, the family's gold refinery, and the newly formed salvage operation. At length, they discussed the Marsh family's efforts to rebuild the once moldering town. Dinner over, they returned to the library. Over after-dinner drinks, Gregory asked and answered many questions.

"You really must tell us how you came to find out about Innsmouth and the family," requested Judith Ann.

"As I've told Ethan, after my mother passed away, I was going through some of her papers and came upon her birth certificate and her marriage license. When I came across her birthplace, I thought perhaps there might be some relatives living here. And here I am, so to speak." After a brief pause, Marsh decided to try his luck and see what reactions he might garner with a few well chosen words. "I had also just come upon a few paperback books that mentioned Innsmouth. You may be aware of their author, Howard Philips Lovecraft."

All eyes in the room fell on him as responses flew like projectiles.

"A damn *liar*," spat Merrick Marsh.

"The spawn of bastards," enjoined his brother Avery.

"Lovecraft was a horrible little man who seduced this family with lies, and then set out to ruin our good name with his tasteless little stories. Lies, all lies. May he rot in some hell forever," condemned Ethan.

Clutching her twin's hand, Seton added, "All that horrible filth about the plague of '46. He should have been dealt with sooner. "

"Daughter! Enough," came the harsh, yet tightly controlled, utterance of Judith Ann.

"I should have let him drown in Devil's Reef that day he fell in," hissed Warden Marsh from below dark reptilian eyes.

Gregory was thrilled. Their responses were more than he'd hoped. *Yes*, he thought, *there are secrets here. Secrets that will solve this puzzle for me. It's now just a question of time.* "But what about the statements of Horvath Blayne, Asaph Waite, and Joseph Curwen Marsh? And what of these books? Here sits *The Book of Eibon* and Remigius' *Daemonolation.*" Pointing to the shelf of arcane texts, he removed one they all recognized and held it before them. "And is this not the testament of the mad Arab that I hold?"

"Surely you do not believe in Lovecraft's hardly amusing tales? Why, that's insane," Ethan probed.

"Is it more insane than Allah, or Yahweh, or Buddha? Which God do you serve? I have seen the temple of Dagon sitting at New Church Green." Their eyes were suddenly hard. "Well? You obviously seek something from me, some sign perhaps? Shall we raise the curtain? Ask me what you will, but remember I seek answers myself."

"Might we have a few moments among ourselves, cousin?" Ethan asked.

Ida rose from her chair and walked to Gregory's side. Taking his hand, she spoke, "There is no need for discussion. This game tires me. Answer his questions that I may see that which I seek to know," commanded the young matriarch of the secretive clan.

"Thank you."

"It is my pleasure," Ida whispered to Gregory as her fingers entwined with his.

"Tell us who you are. In what do you believe? And why are you here among us?" Ethan demanded.

"I am the last piece of your puzzle and you are the picture I require to assemble mine," he replied. "I believe in the Outsiders and so do you. I seek the door to which you hold the key."

"Well spoken. My dear cousin," Ida said as she brought his hand to her lips and kissed it. "You will receive your answers, but not tonight. I tire. Gregory, would you be so kind as to escort me to my room."

"Few things could bring me more pleasure."

* * * * *

Mid afternoon in a widowless office. Beckett was going crazy. He'd torn up three drafts and was about to toss the fourth. *Two in one day? Two! And this one's a nurse, not a hooker. Maybe Stewart was right. The wackos think the millennium begins the end. This monster wants it, and he's starting early.*

"Beckett. Stewart. I'll make this short. You've heard about the woman? Okay. It's more of the same. Same MO only it's not a prostitute. The killing occurred uptown on a quiet residential street overlooking the park. You understand what I'm talking about? Now write. Get me this bastard and get him quick. And one more thing. You're working with us now and if we lose, you go down as well. You got that?"

The phone slammed in Beckett's ear. "Yeah. I got it. And fuck you." *Okay, Stewart, you want 'em. You got 'em.*

* * * * *

"Hey, Joe! You've got the con. Close up, will you. I've got some things to take care of," Pat Price said, grabbing his coat and heading for the door of his restaurant. All morning he'd listened to reports on the radio about the murdered man they'd found and now they'd reported discovering a second victim, a woman who was not a prostitute. *Hell!* "He'll be ready to burst an artery. I'll bet money he's screamin' louder than the fuckin' mayor." Pat hadn't seen Chris in six days. He was all too aware of how this series of murders was driving Chris and if anyone knew how possessed Chris could become, it was Pat. After touring 'Nam together, covering each other's butts, there were no secrets left between them. When Chris was on point, all his senses were directed toward only one goal, survival. Pat knew Chris felt this freak threatened his survival.

His thoughts lashed to the wheel of concern, Pat tried to contact Chris at headquarters. Rolly informed him Chris was out, tied up in a meeting.

"How's he takin' it?"

Rolly dropped a little background regarding the two victims on Pat.

"Shit. Thanks, Rolly. Yeah. Bye."

Pat drove the six blocks to the main branch of the public library hoping Laurinda might know something. At the reference desk he was informed that she'd taken a few personal days. "Personal days?" he asked, adding Laurinda's name to his list of friends to worry about.

Back in his car, he drove to her flat off upper Union, hoping she was okay. *If that fuck Kenny is bothering her again, I'm going to—Shit! In the mood Chris' in he'll kill the bastard*, Pat thought, recalling Chris and Kenny's last meeting. *It's too bad Chris and Lauri can't get over their fears and get together. Hell, it's twenty-five years now.*

Pat parked the car and walked up the porch steps. He rang the doorbell three times and waited.

Maybe she's sick. No, they said personal days. "I wonder where she is. Damn. I'll call her later."

* * * * *

At 8:45 p.m. Chris, exhausted and wishing he could put this off, pulled up to Laurinda's flat. *Guess it's time to meet cousin Henri. Remember, just take the dumb thing and shut up. And don't forget to smile.*

You don't need to rile her up again. And for God's sake, don't laugh at any of his voodoo mumbo jumbo. "Here we are, Misty. Now, Lauri's already got a cat. Name's Plato. He's a nice old guy, so I want you to be nice too. Tomorrow I'll take you to our house." *Wonder if I'm going to be staying tonight with Henri here? Guess I'm gonna find out.* "Well, it's showtime," he said to his reflection in the rearview mirror before he got out of the Taurus.

"Hello. Anybody home? Lauri, you home?"

"Hi there, handsome," Laurinda said as she kissed Chris. "Oh. And who is this? Hi, little one. Is he for me?"

"Well, yes and no. He was at the murdered woman's house and I didn't want to see him wind up in the shelter. So, I decided to keep him."

"You're sweet. Now what about you? I heard about the slayings. They're all over the news. Was it a bad day?" *That was stupid. Just look at his face.*

"Feels like hell is in session again. Heat's unbearable downtown, and the national press hasn't even shown up yet, but I'd bet they'll be here by this time tomorrow. Ivanelli and Carroll are already havin' babies down at City Hall. They want the state boys brought in, and there's talk about maybe even bringing in the Feds. But we'll talk about that later. Did your cousin show yet? Before you say anything, I promise to be good."

"Thanks. I knew you would," she said before rewarding him with another kiss. "He's in the living room. Would you like a beer before you meet him? I bought some Coors today. If you're hungry, I've got some baked ham and there might be some turkey for a sandwich."

"Just a beer. I'm not too sure I could eat right now."

"Ah, Christopher! *Bonjour.* I am Henri, Laurinda's cousin. I am so very glad to finally meet you. Please accept my apologies regarding the unfortunate circumstances surrounding our meeting. I had always hoped we would meet under, shall we say, more festive conditions," he said, offering his massive hand to Chris with a glowing smile. "But I could not ignore my *grand-mère's* wishes in this matter. I hope you will understand."

My god. This guy could play for any team in the NFL. Is everybody in the family this big? Chris wondered, recalling the size of Laurinda's three older brothers. "Uh, yeah, I understand. Glad to meet you. How about a brew? I was just going to have one."

"Thank you. I would love one."

"Why don't we sit in the living room? I think we'd be more comfortable while we talk," Laurinda said as she took three bottles of Coors from the refrigerator. "Here we go," she said, handing the beers to Chris and Henri. "Where should we start?" asked an-ill-at-ease Laurinda as she wondered how uncomfortable Chris was.

"Laurinda has informed me that you have discussed my reasons for coming, so perhaps we should talk about *Grand-mère's* charm first?"

"Sure. Let's get it out of the way."

From his jacket pocket, Henri removed a case that matched the one that he had handed to Laurinda just a few hours earlier. Opening the case, he handed it to Chris. "This is *Le Pierre du dardien du ciel*. It is French for the stone of heaven's guardian. If you would please put it on, I will explain why *Grand-mère* feels you need its protection."

"Sure," Chris said as he placed the stone around his neck.

The crude star hung just below the silver crucifix that had hung there for over two decades. He could feel its warmth. *Odd*, he thought. *Shouldn't a piece of stone feel cold until it absorbs some body heat? Well, if it makes her happy. I guess it can't hurt.*

Laurinda nodded and mouthed a soundless "thanks", followed by a blown kiss and a smile. Silently she added "I love you."

"*Merveilleux*! It is done. Now, where should I begin? Yes, with *Grand-mère*. As you are aware, I believe Laurinda has filled you in somewhat, *oui*? My *grand-mère* practices voodoo. *Blanc* voodoo. Not the dark blood-filled magic used for greed and power. Her work serves the light. She honors tradition and respects the loas. You would call them spirits. She uses her gifts to give aid to the needy, to help those whose lives have been touched by trouble or despair. You must understand that she is an old woman who has spent a lifetime working for good. When she senses trouble, she tries to help in the only way she knows. I am here at her behest to aid you in any way possible. Please do not feel offended by my presence here. I am aware you do not believe in our ways, but among her peers *Grand-mère* is considered a very powerful priestess. To us this is a serious matter. If we did not feel it so important we would not ask this of you."

"When Lauri first told me you were coming I didn't like the idea, but it's okay. I'll go along with things, but you have to understand that I don't believe in this stuff."

"There is more I must tell you. *Grand-mère* asks that you promise never to remove the charm from your neck. It must remain there at all times until this matter reaches its conclusion. Will you give me your word of honor on this?"

"Sure. As far as this is concerned, yes. I promise," Chris said, holding the stone up.

"Thank you. You have made an old woman feel more at ease with your pledge. Now, if you would like I shall explain what she has seen," Henri said.

"I'd like to get another brew first. Can I get you another?" Chris asked.

"No, thank you."

In the kitchen, Chris suddenly realized how little he knew about certain members of Laurinda's family. *Guess I'm gonna find out.* As he turned, he found Laurinda's arms coming around his waist.

"I love you," she said, kissing him. "Thanks for being so understanding. It means a lot to me."

When they returned, Henri said, "I must tell you how good you two look together. It is unfortunate *Grand-mère* could not be here. I am quite sure that you would like her. She is a very special woman and I am quite certain she would like you." *Yes, she would like you a great deal. I can feel the powers of light that reside in your heart.*

"Thanks." Uncomfortable, Chris changed the subject. "About the stones?"

"This began when *Grand-mère* was visited by a sensation of foreboding. Her premonition was saturated by darkness, by an evil obsessed by hunger. The malevolence she felt pressed both Laurinda and you. *Grand-mère* felt your deaths. It was at this point that she questioned the tarot. You must understand the accuracy of the tarot diminishes when the person you wish to read is not present. Yet she read the cards. What they revealed terrified her. Then the next afternoon, Laurinda called, and here I am. I have already read the cards for her today at *Grand-mère's* request. If you would permit me, she has asked me to read yours as well."

Chris looked to Laurinda for help. He could see she wanted him to go along with this. *Maybe she believes some of this stuff. I know she lived with these people for four years, some of it must have rubbed off.* "I don't believe in this stuff. Does that make any difference?"

"This is not your fortune in an astrological sense. We will be asking the loas to answer one question, not to divine the whole of your life. This question will be of your choosing. I shall not know the question. I shall merely explain the answer the loas provide you through the cards. Are you ready to begin?"

"I guess. What do I have to do?"

"First we will have to prepare. I understand you place no credence in this, but I shall ask you to not disrespect the spirits. There are a number of elements you will perhaps find strange. Please just accept them as part of the ritual. They will not harm you. Your task is to concentrate on the question. Try to set your doubts aside until the ritual is concluded. There is one other thing the ritual requires of you. You must offer the loas a sacrifice."

"Lauri's explained sacrifice to me," Chris said instantly recalling his unfortunate chicken joke. "Is there something I should give? Anything in particular?" he asked, a bit fearful of the answer.

"You may give the loas food or drink. *Grand-mère* and I normally donate food or money to the needy."

"Something like a banana and one of these?" Chris held up a can of Coors.

Henri smiled. "That would work. If you will give Laurinda and I a few minutes to gather the items we shall need for the ritual."

"No problem." *See, that wasn't too bad. You managed to behave and what can this really hurt. All it costs is a few minutes of your time. Besides, Lauri seems happy.*

Watching Plato and Misty at play, an idea came to him.

While Henri and Laurinda were gathering the materials they needed, Chris went into the kitchen and brought back a banana and a beer, which he placed alongside three cigarettes and his check to the animal shelter for for twenty-five dollars.

Henri beamed as Laurinda bent to kiss Chris. "Yes, *mon ami*. Your sacrifice is in the proper spirit. May our quest have the blessings of the loas. We will be ready to begin in a moment."

Henri cleared the table and placed a mirror in the center, along with a red candle, three sticks of incense, a glass, and a cup of water and some potting soil. The dining room lights were extinguished and the candle lit, as the ritual of honor was performed and the ritual of sacrifice began. As the room filled with spirits and hopes, Henri removed the Significator card, *Rada Houngan*, the storms of heaven, from the deck and placed it in the center of the mirror. Chris then shuffled the deck. "Concentrate, Christopher. Concentrate on your question," Henri instructed.

Chris found it easy to focus on catching the killer. Very little else ever entered his mind these days. As if it were a frequently repeated mantra, Chris silently asked, *Will I catch this beast?*

"Now. Cut the cards, use only your left hand, and make three piles."

Henri picked up the cards with his left hand and placed the first card on top of the Significator. "This covers him," he said as he then turned over the next card and placed it on the two already there.

Laurinda gasped as she saw the card. Hours earlier the identical card had crossed her.

"This crosses him," Henri fearfully whispered.

Before the seated trio sat *Congo*, the Place. Laurinda knew Congo. Calm outside, a demon within—crafty and filled with secret violence. Danger and evil stood in Chris' path, as well as her own. Henri continued until before them on the table ten cards formed the Celtic Cross, which Henri, with the aid of the spirits, would use to answer Chris' question.

The loas, through Henri, told Chris that yes, he would meet Congo, his adversary, and that grievous danger awaited. The horizon before him was covered in darkness. The loas saw him, horns locked in ferocious battle with the titanic forces of evil. The final resolution could be positive if Chris brought all his strength and courage to bear for the forces of light and purity. Yet there was a great chance that if his faith and determination faltered, he would lose everything dear to him and all around him. Finally, the loas foretold, even if he succeeded, he would give up some part of himself or those around him.

After a short period of silent meditation and thanks the ritual was ended. Henri collected the cards and reverently returned them to a white piece of silk. There was little conversation as Chris excused himself to retire for the night.

❦ Chapter Eleven ❦

Gazing out the window of her sixth-story penthouse overlooking the Isar River and toward the west and America, Christa Liebezeit, ex-devotee of astrology and the tarot at twenty, ex-witch, ex-Satanist at twenty-six, waited. Her luggage was packed and sitting by the door. In three hours she would embark for America and him.

This would be her greatest venture—years beyond Agrippa, Crowley, Atlantean magiks, and Dees, an ocean away from the half submerged shore of *don-wiche* in Suffolk. Finally closing her brittle-paged grimoires and turning away from Murrey, Frazer, and Barrett, she was prepared to embrace the New World.

Rarely in her thirty years had she been more excited. The last time it had been her marriage to seventy-eight-year-old Irmin Liebezeit, six years ago. Liebezeit had been the most powerful Satanist in Europe when she first met him at a black mass on Brocken near Blankenburg, in the Harz Mountains of Germany. The mass had been celebrated on April thirtieth, the feast of Saint Walpurgis.

Christa Liebezeit craved only two things in life: pleasure and power. Pleasure came in any form she could find. The night life, mind games, petty cruelty, narcotics, and sex: with men, young or old; with women; in groups, large or small; and on two occasions with animals. Power on the other hand was not derived quickly or found on the edge. Acquiring power took time, learning, and skill. It came from deception, cunning, and patience, as well as from shrewdly utilizing her formidable sexual skills, which she had long ago honed into a weapon few could resist.

Seizing opportunity, her skills were applied with the mastery of an expert on Irmin Liebezeit. Within two weeks of meeting him, she was a member of his coven and his mistress. Less than a year later she married the warlock, who'd become addicted to her sexual ardor and beauty. It was a marriage made in hell. Fueled by a rabid devotion to evil and burning lusts, the coven-master poured his resources into the one-sided relationship, catering to her multifarious appetites, supplying her with men, watching her with women.

Unfortunately, her husband's pact with the devil did not include immortality, a fact Christa was blithesomely aware of. Within a year of their nuptials he expired, leaving her his unwholesomely gained power, his illicit connections, and his bloated fortune. It was after his death, while chasing down a young Englishman from Bath who had aroused her lust, that she came upon her next addictive pursuit. The figurines.

She discovered them in a small antique shop, in a town to the southeast of Bath called Trowbridge. Adorned in filthy windows and peeling paint, it wasn't much, but something about the dilapidated store front compelled her; perhaps it was the name, Pharaoh's.

Inside were the usual. An old bird cage, a few chairs which might have been nice if they hadn't needed so much work, an assortment of supposedly antique vases, a purported piece of Stonehenge which someone had carved into a druidic rune. Overseeing the dusty assortment was a kindly old gentleman with an odd smile and an ever-present stare. As she was about to leave, she was asked if she would like to see some "unique and alluring" items. Yes, yes, she would.

With a gleeful step the old man locked the shop and took her upstairs, where behind a locked door she found her new calling. For almost two hours the old man showed her the instantly magnetic figurines and related fantastic tales regarding these deities to her.

Often during his discourse, he would stop to show her drawings of the same deities in a rare book, *Les Douze Déités du Couchemar* by Meridiana Montevecchi, who he explained to her was an expatriated Italian witch and occultist whose writings (this book in particular), drawings, and sculptures were well known in certain Parisian circles in the late 1800's. The notorious British demonologist and occultist Charles Bishop had shot her dead at a lecture in 1901, screaming she had betrayed holy secrets. Six months later he took his own life at the de Grandin asylum outside Paris. The affair had caused quite a stir in London, where it was common knowledge that Bishop's half-sister was married to the queen's third cousin.

Before sunset she was the new owner of the twelve figurines, each representing a deity she had never heard of, and Montevecchi's banned book. Eleven of the twelve she arranged to have shipped to her home in Germany. The twelfth, along with the worn old book, she took with her.

As she left the shop, the dark-skinned old man quietly laughed.

Upon returning to her hotel room, Christa placed the figure on a table and spent almost an hour transfixed by it, occasionally stirring to read of the other Great and Holy Old Ones in Montevecchi's book. From the instant she'd seen the sculptures she had been drawn to them, and now, sitting before the knotted, dark figurine, she wondered what the future would bring. "What I deserve . . . more power."

For years, Christa often had been captivated by the creations of the young American surrealist Randall Marsden. Death, alien architecture, unbridled sexuality, and destruction, all were present in his powerful other worldly paintings. Many times she'd wondered where this genius and his idol and gifted predecessor, the renowned H. R. Giger, came upon their inspiration. Now she had the answer—here in the small, gray-blue marble sculptures of Meridiana Montevecchi.

Christa had a sixth sense when it came to occult phenomena. She used this sense as a barometer for detecting power. This figurine was powerful. It had taken her years to determine what purpose it served. Finally, in possession of her answer, she was on her way to America. Before the blight of spring could taint the earth, she would join in another ceremony, this one darker and more malevolent than any she'd attended before.

* * * * *

The fatty tissue of Donnalee O'Donnell's breasts had been removed and thrown in a dark green plastic garbage bag for disposal, along with rags and old newspapers. Tomorrow Gregory Bradshaw Marsh would find an out-of-the-way dumpster, perhaps the one behind Strawberries Records and Tapes on Clifton Country Road, and deposit them. The skins taken from her breasts were being stretched by handmade frames. Looking up from his work table, Marsh stared at his newly acquired treasures. *Everything's right on schedule*, he thought, as his finger reached out and traced the outline of what had hours ago been Donnalee O'Donnell's areola. As his finger continued to trace the dark circle of flesh, Marsh began nervously wondering about tomorrow.

The cause of his anxious uneasiness was a woman he'd yet to meet and a photograph of a small statue. Both were due to arrive at the Albany County Airport at 8:35 p.m., on American Airlines flight 519 from New York City.

Finally! Why couldn't that bitch have sent it here sooner? If she's playing with me, I'll carve her up and feed her blood to the Holy Mother. Maybe I'll do that anyway. It would serve her right. "This picture is horrid." *It's too fuzzy to make out the details. Rich whore, it better be real, or I'll sacrifice you, witch!* Enraged by delays, Marsh envisioned Christa Liebezeit ripped from vagina to jaw, her entrails exposed and her heart still beating. *Keep me waiting! No, it's real. That toad Roaker checked her out. He wouldn't dare lie to me. Not about this. He knows the price of failure. I wonder what her tits are like?*

As he continued to trace circles around the dark ring of O'Donnell's areola, he tried to imagine Christa Liebezeit's breasts. Heavy? Round? Dark nipples? *Stop! Don't get ahead of yourself. The plan! Stick to your plan. If she's right, then maybe? For now, concentrate. Focus! The other shipment is due. And then there's the calfling. Now's the time to plan taking the kid. Tuesday. No, Wednesday morning will be better? Remember to check tomorrow's paper. That pig Beckett hasn't responded yet. He won't have any choice after today. Maybe he'll get the letter tomorrow. Concentrate! Tomorrow's a busy day.*

* * * * *

"Breakfast is served," the Wizard said, handing a beer to Cosmo.

"Thanks, man. I'm tired of going over these." Cosmo held up two loose leaf binders of his notes on the Mythos encyclopedia. "I could use something. Too bad we abstain from chemicals these days. Christ! I'm as exhausted a rat at a fresh garbage convention. Had any luck so far?"

"None to speak of. But I'll tell you something. I haven't read any of this Mythos stuff in what? Ten? Fifteen years? It's kind of funny— I'm not sure, but I think I might have missed the boat. Some of Desmond's stuff is good. Not just the writing."

"Praise the lord. There's hope for you yet. Maybe you'll finally realize that Poppy Z. Brite and Dan Simmons aren't the only current practitioners of horror."

"Slow down, Cos. I said some, and good. Remember it was you who said that Simmons was a goddamned wizard with a pen? Know what piece of Desmond's work I really liked? His novella about the cosmic civil war that occurred between the Elder Gods and the

GOO. He did a nice job. It read more like a tale from classical mythology than a horror story."

"I can see it now, Edith Hamilton having tea with Lovecraft, as she takes notes for her new book *Unclassical Mythology*, the mythology of . . . what? Lovecraft's New England."

"I guess. Listen to this," the Wizard read. "'Unlike the as yet created gods of man, he liked to sleep, to dream. Not long periods of hibernation, just short little naps. A millennia or two. It was while he was lost in his warm dreams, they came. In their wake, they left only the stark remains of brutal savagery and despair. Quickly, he was awakened by the survivors to see the destruction they had unleashed upon his once fair city. And to face the loss of his beloved sons, and the body of his raped and beheaded queen, Sk'tai. On the ground before him lay the still and lifeless shell of his first born, Eppirfon, who once breathed joy and laughter into the universe. Tears ran in rivulets over his once light countenance, as he grieved. Then came the rage. A brutal anger, onethousandfold the force of the most devastating storm ever known, rose within Kthanid. They would pay. Until the universe collapsed back on itself, they would pay. The damnation of the king of the Elder Gods was vowed to every orb that lit the heavens. The Great Old Ones and their bestial tyranny would be brought to justice. Roaring, his anguished cry split the cosmos as he declared war upon the Great Old Ones. Thus began the war of the gods which ended with the Great Old Ones imprisoned for all time.'

"Nice beginning. Charming idea. No men, no Earth. Just a tale of the Elder Gods and the GOO. I didn't realize this story told how and why the GOO became imprisoned. I'd love to see Campbell, or Lumley fill in more of the Mythos this way. Bet Ligotti, or McNaughton could whip up a wonder, maybe a creation myth, or a tale of the Old Ones before they came to Earth. Ever wonder what their society would look like? Might be fun to read a GOO thriller filled with familial betrayal and cosmic intrigue. I'm starting to think this is fertile soil."

"That's high praise coming from you. Maybe the next time I see Des I'll pass along your ideas."

"Odd you haven't heard from him."

"Yeah, but he's vanished before. One sunny afternoon he'll just pop up."

"I guess so. Still, it's been a long time."

"Not really. You figure he went off to Europe on the promotion tour for *Eyes of Stone* and then was attending the convention in London. Plus he was going to meet McKennitt about turning *Fears and Lost Voices* into an opera."

"That's the part that bugs me. He's sitting home in Saratoga when the phone rings, and it's a world-famous composer on the other end saying he adored the book and has some ideas about turning the book into an opera. Then McKennitt invites Des to Ireland to discuss the idea. Hell, as soon as he hung up he called you. You guys were on the phone for, what? Three hours. He was on cloud nine, who wouldn't be? McKennitt was calling him almost every day about project ideas."

"So?"

"They were both so hot on the idea, I can't see either one backing out. It had become a labor of love for both of them. They were getting along great and both of 'em loved each other's ideas. So, why hasn't he called to fill you in?"

"He's busy."

"He always calls you when he's busy. You're his sounding board."

"True. Maybe he met a girl and fell in love. You know how much he loves redheads, and he was, or is, in Ireland. And they got a couple of redheads over there, you know, or maybe he came up with a great idea and he's locked himself away to write."

"Still, seems odd. If a world-famous composer called me, especially if he's almost as famous for being a reclusive mystic, I'd want to toot my horn or something. One other question. I know Derleth came up with the idea of a war between the Elder Gods and the Great Old Ones, and I know he was Tom's mentor, but what did he think of Tom's story?"

"He loved it, well, the idea anyway. Derleth died long before Tom finished the story. Tom didn't have the heart to tell him it wasn't all his idea."

"You lost me."

"In '67 Tom's parents took him and his sister to Spain for a summer vacation. While he was there, he found an old handwritten page in the house they were staying in. That partial page became the basis of the quote and the tale you just read."

"He stole it?"

"Adapted. The page was old and it was only some names and a statement that the GOO started the war. The rest was his, but years later he started to feel guilty about it. He wanted to thank, or pay tribute to, whoever created Sk'tai, T'ith, and Eppirfon. So we tried to find out who wrote the thing, but never had any luck. As far as we can tell there's no part of any published story like it, nor is there any mention of the names before his tale saw print."

"I guess this isn't getting us anywhere, maybe we should hit the books again."

"Bugs the hell out of me that I haven't found anything to help Chris. It's pretty hard readin' this stuff knowing every minute counts. Takes all the fun out. Damn, if we can't find anything about this crap, how can anyone else?"

"Just keep pluggin'. We'll find something. It's in here somewhere, I know it. Whadaya say we take another crack at these books?"

"Sure."

"The next story looks good. At least I like the title, 'Footprints in the Wind.' Sounds like one of those damn ECM CD's you're forever playing. Christ, what a diet. Kancheli, Bryars, and— "

"You're bustin' me for playing ECM laments. Mr.-'Turn Out the Stars'-is-my-anthem is gonna tell me *Three Viennese Dancers* isn't a rarified gem, and if you say anything, anything at all about Eleni Karaindrou, we're gonna have a battle that apes the Thing and the Trapster goin' at it. Dig?"

"Forget I said anything. I assume 'Footprints' is about Ithaqua."

"Sure is. You're gonna love it. It's set in Umanak in Kalaallit Nunaat. In January no less," Cosmo's laughter burst into the room as he thought of his reptile-adoring friend reading of the cold Arctic wastes of Greenland, stalled in an endless winter. All too well he knew of his friend's love of darkness, but curse-bearing hatred of temperatures under seventy-five degrees.

"Yours is coming, Cos. Hey, before I get back into this stuff I'm heading over to the Mini Chopper. I need some smokes and a candy bar. Want anything?"

"Yeah. The answer we're looking for," Cosmo replied.

"I hear that."

❦ Chapter Twelve ❦

How long is she going to make me wait? She's not like them, not like her brother. He's a cold one. Friendly outside, or so he'd like me to believe. Why was he so probing? So resentful? He's jealous of the way she looks at me? How much does she know? She wields all that power, and she's only seventeen. Yet she's here, among these people, surrounded by all this knowledge. This would have all been mine if that bitch hadn't run! If I was raised here, I wouldn't have spent all those years in pain. When do I get my answers? When?

"My dear Gregory, good morning. I trust you slept well? Have you had your breakfast?"

"Good morning. Yes, I've eaten. I was hoping I would see you this morning. I have so many questions. And—"

Ida Louise Marsh placed her fingertips to his lips. "Be patient. I promise that before you leave here you will know all I know. First you must understand who we are now and what we Marshes were before. There is a lengthy history to our family and you must learn it. Before your answers can be given to you, you must learn how to deal with what you will encounter in the coming days."

"I'm ready, Ida. I've spent years waiting. Learning. I've read Lovecraft and the others. And I—"

"You've read fictional half-truths and lies. Listen to me. Here I hold the throne, as shall the one that comes after me. Your knowledge is minimal, nothing more than a spark. I am the wood to build your fire with. You have just started down the road you must travel. For a short period of time I shall drive your coach along the road. I am your teacher and your navigator. You are right about knowing your destiny, but at the moment you do not possess the knowledge to implement it. In the coming months I shall turn you into a dark warrior who shall deliver victory to our crusade against order and light."

"I'm not completely sure I understand."

"You shall. We'll begin your education with a tour of our scenic town. As we go along, I will correct the lies Lovecraft has filled you with. I have the car waiting. Ethan will be our chauffeur. Are you ready to begin?"

"Ethan? I thought we might have some time alone."

"We shall. Later on we will find some time."

From the palatial, three-story Marsh mansion the black limo regally traveled the three short blocks to New Church Green and the old Masonic Temple that had housed the Esoteric Order of Dagon forty-four years ago.

"I thought Innsmouth was decaying, almost dead, but this—"

"Old stories fleshed out with shards of truth. At one time Innsmouth was a town of fog-enshrouded shadows and shaded secrets, its buildings little more than crumbling red brick, decaying mortar and damp, salt-eaten, rotting wood. Beneath painted facades, ruin caressed her streets like a cancerous lover. A hundred years ago the deep ones roamed her darkened streets by night as if they were powerful emissaries of a king, and they were. But before that, Innsmouth was typical of many small New England villages.

"Or should I say almost typical? There were no puritanical witch hunters here. Here, no petty power-mongering glory seekers assaulted us. The self-righteous, fear-embellished rantings of Mather, Parris, and Phillips did not find their way across the dense salt marshes that surround Innsmouth. No, here something else, something far older than man, was rising. The seed of a second genesis was sending its roots out, preparing to once again burst through and cover the earth. The salt marshes that surround Innsmouth made her far more isolated than most. And isolated she remained, until Obed took his fishing vessels and turned her destiny. A fishing village no more, she became a seaport. Bountiful harvests of fish and gold flowed from beyond Devil's Reef into the harbor and our awaiting hands. Gold that filled our coffers beyond the imaginings of kings.

"To our neighbors in Falcon Point and Boynton Beach, Innsmouth appeared the cold face of age and the unknown winds of desolation. To the stranger, Innsmouth looked as old as the shadowy pine forests of New England and smelled like the depths of the sea it sits beside. But with the crashing salt waters of the Atlantic came the deep ones, the oath, and the price. The plague and the government tried to burn it clean, but like the mythical Phoenix it has rebuilt itself, stronger and more determined than before. Marsh blood, as well as the sea's salty spray which covers the docks, flows in our veins. History stalks her streets on damp dark nights, history as old as the cosmos itself. Marsh history. Remember Innsmouth, she is in your blood. Blood that descends from the spawn of Xoth. In her dreams, Destiny whispers your name. Listen to her soft voice speak your name as if it were a prayer. Listen," she said in a husky whisper. The heat of her breath warmed his ear and his loins. "Can you hear her?"

With his head reclined and his eyes closed he replied, "Yes."

Shortly before one-thirty they returned to the Marsh mansion on Washington Street. Gregory Bradshaw Marsh's morning had been filled with Ida's continually informative commentaries on the town, its inhabitants, and its real history.

Yes, Captain Obed Marsh had indeed brought back dark secrets from the south seas, and, yes, he had brought the deep ones here. That which Lovecraft had spoken of had been called to Innsmouth, but only a few had remained after the destruction the Coast Guard and the Navy had unleashed in Devil's Reef during the winter of 1927-28. Y'ha-nthlei is still there, or what little is left of it. Someday it would be rebuilt to its former glory.

"And what of the deep ones?" he'd asked.

The family practice of worshiping them stopped shortly after Barnabas had completed his transformation and departed for the seas.

"When Barnabas' cousins Zebulon and Warden, along with Zebulon's son Ernest, took control of the family's fortune and future, they broke the oath the deep ones had forced on Innsmouth. They outlawed both the offerings to, and the coupling with, the hideous deep ones. Not that the worship of the deep ones could have really continued, only a few survived. Nor were many Marches left in Innsmouth. Most had been taken to the camps, never to be heard from again," she said.

Repopulation, she'd explained, had occurred slowly by calling home Marshes and Waites from Newburyport, Dunwich, and Redding, Connecticut. And of course the family members who had settled near Middlebury, Vermont, and the Upper Red Lake region of Minnesota returned to their ancestral home. Naturally, some Eliots, Gilmans, and Ornes returned as well. Ernest then decided that the family's interests would be better served if they poured their energies into rebuilding Innsmouth and the releasing of all of the Holy Ones.

"Ernest felt it was mere folly to frolic with the deep ones, when all the power of the cosmos lies chained with their Masters. He was a bold man, filled with wisdom and self confidence, who envisioned a future where the Marshes would be the conduit through which the power of the Holy Ones would flow. Can you comprehend the scope of his desire?" she asked before continuing.

Ernest had found revelations in Navarre's *Las Reglas de Ruina*. The Spaniard had foretold of a messiah of destruction, who would be born in the western land of the red savage across the great ocean in Columbus' New World. A family of fair-skinned men, born in the land of Shudde M'ell, would settle on the rocky northern coast of this new land, and sometime after the heavens were touched by the footsteps of man, in five centuries, the messiah of evil, the human key, would be born to unleash terror from the stars above on mankind.

"We Marshes, my dear Gregory, are that family of fair-skinned men and the soiling of the heavens that Navarre spoke of was Apollo 11. You are Navarre's messiah."

"Me! I thought—well, I'm not exactly sure, but this, this . . . messiah? I—"

"You need not be sure at present. I am certain, and for now that is sufficient. I will teach you all you need to know to open the way for the Holy Ones' reemergence. Their Great Arrival will occur soon, and I shall ensure you are ready to unlock their prisons. Now before we continue, come, I am famished. We shall have lunch? After we've eaten, I have a surprise for you."

They dined on a salad, baked sole, asparagus tips, and a ten-year-old bottle of Pouilly-Fuisse. As they finished Ida removed a large brass key from her expensive Italian handbag. "This is the key for the oak door in the hall outside the library. Only Ethan and I use the chamber below, although there are occasions when other family members attend us. After today's instruction you will have free access to the chamber and its pleasures. But first I think we should enjoy a little more of this lovely burgundy."

Following Ida's pale contour, Gregory began his descent into the cavern below the family's expansive New England mansion. Marsh paused a third of the way down the seemingly endless stairway of unevenly worn stairs. For the merest second, he had the impression he'd stepped onto the set of a Hammer film. Fungi cloaked the damp walls as if it were leprous skin. Spidery fingers of a mucus-like film clung to the crudely hewn, cracked stairway, making the footing treacherous.

Anxious, yet ever cautious, he reaffirmed his grip on the iron railing, silently cursing the scant few torches and their dim bays of fragile light, which futilely attempted to illuminate the ocean of dark below. "Is this my surprise?" he asked.

"My, you are the impatient one, aren't you? The bottom is just a little further. I assure you it will be worth both your time and effort."

"I never doubted that for an instant."

Truly she commands here, he thought, noting for the second time that her hand had yet to touch the railing. Whatever experience or thing lay below, Gregory knew Ida had no fear of it.

Nearing the cavern's floor, he began to discern vague forms and the enormity of the natural structure. Scanning the few harbors of feeble illumination, he was struck by almost-faces petrified in the fanged outcroppings of rock. Below, a trio of candelabras cast wavering shadows across a small arena of mounds. A gust of rank air cast its breath across the candles, sending their shadows into a twisted dance. Watching the waltzing silhouettes embrace, Marsh quickened his pace, anxious to attend whatever festivities awaited. Moments before reaching the bottom step, he slipped while trying to discern a large object dominating the center of the cavern floor.

That can't be a natural structure, can it? Maybe it's a sculpture? Damn, it's so dim down here.

Holding his questions, Marsh peered into the darkness as they traversed the uneven floor, occasionally skirting brackish pools of indeterminable depth. Nearing the ring of loose soil-covered mounds his hopes flared. Were these graves? Again he wondered about the cavern's enormity and age, as he looked up and he saw the tips of giant stalactites, many hanging low enough to be caught in the torchlight; one would soon join the monolithic phallus jutting from the floor to meet it.

"Ida."

Taking his hand, she whispered, "We're almost there."

The electricity of her touch, the heavy perfume of salt, and the muffled sounds of the sea heightened his expectations.

Startled, he'd been dreamily preoccupied with Ida's profile, imagining pressing his lips to hers. He drew back slightly, realizing they were not alone.

Before him, on a massive dark stone crudely carved to resemble a throne, sat Ethan Marsh, legs crossed, a cigarette in one hand, a snifter of golden liquid in the other. Beside the black-clad figure, bound and gagged upon an ornately carved black stone altar, was a naked young woman, whose reddened eyes revealed the terror she'd experienced. The woman continually squirmed, as she tried to loosen her bloodied bonds to no avail.

"My dear cousin, welcome to our temple. I shall leave you two to your little lesson. I hope you will relish your first taste." Ethan rose and took his sister's hand to kiss it. "The other items you requested are on the table. Enjoy," Ethan said as he walked up and paused before the terror-stricken woman. Reaching out he gently caressed her left breast with his forefinger before slapping her with his other hand. "My poor frightened fawn, I regret our brief encounter has ended." His smile melted into cold hate. "Did you enjoy our time together as much as I? I trust it was as pleasurable as you imagined it to be when you accompanied me. Please treat my cousin and my sister as lovingly as you treated me." Bending over the girl, the heat of his breath filling her ear, he, in a tone drunk on bitterness, whispered a passage from Baudelaire's "L'Héautontimorouménos."

> "'Et je ferai de ta paupière,
> Pour abreuver mon Saharah,
> Jaillir les eaux de la souffrance.
> Mon désir gonflé d'esperance
> Sur tes pleurs salés nagera
> Comme un vaisseau qui prende le large,
> Et dans mon coeur qu'ils soûleront
> Tes chers sanglots retentiront Comme un tambour qui bat la
>   carge.'

"Adieu, cheri." Ethan's callous laughter echoed through the dark as he walked, periodically disappearing in the lightless shroud, to the steps. Whistling a passage from the fourth movement of Berlioz's Fantastique he leisurely ascended the stairway, entertaining the idea of observing Gregory's lesson. Dismissing his voyeuristic thought he exited the chamber, closing and locking the door behind him.

Ida stood like death herself, cold, waiting, her eyes on Gregory during Ethan's exit. He seems ready for this. Ghoulishly hungry eyes smiled at him as she took his hand. "This is your surprise," she said, while her finger gently traced the outline of Ethan's handprint on the woman's face. "There are three parts to today's lesson. The one I hold is the first."

"What is it?" he asked, looking at the tiny purple, barrel-shaped pill she held between thumb and forefinger.

"Lysergic acid diethylamide. The hallucinogenic drug, LSD. Have you heard of it?"

"I don't believe in drugs. They're for those unwashed fools who yearn for peace and beauty. I need to be able to think clearly."

Her quick, sharp laughter was bell-like. "That is precisely what this chemical allows you to do. It will strip away all the interference you've encountered. Shamans and mystics throughout the ages have used hallucinogenic substances to peer through the mists that deaden persception, to uncover the secrets that lie beyond the limited sight of man. You must follow them into the beyond if you would converse with truth. Today, with this cleansing agent, you will hear and see, without distortion or disguise, your true calling. Unfettered revelations shall come to you in today's lesson. Do not fear your journey, for wherever you travel, I shall be with you. Your hand will not leave mine. Do you have any questions?"

"Will I hear or see things? What will I find?"

"The truth that waits Outside. You will witness the birth of death as it sheds the skin of sleep. You will hear it cry out in agony. Even now it waits, inside you, below all the teachings of man. This drug will open the portal to your desires. It will turn you into a dark bird of prey whose talons stand ready to grasp the truth as you wing the infinite. Here lies your path. Take it."

Gregory took the purple pill her outstretched hand offered. As he raised it to his lips his eyes asked her to abolish his fear.

"I am here. I shall be the mother she-beast, fangs bared, standing over her young. Fear nothing," she responded, caressing his cheek.

Into his mouth went the bitter tablet. For a moment he sucked on it, then he swallowed. Nothing. No blast rent his vision. Only the torchlight wavered. No sound fractured the hesitant silence. In the still cavern he waited. His mind and body rigid, tense, expecting anything. Hoping for answers.

"I don't feel anything. Shouldn't something happen?"

"You must be patient," she said, taking his hand. "The effects of the drug take almost an hour to occur. During that time we have preparations to make before the visions come upon you." Turning from him, she walked to the woman bound upon the altar. "Have you looked at this?" she asked, her hand stroking a curve of the finely carved table of offering as oddly bent as the victim's bound arm. "This is Her table. For centuries it has been anointed by her faithful priests. Consecrated with nourishing blood. On this altar we feed her hungry dreaming with human blood. Notice how the apertures and cavities have filled with dried blood over the ages. As the light of her path, you must consecrate this vessel. This is your second lesson.

"I have tended her holy table for the last five years. When I was twelve mother placed the blade in my hand. Now the task falls to you. Three times you must anoint the altar before you become her chosen priest. This flesh before you is your first offering to the Holy Mother, Kassogtha. Yes, she is the voice that calls to you. She cries for you to release her from her damnation."

Ida withdrew a long-handled blade from inside her jacket. Handle-first she offered it to her hesitant, wide-eyed cousin. Slowly his hand reached out and took the knife. The sacrificial blade was old and razor sharp despite being covered in dried blood. On the blade was a single mark, which resembled teeth. Ida called it the mark of the three.

"Can you hear her?"

He exhaled. Then inhaled. Searching, reaching. Tension heated the damp air. The pressure of a silent moment changing, found a voice—the voice of ravens no longer concealed. He was immersed in the breath of God. There was rapture in the drowning.

"Yes, I hear the agony of her cries. What must I do?"

"Feed the queen of abominations. Show her your devotion. There are no formal steps to the consecration. Simply let the blade sing upon this canvas of flesh."

And the blade sang, filling the butchers' temple with its unholy song, as death's dark dance began. One slash to the inside of the victim's right breast and the blood began its gravitational flow downward to the white valley between her breasts, where it began to branch out and run in rivulets toward her spasming abdomen. In the wake of its downward arc, a delicate path across her soft belly created a twisted red rune. Up—skyward—rode the blade, to perch momentarily at the apex of a pale monolith. Then plunging furiously down, propelled by a heart colder than the dagger's metal, in a lightning-sharp bolt to pierce her inner thigh. When the blade was retracted the wound erupted; hot blood ran like lava toward the delta of her sex.

As the blade continued to paint bloody furrows across the once unspoiled pale canvas, Ida removed the gag to allow the young woman being offered to enjoin the chorus of Marsh's joyous moaning. Rapt in creation, the deflowered butcher's lips curled back to form a mask of bestial intensity. Hellish laughter erupted to mix with tearful wails, wails which permeated the blackness as they reverberated off the walls and ceiling of the cathedral of tortured unholiness.

Ida quickly shed her clothing and moments later had stripped him. Soon the three naked figures were spattered in a blood-colored mockery of abstract art. Ida's slim hand wiped the blood pooled between the young woman's breasts and rouged her own lips and nipples, as well as his engorged penis, with the crimson paint. As Ida smeared blood across her abdomen her voice erupted to join the harmonic discord that filled the cavern. "*Isskaktuum! Kassogtha! Hptugh! G'ghna Ni'zos I'gaq! Iä! Kassogtha!*"

As if it were the desert itself, the ancient blade drank the ceremonial wine poured into its unquenchable maw. Fifty-seven times the cannibal blade feasted on tender flesh before its final bite severed the dead woman's head from its former resting place. When the frenzied blood dance reached completion the two destroyers turned to face each other.

"Soon the chemical that races through your blood will take you to her. Heed her commands. You have proven your devotion, and shown your worthiness. Now come and sit beside me until your journey begins."

Weighted by the ghosts of unanswered prayers, he sat beside Ida, anxiously anticipating revelation. Her eyes, hawkishly darting from stony face to quivering hands, cautiously monitored his reactions while her finger traced unintelligible designs in the blood covering his chest. Slowly the fluid flames of the torches froze, as the acid wave washed over him. Horribly strained, but not torn, his elastic flesh expanded to house the new sensations. Somewhere in the multishaded darkness to his right a massed buzzing sound composed of sharp short pops drew his ears. The chemically distorted butcher turned in a series of puppet-like, strobe-light-fractured motions to the remains of what once had been a human being to find gray, unevenly red-striped, wormish shapes feeding on the mutilated carcass, their bladed teeth hewing flesh from bone with the efficiency of a machine. Like *marabunta*, the South American army ant, they undulated across the ripe flesh, leaving only polished white bone in their wake.

Are they real? She said this was a hallucinogenic chemical. They're visions? "Ida?" The word issued from him sounding stunted and flat.

"I'm here. I have your hand. Let yourself flow with the drug."

I can't move. What did she say? Flow with it. Wait? I am waiting. Standing ready. The sentinel watching, bearing the weight of his charge.

Cast from stone he stood, cocooned in a darkness as constricting as the wrappings of a dead Egyptian king, at the edge of a black carbon desert where shimmering clots of black maggots feasted on the cobwebs of his consciousness. Joined to the black surface he stood upon, he continued his vigil, scanning the time sponge of motionlessness, inch by tentative inch, waiting for the coming of—

What? His question searched the void of black before dissipating.

"Her!" breathed the foul stench of no longer silent air.

Inky clouds of darkness settled over him as his mind reached out in a kaleidoscopic arc. Bending, pushing, reaching. Straining. Whirling around a splintered shadow of light cast by a broken moon, the acolyte, consumed with the addictive fire of desire, became a vessel of conception.

Storms soothed him.

Light fled.

In the distance, beyond the limits of his sight, a scratched, flattened quacking faced a lower-toned twin that laughed its reply. Beneath the unintelligible conversation, a repetitive monotone of lilting volume, a primal drone, filled the aural panorama. Sensation married to a new perception transformed him. His vision cleared and he beheld shadows filled with lines and angles, broken by curves and holes. Within the shadows, withered fingers flexed and spiders of shade crawled. Inside was motion and menace. Shapes slithered and oozed and almost-shapes fluttered. He was almost there, although he was uncertain were *there* was.

Then silence and stillness bound him anew.

Above him a warped stem rose up. Hovering above the land-scape of ruin, a supple form, a cobra sculpted from nightmare, softly rocked. Bending and swaying as if it were responding to the vibrations of some primal music, it seemed to summon him. Caught in a slice of moon-colored light, appendages, from the curvaceous shaft, danced. In arcing motions, the black flower bloomed.

Ida? he wondered, almost knowing the answer, yet uncertain.

Slowly the shaded form compressed and settled before him, as a hobbled dance of seduction set to a disjointed rhythm began. Free of the dark trunk its arms fully extended; it searched, groping the barrier of space between them. As if magnetized by its efforts, he extended, establishing contact. Meshing. Desire flowing into desire, energy bonding to energy.

Marsh, blurred and electrified, felt himself melting, metamorphosing as her arms, hands, and fingers spread like blackened tree limbs to entwine about his arms. Beneath him, low on the body of the swaying form before him, a hungry lightless slit appeared. Small fangs emerged from the soft mushroomish flesh of Ida's puffy lips as her open mouth widened and a trio of balletic tongues darted out, beckoning to Gregory's loins. Accepting the rhythmic invitation, the segmented tentacle dangling between his legs began its hungry ascent.

"Give it to me!" demanded Ida's screaming voice. Her mouth engulfed him.

He was lost in the swirling haze of chemical ecstasy as the black face cracked, curled, and flaked away, revealing pocked, pallid skin stretched over another layer of shiny darkness. Teeth-like claws smiled as her tongue worked on his engorged member. Marsh's brain, a polluted waterfall of consciousness, dissolved, pouring into his chest.

Somewhere below pressurized novas expanded; he felt energized, animated by this new experience. Suddenly he felt full, as a sharp, roasting pain ripped his membranous outer jacket from him. Shucked of his confining sheath, now a pale flimsy husk laying below him, he became lightning, a piercing bolt which burst into the pulsating maw gently chewing at him. He was born, a radiant new entity of fire—exploding into the black mask.

Wobbly and uneven, he shook as the feverish pulse of carnal felicity ceased. He gasped, once again sensing the powerful blood that sent streams of heat through his new body. Beginning to settle, he felt alone. Fear overrode desire and expectation. He extended, searching.

"Ida?"

"I'm here," she whispered.

Her warm arms enfolded him and he quieted, now safely moored to her motherly presence.

As the pair held each other, bloody breast to bloody breast, he felt her small breasts elongate and burrow like curved metallic worms, into his chest cavity. Inside him the two writhing forms balled before expanding, displacing his lungs. No longer did he breath air. From her came opaque fluid, thick, lumpy, and hot. The sustaining, curdled black milk of hate.

"Drink! Grow!" came the razor-toned order as her breasts were ripped from his chest and forced into his awaiting mouth.

His teeth and tongue covered her nipples like an insatiable cascade of heat as he drank the pasty fluid.

Power. She's feeding me her power and determination.

After a time his frenzied tongue and teeth stopped feeding and the pair sat waiting.

Suddenly light extinguished the darkness that held him; then it faded. Shades of shadows appeared and grew to become a womb of black. Some presence beckoned to him from the multihued depths of inky darkness.

"Wait!" he yelled to the failing light.

Cold caressed him and he turned to face it. There it was before him, clothed in a nimbus of charged, blurry vapors, a gray-blue knot of slithering motion. Miles and miles of twisting, writhing coils. Knotted, flowing over one another. Closer it came.

A millennium passed as it danced before him.

Into the searing melting pool of his bubbling, drug-irradiated thoughts came visions. Lightning, splitting clouds of uncertainty, illuminated the creature of his need. Arms uplifted to the void above and before him, his voice, a broken croak, praised and prayed, "IÄ! KASSOGTHA!"

Twelve times the universe cracked and reformed before him. Heat filled him, cold stripped him. Novas rained down upon his mind, now a crumbling shell scurrying for refuge. He stood naked. Aware. Before him, poised as a black star limitless in its ravening dominion, shimmered the twisted gray-blue snake, an orgy, rubbing against its own flesh. Cold scales grinding hot sparks against the colorless void. Like black lava writhing, brutally caressed by its own motions, gliding, jerking, fast as an eye blinking. Flickering, shimmering, oozing—almost frozen—still. Moving again, the stench of dead sex and rotting carcasses.

Then came the noise, a tuning fork struck in a million hells, stone rending flesh, the tears of banshees and broken angels striking him like the harsh backside of his stepfather's hand. As the thunder ceased the momentary ring of silence echoed into a pulse, assaulting then kissing his ears. Bathed in the hurricane of god's breath he was too rigid for tears, too blessed to speak. Contorting, the open maw of the goddess spoke.

"FOOD! SUSTENANCE! DEATH!" came the deafening volume of her plea/command. "DARK-HOLLOW . . . WORLD-PAIN . . . BACK! RULE-OWN!" the she-being wailed, thrusting an image of Kashkash into his mind.

He saw the alien city looming like a geometrically twisted Babylon above the blasted desolation surrounding it. Black and gray blockish shapes the size of buildings were arranged in forms unfathomable to human perception.

"I! ISSKAKTUUM! QUEEN! OWNED, HELD-SQUEEZED . . . ALL! PAIN! BURNING! . . . ELDER LIGHT-PAIN! BLOCK-TRAP . . . FROZEN . . . HUNGER!" At each word a blue vein of jagged light coursed through the energy nimbus encasing the goddess, and as her words fell silent and the lighting reached the outer rim a small explosion, the pop of a cosmic bubble, sent a rank odor through the heavy air. "PAIN! NEED-WANT FEED! NOW! CAU MO! PLACE-MINE! CTHULHU NELEH VTIIV I! JOIN-ONE! I NOW!"

Again an image formed in his mind. The she-being, Kassogtha, locked together with the octopoid god Cthulhu. Mating.

"CRUSH STAR SEAL! PAIN! WEIGHT-BARRIER! HOLD! PAIN! IMPRISON I-KASSOGTHA! RULE-GLORY! NOW! SEED-YOU! BREAK-FREE . . . DARKNESS! KEY! TAKE! HOME-RULE! I NOW! KEY! TAKE-FIND! OPEN! NOW!"

Time spewed from her.

Before him flashed blurred pictures filled with stark shadowed images.

"SEE! KNOW!"

There was the book, the key to her prison. He saw a jungle-nest of dense green and a stone building. Inside, behind the accursed stones of Mnar—the name burned his mind as it came into contact—lay the book. The *Zhou Texts*.

"TAKE! KEY! WAY-CEREMONY! NO! LIGHT-BURNING! HATE! EVIL! LIGHT! HURT! PAIN! FREE! HOME . . . KASHKASH UBH'SOTTI R'LYEH! I NOW!"

His mind, a dry spongy vessel, recorded the pictures.

"USE!"

Knowing/understanding. "When? How?"

"FILL I! ALTAR! BLOOD-FOOD! BURNING ORBS! POINT-STRAIGHT! HOME-RULE! BREAK LIGHT! NO PAIN! SLEEP-DEATH-PRISON FREE! I—YOU . . . SEE-JOIN-SPEAK! DREAM-WANDER-DEATH!"

"We will communicate—understand. Yes. In my dreams you can come to me. I am ready. I'll be waiting for you."

"GONE-NOW! PRISON! PAIN! BACK! I NOW!"

With an odd jerking flip the writhing mass Kassogtha withdrew, and he was alone again.

Find the book! Find the book! The book holds the key. The ceremony is in the book.

Wearing his answers as if they were armor, Gregory beheld bas-relief hieroglyphics burned onto the inner walls of his brain. He understood the charge carved by torment. Below his feet the floor of his mind became a path through dense jungles, a map to her book of passage.

Drained, he lay down on the floor of his mind to pray. He was now one with revelation.

He awoke naked several hours later beside the carcass he'd butchered. Bloody and weak, he walked to his cousin.

"I remember. I spoke with her."

"Yes. I know."

"There are things I have to do. I'll have to find the text."

"Not quite yet," she said, pulling him down.

She was violent and he was cruel. Her lusts fed off his cruelty as she screamed and he moaned. When he finished, they slept.

Three hours later, Ethan woke the blood-covered pair. Ethan reached out and stroked his sister's breast, sucking the blood from his fingertip after the caress. He smiled. "Sister. Cousin. I trust the lesson was fruitful? Perhaps you two would like to clean up for breakfast?"

When Gregory had dispensed with showering and breakfast, he found himself once again coupled with his cousin. Later, while Gregory slept, Ida Louise Marsh rose from the bed and stood over him. Walking across the room, she seated herself in a pine rocking chair, the one her mother had rocked her in. The candlelight coming from the marble sconces on the wall cast sharp shadows on her smiling face.

❦ Chapter Thirteen ❦

All the way through boot camp Chris was known as Private Hollywood, thanks to his drill instructor, Master Sergeant Jonathan Rivers.

"Christopher—*James Stewart*? What, did your mommy want to fuck Jimmy Stewart, Private?" Master Sergeant Rivers venomously inquired.

Dead silence. Chris' eyes went cold. It seemed as if even the wind stopped to listen. In his mind, Chris was about to rip this man's head off for defiling his mother.

"Can't you hear me, Private?"

"SIR! YES SIR! The private can hear you, SIR. It's just the private's mother liked Jimmy Stewart, SIR."

"I'll bet she fuckin' did. Now drop and give me twenty, Hollywood."

And it stuck. For the next eight months he was Hollywood until one night in 'Nam.

Echo Company was sitting on a small hillock about two and a half clicks south of Chu Lai. The full moon was riding high and Chris was in a foul mood. It seemed to Pat Price that Chris was always in a black mood while the full moon reigned. "Connie" Costansa had been riding Chris for almost an hour, when he stepped over the same line that Master Sergeant Jonathan Rivers had. When it was over Pat Price had dubbed Chris "Mad Mutha Moon." From that point on Chris was no longer Hollywood, he was simply Moon.

* * * * *

If there was any drawback to staying at Lauri's flat it was that she didn't receive the morning paper. After he promised Laurinda that he would eat something ("sometime today") he drove off. It was only a few blocks to the Stewart's Shop on upper Union Street, and they did receive the morning paper. Chris left the Taurus running, went in, and plopped down his thirty-five cents for the *Times-Herald*. Chris had okayed the article but he still wanted to see it in print. He didn't trust Beckett. Lighting a cigarette, he read Beckett's handiwork.

Nightmare's Disciple Claims Two More Victims
By JACK BECKETT
Staff Writer

SCHENECTADY – At 6:35 a.m. yesterday, the ninth victim of the butcher I had previously dubbed the Mastectomist was found in a parking lot near Sprees. Shortly after 1 p.m. his tenth victim was discovered outside her home on Londonderry Court, near Central Park.

The victims, a twenty-year-old white male and a twenty-nine-year old white female, had no ties to prostitution. As in the previous eight slayings, both of yesterday's victims were discovered with their throats slashed and their torsos mutilated.

The Schenectady Police Department has uncovered new information regarding the murders that have plagued this city over the last fourteen months. These new facts are being released to the public in hopes that someone may have further information regarding the murders or the murderer.

Last Thursday, January 6, this reporter received a letter from a person claiming he was responsible for the deaths of all eight victims. The letter is being printed here in hopes that it will aid in his capture.

Chris scanned the letter he'd already read too many times. Beckett had come through. There was Chris' name prominently displayed, as well as his inflammatory statement regarding the homicides. Beckett had tied Cosmo and the Wizard to a flagpole with their asses whipping in the wind. The store, as well as its location, was prominently mentioned. Beckett had really jumped into the fray. He had also placed himself as a target. The Lovecraft connection, complete with a prominent error and two misspellings, were there.

Okay, you fuck. React. I'm waiting. We've given you plenty of reasons to want to talk to us . . . . You shouldn't have any shortage of targets now.

After he had finished reading Beckett's piece, he drove downtown to see Cosmo and the Wizard. Chris pulled into The Horror Corner expecting them to be sleeping. He felt bad about waking them up, but there was no way to tell just when this asshole would react to Beckett's article. They would need to be ready for anything after Beckett—with Chris' okay—had positioned the store as one of the primary targets. As Chris walked to the front door he noticed lights on and the two musicians-turned-police-researchers sitting reading. He knocked and was greeted by waving hands and two weary faces.

"Morning, Chris. What's happening? It's a bit early, isn't it?" asked Cosmo as he opened the door.

"Not for me, but I thought you guys were nighthawks. Seen the paper? We're all in it. I thought you guys should know Beckett's placed you as point men on this little gambit."

The Wizard smiled and patted his .30-.30. "She's locked and loaded. Been giving Cos here a few tips just in case. But wait, it gets better," the Wizard said as he pulled a twenty-gauge Remington and a box of number four shot from under the table where he was seat-ed. "As it happens, I'm a pretty fair trapshooter too. Started in the Scouts. Got an old P. F. Flyers box full of dusty medals for sharp-shooting upstairs. So, bring 'em on. Let's see what this freak will look like with a couple of rounds of number four in him. Hope you guys have plenty of blotters. Ever shoot trap?"

"Just people." *Shit! That came out wrong.* "I toured 'Nam on the ass end of Tet. But, that was another life."

"Army?" Cosmo asked.

"Marines."

"Really? The Marines. Wow! Tough bastards, I hear. See much action over there?" the Wizard asked.

"Too much," Chris replied while looking at his shoes.

"Sorry, man. Didn't mean to dredge up bad memories. It's just, well, curiosity. Cos and I coulda . . . it's like Phil Ochs' song 'There But For Fortune.' Know what I mean?"

"Yeah. Look, about the weapons. I—"

"Don't worry. I really do know how to use these. Besides, we've worked out a little plan."

Over tea and the morning paper, Cosmo and the Wizard ran down their plan. "Here's how we got it figured. First off, almost everybody that comes in is a regular. They're pretty much like Mike. Most of 'em know us, at least to some degree. They hang out and chat for a while or have questions about books, movies, and models, or they want to know if something is available. So if anyone comes in that we don't recognize we'll be on the alert. Now we also know the bastard that you're looking for is about six feet tall, he's well built, and has black hair. The Wiz and I have been thinking about our clientele, and we can't think of anyone who fits that description. So, if he comes in there's a damn good chance we'll know it. Whadaya think?"

"You can't just shoot someone because you think they might this butcher. There must be a thousand men in the city that fit that description. Be careful with those," Chris said, pointing to the guns. "Most of your customers are kids and I don't need any more dead bodies floating around. Except one."

"In fact, most of our customers aren't kids. Sure, we get quite a few. But for the most part they're men, twenty-five to well, let's say forty. And you'd be surprised how many women come in," Cosmo said. "They seem to love vampires and serial killers."

"Don't worry about these. I'll make sure they stay out of the way," the Wizard said, patting his weapons.

"Just be careful. As to this monster coming in here, I want to install a closed-circuit camera and wire the store for sound. That way if he does, maybe we'll get a picture and his voice on tape. Cos, remember when you said that you thought he probably went to Innsmouth or Arkham because they're so close? Well, I think if he reads Beckett's article he's gonna have to check you guys out. Like you said, it's so close I don't think he'd be able to resist. There is something else. I want to put one of the task force members in here. We can pretend he works for you. You two guys can cover for him while he's watching your asses. If our boy were to really come in, there's no way you two could do anything unless he tried something. Besides, even then you two don't have any legal authority."

"When's this stuff getting installed?"

"In about an hour, if you agree."

"Let's do it. But your guy stays out of the way. We handle the customers. Remember, most of our clientele know their stuff. We've got one cat who comes in that can quote Anne Rice's vampire chronicles verbatim and another one who knows more about werewolves than I know about the Mythos. And there's a woman who comes in who knows more about cannibal flicks than our resident ghoul here. I'm talkin' encyclopedia—directors, actors' names, the whole smear. I don't suppose you're sending us someone who's a horror buff? If not, he only comes into the picture if someone fitting your description comes in," Cos said.

"He'll be quiet as a church mouse. Have you come across any more bait yet?"

"No, but we won't stop looking. We'll find something for you. Promise."

"I hope so. Look, I gotta run, but I'll check in later. You have my beeper number if anything comes up. One last thing, don't let anybody in the store until my guy gets here. There's no way to tell when this asshole might show up. The investigator I'm sending over's named Stanton. Willie Stanton. Please listen to him and do what he says. Remember, he's here to protect you. He's a good guy, I think you'll like him. Later."

"We'll yell if anything comes up."

Cosmo locked the door behind Chris and went back to his desk more determined than ever to find something to help Chris catch his monster.

"There goes one tired and wired cat," the Wizard said, as he went to make another pot of tea.

Sitting there, Cosmo's mind began wandering. Murder, mayhem, and revenge stalked freely. Before too long he started ticking off the weaponry mentioned in Willie Dixon's "Wang Dang Doodle." "When we nail your freako ass, we're sure gonna pitch something all night. It's gonna be romp, tromp, and bash and stomp . . . ."

* * * * *

Gregory Bradshaw Marsh was up early and ready for the day's first task. He had already gone through the phone book and studied a map to determine which elementary school would become today's hunting ground. He'd decided on Zoller School. It was perfect. Zoller was less than a mile from Donnalee O'Donnell's home. It was the last place they'd think he'd strike. He'd played with the idea of Howe School for a while as it was even closer to her home, but Zoller's location gave him a faster way out of the city after he acquired one of their children.

At 7:30 a.m. Marsh found an ideal vantage point, directly across the street from the school on Lancaster Street. *Who knows?* he thought. *I might get lucky and be able to grab one this morning. They're too young to really be wary.*

At 8:27 a blonde girl Marsh suspected might be seven or eight years old turned the corner of Regal Street and came walking toward his van. He quickly looked around. He saw no one but the child.

This is as good a time as any, he thought. *Let's try it.*

He started the van's engine and went into the rear. Opening the side door, he called to the girl, "Hi. Could you help me? I've lost my puppy. Have you seen a little black puppy around here this morning? He's been gone all night and I'm really worried that something might have happened to him. He might be hurt."

Joni Holland approached the van. "Hurt? What does he look like?"

"Here, I've got a picture. Maybe you could show it to your friends? You could be a big help. Maybe one of them has seen my lost puppy," the gently smiling monster said in a soothing tone.

Worried about the puppy, the unsuspecting child walked up to the van. Before Joni Holland could see the photograph Marsh was holding, his hands were on her and she was being hauled inside. Marsh pulled a rag from his coat pocket and stuffed it into the child's mouth. The helpless fifty-six-pound child was too terrified to utter a sound or move. Twice his fist pounded the small child's head before he reached up to the hammer that was laying on the seat. His arm rose and descended twice as the girl lay still, unconscious and bloody. He quickly bound the child before covering her with a blanket. Jumping into the front seat, he drove away.

Five minutes after the second descent of the hammer, Gregory Bradshaw Marsh was two miles beyond the city limits, headed home with his bloody prize.

That was easy, he thought. *Sometime this afternoon I'll have to come back and find a suitable place to deposit the carcass.*

* * * * *

Chief of Police Michael Carroll and task force commander Lt. Marlin Matthews stood before the investigators and officers assigned to the case. Invanelli had screamed at Carroll and Matthews for twenty minutes, thus the scathing decree to assemble.

Chris could do without the venomous speeches that were about to be delivered. *Christ! We're not gonna catch anyone sitting in here listening to this bullshit.*

Carroll preached for ten minutes. Just as Chris thought he'd made it through unscathed, Carroll turned his wrath upon him. "Stewart! You're the primary on three of these murders. You have anything to add to this?"

"No." *You dim-witted asshole.* "Hopefully, once the killer sees Beckett's article something will break. Everything we have at the moment is in that report you're holding. Our artists have tried to come up with a composite of the killer's face, but the bartenders and waitresses from Spree's all gave conflicting descriptions. At this point, all we have is a general description. Black hair. Dark eyes, maybe? Six feet, two hundred ten pounds. Those are estimates based on the killer's shoe impressions and their depth. At the moment our best bet is Beckett, or the owners of the bookstore we have positioned as bait."

"I really hate this, Stewart. I really don't give a shit about a few hookers or the fag, but now we've got a *decent* woman butchered in her fucking driveway. And you've got two forty-year-old hippies that fucking play that rock and roll noise, not to mention they operate a store full of shit that should be outlawed, working with us. If the press starts making us out to be monkeys because of your so-called experts, I'm going to have your ass. I want something done about them soon. And one more thing, I want some fucking suspects. And I want them fast. Does everyone in this room understand what I want?"

Chris lit a Salem as he watched the door close behind Carroll and Matthews. *Fuck you! You two bastards probably sucked more cock than that poor dead kid. At least he did it for pleasure. You don't care that a few hookers and a gay kid are dead. Well, fuck you! They were people whether you like it or not. They didn't deserve to die. Not like that! No one deserves to die like that.*

* * * * *

While Chris and the rest of the task force members were having their asses chewed out because they weren't seers or magicians,

Investigator Willie Stanton parked his wife's '72 Maverick in front of The Horror Corner.

"I hate this car." *Damn seat is uncomfortable. No wonder she yells about buying a new one all the time. But Chris was right, this one looks like it belongs here. Twenty years of rust. Probably wouldn't get a dime on trade in. Why did he pick me for this assignment? Last time I read a scary book was back in high school.* Frankenstein. *Is that even a horror book? Maybe it's a science fiction book? I'll have to ask.*

Cosmo and the Wizard saw the rusty brown Maverick pull into the lot. They exchanged questioning glances as the Wizard took the safety off the shotgun.

"Can't be the cop Chris said is coming. They don't drive junk like that," the Wizard said.

"It's not the killer. The driver's black. Any guesses?"

"No. Let's go see who it is. I'll cover you."

"I'm not sure that's necessary."

"Neither am I, but we've been running for days now with little sleep, and I'm not taking any chances. Even though Chris is sure there's only one killer, there's still the outside chance he's got a friend or two."

Cosmo unlocked and opened the door as the unknown man walked to the store. Taking note of Cosmo's bat and the Wizard's shotgun, Willie stopped three steps short of the door.

"Good morning. Name's Stanton. I believe Sergeant Stewart mentioned I was coming."

"Sure did. Can you prove who you are?"

Willie Stanton set down the two large bags he was carrying and showed Cosmo his shield and ID.

"Great. C'mon in. My name is Cosmo and this gentleman here is the Wizard."

"Hi. Heard a lot about you two from Chris. Could you guys help me bring in the rest of my equipment?"

"Sure. All high-tech gadgets, I suppose. The kind of stuff that makes mouse farts sound like thunder claps?"

"Uh, yeah. I guess," Willie replied, grinning and shaking his head. "I should be done setting up in about an hour. Can I ask you guys a question?"

"Sure."

"This might sound dumb, but is *Frankenstein* a horror story or is it science fiction?"

Cosmo and the Wizard laughed.

* * * * *

Gregory Bradshaw Marsh sat admiring his handiwork.

Too bad I had to use a hammer on the little bitch. It would have been better if I could have just ripped out her throat, like the others. No, this is much better. The mindless herd will be petrified once they see what the hammer did to her skull. Hahahahaha. I think I'll leave the cop a little present. Yes! Detective Sergeant Christopher Stewart, see what you think of this! Put this in your next newspaper article. Just how stupid do you think I am? I can smell your little Horror Corner setup. Once her holiness arrives, I'll deal with them. We'll see how much they like playing with horror after I show them the real meaning of the word. But first it's your turn to suffer.

* * * * *

Chris walked into Pat's restaurant. He hadn't taken three steps when Pat started. "Where the hell you been? God, you look like hell. Joe! Get this man some tea. Well? No, no, wait a minute. Joe, we'll be in the office. You've got the con. C'mon, Moon."

Chris followed Pat into his office. Once seated, the questions began.

"I haven't seen your sorry ass in days. You all right? Christ, Moon, I've been worried. Two more dead. You must be tearing your hair out. Anything new?"

Chris sat there with a haggard smile, "If you want me to answer any of your six million questions, you're going to have to shut up for a minute or two."

"Yeah, yeah. I'm not talkin'. So start talkin'."

Chris spent fifteen minutes filling in his best friend on the two new murders and the killer's letter to Beckett. He told him about the Lovecraft connection, and Cosmo and the Wizard. Pat sat quietly and listened to Chris, until Chris mentioned Laurinda.

"Hot damn! I knew it! It's about time you two got together. I been hearing you talk about her for twenty-some years? Bet you still have that picture, you know the one from that album cover? You do, don't you? I can tell by the look on your face."

Chris recalled twenty-plus-year-old fantasies mixed with the last few nights' memories. He could smell the fragrance of the bountiful earth as she exhaled. He heard the sultry song of the wind as she sighed.

"'Made love to it, prayed to it . . . . Called it our beloved, called it—'" The words escaped without him knowing he'd verbalized them.

"*Abraxas*! Hot damn. Dreams do come true. I guess Lindy can finally stop trying to find a nice girl for you."

"Thank God for that!"

"It's your own fault, and you know it. You two belong together and you damn well know it. I can't wait to make the toast at this wedding."

"Whoa! Let's slow down. I'd hate to have to write you up for speeding."

"Speeding, hell. We both know where this is going."

"Look, you big shithead, you're probably right, but would you mind if we take it at my pace? Oh, shit! Is that the right time? I've got to run. I'll talk to you as soon as I get the chance. And stop worrying about me. I'm a big boy now. Okay, Mom?"

"Later, bro'. And don't forget to eat. You hear me?" *No wonder Lauri's taken some personal days. She must be on Cloud Nine. I gotta get over and see her. Better call Lindy and give her the good news.*

"Hi, hon, it's me. Are you sitting down? You won't believe this."

Chapter Fourteen

Gregory Bradshaw Marsh had placed one dollar and twenty-eight cents postage on the manila envelope, wanting to be sure it would arrive. Marsh had then driven to Schenectady, to deposit the letter in a mailbox, directly in front of the main branch of the post office. Now, forty-eight hours later, Beckett was two letters from discovering it.

There was no mistaking the mark in the lower left-hand corner of the envelope. Bile started to claw its way up Jack Beckett's esophagus. The last letter he'd received was signed with the same mark. Beckett was afraid to touch the thing. Twenty seconds inexorably passed, while fear held the hairs on Beckett's nape captive. Beckett reached for the phone.

* * * * *

"The Wizard? Does that have something to do with these books?"

"No. My given name is Roy, never use it though. Cos dropped the Wizard on me back in high school. There's a guitar player named Roy Wood I've always loved. He played in a band called The Move. Later he played in ELO, the Electric Light Orchestra, and with a band called Wizzard, that's with two Z's. Since high school, Cos has always said that I'm a magician with a guitar. Hence the moniker, the Wizard."

"Ah. That's better than mine. Willie is just short for William, always hated Bill. How about you, Cosmo? Is there a story behind your name?"

"I was named for my father's father. Papa Cosmo."

"Chris said you guys have a band. I saw all the equipment. Is it a rock band?"

"Blues. We play blues," Cosmo said.

"What type? Chicago? Country?" Willie inquired.

"Type! You know something about blues? Chicago mostly. You know. Muddy, and the Wolf. You like blues?" Cosmo asked.

"My father was a big fan of Blind Lemon Jefferson and J. B. Lenoir. I can remember him singing 'That Black Snake Moan' all the time. I like the music, but I'd rather hear r&b or sweet soul. James

Brown or the Impressions. I dug Kool & the Gang and Parliament when I was younger."

"Fantastic! I own every Funkadelic and P-Funk album. Eddie Hazel was a motherfucker. Talk about someone who knew his way around a guitar. One of my favorite players, after Jeff Beck, of course. We play 'Maggot Brain' and 'Funky Dollar Bill' once in a while at the end of the third set," the Wizard said.

"Yeah? Great! I think we'll get along fine. You guys like Johnny Guitar Watson?" Willie asked.

"Sure do. 'Ain't That a Bitch' is pretty much a staple in our third set."

"I'll have to catch you guys sometime."

"Just let us know when. We'll make sure you get in free."

"And buy you a brew," the Wizard added.

"Thanks. The equipment's set up and ready. There isn't really much you need to know. The cameras are set up to record every time the door opens, and all the mikes are recording, and being monitored at all times. We also have a tap on the phone lines, just in case he calls. Chris said you understand I'm staying here until this is over. And if either one of you leaves the store, you'll be tailed. Oh, I almost forgot. Chris said to tell you all tapes and videos will be given to you when this is resolved. Unless they contain evidence that could be used to convict this psycho."

"Evidential omissions." The Wizard faked a scowl. "And just as I dared hope we'd wind up with our own episode of *American Justice*?"

Cosmo laughed and shook his head. "We figure we'll tell anyone who asks that you're an old friend. You've just moved back to the area, and you're staying with us till you can find a place. We'll deal with the customers. Anything else?"

"Chris said I should help you in your research. I guess he meant read. Where should I begin?"

"Pick any book on those shelves."

"What am I looking for?"

"Angles," Cosmo said.

* * * * *

Chris opened the envelope with the finesse of a surgeon. "There's more than just a letter in this," he said to Beckett. "Do you have any idea how many people here have touched this?"

"At least two, I guess. Whoever sorts the mail and the guy who delivers it. When I saw the mark, I didn't touch it. To be honest, I was too scared. I knew there was something in there other than a letter, and well . . . I was afraid of what that something might be. The whole damn thing jarred me pretty good. I wasn't expecting a response to the article this quickly."

Pressing the ends inward, Chris looked into the envelope. His head involuntarily backed away from its contents. He didn't need to be a seer or an astrophysicist to know that he was looking at a piece of human flesh. "Shit! Jack, call Rolly and tell him to get the lab boys here now."

"What's in there?" Beckett asked, although he had a pretty good idea.

Chris' gloved hand removed the baggie. "Skin. And if I'm right it's from one of the victims. Now make the call!"

Chris placed the sandwich bag on Beckett's desk. Inside was a small swatch of tanned skin. A brief pause occurred, as both men stared at the flesh, lost to their grim imaginings.

"Jesus Christ! Does this son of a bitch think he's Jack the Ripper? Sending us pieces of his victims. Do you think that looks, I don't know? Odd?" Beckett asked, pointing to the skin.

"I think it's been tanned," Chris said.

"Tanned? It's pale."

"Not suntanned. Tanned as in prepared. Like a deer skin."

"Taxidermy?"

"You got it."

"Shit, he's saving this stuff? These predators are showing up everywhere. Ed Gein, the Dunwich Cannibal, Dahmer, the Headhunter in British Columbia, Dale Vernon Chadbourne in Phoenix, and our monster . . . Good Christ, we're breeding angst-ridden isolationists, which we strain through emotional alienation and trauma, social decadence, paranoia, and God knows what else. You'd think there was something in the water," Beckett asserted.

"It's in the culture. Man used to aspire to the heavens, he tried to be moral. There was a Big Picture. Now, we're looking down and inward—it's Me. We've stopped looking skyward. Our goals have become personal; they're no longer national or cultural. Nowadays it's the trees. Nobody sees the forest anymore."

"Too true. Do you think this asshole is making something?"

"I've thought about that. A lot of these types of freaks do just that. The Dunwich Cannibal had sheets and pillow cases made from skin. Some make spoons or bowls, furniture, or . . . did you see *The Silence of the Lambs?* Harris has his killer making a girl suit. Shit, I wish I knew what this fuck is doing. Maybe he's just making sure his trophies don't rot away. That's what I think. Flesh decomposes, and he wants to preserve it for later on. Christ, he could be wallpapering his living room for all we know."

"I hadn't thought about anything like that. You've got to get this asshole," Beckett said, shuddering as he envisioned wallpaper patterned with human nipples.

"What the fuck do you think I've been doing?"

"Sorry. How about the letter? What does it say?"

Chris read the letter to Beckett. "Your name, by the way, is spelled with all lower case letters. He must not think too much of you. Basically it's the same, except for the ending. What the hell does *Cel Gor'ro Gr'xum Fng'i* mean? Maybe it's some kind of title? I'll have to call Cosmo, he may know. Look at the first three lines . . . he's pissed at you. One thing's clear. His farm can be bought. That's the first chink in his armor. And that's what we have to prey on."

"If that's true, he's not going to like the errors in my piece. We had the typesetter misspell this Kassogtha thing with a C instead of a K, and we're leaving out an S, too. And I'll bet he won't like the way I've compared him to other dangerous fanatics who had apocalyptic visions. So we'll be hearing from him again. He won't be able to stand the fact that things still aren't exactly as he wants them. If he's as devout as Cosmo thinks, just the misspelling of Kassogtha is going to send him into a rage. He's a power freak. It's his way or no way. So what now?"

"When the lab's done, you'll get a copy and write your next article. While you're doing that I'm gonna run this, Cel Gor, whatever, past Cosmo. I think we're off to a good start. We're under his skin. Now, let's get this bastard to start scratching. Let me use the phone while I'm waiting, I'll call Cos, and run this by him . . . . Cos. It's Chris. Beckett just got another letter."

"Does it say anything different?"

"I'll read it to you."

"Wow! This one is more Cthulhuvian than the last one. Can you do me a favor? Spell the words to the closing line. You're not too good with the pronunciation of Mythos words and phrases yet."

"That's because my mother sent me to school to learn English." Chris spelled the last line. "Recognize it?"

"No. You said it's directly under his mark. My guess it's a title he's given himself. I'll have the computer look for the words. I have all the words, names, people, things, and places that have been made up for the Mythos listed in files. It won't take long. Maybe it's in there, but I don't think so. You wanna wait?"

"No, but can I get a copy of the file? It has something to do with the encyclopedia you're writing, right? We may encounter other words before this thing is done, and it might be a good idea for the task force to have a Lovecraft dictionary. I'm gonna run. There's other things going on here. I'll get back to you, or you can beep me if you come up with anything. Talk to you soon."

"Okay. Bye."

"Can I get a copy of that when you get it?" Beckett asked.

"No problem."

* * * * *

The inside light of the refrigerator shone on the lunch bag. "Again! That's the second time in the last eight days she forgot it. Why didn't I check to make sure it was in her backpack." Joan Holland collected her car keys, purse, and the brown paper bag, and drove the three blocks to Zoller Elementary School.

In room number six, she was asked how her daughter Joni was feeling by Miss Jacqueline Lee Bouvier Thill, Joni's second grade teacher. During the brief exchange between parent and teacher, it became apparent that Joni had left for school this morning and never arrived. Ten minutes later the police arrived and the search for seven-year-old Joni Holland began.

An APB was sent out: Female. White. Seven years old. Four feet tall. Fifty-six pounds. Blue eyes. Blonde hair, long, ending just below the bottom of her shoulder blades. Missing one tooth, the front left lateral incisor. Wearing white high-top sneakers under white rubber boots, dark blue wool coat, blue jeans, and a white sweatshirt with Baby Shamu on the front. Possibly abducted on her way to school this morning. (Possibly, hell! Definitely! Her mother had screeched.)

* * * * *

Marsh's maroon 1988 Grand Marquis GS slowly cruised the lot. *Only one street light on the block. Perfect! One block from the highway, drop the body, and one block back. The bridge above makes the chance of anyone seeing me nearly impossible. And there's not a damn thing around. I'll be back. Around 7:30. That sounds about right. It gives me an hour to get to the airport. Home to package up my little prize.*

* * * * *

Wednesday afternoon only the rain reported.

The latter part of the day passed in frustration for Chris and the members of the task force. A few blocks away, Cosmo and the Wizard fared no better, as gloom and depression gripped them.

In the basement shrine of his mansion Gregory Bradshaw Marsh sat smiling, one step closer to the fruition of his dream.

❧ Chapter Fifteen ❧

"How about locking up and grabbing a bite?" Willie asked.

"Do you like pizza? We could order a pie and have it delivered."

"Sausage and mushrooms would be good, if that's okay with you two."

"Around here there are three things on the menu. Pizza, subs—the Wizard only eats subs from Subway; he's got a thing for olives—and girls."

"Please don't take my hirsute friend too literally. What he means is that due to the fact that neither of us can boil water, we are fond of women who can cook. Unfortunately they seem to be, if you'll pardon the expression, hard to dig up."

"Are you trying to say that I only date women with culinary talents? What about that professor from the community college. One night we're sitting around discussing the lyrics of Dylan and the next thing I know she'd got me turned on to poetry. Man, she was crafty. First she lured me in with Leonard Cohen, then POW! Knowing I'm a horror freak, she hits me with Poe, not that I hadn't encountered 'The Raven' earlier. A week later, it wasn't really a week, I'm reading some Yeats, and Alice Walker. I wish I could remember how the one about our mother's lap goes . . . and Ernest Dowson, *I have been faithful to thee, Cynara! in my fashion.*' Willie, wanna hear my favorite poem? It's by James Elroy Flecker." Without waiting for a reply, Cosmo's eyes brightened and his voice lowered, its tone round and ringing as if to impart a proverb ripe with wisdom or share a favored story.

> "*We who with songs beguile your pilgrimage*
> *And swear that Beauty lives though lilies die,*
> *We poets of a proud old lineage*
> *Who sing to find your hearts, we know not why,—*
> *What shall we tell you?*
> *Tales, marvellous tales*
> *Of ships and stars and isles . . .*'"

"Hey, Bullwinkle! We're not gonna' go moony-eyed and spend the rest of the night stuck in the Poetry Corner, are we?" the Wizard sarcastically inquired.

"No, we're not, Mr. Know-It-All. I just wanted Willie to understand that I love women for more than their ability to cook. You know damn well that she was a hell of a woman—brilliant, attractive. The last thing I cared about was her inability to tell black-eyed peas from pork and beans. Hell, she didn't know beans about any aspect of the culinary arts. Her idea of cooking was to take it from the freezer and nuke it."

"Sounds like a marriage made in heaven to me," the Wizard quipped.

"The hell you say."

"Gentlemen, please. My stomach is starting a revolt. Are we going to order that pizza or what?"

"Okay. Okay. Two pies, with cheese, sausage, and double mushrooms?"

"Dial, bro', dial," the Wizard commanded. "And have them send some root beer or cream soda with those pies."

* * * * *

"Bug" Pierce had put in his thirty years with the Schenectady PD, and retired at age fifty-four. On Tuesday, Wednesday, and Thursday evenings, while his wife played bingo, he supplemented his pension by working part-time as a security guard for Schenectady County Community College. Bug liked the kids and the quiet. During the spring and summer sessions he leisurely walked the grounds, taking in the fresh air. In the autumn and winter he drove. Tonight he was thankful for the car's heater; which he'd cranked up to high. The winds blowing across the massive parking lot were a bitch.

At 8:30 he thought it would be a good idea to check the college's access ramps. Often, when the winds raged this badly, the circular ramps became impassable due to snowdrifts. On three occasions this winter, students had needed to be pulled out of the banks. Driving under the Western Gateway Bridge his eyes caught a patch of blue in the right bank. Against his better judgment he stopped the car and got out. *Looks like material from a ski jacket*, he thought, while shining his flashlight on the patch of blue. Bug pulled on the material that encased what became an arm with a small hand in a red mitten. Thirty years of police training instantly kicked in.

* * * * *

Chris and Misty had settled on the sofa with a Coors and *84 Charing Cross Road* in the VCR. He'd been dragged by Laurinda to see the film in '87, and in one of life's ironic twists, he had loved it. Laurinda on the other hand found the film a bit pretentious and in some parts superficial. To this day it drove her nuts that he could watch the movie, along with *Singin' in the Rain*, half a dozen times a year. Twenty minutes into the film both he and the kitten were curled up with their dreams. His were to be short-lived.

* * * * *

Marsh parked his car in the short-term parking lot and walked briskly into the airport. At the American Airlines desk he was informed that flight 519 from New York was delayed. Snow had forced Kennedy to close. It was now 8:45 p.m.

What am I supposed to do until 11:00? It's a good thing that the body isn't still in the trunk. Ahhh! What an insipid place. Look at them, running like they have something important to do. Witless cattle. Soon you'll busy.

Marsh found a seat. Closing his eyes, the click-clack of time-driven heels on tile slapped his ears. *Running, they're always running,* he thought.

> She was running, an infant clasped in her left arm as she half-dragged a small boy with her right. In another world her beauty might have been awarded riches or fame, but here she was nothing. Covered in filth and scratches, with snarled, ragged hair, she was merely an animal. A terrified animal trying to protect its young.
>
> Terror pumped adrenalin through her veins as she fled the winged predator that hovered above her. If only she could find some cave to escape into in all this rubble. Yet no sanctuary appeared. Soon the two children would be too heavy to bear. This fear momentarily redoubled her efforts to escape. In the failing light of dusk, fear devoured her determination. Above the desperate trio, a hovering abhorrence consumed the banquet of despair conveyed through thought, emotion, and pheromones. Soon she would be forced to abandon one or both of the children, and another type of feast would commence.

Gregory Bradshaw Marsh, consumed with the paradisal images in his head, began to laugh as the play of terror concluded. More than a few turned to look at the man seated alone, laughing at his own thoughts. Quickly they passed by.

* * * * *

Chris was in a small book shop on Charing Cross Road, buying a lovely old volume of Lord Byron's *Hours of Idleness* for Laurinda. It was a slim, dark leather copy that had been worn by loving hands. *Hands much like hers*, he thought, tender and thoughtful.

The phone took him from his dream. "Sweet mother of God! Fifteen minutes. I don't give a rat's ass how cold it is. Bye!"

It took Chris less than two minutes to put on his shoes, hit the can, and grab his coat and keys. In the blowing snow the driving was slow going, especially down Broadway's treacherous curved hill.

"You rat-bastard-motherfucker! A seven- or eight-year-old girl. You're dead! Can you hear me! You're fuckin' dead!"

As the Taurus pulled onto the access ramp of Schenectady County Community College Chris took note of the press. "Christ, look at 'em. There's more of them than us. They're like flies around a carcass." *Blood-suckin' vultures!*

Raging as hard as the wind, he stepped out of the car. His eyes found Rob Kramer. *Are those frozen tears? Dear God, help us all.*

"She's about the same age as my Sandy. God! I'd give anything for ten minutes with this fucker. *Anything*," Kramer said.

"I know exactly what you mean." Chris' daughter's face appeared before him. "Don't suppose there's any chance—"

"No, it's him, and this one's worse. There's all, God help me, the usual. But he's beaten in her skull with a . . . hammer."

"*What?*" Chris saw his daughter's bloody face lying on the coroner's table as he IDed her broken body.

"There's something else. He left you the hammer."

"Huh?"

"The hammer. And there's a note for you attached to it."

Chris fought back the welling tears as his anger rose. "A note for me? I want it."

The note had been placed in a sandwich bag, to protect it from the elements. It had then been taped to the handle of the hammer, which had been stuffed into the waistband of the girl's jeans. Chris read the handwritten note.

MY DEAR stewart.
THE GAME'S AFOOT.
I ALMOST FUCKED THIS SWEET LITTLE ONE
JUST FOR YOU.
MAYBE THE NEXT ONE. THINK ABOUT THAT.
SOON WE SHALL MEET.
UNTIL THEN, THINK OF THE PLEASURE
I TOOK WITH THIS LITTLE BITCH.
SOON, stewart, SOON.

CEL GOR'RU GR'XUM FNG'I
P. S. MAYBE I COULD INTEREST YOU IN ONE OF HER NIPPLES?

Rob Kramer stared at his rival, wondering what was going on behind that expressionless face. He felt he was looking at an empty shell. "Chris? You all right? Chris . . . hey!"

Slowly something came into Chris' eyes. Whatever it was, Rob Kramer didn't want to meet it. The eyes of Christopher Stewart were now colder and more savage than the raging winds he was standing in. Without a word, Chris walked away from Kramer. When he reached the body bag that contained Joni Holland, he unzipped it. Trussed in a skin of rage, Chris opened her winter coat and looked at the incomprehensible mutilation that had been forced on the inno- cent child. Chris looked into the unfocused doll eyes, now forever fixed on black nothingness, while in his secret heart he said a prayer for the child who hours ago had lived in this shell.

All who watched understood the rules had changed. There would be no turning back. Chris zipped up the bag and crossed himself. Those around him could see his lips moving yet no sound emanated from his mouth. As he silently walked away, Kramer imagined he saw Chris surrounded by a raging black fire. Kramer knew that no man

should now bar Chris path to this monster. An Avenger steeled to
destroy the evil that walked among them had been unleashed.

* * * * *

After spending an hour trying to amuse himself with visions of the
airport being descended upon by the Holy Ones, Marsh was
informed that flight 519 had been canceled. Kennedy was closed
until morning. In a fit of anger he stormed out of the airport.

*At least there's time to watch the eleven o'clock news and see if they've
discovered the little bitch. I'd love to see the look on Stewart's face when he sees
my little present.*

Entering his house, Marsh found the message light on his
machine blinking.

". . . tomorrow morning. Nine-seventeen. American Airlines,
Flight 502. If you need to contact me tonight, I'm at the Plaza, room
908. The number is 2-1-2, 5-5-5, 3-0-0-0. Until tomorrow."

"It's here and safe. I can wait until morning."

* * * * *

"That was quite enjoyable. I do not seem to be able to find time to
attend the cinema at home. Truly a wonderful performance. And to
think I had not even heard of this film regarding Lewis before
tonight. Nor had I ever heard of this actress Debra Winger, she is
quite talented. Once or twice, I felt her facial mannerisms were per-
fection itself. One might say, tiny marvels."

"She was also in *Cannery Row* and *The Sheltering Sky*."

"Ah. Bowles and Steinbeck, that is superb company. Perhaps we
should top off our evening with a couple of those hot dogs you
described to me earlier. They are from Mike's, I believe you said."

"Yes, Mike's. Almost the best in town. Pat's are better, but he's
closed at this hour. I wish Chris could have come with us. He pre-
tends not to like romantic drama, but down deep, he's really a softy.
I wonder why he didn't call today."

"*Chère*, I am certain he was simply too busy. These murders must
create unbelievable amounts of pressure for him. Look at the media
attention given to these horrible crimes. This area is not used to this
type of terrible event. It is much quieter here than at home. Do you
realize that we have almost one murder per day in New Orleans? The

frequency of these murders must make things hellish for him. I am sure he will call you as soon as he is able to."

"You're right. I guess I just miss him."

"Perhaps those hot dogs will help."

"Are you always this hungry?"

"Yes. *Grand-mère* says that I eat enough for three."

"I can't imagine why she'd say a thing like that."

* * * * *

Gregory Bradshaw Marsh paced as he watched the newscast on WRGB, while videotaping WNYT. He was elated. At 11:30, WRGB, Schenectady's hometown television station, was going to air a half-hour special on the murders.

Finally! It has taken them long enough to properly cover this. Now the herd will truly embrace fear. How easy it is to play with their emotions. First the whores, then that faggot, finally that woman and one of their precious babes. Now even their protectors understand no one is safe. The strong weaken as my victory draws near.

* * * * *

Chris sat in the darkened family room of his once joyful home looking out on the snow-covered backyard. He'd spent the night in his chair with only cigarettes and tea as company, although the moon, an unwanted silent companion of stark observations, thrice appeared from behind dark clouds to sneer down at him. Twice he had fallen asleep, but awoke quickly. Disturbing dreams reared up to haunt him. Years ago he had dried out the bottoms of what seemed like a thousand beer cans in an effort to banish his demons. The moment before he looked into the empty eyes of Joni Holland, his demons reappeared, banished and repressed no longer. No longer was the lawn covered in green. No laughter erupted from Pat as they played horseshoes. The Japanese scarecrows that frightened the birds from his summer garden were now the taunting, demonic eyes of the man-beast that laughed at him. Repeatedly, the lifeless eyes of Joni Holland flashed before him. Begging. Pleading from her drawer in the morgue, she begged for justice. He could not escape her eyes. Chris had seen the same eyes before in the morgue when he had identified his daughter's crushed body.

It was all death, nothing more. That's what he was afraid of, so afraid he was immobile. His heart was full of it. His mind, a confused aggregate of kaleidoscopic what if's, Dear God why's, get a grip and get on with it's, and I can't's, threw up bloody, tortured memories accompanied by frightened, anger-distorted voices. Butchered lamentations of outrage provided a stark soundtrack to his memory montages of gore-soaked pain. As dawn broke, he could find no hope. Only the pain and anger of eleven butchered innocents seethed within him.

* * * * *

Lindy was trying to get Anne dressed for school when news came over the radio. Pat Price almost dropped his Daddy's Alarm Clock coffee mug as he looked at his daughter.

Saints preserve us! A girl! The bastard's butchered a child. "I want you to keep her home today. And I don't want her outside. There's no telling where or when this asshole will strike again."

"*Dad.* You said a bad word. Mom says we're not posta say swears. Member?"

"Sorry, darlin'. It won't happen again."

"Promas?"

"Promise."

"I'm not sure her staying home from school is a good idea. After finding that girl, I'm sure the schools will be on alert," Lindy said.

"Just for today, okay? Look, I need to find Moon. You know how he gets. And I don't want to be worried about Anne. I don't want to go through what he went through when Sue and Meredith died."

Pat vividly remembered the photographs of the automobile Chris' wife and daughter were killed in. He hadn't seen that much blood since 'Nam. Chris had spent months half-drunk and completely shattered.

There's no way I could go through that. Christ almighty. A seven-year-old girl. Meredith was seven when she died. Moon's gonna destroy anything that gets in his way now. If he doesn't drink himself blind.

"She can stay home today. And you're right about Chris. You're the only one who'll be able to talk to him. Do you think he knows about this?"

"Damn right, he knows. Didn't you hear what they said? The killer left a message for him. I gotta find him. Call Joe and have him open up for me. Tell him to call Bobby or Sal if he needs more help. By the time this is over I'll have to make him a partner."

"Dad. Is Uncle Chris okay?"

"He's fine." *I hope, but I doubt it.*

* * * * *

Angered faces under umbrellas of protest clogged the storefront. The first shots in a war of morality had been fired at the evil which was sold from behind that glass door.

Behind the plate glass window, copies of Michael Slade's *Cutthroat* and *Ghoul* bookended a copy of Bret Easton Ellis' *American Psycho.* The three stark novels of insanity-driven violence—human predator hunting human prey—glared out at the conservative mob. To the angry eyes of the throng, there was no difference between the grim novels of reason battling razors and the Wolfman and Mummy models that flanked them. Reverend Stephen M. Davis, Jr. and his fear-whipped followers believed all the merchandise in the store's windows had been spewed from the open maw of hell. What appalled Reverend Davis most was the serial killers collectors' cards that sat in the window beside a copy of *Eroticism in the Horror Cinema.*

"FILTH! It's all filth and pornography! These demons are placing this filth into the hands of our children. It's no wonder they are growing up without any sense of moral direction. 'Ask not what your country can do for you' and the golden rule have been replaced by this, what do they call it, *juice*, and a generation of always open mouths screaming, *Me! No, me! No, me! Me! Me! Me!* Where does it stop?

"Not on MTV, or *N.Y.P.D. Blue.* There are serial killers and Satanists on the 6 o'clock news. There's NC-17, crack, and the Homosexual Plague! All these things should be exorcised by a proper fear of our LORD JESUS CHRIST and The Strap! Not to mention abolishing all plea bargaining and establishing and executing the death penalty in this state. In *all* states for that matter.

"They teach our children science while they ban prayer! They outlaw *prayer* while our streets are transformed into speedways leading our innocent children straight into the awaiting jaws of Hell! John Wayne has died, so no one will ride to our rescue. *No one but ourselves can rescue us from this filth*!" preached Reverend Davis as he cast his accusing finger toward the store's interior.

From his crowd of followers someone shouted, "Close it down!"

"Close it down!" enjoined two more energized voices.

Within moments the crowd, almost fifty strong, lifted their voices in the chant, "CLOSE IT DOWN! CLOSE IT DOWN!"

* * * * *

"Cos! You better come see this," the Wizard yelled. He looked at his shotgun, hoping he wasn't going to have to use it to protect them.

"Not again! How many times are we going to have to deal with these bible-thumpers? Motherfuckers are comparing us to rats! *Fucking rats*! Goddamn it! Don't these people have lives?"

"Small and overly narrow ones, I'm afraid. This is the anger of the weak, not the righteous," the Wizard explained in an even tone, hoping to calm his angered friend. *If he goes out there we're gonna have a battle scene worthy of the Hulk*, he thought.

"Righteous? Bullshit! This isn't a maggots' hive."

"But they think we peddle the flowers of evil—"

"We're not depraved diabolical corrupters."

"No, we're not. But these are mere children who fear leaving the security of their fathers' homes and entering the world. A world they see as fraught with temptation and desires. Their fear is born from the allure of perceived corruption. They fear their senses and the desires they secretly long to embrace."

"Embrace? The only thing they embrace is a much talked about angelic devotion. Showing off their Sunday finery is more like it. We both know what happens to their devotion and their morality come Monday morning." Cosmo's anger was being fueled by a small blue-eyed redhead, with a face more cherub than child, dangling two Halloween prop, dead rubber rats (by their tails) and a large sign, facing inward, that had been taped to the front window. It read: "Feed rat poison to the RATS who sell it, not to our CHILDREN!" Cosmo was terrified of rats and mice. Monsters, blood, and guts, he could handle, but not rats. The mere mention of the word brought a chill to him. To be referred to as one caused his anger to erupt.

"Some, perhaps, but that's not the point here. These are people who are desperate. They are being driven by the fear that their world is no longer safe. You and I have encountered these exact feelings lately. We have both felt rage over the security of our world being violated by this butcher. They're only lashing out at us because we're here. We're as close to this monster as they can get. If the true source of their rage were present they'd tear him apart."

"What's that noise? Holy shit!" Willie Stanton exclaimed as he entered the store. "I better call Chris. This kind of thing will mess things up."

* * * * *

Twenty-two minutes later Reverend Stephen M. Davis, Jr. was seated in Michael Carroll's office.

"Chief Carroll, I don't appreciate being ushered in here like some common thug. I play golf with the mayor. It might interest you to know that I have some clout around here."

"That may well be under normal circumstances, but these are not normal circumstances. This is an election year and if this killer is not caught it won't make a damn bit of difference who you know. As I've explained, at the moment we have only two chances of stopping this monster, and that store, whether you or I like it, is our best opportunity. If you and your congregation don't leave that store alone, you'll all be arrested for obstruction of justice. And if that doesn't work, Jack Beckett at the *Times* will find out you've jeopardized a police operation to apprehend this killer. I'm sure you're aware of Beckett's influence in this community. It's greater than yours and our mayor's combined. Now, have we reached an understanding?"

"I don't like this at all, but for the moment I'll go along with it. But I warn you, Chief Carroll. I want results and I want them soon."

You and everyone else in this city.

* * * * *

Christa Liebezeit disembarked from her flight. She had spent an anxious night in New York, wondering about her first meeting with him.

This close, and still suffering delays. I must have enough time to implement my plans. Before leaving the airliner she checked her makeup. *You look stunning. It should prove easy to seduce this, what does Roaker call him? Lord Marsh. This self designated messiah. Shortly I will be the power behind the throne, the governor's consort, and after a period of time . . . I must go carefully with this one. Roaker says he is devious and brilliant. He must not ever gain the slightest inkling of what is to come. And he must never become aware of Roaker's devotion to me.*

How easy it was to supplant Roaker's will with my own. He folded beneath my skills in a single night. These worms, *how full of themselves they are. Marsh thinks to use me to gain power and then discard me. And his bloated sycophant Roaker believes I have become nothing more than chattel, a quivering toy, devoted to his repulsive caresses. How simple he must be to believe that I shall use my talents to dispose of Marsh and then install him as the human power on earth.* Dummkopfs! *All they see is a beautiful face with tits. Let them dance upon desire's playground for a time. When they're comfortable within my writhing coils, I shall remove this mask.*

Waiting for her luggage, she began to wonder why Marsh had not met the plane. *Where is he? Twice last night I left messages on his machine. I wonder if something has held him up? I have been standing here for twenty minutes. Where could he be? Perhaps he's making me wait as some form of punishment for being delayed. This game we are about to play may prove more interesting than I thought.*

"Excuse me, are you Christa Lie-be-zeit? I'm Gregory Bradshaw Marsh."

"Mr. Marsh, it is a pleasure to finally meet you."

"The pleasure is all mine."

Is it really? Soon we shall see whose pleasure it is.

"Shall we go?"

* * * * *

Hand in hand the two young lovers walked through the garden.

"When we, ah—"

"Please, not quite yet. Let's just enjoy the garden a little longer. I do so love to walk here. The fragrance of lavender and lilacs filling the breeze. Don't you just love the smell of the earth after it rains?" Ida asked.

"No. This is not the earth I desire," Gregory replied.

"You must learn to take the best from both worlds. Did you not take note of my brother yesterday? His hand tender as a rose and sharp as a blade. You must learn the fine arts of pain and pleasure. They will serve you well when you rule."

"When we rule."

"I am merely your first teacher. I fear you will outgrow me."

"Never!"

"There will come another; Mother has seen her. She is to be your bride," she whispered, turning her head down and away from him, "and your bed mate."

"I have just found you. How can you think I would leave you? Who could give me what you do? Do you think there could be another who could understand, let alone share, my aspirations?"

"I am only the road to your manhood. She is your destination. You may not change what is written."

As the lovers continued to walk, his thoughts were as scolded puppies, filled with hurt and longing. *There must be some way to show her my devotion.*

Things progress nicely. Another cornerstone has been laid, she thought.

Seated in the library, over cognac, Marsh held back his questions as he held her hand.

"Gregory, you seem nervous. Please relax. You are perhaps wondering if there is to be some lesson this evening? Tonight I thought we might just sit quietly and enjoy each other's company. We shall continue your lessons tomorrow."

❦ Chapter Sixteen ❦

Pat looked at the car sitting in the unshoveled driveway. *How many times does he think I'm gonna ring this damn thing.* "Fuck me, if he's not gonna answer the door I'll let myself in. Moon? You here?" *You sober?* "Moon!"

"Yeah . . . back here."

At least he looks sober. "Sleep?"

"Not really. Sorta drifted off. Once, maybe twice. Nightmares. Couldn't relax."

"Sober?"

"That's a dumb question. I take it you've heard?"

"I heard and you still haven't answered my question."

"Yes, Mom, I'm sober."

"Good. How about I make us a pot of tea?"

"Us? You hate the shit."

"Okay, you." Walking into the kitchen Pat asked, "Got any coffee? Never mind, I found it."

"Aren't you supposed to be at work?"

"Aren't you? Now cut the shit. After all these years, let's not start running in circles. When I heard about the girl I had a pretty good idea how you'd take it. Looks like I was right. So start talking. If anybody knows what's going on in there it's me. And you're too fuckin' old to spend another six months in the bottom of a bottle."

"They were cans."

"Don't correct me, just talk."

"I haven't heard the news. What are they saying?"

"Huh?"

"What are the news reports saying?"

"That you found a seven-year-old girl carved up by this motherfucker. Why?"

"Anything else?"

"Like what? Christ, Moon, this ain't *Jeopardy*. What are you trying to tell me? What else?"

"He left me a note."

"What do you mean, left you?"

"The note said, 'My dear Stewart, I almost fucked this sweet little one just for you—'"

"Christ almighty! He actually called you by name? Maybe we should both have a drink?"

"No. No booze."

"How does he know your name?"

"Beckett's article. Remember? We set up Beckett, the store, and yours truly as targets. It seems he's zeroed in on me."

"Christ, this fuck's luck is spooky. He scored a direct hit first time out?"

"He also said we'll meet soon."

"He's coming for you? What's he, fuckin' nuts? No man in his right mind would fuck with you now."

"I want him to come."

"Fine. Take a couple of weeks off. You sit here and I'll watch your back."

"No can do. I've got to be in the open. I've got to let him get close."

"That's bullshit. You want to be point man with no one covering your ass. Christ, Moon, you're crazier than this asshole. There ain't no way in hell I'm gonna let you hang your ass out there by itself. You're a member of this family, and we're not ready for any more tragedy. Lindy went half out of her mind when Sue died. They were like sisters. She's not ready for you to get yourself killed."

"I know that. But there's nothing you can do about it. This ain't the 'Nam. Besides, I have Rolly covering my ass."

"Look, Rolly's a good guy and all, but this is out of his league. You're not dealing with some stupid S-O-B who shot his wife because he thought she had a boyfriend. This is a fuckin' psycho, a spook who comes and goes at will. I don't want to see you in a bag marked KIA. Damn it, Moon! I thought we escaped the insanity. Will you think about this for a minute?"

"I've been thinking about it all night. There's only one way to get this freak, and it's me. He wants me, so let him come. I'll be ready."

"I fuckin' hope so."

"Just drink your coffee and shut up."

"Whether you like it or not I'm gonna' be watching your sorry ass."

Yeah, I love you, too.

* * * * *

A smile appeared on the Wizard's face. Insight had arrived.

Hot shit! Why didn't it occur to anybody before this? This freak's gonna go ape-shit. Hope they let me buy a ticket to this cocksucker's execution. "Hey, Cos! I think I found something. Something that just might break things for Chris."

"Figured if anyone would, it'd be you. We all know when that intellect opens up things happen. Ain't a better idea man walking. So, what's the deal?"

"It's still rough, but you'll get the gist. I was flipping though this," the Wizard held up a paperback copy of Brian Lumley's novel *The Spawn of the Winds,* "and I came across this idea. Look here on page one hundred. I wasn't reading it, I was just browsing, but shit. There it is. The stone."

"The Stones from Mnar. Holy shit! How in the hell could I have overlooked the stones? How many times over the years have you heard me bitch about Lin Carter's book about the stones not being published."

"You're not by chance referring to that book Carter wrote that was supposed to actually be a small fragment from Lovecraft's fabled *Necronomicon*, are you?" the Wizard asked with a poker face.

"Yeah. The one Mirage Press was going to publish in '76. Wait a minute, you're busting my ass. You remember."

"Of course I remember. I'll probably remember the damn thing after I've been dead for twenty years. You've only told me about the thing, what—eight thousand times."

"I can't believe I missed this angle. Man, I think you're a fuckin' genius. Some days I wonder why you hang with me. How could I be so stupid? Derleth, Carter, and Lumley, not to mention a dozen other contributors, have all written about them, and Lumley musta spent the first fifty or sixty pages of *The Burrowers Beneath* seeding them in the plot. Next thing you know I'll forget the words to 'Baby, Please Don't Go', or worse yet, 'Mannish Boy.' You must think I'm an idiot."

"Nah, some days you just misplace your thinking cap. Can happen to anyone. Hell, it does to me all the time. Now, here's my idea. This asshole believes in the GOO, right? So it stands to reason that he'd believe in the stones as well. They probably secure the doorway he's looking to break down or through. So he hates these seals. They hurt his gods, either physically or psychically. They're shaped like the sign of the Elder Gods. Like the cross, they represent the powers of light, of goodness. The powers that defeated his precious Old Ones. Now this is where it gets a bit rough. This guy is nuts, right? So maybe he'd go out of his way to get rid of these stones if he could.

"You got tons of the stones upstairs in the spare room. Remember that collection over in Scotia you bought a few years back? Well, there's a ton of 'em in it. I know you said they're phonies. Just toys some Lovecraftian had made up, but our freak doesn't know that. All we need to do is find some way to get them where he can see them. Maybe Beckett could put a picture in the paper, or something like that. Or maybe we should fill the window with them— maybe something like an outline of the Elder Sign made with your Cthulhuvian talismans. We've already set the store up as a target. He might drive by and see them, or Chris could go on TV holding one or something. One way or another we've got to find a way to bring these things to this bastard's attention. I don't know how to use them yet, but I think they're the only ammo we've got at the moment. Whadaya think? Good idea?"

"Why the hell didn't you listen to your mother and become a doctor or something? You're brilliant! And how come this never occurred to me? Shit. I'm the one who's supposed to be the Lovecraft devotee around here. Damn! Where have I been? This is great! We've gotta call Chris. Man. He's gonna give you a kiss and probably a medal. Do they give medals to citizens? Christ, they'll throw you a parade. Mayor's gonna have a Wizard Day. You'll be famous. Imagine the grandeur."

"Grandeur, parade, and medal be damned! How about a case of tall boys. Cold ones. No, make that two. I'm worth it. And I want to sleep till noon for a whole week. Cos, you call, I'm too excited. Let's have a brew. Man, I feel like playing. Poor Stacia's starting to feel neglected," the Wizard said, looking at his black '55 Strat, lovingly named for a well endowed topless dancer who'd performed with the space-rock band Hawkwind in the '70s. He regretted he'd been too busy to have touched his beloved instrument in the last four days.

* * * * *

Just as Pat was about to leave, Chris' beeper went off. Chris' face went white. He looked at the number displayed. "Thank God. It's Cosmo or the Wizard."

"Who?"

"The guys who run the store we're using as a target. I gave them my number if anything came up." *Saved by the beeper*, he thought as he dialed The Horror Corner. "Cosmo, hi. It's Chris. You called."

"Hey, thanks for getting rid of all those assholes. I was ready to go out and kick some ass. We've got this idea. Maybe you should come down here. You might like this."

"What assholes are we talking about?"

"The holy rollin' picketers that were outside the store an hour ago."

"Picketers? I don't know anything about them."

"That's odd, well, never mind. We'll talk about it when you get here."

"What's your idea?"

"It would be better if you came down. We've got something to show you."

"Give me a few minutes." He hung up and turned to Pat. "These guys have some kind of idea they want to run by me. Gotta run. I'll call you later."

"You better or I'm coming to find you. One other thing, Moon. Be careful. I've got a bad feeling about this," Pat said. *Real bad.*

You're not the only one, Chris thought as he left Pat standing in his kitchen.

"He's on the way. Ten minutes. Must be nice to have one of those red lights." Cosmo said to Willie.

"They're handy. Could one of you fill me in on this stone? I think I missed something. How are you going to use a stone that's not real to catch someone who is?" Willie asked.

"These are just stories to you and to me, right? Well, to the killer they're real. So, he might think that the stones from the stories are real as well. In the stories these things can hurt his gods."

Draw him out. Proactive techniques often ensnare these animals. "Not a bad scheme," said the recently-promoted-to-homicide-investigator.

Fifteen minutes later Chris pulled into the parking lot of The Horror Corner. As he reached the door, Cosmo opened it.

"What's up? You guys find something we can use?" Chris asked.

"We think so. Go ahead Wiz, it's your idea. You tell him," Cosmo said.

"Yeah, tell me."

"Well, Cos asked me to read some stuff, a few Mythos books, kinda see if I could maybe dig up something. And I did, here in this one novel *The Spawn of the Winds*. It's about Ithaqua, the Wind Walker. He's the Great Old One that roams the Arctic wastes from British Columbia to Kalaallit Nunaat. That's Greenland. It sounds like a Mythos name, doesn't it? One for me, huh, Cos?"

"I give you two for that one bro', but when yer talkin' bout Greenland, don't forget unihorned Gnoph-Ken," Cosmo replied.

"Right. In Lumley's novel these guys defeat Ithaqua by using these star stones," the Wizard said, holding up one of Cosmo's fake Mnarian wards.

"Where did you get that? Take a peek at this," Chris said, showing them the charm that hung from his neck.

"Where did I get it? Where the hell did you get yours? And when did you get the idea, and from what story?" a very bewildered Cosmo asked. "Damn. Everybody here seems about ten steps ahead of me on this."

"I'll tell you about mine in a minute. First, let's step back. You guys know what these things are? Look, you tell me what you know about these, what did you call them, star stones?"

"They're called Stones from Mnar," the Wizard said.

"Right, Mnar. When you're done I'll tell you about this," Chris said.

"Fine. In the Mythos these star stones are shaped like the sign of the Elder Gods. Remember them, they're the good guys. These stones sometimes hurt the GOO, but more often they're used as locks or seals on the prisons of Cthulhu and his cohorts. They have great power and are rare. Now, here's our plan. We've got maybe two hundred of these things, see," the Wizard said as Cosmo held out the box he'd picked up from the floor. "What if we plaster these stones all over our front window or something? Maybe this asshole will want to check them out or try to destroy them. We'll use the stones as a cask of Amontillado."

"'The thousand injuries . . . I had borne' . . ."

"What are you guys talking about? I've never seen anyone who can go off on tangents like you two."

"That's us, the new Doctor Tarr and Professor Fether," the Wizard said.

"Quite so! A heady *Clos de Vougeot*, good company, and women, with their bright eyes—" Cosmo boisterously added.

"Whoa! Let's get back to the stones," Chris commanded.

"Right. What we were trying to say was we could use the stones to lure this fuck here, then we—you—pounce. That's why we made the Edgar Allan Poe reference. See, in Poe's story Montresor uses a cask of Amontillado to lure Fortunato to his doom," the Wizard explained. "Then once you've got him, you can use the stones like a cross, or a silver bullet."

"Your turn. Where did you get that thing from? Nobody's ever made them up commercially. If they had, I'd know about it. At least I think I would," Cosmo said.

"Are those things real?" Chris asked, his mind racing, considering and dismissing possibilities.

"Real! Nah. They're just toys some collector had made up. For fun, I guess," Cosmo said, explaining he'd acquired the stones when the widow of a local Lovecraft enthusiast had called him, asking if he were interested in purchasing a small collection of Lovecraft's books, letters, and assorted items.

"Give me a minute to think about this," Chris said.

"But what about the one you're wearing? Where did you get it?" the Wizard asked.

"Came from my girlfriend's cousin. He's here visiting. He's from New Orleans. His grandmother is some kind of voodoo high priestess. She had a premonition that something bad was going to happen here and sent this. It's supposed to be a voodoo charm. It even has a name, something French, something like the star of heaven's, ah, protector. No, that's not it. Guardian, that's it."

"You're into *voodoo?*" Cosmo asked, his mind blitzing through its catalogue of Dr. John quotes but not finding one he deemed appropriate.

"No, not me. My girlfriend's cousin is involved in voodoo. White voodoo."

"Damn. You get around," the Wizard said. "Voodoo. Dope and prostitution. Vietnam, serial killers. You ought to write a book."

"You don't suppose this guardian could be Kthanid?" Cosmo asked.

Three bewildered faces looked to each other for help. Chris shook his head, the Wizard shrugged, and Willie again wondered what he was involved in.

"Who?" Chris asked.

"Kthanid. Sorry, I guess we haven't got around to him. We kinda skipped over the Elder Gods. Kthanid is the Elder God Eminence, the king of the powers of goodness, love, and light. He rules the Elder Gods from the Hall of Crystal and Pearl, beneath the polar region of Elysia, which is somewhere near Orion. He's Cthulhu's cousin," Cosmo explained.

"These Elder Gods are direct relatives of the GOO?" Chris asked.

"Yup. I wish I knew something about voodoo, 'cause this strikes me as odd. Look at the shape, it looks just like these. Same color, same shape and size. Hell, the texture is even similar. How does a voodoo priestess in New Orleans know about the Stones from Mnar? How does she get one? And how come it shows up now?"

Chris and the Wizard looked at each other. "There's *something* going on here. I don't know what it is, but something is definitely going on," The Wizard said.

"You're not kidding," Chris added.

"Maybe we should talk to this guy from the Big Easy," Cosmo said.

"He doesn't know anything. Lauri, that's my girlfriend, and I were discussing the Mythos the other day and he hadn't heard of it. He'd barely heard of Lovecraft. Said he'd never read 'em."

"Maybe he hasn't, but he knows more about these stones than we seem to. And more importantly, he thinks these things, or at least the one you have, are real."

Chris called Lauri's but no one answered. He left a message. "Let's kick around your idea about the window some more. If we could lure this bastard into the store, we could nail his ass."

"True, but there may be a problem here," Cosmo said.

Chris asked, "Like what?"

"Let's assume that this demonic fuck knows, or has read, most if not all the Mythos material there is. So, he knows all the GOO, their minions, all the dates and places—everything. He's a walking encyclopedia. He shits, shaves, and showers the Mythos."

"Cos, I love yer ass, but is there a point here?" the Wizard asked.

"Yeah, there is. I don't think we've discussed the differing schools of opinion regarding the Mythos."

"The what? These are just stories. They're, what—pop culture? This stuff's not Mark Twain or Hemingway, and it's sure not Shakespeare." Chris flatly stated.

"To some people it is," the Wizard said, grinning and pointing at Cosmo.

"I know you said some guy in France did his doctoral thesis on Lovecraft, but that's just one guy, right?" Chris asked. "Goddamn it. First I find I've got some sick son of a bitch who believes the stuff in these books is real, then you tell me some of the places really exist and they're practically in my own backyard. And now you're telling me that there are opposing schools of literary criticism on the Mythos. Is this ever going to end?"

"Just listen. What I'm trying to say is, what if this freak doesn't believe in the war the Elder Gods fought with the GOO, or in the stones from Mnar?"

"Huh?"

"The schools, and please understand that they're not hard and fast schools, they're more like differing gray areas of opinion, often heated. See, Lovecraft never mentions a war between the GOO and the Elder Gods. The war was the creation of August Derleth, and some, many, discount it altogether."

"Are you saying this beast might not fear anything? He's like a Satanist who has no fear of divine intervention, because there's no God."

"Not exactly. There are powers of light, the Elder Gods, but they're not at war with the evil ones. They have no reason to be. Look at it this way, in the cosmos, we're just insects. Earth is one small speck in an infinite ocean of entities. Why should the Elder Gods be concerned with what happens to a bunch of fleas? Did you ever read the *Fantastic Four* comic when you were a kid?"

"Sure did," Chris replied.

"Do you remember Galactus?"

"Yeah, he was one of the FF's enemies. I really loved the Thing. I had an *'It's Clobberin' Time'* sweatshirt. As I recall, Galactus was something like thirty or forty feet tall, and as old as creation itself. He was going to devour all of Earth's energy, leaving it a dead rock."

"You got it. When he first arrives here in *Fantastic Four* #48, he's only come to Earth to feed, to sustain his biological needs. He's god-like to us, but not a god in the true sense of the word. We're nothing but ticks on a dog. So why should a much higher form of life, one that's godlike, and we'll skip the moral and theological questions involved here, concern itself with organisms which are inferior? We're dealing with hungry predators here. Remember the GOO are alien beings, not true gods. They're not Odin or Yahweh. They didn't create the universe, they just exist in it, like we do."

"Christ! He refers to us as cattle, and cows certainly don't have a god. We don't think about them, they're just food. We're just a few steps down the food chain to these things," Chris realized.

"Right. Fish, plants, nobody thinks of them as anything other than food. So, depending on what this psycho believes, he might not care about a few little stones."

Shit!

"But then again, he could be very concerned about the effects of these stones on his gods. Maybe he thinks they could interfere with, or completely disrupt his plans," Cosmo said. "I'm gonna go clean out the window and fill it with these babies. And you should figure out how to leak them to the press so he'll know about them. Maybe, something like we've discovered a talisman against his gods."

"How about we say a psychic's come forward with a warning from Kthanid and we're arming ourselves for the coming battle with evil. If you get something prepared the local TV stations can disseminate it on the noon, six, and eleven o'clock news. Three stations, nine broadcasts, there's a good chance he'll see it today," the Wizard said. "And how about a picture or something in tomorrow's paper."

"I'll get together with Matthews and Beckett and put things in motion. We'll roll the dice and hope for a seven," Chris said.

* * *

"Did you sleep well, my darling?" Ida asked Gregory as he entered the library.

"Yes. I dreamt of dark landscapes where black angels winged through gray shaded skies. Below them, the Earth burned and heaved."

"You've beheld the future."

"Why didn't you wake me? We could have had breakfast together."

"I thought I would let you sleep while I organized my thoughts. You have much to learn and the coming weeks will be hectic."

"I understand that I have a lot to learn, but before we get to my instruction I have a question. The other night when I was introduced to your mother she said her name was Waite, not Marsh. And yet both you and your brother use the Marsh name."

"That's really quite simple. Great-grandfather's will stipulates that if the beneficiary of the Marsh estate is a woman, she must use the Marsh name, even if she marries. If she does not continue to use the name she forfeits the inheritance. When mother married Thomas she kept the Marsh name until Ethan was born. Once a new Marsh heir was born she took her husband's name. Few of the Marsh women have changed their names after marriage. Retaining the Marsh name seems to have become a tradition."

"Will you keep the family name?"

"I'd like to, but—come now, there's no more time for idle chatter. You must learn in a few short months what it has taken this family over a century to discover."

"Why do I only have a few months? Is the time of their arrival so near?"

"No, I do not believe so. By summer's end you must begin your preparations, and there is no way to know how long they will take. Once you have learned what I know, you must find the *Zhou Texts* before you can proceed further."

"Why?"

"According to Navarre, the text contains the rite which will open this world to Kassogtha. Where and how to perform this ceremony lies on the pages of a book we do not possess."

"She showed me the book. It was in a crumbling temple or palace. Somewhere in a dense and overgrown jungle. Am I to go there to find it?"

"Ethan and I believe you must. We believe a copy, perhaps the only copy, resides in Thailand, in avaricious hands. It falls to you to obtain the text."

"Then I will find it and bring it here to you."

"No. You must not return once you have left us."

"Why? What about the feelings we share?"

"I did not want to tell you this, but it seems I must. As you are aware, Ethan is quite devoted to me. Even now his jealousy of you deepens. There will be an event occurring here after a time. Once it happens, Ethan will not allow you to return. What I am trying to tell you is that I am about to . . . die." Her last word *sotto voce*, and delicate as if it were the aching caress of a tear.

"Die! I—"

"Please, let me finish. I have suffered headaches over the years, much like the ones you suffer. Now I am informed that I have a brain tumor which will kill me before the next spring comes."

"But there are doctors, who—"

"I have seen almost every neurosurgeon in Boston, and a few in New York City. Each has told me the same thing. My condition is inoperable and terminal. It is solely because of the feelings that you have mentioned that you must leave. I do not want you here when death comes for me." With a practiced sorrow shading her words like late afternoon autumnal sunlight filtered through sheer drapes she maneuvered his feelings.

"I won't leave."

"I do not want to die knowing that everything I have worked for will not come to pass. If you do not learn what I must teach you and take that knowledge and use it, then all my efforts and dreams are worthless. If you have feelings for me then allow me to die knowing someone will eat the fruit of my toils. You will give my life meaning. But there will be no more talk of this for now. We have much to accomplish and I would like to have time to spend with you, time for walks and the like. Now, shall we begin your education? If you are to be the commandant of Earth, there is much you need to know. You have little real knowledge of the Holy Ones, their history, and how men have worshiped them through the ages."

"But—"

"There will be no buts! Can you name the three mates of Cthulhu? Which one is dead? Which was abandoned on Xoth? Do you know of the ancient priests Tchotghtguerele, Hnas-ry-Gij, Kreuhn, Ankn-f-n-Khonsu, or Vatnsenda-Rasu? Have you read Clithanus' *Confessions*, the *Celaeno Fragments,* or the *Occultus of Hieriarchus?*"

"No."

"No? What about Mulder's *Secret Mysteries of Asia?* Or *Ghorl Nigral?* Who are the Nestrarians? Where is Enten Terrace? Yatta-Uc?"

"I—"

"Do you know the name of the lake that the twin suns set behind? Have you ever heard of Bordighera's opera *Massa di Requiem per Shuggay?*"

"I—"

"Where in the pantheon lie serpent-bearded Byatis, Rhan-Tegoth, Othuum, Vorvadoss, or Chaugnar Faugn? What did the Turks call Beled el-Djinn? Where will the Torch of Nug appear? And for what reason? Can you name the guardian of the Chaos Stone?"

Her rigid stance and chilled glare stung him as he fumbled for an answer. He longed for a response, any response that would lighten her reproachful countenance. Demeaned by his ignorance he lashed himself with insults and averted his eyes to escape her disdain.

"No? These things you must learn, as there will be barriers on the path you travel. You will need to be wary and cautious. There are many who will use any means necessary to stop you."

"Like who?"

"The damnable Sutherland Foundation, or even worse, the accursed Order of the Sword of St. Jerome. Beware them! These ascetics will stop at nothing to destroy anything they deem evil. If either of these witch-hunting fraternities learn of you or of your design they will kill you."

"I've never heard—"

"The Sutherland Foundation was created in 1921 when real estate and oil magnate Martin Barriemore Sutherland's only daughter, Genevieve, was kidnapped by the Dark Nursery Guild and sacrificed to Shub-Niggurath while on holiday in Wales. Sutherland was shattered by his daughter's death and vowed to eradicate the evil stain of occult worship from the face of the Earth. When he became aware of the existence of Shub-Niggurath and the other Holy Ones, he created the foundation and focused all of its energies on destroying them. To date, the Foundation is suspected of assassinating over two hundred members of various denominations devoted to the Holy Ones. Both here, and in Europe, several assemblies have been hunted down and murdered. The Foundation seems to have close ties to the governments of the United States, Canada, England, and France. These governments appear to turn a blind eye to the Foundation's covert activities. We believe them to be responsible for the eradication of the British and Italian sects of Her Maidens of Sorrow, although we have little more than circumstantial evidence.

"When Sutherland was killed in 1951 in an airplane crash, his son Jeffrey assumed the foundation's directorship. Jeffery Sutherland believes the Holy Ones were responsible for his father's death and has redoubled the foundation's efforts. The agents of the Sutherland Foundation are deadly. Each agent is judge, jury, and executioner. Like the film hero James Bond, they have a license to kill, and you can be certain they will use it."

"Where is the Foundation located?"

"Its headquarters is located in New York City, on Central Park West, but they maintain dens the world over. You must also fear the Order of the Sword of St. Jerome. Pope Leo XIII banned the order almost eighty years ago for its secret activities. Before it was banned, the bulk of the order worked within the Church for five hundred years amassing and collating the Vatican library's vigorously concealed 'Z collection', a collection rumored to house the most extensive library on the occult in the world. Some believe the collection even has the bones of the mad Arab himself. In 1959 a dying brother described a fossil the collection houses; based on that description we know they have the remains of an Elder Thing."

"Fossilized proof of their existence—that's incredible."

"We know very little about the collection. Rumors abound in Europe regarding other items the collection holds—everything from werewolf skulls to Dracula's ashes. Because of the knowledge they have amassed, these robed zealots are more powerful than you can imagine. Over the centuries many of the order's members participated in the Inquisition. They consider Conrad of Marburg and Robert le Bougre saints. To honor them, many brothers bear the epithet *Malleus Haereticrum*, the Hammer of Heretics, or *Inquisitor haereticae pravitatis*, inquisitor into heretical depravity. Since the Inquisition ended, a faction within the order has secretly traveled the world seeking out and destroying evil wherever they encounter it. Today this faction rules the order. You must understand that the order believes the Holy Ones to be the demonic spawn of Satan. Because they are shrouded in secrecy they are the most deadly adversaries you may encounter. These Christian witch-hunters will, without a second thought, willingly give their lives for their cause. Always remember each brother is a highly trained assassin completely committed to his vow of Satanic eradication."

"I can take care of myself."

"Can you now? You know enough to protect yourself? Then tell me of Bugg-Shash or Cynothoglys. Describe Ythogtha to me. What happens to those who look into the Mirror of Nitocris? Well? . . . Are you aware that Lovecraft was not the only great liar? There are many others who have taken the truth and distorted it for profit and fame. You have spent much time reading and absorbing the misleading tales reported by Lumley, Bloch, and Carter. And how many of Campbell's or Derleth's lies have you swallowed whole?"

Marsh said nothing as she waited for his answer.

"From the beginning we will start righting the erroneous words of these false profiteers. These infidels who pray to false gods take what is holy to us and blaspheme against the true gods. These loathsome fools take snippets of fact and weave in Atlantean and Egyptian mythology, or Arabian legend, along with their own inventions to create lies, many of which you have taken to be gospel. They have salted their stories with sorcery and science. Most of what you have read by these demons are lies. Lies they perpetrate for mere coins, or literary fame. They play literary parlor games with the true bible, Alhazred's *Necronomicon*, and Navarre's *Laws of Ruin*. Open the words of Navarre that now lie before you and read. Read the truth!"

Shamed, the student did as he was bid. "'I, Philip of Navarre, *Inquisitor haereticae pravitatis*, was taught by saintly priests. In the beginning there was God and God created the heavens and the earth. Charged by Saint Dominic to deliver the word of God to the lost, "to go humbly in search of heretics and lead them out of error", I have failed. Temptations abound; false words, dark pleasures, and graft assail me. Helpless, I watch my brothers fall victim to darkness. De

Paramo in Aragon has recently been seduced. Now I have fallen under the dark influence of those I was sent to deliver. Would that I could have followed the example of Blessed Giordano of Rivalto.

"'Saint Dominic preserve me, I no longer have my faith in God to protect me as I sit here to warn you of the abominations I have seen in the plague city, Ba-Venze. Listen, and heed my warning, as I tell you how the crucifix I held out to shield me melted in my hand before the blasphemous horror of Brl'trun, the yellow worm of Belane. Heed the words of this tormented witness, now eternally damned. Although my faith in the Almighty has been shattered, I have found a way to save you from the horrors that will befall all the lands of the earth. Listen to the words I learned on the red road to Iff'issa. One hundred days I was held, a prisoner in the land of the Eni. Know I spoke with Dim'mada, the Matti of Atbu-nr'ol, and watched the Dance of An'Tuul in the valley of Celmosus. Would that I could have faced the three rending maws of mythological Cerberus, or walked through the burning valley of Gehenna, instead of, God forgive me—'"

"Can you feel Navarre's conviction, his fear? In your hands I now lay the truth. You sought answers, read and learn the law."

On the wall the clock charted the lost hours of morning as he read Navarre's words. On the table before him lay the symbols of the lost Eni, and the rite used to enter the loathsome city of Iff'issa. Lunch was brought to them as the hours continued to pass. He read with great joy of the horror that befell Navarre in the Temple of Sy'tious, where half-lizard, half-walrus-like creatures gorged themselves on rotting flesh served to them in bejeweled golden bowls. When he reached the fortieth page her hand shot across the table.

"And here is Navarre's recounting of the tale of their doom at the hands of the vengeful gods of light. Read it and learn!"

Unable to ignore her command, he read.

"'I sat under a pregnant red moon with the Matti, Dim'mada the fallen mistress of the seven moon gardens, in the unquiet wastes of Atbu-nr'ol, and she spoke in broken whispers of Cthulhu's loss. How Kthanid had wooed Sk'tai away from her betrothed Cthulhu, and made her his bride, even while she was full with Cthulhu's seed. The Matti told this frightened traveler how Cthulhu had taken his vengeance upon his Judas and her spouse. She told me of the hatred that still beats in Cthulhu's heart for Kthanid, who seduced Cthulhu's son, T'ith, with the powers of goodness. She spoke of how T'ith, born of evil's unholy seed and weaned on the chalice of love, devoted to his adopted father, Kthanid, stood before Cthulhu and said he would rather join his mother, Sk'tai, and his beloved half-brother, Eppirfon, in death, than kneel before his butcher sire. Then in a low fearful whisper, as if she feared some hidden presence might hear her words, Dim'mada told me how the angered god, Cthulhu, then reached out and drank his own son's life. All this and more, she spoke of as the demon moon bled its perverse light down upon us.'"

"Do you now see how your writers have lied and twisted the truth? They make the Holy Ones out to be a cancer that chews at the core of the universe. The exalted Holy Ones did not invade the city of light! They simply went to render justice upon the Elder Gods. Do you now see who the real betrayers are? The Elder Gods do not serve the Daemon-Sultan—He Who Creates Without Cause Or Reason By Idle Thought And Breath—or Yog-Sothoth, The-All-In-One, The-One-In-All. They do not serve the laws of confusion and chaos. Even today's scientists unknowingly acknowledge the law. Look at physics. Action causes reaction. It's push and pull. All things move. It does not matter if they are fluid, liquid, solid, or plasma. They vibrate. There is no stability. The universe is at war. The Elder Gods, like mankind, wrongfully seek to pacify our convulsive universe with order and their blissful calm."

Ida stood above him, her hands clenched, and he felt the fire of knowledge. Her fingers pointed to passages, and he felt his ardor strengthen. She stood before him; her words caressed and cajoled, driving him on. The sky grew dark as he poured over the maps and spells she spread before his voracious heart. When weariness rubbed his eyes she would smile to restore his waning energy.

"Read! Learn," she commanded, imposing sensations and demands. "You must be ready for *Li-ure*, the night of white shadows."

🍃 Chapter Seventeen 🍃

Cosmo, Willie, and the Wizard turned as Chris entered the store and flashed a thumbs-up. Faint smiles crossed their faces and their nerves ratcheted up a few notches.

"Matthews is holding a press conference in an hour. The press release he's going to read is salted with the nonexistent psychic, your store, Kthanid, and the stones. It'll be all over TV and radio this afternoon," Chris informed the trio.

"So, now we wait," Willie said.

"Yahoo," the Wizard said satirically, looking to the door. Fingers massaging his eyelids, he let his questions take flight from the hard cloak of dread woven by apprehension. *What if this asshole really comes in here?* Settling back into his chair he mulled over a number of quick and bloody scenarios, two of which cast him as the sharp-shooting hero. As he considered confrontation, the liquid keyboard and the heavy plodding of Led Zeppelin's "No Quarter" provided a just underscoring to his envisioned bolt of retribution.

* * * * *

"Please, come in. I have a room prepared for you. I hope you will be comfortable?" *You scheming bitch, are you intent on making me wait all day to see it? You didn't say ten words in the car. Are you playing a game with me? If so, be careful. Once I determine the rules, I'll win. I always do.*

"I am sure I will be, thank you. Please forgive me for being so quiet on the way here. I still seem to have a touch of jetlag. I apologize if I seem ungrateful for the honor you have so kindly bestowed upon me. Hopefully, after I've taken some aspirin and had a shower, I will feel better." *Even the cruel ones occasionally succumb to my weary-little-girl routine.* "I hope you will accept my apologies. I know how tiresome waiting can be. Please feel free to inspect the package while I settle in," she said under the cover of a dark smile.

I need some time to assess you and your surroundings before I begin working on you. My headache will buy me time, and a few reactions. Yes, Mr. Marsh, I do have wonderful tits. You're having a hard time not looking at them, but you have not looked at my legs or at my crotch. Yet you seem fascinated by my hands. And you seem drawn to my face. This should not take long at all. Perhaps by Sunday, I will have you ready to beg me . . . for what? What do you like to do in bed? No, this one has no use for beds. Do you enjoy urinating on your partners? Blow jobs? Perhaps you would like me to be your mommy? No, this one would never give up that much control. Would it make you happy to slap me around? I can see how tightly you grip yourself. You love violence, I can feel it. Maybe S & M. Yes. Something dark. What will make you my pawn, Mr. Gregory Bradshaw Marsh?

"I can wait," Marsh said. *I don't like this at all. She isn't what I expected. She reminds me of Ida. Her skin, those lips—her breasts. If I could only see her eyes. Ida, why did you have to die? If you were here now, everything would be perfect. Is she the one you told me would come? Is she to be my mate?* Stop it! *You're far too close now to lose sight of what needs to be done, and you really don't know that much about this woman. Walk slowly in the darkness she presents to you.* "Why don't you rest awhile and we'll open your gift at four. I have always enjoyed that time of day. Here is your room."

"Until four then. Again, please accept my apologies for all the delays."

* * * * *

"Heard the radio report. It should piss him off, or at least make him curious," Cosmo said.

"Good," the Wizard said.

"Over the weekend we're gonna hit him again. Beckett's about to run a large feature on the Mythos and all three local TV stations are running specials on the murders as well as segments on the history of serial killers," Chris informed the pair.

"Don't forget CNN, they ran a small segment on this yesterday, and they've brought in a self-proclaimed expert. A small potatoes hack named Ian Bruce. Doubt he could write his way out of a wet paper bag."

"He'd never have gotten published if his father didn't own a publishing company. One of the largest in England, no less," the Wizard injected.

"CNN bringing in an analyst turns up the heat, even if their expert has written a shitload of poor Mythos pastiches, but I'm not sure that's relevant here—if they had gotten someone like Bob Price, now there's an authority, but we're saddled with Bruce," Cosmo said, pausing to light a cigarette before continuing. "So like I was saying, CNN thinks enough of this story to bring in someone to add literary background and color to these atrocities, so they must believe this story is good for some long-term ratings mileage. I think they're betting on this going all the way to a gore-soaked trial. Why else hire this guy? And I bet he came cheap."

"For the domestic exposure, probably free," the Wizard added.

"CNN's been here twice, trying to get an interview. Let's face it, Beckett's got us positioned as major players after his last article, so once we place the stones in the window to lure this asshole here, and Beckett runs his next story, which is going to lay the stones on thick, we know CNN will have their expert. Shit! I hate calling Bruce an expert, but, well, Bruce is going to pick up the ball, in this case the stones and run with them on national TV. I don't see how this psycho fuck can avoid seeing them or the store on TV," Cosmo said.

"I agree," Chris said. "He must be following the news. In case you didn't know, the networks and about a dozen things like *Hard Copy* are in town. I heard we got reporters here from Tokyo and London. Wanna bet before this thing is over, Hollywood's going to be here filming the movie for TV. So, let's go over the ground rules.

"One, neither of you two go anywhere outside this building without my permission and Willie as your bodyguard. If you go to the market or to the post office, anywhere, only one of you goes, and it's with Willie as an escort. If you're out with him, you stay with him. That means he goes into the bathroom with you if you've got to take a leak. I don't care what you're doing outside this building, even if you just open the back door to take out the garbage, he's with you.

"Willie, when they're out you keep your eyes on them every second, even if exotic-colored, candy-cane-striped Martians with three breasts start striping for you.

"Two, and this is not open for discussion, I'm moving in. You're going to have your regular customers coming in, as well as the media and the curious. And after this morning's incident with the religious right, we don't know who else. So I want to be here. Besides, I want this motherfucker. By the way, what happened to the snake?"

"I moved him upstairs in case of a problem. There's no way I'd leave him down here in the line of fire. If you had a dog you'd do the same."

"Don't care for dogs—too messy. I've got a cat," Chris said.

"Really. I wouldn't have thought you'd be a cat lover," the Wizard said.

"Do you really think he'll come here? It makes sense to me, but what do you think the odds are?" Cosmo asked.

"These monsters often show up at funerals, and return to crime scenes to re-experience the rush. They try to find ways to find out what's going on. I think the odds are fairly high he'll want to inspect our hand." *At least that's what I'm hoping.*

* * * * *

"Do you have any idea how many times last night I wondered about how events here were unfolding? I wish you had informed me that you did not want me here. What did he say, when you told him about your demise? You did tell him, didn't you?"

"Yes I did, and naturally, he was deeply saddened. Would you have expected otherwise?"

"Of course not. Are you certain he believes you're going to die?"

"Yes. The fool actually wanted to stay, so he could comfort me on my deathbed."

"He will leave, won't he?"

"Yes. He believes everything I've told him; he suspects nothing."

"Then everything is working perfectly. His feelings for you are fast becoming what appears to me to be an addiction. When you are finished instructing him we will unleash your *enfant terrible* on the unsuspecting world. Where is he now?"

"Lost in the footsteps of the mad Arab. He will be tied up for hours with Angelopoulos' weighty transcription. Do you remember wading through all of his protracted annotations?"

"Yes. There were occasions when I thought the annotations were longer than the *Necronomicon* itself. Do you remember me calling them the sermons of Christos? Do you think dear cousin Gregory can handle the reading without your assistance?"

Walking over to her brother, Ida slipped her arms around his waist. Her lips brushed his neck as her hands, full of pressure, slid up his back, pulling him closer.

"Speak no more of him. It sickens me to touch him, but I do what I must. Do you know how much I've missed your caresses?"

"Show me," he said as his fingers left her breast and began slowly unbuttoning her silk blouse.

* * * * *

Chris slumped in an old armchair shiny in places from years of use. Frayed edges revealed its cigarette-yellowed stuffing. Behind and above him an old floor lamp burned. Slowly, interrupted by a shudder, he came out of the blank fog of fitful sleep that had enveloped him, opening and closing his eyes as he tried to focus them, while rubbing the heaviness of the upper lids. There was pressure grinding behind his eyes and the clamp affixed to his temples was tightening. It seemed that in the last week or so he and the headache were rarely parted.

From a shaded, dusty recess, deep along some seldom used corridor of his mind, an idea began to creep across the bedrock of rationality toward the center of his consciousness—the GOO were applying some kind of pressure, aimed to deflect him from his goal.

"Maybe a couple of brews would cut this? No! That's what they'd like." *Yeah, they would love to see me in a daze. Things would be unclear, and I won't be prepared to face their emissary. C'mon, Stewart. Snap to it. Where'd you get a dumbass idea like that?*

The coffee table before him was strewn with books. Books with titles like *Strange Eons, The Clock of Dreams, Tales of the Lovecraft Mythos,* and *New Tales of the Pallid Mask.*

"That's where." *All these stories about the Mythos, and the GOO exerting control over the minds of men. What a bunch of bullshit.* Chris rubbed his eyes again, and started to massage the back of his neck. *Another few days immersed in this crap, and I'll be ready for the Arkham Asylum. I'm beginning to feel like one of the narrators. It's like I've witnessed some terrible evil and now I'm awaiting some demonic being to come and grab me. You ass. Go wash your face and wake up.* Yawning, he stood and lit a cigarette.

Returning from the bathroom by way of the kitchen, he sat down to his iced tea and stared at the surveillance monitors that revealed the interior of the store below. Everything seemed calm.

Looks quiet. When will the shit-storm hit? I know he's out there, and he's headed this way. But when? Reaching across the table his finger depressed the intercom's talk button. "Hey guys. Looks peaceful."

Cosmo looked up at the camera.

"Yeah. Haven't had a customer in over an hour. How's your reading comin' along?"

"Okay. I seem to have dozed off. Had a strange dream. I guess I'm reading too much of this narrator's dreams haunted by the GOO shit."

"I know what you mean. Reading this stuff, with a specific purpose in mind, well, it seems different from when I've read it before. Maybe because I'm trying to read it like the killer would. You know, as if it's real—like reading a newspaper. Facts, dates, names and places. Suspension of belief is one thing, but—"

"If this stuff was real, I sure hope the school of the Mythos you told me about, the one that throws out Derleth's war between the Elder Gods and the GOO, is wrong. I'd hate to be some puny little human facing these monsters without hope of divine intervention, or without the Elder Sign. How the hell would we battle alien demigods who can't be drowned, frozen, or incinerated, and who can exist in the vacuum of outer space? Would lasers or tactical nuclear weapons have any effect? Cthulhu's so damn big he'd make a grizzly bear look like a kitten embryo. Our asses would be in sorry shape," Chris said.

"True, but don't forget the GOO are alive, and anything that's living can die. Vampires are the only beings that I know of that are immortal, and they die, even if it's not by natural causes. Maybe a virus could take him out."

"Biological warfare against demigod aliens?" Chris laughed at the idea.

"Sure, why not? Balder was killed by a sprig of mistletoe. I know it's different, but it could be construed as mythological precedent."

"Better run, you've got a customer coming." *Viruses, mistletoe, and mythological precedents, not to mention a secret religion filled with dozens of evil gods almost as old as the Earth itself—what a strange world he plays in. Too many comic books, I guess. Why can't I be dealing with a nice jealous-*

husband-shoots-wife slaying? At least that makes some sense. Christ, what am I thinking? There's nothing rational about that, either.

Across from the battered relic of the chair Chris sat in, affixed to the solid two-panel door of his temporary bedroom, was a placard which read

ARKHAM ASYLUM
Within these walls there are no silent places.

He thought the sign was both a warning and a taunt.

Damn! This place is spooky. I wish these guys were into model trains or something—fishing, football. Unconsciously he reached for his crucifix, and brought it to his lips. *Our Father, who art in heaven, hallowed be thy name.* As he finished his silent prayer, he crossed himself. "Kyrie eleison," he whispered. *I better try Lauri again. We should talk to Henri about this stone.*

* * * * *

The scalpel continuously moved, rotated by strong fingers, as if controlled by a master baton twirler, and the carpet began to flatten under the steady footsteps that circled the table and its package. For the fourth time in an hour he performed the mental equivalent of a leper's Visual Surveillance of Extremities Test. Patience, control, determination, all were present and accounted for, yet he continued to have difficulty quieting the rage that battered upon the door of its cage.

What is keeping that cunt? Is this part of her game? Can she really be playing a game with me? That would be suicide. No! If she is the one, that's exactly what she'd do. Seeing herself as an equal, she'd be unwilling to bend. She'd test, watch, and wait. Ida said I would know her by her eyes. Damn those sunglasses! She won't have them on when she comes down here. Then I'll find out. 3:43. Less than twenty minutes, I can wait. I can wait.

"Mr. Marsh, I hope I have not kept you waiting too long."

Quickly slipping the scalpel into his pocket and looking at his watch, he answered, "No, not at all." *Five minutes early. She has mastered the art of a staged entrance. Her eyes. Can she be the one? Those eyes. Ida said I would know her by her eyes.* "Do you feel any better?"

Too late. I saw your little toy. Fool. You were so lost in your thoughts you did not even know I was standing here watching you. "Yes, thank you. Just laying down and closing my eyes helped a great deal. It was a long trip. And the honor of being allowed to participate has made me a little nervous. Again I hope the delays I have caused you were not too distressing, but I could not allow myself to be parted from this," she said, placing her hand on the package. "Since I found her, she has never been out of my sight. You of all people should be able to understand that."

"I certainly do. Since Roaker first sent me the photographs eighteen months ago, I have felt compelled to own it."

"Surely this close to the ceremony, and seeing her restored to her rightful stature, this *objet d'art* does not hold the same sway over you as it might have before?"

"There is some truth in that, but after waiting so long, well, I still must possess it. Can you understand that?"

"Perhaps you should open it now. Later, if you would permit me, I have another small gift for you."

Gift? That's the same look that Ida had when she said she had a gift for me. Just what do you have for me? "Another gift?"

"It is just a small token of thanks for being accepted into the circle. I hope you will enjoy it. Would you care to be alone while you open this?"

"No. You may remain."

Marsh removed the scalpel from his vest pocket and began opening the package Christa had brought. Moving aside the Styrofoam popcorn, he reverently lifted the figurine. He almost found it impossible to quell the minute tremor in his hands as he held the weighty sculpture. Carved from gray marble, slightly tinted and veined with blue, it was as finely rendered as Her altar in the shrine below. As he pored over the work, absorbing the dark passion of the form, she related the tale of how she had found the figurine.

"I shall never forget the sound of that old black man's laughter as I left the shop. It was chilling. For a time I thought it inhuman. Perhaps if a demon were capable of laughter."

He froze. Could it be possible? Was the black man in the antique shop Nyarlathotep? Had the messenger of the Outer Gods really appeared to this woman?

It makes sense. Many of the connections I needed to obtain the Zhou Texts *and the candlesticks seem to have originated with her and Roaker. My every effort was squelched before the rumored discovery of these figures. Then suddenly, wheels begin to turn and I possess the text of Fu-Shen, and the other items I need for the ceremony become accessible to me after lengthy frustrations.*

Suddenly his knees buckled under him. Pain crushed his temples.

"Gregory! What's wrong?"

"She is . . . in pain. Head . . . AHHHH! Aches. Help me . . . . Couch. They pass."

Roaker had told her Marsh suffered debilitating headaches. Sometimes he experienced the Queen Mother's pain, he'd explained. They passed, and as the ceremony approached they seemed to be lessening in their length and intensity.

"Can I get you aspirin or something?"

"No . . . nothing helps . . . . It will pass."

Perhaps it's a mistake to consider crossing this man. If he really suffers the pain of the Queen Mother what form of retribution would befall his Judas? Roaker truly believes he is her *chosen. Is it possible our plans place me in greater jeopardy than I had thought?*

🍎 Chapter Eighteen 🍎

Car's here. Guess she's home, Pat thought, climbing the steps to Laurinda's flat.

"*Bonjour,*" Henri said, opening the door in reply to the buzzer and quickly determining that this man did not fit the description of the killer Chris had given him. *Red hair, and much too short; this is not him.* Henri's hand left the knife strapped at his side. "May I help you?"

Pat stood frozen.

Who the hell is this monster? Hot damn, he's big. I thought Moon said that they were finally getting together. So who the hell is this? Look at this guy. And who the hell walks around with a K-bar like that? Damn! "I was hoping Lauri was home?"

"Laurinda is here. Might I inquire who you are?"

Tall, dark, and handsome, not to mention well spoken and mannered. Who the hell is this guy? It can't be one of her brothers, they don't get along. "I'm Pat, a friend. Like I said, is she home?"

"One moment please. *Chérie,* you have a guest."

Chérie? Ain't that French for honey or something? What kind of friend calls someone honey, and how come Moon ain't mentioned this friend? He must know him.

"Hi, Pat. Is everything all right? Is something wrong with Chris?" Laurinda asked in a voice tinged with concern.

"With Moon? Nah. I just saw him a few hours ago. He's actually taking this pretty good," Pat replied, never taking his eyes off the giant standing beside her.

"Well. Don't stand out in the cold, silly. Come in before we all freeze. Pat Price, this is my cousin from New Orleans, Henri Freniere."

"Cousin? Ah, great! I mean—"

"Patrick Price! Just what were you thinking? You of all people should know better."

"Sorry. I just thought, well—hi, I'm Pat Price. Call me Pat," he said, feeling stupid but relieved.

"Hahahaha. I am quite pleased to meet you, Mr. Price."

"That's Pat."

"Pat. I apologize if you thought that Laurinda and I were, shall
we say, entwined. Now I understand that look you gave me," the
smiling giant said.

"Pat, you'd better behave or I'll have Henri fix your wagon. Do
you understand?"

"Yeah. Got it. Just go easy on me, okay, Juma?"

"Pardon me? Who or what is Juma?" Henri asked.

"Juma. You know, Conan. Robert E. Howard. Sword and sorcery.
Arnold Schwarzenegger?"

"The actor? I do not understand? What is Juma?"

"Not what, who. There's these books by Robert E. Howard
about a warrior named Conan. Arnold Schwarzenegger played Conan
in the movie a few years back. Well, in the books he's got this bro'
named Juma. He's a giant black warrior. A human mountain. One of
the good guys. Sorry if I offended you. It's just you seem, well, if I
had to be deep in the shit, I wouldn't mind having you on my team,"
Pat said.

"Now what brings you to this side of the city in the middle of a
work day?" Laurinda asked.

"Like I said, I saw Moon this morning and, well, after we heard
the news on the radio, I figured maybe he'd hit the bottle again,
so—"

Bottle! "What news? He left a message on my machine earlier
and he sounded fine. What happened? Why did you think Chris
would start drinking again?"

"The girl. You haven't heard the news? You haven't heard about
the little girl?"

"No."

"The butcher murdered a little girl."

"Oh my God!"

"*Dieu nous aide*! You say he butchered a child?"

"She was seven."

"Meredith's age." *A girl Meredith's age. Dear God!*

"There's more. They found a note on the body for Moon and . . .
this animal beat in her head with a . . . hammer." The last word an
angered whisper.

Many of the people who knew Henri St. John de Baptiste
Freniere would have sworn on their mothers' graves that the smile on

his face was an indestructible fixture; they couldn't have been more gravely mistaken.

Pat watched Henri's eyes grow cold. He'd seen that look before in the eyes of his best friend. It had been there this morning. *Holy shit! Another one. Christ, I don't think I can keep the lid on two.*

"Where's Chris now?"

"Work, I guess."

"I better call him."

"Wait. He's fine. At least he's holding together for now. When this is over he'll fall apart, but for now he's fine. Let him call you."

"How can you say he's fine?"

"Cause I've been with him every time the shit's hit the fan. I know the signs. He's got a grip. He's been a Marine and a cop for too long to lose it yet."

"But—"

"No buts. Henri. Hey! You okay?"

"Yes. I'm sorry, I was . . ." *This monster has mutilated a child! A girl.* "*Un innocent. Chère et douce mère de Dieu. Quelle folie marche sur la terre? Si j'aurais cinq minutes seul avec se . . . je . . .*"

"What?" Pat asked.

"Forgive me. I was just thinking out loud."

"I can't just sit here and wait. There must be something we can do," Laurinda said.

"Hope and pray," Pat said, "just hope and pray."

* * * * *

"I was thinking about Navarre and the *Zhou Texts.* You said you don't own a copy."

"Unfortunately that is true. We have tried many times over the years to obtain it, but it continues to evade our grasp. Mother began looking for the book while being tutored by my great-uncle Ernest, your grandfather."

"There are questions I have about him and my mother."

"We shall discuss more of the family's history at a later date. For now you need to learn what is contained in these books," Ida said, laying down a yellowed, handwritten copy of *Unaussprechlichen Kulten* along with photostatic copies of the five hundred and fifty-five *Dhole Chants.* Beside them she set a handwritten copy of U Poa's *Black*

Sutra, and the transcribed *Liber Damnatus*. "As I was saying, my mother had been studying Friedrich von Junzt's *Nameless Cults*, not the inadequately translated Bridewell edition of 1845, but a hand-copied, exact transcription of the 1839 Dusseldorf edition. Along with the manuscript, she had copies of the notes that he was using to prepare a second volume of *Unaussprechlichen Kulten*. These notes describe his journey to Mongolia in 1840.

"Within his notes von Junzt first mentions reading Fu-Shen's forbidden text. I am certain Fu-Shen's text held great interest for him, as he was deeply interested in the Tcho-Tcho people and other cults that worshiped Lord Hastur. In the fifth chapter of the first edition he speaks of his journey to Asia and his dealings with the Tcho-Tcho. He also describes the thirty-yard-long living mountain of tentacles, Zhar, and his twin, Lloigor. In addition he quotes liberally from the *Black Sutra*. Had his planned second volume ever been completed we might have further knowledge of the *Zhou Texts*, but von Junzt was found inexplicably strangled in his locked and bolted study, six months after he returned from China. We have tried for years to obtain the sorcerer Fu-Shen's arcane text, but it appears it is not for sale. This war that currently rages in southeast Asia continues to hinder our efforts, but we have managed to procure four pages from the text. Now that you have absorbed Navarre's writings, we shall discuss the Chinese text. One of the four pages describes and discusses the Queen Mother, although too briefly. These pages and Navarre's brief mention of her are the only references to her we have. The author of these pages states he was two hundred and eleven years old when he wrote this. In 1100 BC, the Mongolian sorcerer Fu-Shen made a one hundred and fifty day pilgrimage, by horse, *makhnas*—"

"*Makhnas?*"

"Elephants. He also traveled by river and foot, from a small village on the banks of the Selenge in China, across the burning hell of the Gobi to Burma. There he lived for five decades in now lost and legendary Alaozar, on the Isle of Stars in the Lake of Dread, high atop the Plateau of Sung. Studying under the necrophagous Tcho-Tcho shaman, Mon Katha, he learned of the star-spawned twin obscenities, Lloigor and Zhar. Fu-Shen was also given knowledge of the Brothers of the Yellow Sign, Chaugnar Faugn, and Ghatanothoa. The Tcho-Tcho lama himself instructed Fu-Shen about Our Blessed Queen

Kassogtha, and her matron, Ut'ulls-Hr'ehr, the Black Glory of Creation. To prove his piety, Fu-Shen ate only carrion and opiates in the seventeen-day-long Ritual of Lhas-Tiajin, which is only performed once in the life of each lama. Naked, he cut himself, the bronze blade already red with the lama's own blood, eight times at the Tcho-Tcho conclave beneath Hkan-Kya. Fu-Shen also says the Tcho-Tcho lama called a Tr'kra to rise from the lake's depths, and fed his daughter to it, after her pure flesh had been sexually consecrated by all forty members of the conclave. Here is his rendering of the Tr'kra."

"By Cthulhu and Kassogtha! Is this a Holy One?"

"I do not know, but I would guess, based on my knowledge, that this being is a member of either the servitor or independent races. Mind you, this is only a guess. It could be a Holy One.

"Not even the great library of the Forbidden City has a copy of Fu-Shen's codex. Only the greed-ridden fool, Phyra Thanarat, in Bangkok is said to own a copy. A copy he will not part with, although we have offered a million dollars in gold. The four pages we have obtained—the first, the last, which is numbered 527, and two in between, 38 and 188—came to us from a former vassal of Thanarat, who wished to escape the damnation she endured under his aberrant hands. The pages, all ripped from different sections of the Oriental's grimoire, we've had translated by a sympathetic confidant, the German mystic Eberhard M. Eicher, who frequently lectures at the University of Toulouse on ancient oriental occult documents. One can only wonder what glorious dark secrets lay on the other pages. If you look at this page, here at the bottom, Fu-Shen is about to describe the rite to be performed on the night when white shadows will destroy the seals that imprison *her*. You must obtain the *Zhou Texts*. Without it, the Holy Mother will continue to languish in their hell."

* * * * *

Marsh was livid. The incandescence of his anger overflowed the room. Kthanid dared send a warning to these cattle! Damn his interference!

In a venomous litany of unfettered rage Marsh cursed all beauty and balance, reviling the Elder Gods Nodens and Zehirete, the Pure and Holy Womb of Light. Screeching, he vowed to feed Othkkartho,

Nodens' first born and lordly sire of the Four Titans of Balance and Order, to the unborn spawn of Kassogtha. He called down every destruction upon Eyroix, Adaedu, and Alithlai-Tyy. He blotted out the radio announcer's monotone of the mundane while leveling damnation on the progeny of Dveahtehs, Xuthyos-Sihb'Bz, Ovytonv, Xislanyx, and Urthuvn.

And worse, a cache of Mnarian star-stones had been uncovered here.

Lies!

He was certain the news report on the radio was a lie. Even as he fought to convince himself it was a deception, a trap, the pain in his head grew. The pounding increased as the chaotic fury of his rage lashed out unabated. Echoes of his own shrill maledictions assaulted his ears. Palms pressed to his forehead, spittle covered the insides of his forearms as his condemnations recommenced. Blinded by the crippling pain he failed to see Christa enter the room and gasp. Seconds later he collapsed.

* * * * *

"Hey, Chris! Big brother, you up there? Earth to the eye in the sky. Hello," Cosmo yelled into the camera.

"Yeah, I'm here. I was just trying to finish this story. What's up?"

"We're going to order subs. Interested?"

"Yeah. Get me a pickle and a . . ." *Meatball?* "Italian mixed with hot peppers. Oil and vinegar, no mayo. And extra onions."

"No problem. Want a drink?"

Yeah. Two or three hundred. "See if they got any Vichy water, or cream soda."

"Got it," Cosmo said, turning to the Wizard.

"I heard. Willie and I will be back in a flash."

"What were you reading?" Cosmo asked.

"Robert Chambers' 'The Repairer of Reputations.' Talk about the willies. I don't think any story ever bothered me like that. The King in Yellow, the dread city of Carcosa, and more lunatics. It's no wonder I can't sleep for shit."

"Great story. It doesn't matter if you like horror or not, it just grabs you. Just wait until you read 'The Yellow Sign' by him. It's twice as unnerving. And while you're reading *The Hastur Cycle*, be sure you read 'More Light', by James Blish. It's another King in Yellow gem."

Gems? "Just great. The hair under my collar is already petrified. It doesn't help sitting up here. Your decor makes this place a hell of a lot spookier after dark. Christ, there's monsters and gore everywhere. Like this model on your coffee table."

"Who, Pumpkinhead? He's great. It's one of the Wizard's favorite films."

"Hell, when this is over I'm going to have to take my vacations on Halloween to escape all this macabre shit. And another thing, these pictures you two have on the walls. Holy shit! Who the hell is this woman in the poster by your door? She's demonic. It's like staring at . . . I don't know what, but it's creepy. Real fucking creepy."

"What woman are you talking about?"

"It sorta looks like the Marsden paintings down there, colorwise. The style seems the same. The poster has a woman's face with a mane of Medusa hair made of wiring. The stuff seems to be taking over her whole head . . . it's like her humanity is being replaced."

"By technology."

"Yeah. Her eyes are almost lifeless black sockets, and there's some pattern forming beneath the skin of her cheeks. It looks like the kind of pattern contained in a computer chip."

"It's called *Erased Horizons*, and you're right, it's a Marsden."

"Erased Horizons. Is that what we're doing to ourselves?" Chris thought out loud.

"Or allowing to be done," Cosmo added.

"Scary prospect either way."

"I'm hip to that. But you're missing one of the painting's most important elements."

"I am? I thought I got the point."

"You did, but the eyes aren't completely black. There's something there, you just can't see it. What you're looking at is a very poorly done bootleg some kid traded in for credit a few years back."

"Bootleg—like in stills and corn liquor?"

"Yep. Unauthorized and illegal. Happens to artists of his stature a lot. The guy was a genius."

"Genius? Is that what you call this? I'm no shrink, but this cat's got some ghosts that need exorcising."

"Don't we all."

"True. But, you have to admit this woman in the painting is eerie. C'mon, just look at those empty sockets. There's something, reminds me of the Wizard's snake. Almost worse than empty—dead in a way. And there's something about the lips, and the set of her jaw, call it a cold resolve or final judgment. It's as if she's accepted the loss of her humanity."

"I'll go along with you on that, but the coloring of the poster you're looking at is all wrong, it's way too dark. Try to imagine the poster with the colors lightened. Here. Look at this one," Cosmo said, pulling a copy of Randall Marsden's *Horizons: From Chaos to Xoth* from the shelf behind him, opening it to page thirty and holding it up to show the original print. "This is the picture. Can you see how much lighter it is? With the higher resolution you can see what's in those sockets."

"More computer guts. Makes her face even more menacing."

"Is it? The lips are full, sensual. She's an earth mother. They're alive. They hold promise. Try to think of the set of her jaw as strength. And here, her skin is containing the spread of the technological disease. She's fighting for her humanity."

"I got you. But all this stuff up here is still eerie. I mean, c'mon, vampire models, the Wolfman, them I guess I can understand, I liked monster movies as a kid, but some of this other stuff!"

"One man's garbage and all that. Besides, man has always been fascinated by death, and what lays behind the impenetrable veil."

"I like to believe there's peace on the other side." *Hypocrite. Your faith's as thin as a cloud.* "How can you surround yourself with this stuff? Doesn't it get to you once in a while?"

"One cannot truly envision heaven without first experiencing hell."

He's right about that.

"When you're looking at the posters and the models, look behind the mask. Peel the skin away. You're a cop. You see what looks like decent men in tailored suits commit murders. It's your job not to judge books by their covers."

True. "I'll try."

"How long do you figure we'll sit around here waiting for this asshole?"

"There's no way of knowing. Stakeouts are always boring and uncomfortable."

"Chris, while we're talking about spooky and other-worldly things, let me tell you an anecdote that many of the writers of Mythos stories relate. Quite a few of them say this is a common experience. It varies a bit writer to writer, but you'll get the drift. My friend Tom Desmond has loved Africa, the animal life that abounds there, and its mythologies since he was a kid. Man, he was hooked on Marlin Perkins and the *Wild Kingdom*. To the pantheon of Mythos deities, he's added Ob'mbu the Shatterer and Xu'bea, the Teeth of the Dark Plains of Mwaalba. Ob'mbu, by the way, resembles a bizarrely mutated, half-reptilian giraffe. Xu'bea has never been described. He's also added one book to the Mythos, *The Grimoire of Ile-Ife*. Most of the grimoire tells stories of the lost city of Ln'ranja, buried beneath the Sahara, where Xu'bea once ruled. Ile-Ife is a Yoruba sorceress from the 12th century that Tom created.

"Thing is, every time he talks about the history of the Grimoire, or quotes from it, well, he doesn't write the text. What I mean is, he seems to get up in the middle of the night, and . . . whether he's sleepwalking, which there's no evidence of, or half asleep or something, he must write, because in the morning there are these quotes, spells, and notes on the book's history, which he claims to know nothing about. He never remembers writing these things. It's like channeling; the medium wakes without any knowledge of what the spirit has communicated. Some people would say it's bullshit, but I know this guy. Besides, he's not the only Mythos writer who's experienced this kinda thing. Wendell Shorter has said that he spent days trying to figure out where in space to imprison Kassogtha in his story. Then one day after he continually kept drawing a blank, he walked into his study to write and found a book of star charts open to the Algol system. He liked the name and stuck her there. Here's the weird part. He had no idea that the word Algol meant demon star. Doesn't that seem odd? Does to me. Then there's Colin Wilson who, like Shorter, says he's had more than a few odd coincidences occur while writing, and Maria Houdon, who says that her poetry comes to her while she is sleeping. When she wakes up, this stuff is in her head, full blown. She just writes it down. She doesn't compose it or think about it, she just puts it on paper. Or so she says."

"Cos, you're right, it's bullshit. Sounds like nothing more than a way to gain some publicity, and sell some extra books."

"Look, Tom Desmond is a principled man. He's got faults like everyone else, but when it comes to what he says I'd bet the store on him. He's an honest, decent guy who I've never heard bend the truth outside of one of his stories. If this were part of the Mythos game, like adding deities and books, using other writers' names, or taking real facts and weaving them into events which occur within the Mythos universe, I'd know about it. Lovecraftian writers share—they're a pretty close-knit literary family. Like I said before, it's a literary parlor game where you take this part of mine and do this, and I'll take yours and add this, then do that to it. Torture me, maim me, kill me, transform me, respectfully borrow from me, whatever works."

"What are you trying to say?"

"I'm not sure. It just seems this whole thing is, like you said, getting a little spooky."

"You're not trying to imply there's some real supernatural element here."

"Hell, I don't know. Maybe? I've said it before, this is just entertainment, but still, the damn thing is starting to get eerie. It's like a real-life Mythos story is beginning to unfold and we're characters who are stuck in the middle of it. You're a cop. Piece the facts together. One, the killer believes in the Mythos. Two, some of the places are real. Three, a what may be real star stone shows up from someone who's really into the occult. And four, we've got a few writers who don't write, they just channel information they receive in their sleep. Five, you've got other murders related to the myth cycle. I can see one lunatic buying into the Mythos and killing, but when you add in a couple of cults, a thousand miles and years apart, sacrificing people to Hastur and Cthulhu, well that seems like a whole bunch of weird to me."

"There's a simple explanation for this. We're all tired and under pressure so we start reading things into this that aren't really there. I think we're taking some odd coincidences and making them into things they're not."

"Yeah, you're probably right, but you don't see weirdos trying to bring the pages of Thomas Harris' or Michael Slade's novels to life."

"I don't know Slade's work well, but Harris' books don't create mythologies or religions. Besides, have their books been around for sixty years?"

"No. Hell, I guess we could all stand some sleep and a break from this madness."

"Something I've been meaning to ask you. I thought you mentioned that you had a cat. I've been up here for hours now and haven't seen one."

"She's up there somewhere. Sleeps a lot."

"Is she friendly?"

"Even to the Wiz."

"Huh?"

"He hates cats. It's like some weird antichemistry."

"What's her name?"

"Bast."

"Let me guess, it has something to do with the Mythos, right?"

"What else? Lovecraft adored cats."

"Figures. Suppose it's black too?"

"Absolutely not. She's a big old fluffy orange tiger."

"Did you ever have a Mythos pet name for a girlfriend?"

"No, but now that you mention it, maybe the next one!"

Chris smiled and shook his head. "Cos, you're something."

"Hey, looks like the food's here. You want me to send it up, or do you want to come down?"

"I'm supposed to be out of sight. Send it up."

"Ten-four. Roger and out."

Chris grabbed a beer from the fridge after throwing away the sub's wrapper.

Guess they won't miss one.

Returning to the dining room turned sitting room he lit a smoke. While he'd been in the kitchen one of the floor lamp's bulbs had burned out, leaving only the smaller wattage bulb to combat the gloom. As the darkness of the apartment's dimmed perimeters encroached, he began to feel night burrowing through the windows.

Damn! How much spookier can things get around here? he wondered while looking at the bootlegged Marsden poster a second time.

Maybe Cosmo's right about there being more to all this stuff than just the surface scars, distorted features, and blood. Guess it's like some form of psycho-

*analysis or confidence builder. We grow because we force ourselves to face the
often dire chaos of chance and necessity.*

Coils of blue smoke curled and twisted in the room. Rising as
aimlessly as the smoke, Chris' shifting thoughts slowly began to see
Frankenstein as something more than a hulking film monster. He
became man's struggle to understand creation, birth, and the respon-
sibilities of the god who created him. The predatory Wolfman
became a way to examine and deal with man's fear of returning to his
barbarous origins, and the anarchy that would rise from ignorance
and primal hunger.

Turning away from the coarse-furred lycanthrope, he reached out
and picked up an exquisitely detailed Dracula model. He marveled at
the color and patient workmanship; even the tiny fingernails had a
coat of clear lacquer. "And where do you fit in? Are you a way of looking at damnation? You drink blood. Blood is life, right? So what's
that?" *To truly be alive we have to drink all of life's experiences. The sweet
with the sour. It's not good enough to be just a doer or a thinker, one has to be
both to understand his role. Or maybe you're a statement about men feeding
off other men?* "You live forever and we're afraid to die." *And sex, your
teeth penetrate flesh. Hey, I'm starting to get this.*

He set Dracula down. He knew what lay behind the mask of his
real monster, but he couldn't see his face. His fist ground in his palm
and he cursed the waiting.

❦ Chapter Nineteen ❦

"I was worried. You were in pain for so long. Roaker has spoken of your suffering, but seeing it . . . I was unsure of what to do."

There's fear in her voice. Was she really concerned for me, or simply frightened? Either way, I can use it. "Once Her Holiness is free I will suffer them no more. I'm sorry if I frightened you."

"Please do not concern yourself over it. What is past is past." *Perhaps the best time to take him will be when he is suffering one of these attacks.* "If you would like, I have something else for you. Or it can wait until another time."

"Is it the gift you mentioned before?"

"Yes, but there are really several parts to it."

"I'm intrigued. Whenever you're ready," he said as he walked to a dark leather armchair and sat.

Walking around the large marble coffee table Christa opened her purse and removed a twenty-four-karat gold ring with an onyx face and a gold emblem, which she handed to him.

Looking from the ring to her, he smiled. "The Yellow Sign, thank you. Does this have any significance?"

"None other than I thought it might please you."

"It does, but why of all things did you bring me the sign of The King in Yellow?"

"It has to do with a remark that Kurt Roaker made to me last year. Sometime last March, he called me and requested that I procure the Zoth-Ommog representation you were seeking. So I contacted my source in Cologne and made arrangements to pick it up. As it happens, there was a convention going on in Cologne while I was there."

Marsh watched her as she walked around the coffee table and delivered her oration. He was fascinated by her gracefully fluttering hands as they wove through the air casting a pale spell upon him.

So much like Ida's hands, he thought. *Can she be the one? Her voice and her eyes, the rose petal and the razor.*

"This convention as it turns out was Strange Realms, the fourth European Fantasy and Horror Exposition. Naturally I was curious, so I attended. Upon seeing the list of featured speakers, I recalled a comment Roaker attributed to you regarding horror writers who distort and lie about the Holy Ones. He had told me that you wished suffering and damnation upon each and every blasphemer. He had also said that you thought Thomas Desmond, along with Brian Lumley, was one of the greatest of these malicious fabricators, at least those who are still living."

"When the Holy Mother has returned we shall institute our own inquisition and Desmond and his fallacy-weaving brethren will be tried and burned as heretics," Marsh paused, seemingly lost in thought as he traced the outline of the ring's emblem. "Forgive me for interrupting your story. Please continue."

"While I was at a cocktail party being held to celebrate Desmond's forty-seventh birthday, I overheard the conversation of two fans who were in attendance, remarking about Desmond's ring, the one you now hold. It seems the ring was his prize possession. August Derleth, his idol and mentor, gave it to him when his first novel was favorably reviewed in the *New York Times*."

"You stole this from him? How wonderful."

"Not quite. I discovered Mr. Desmond was a reclusive bachelor. So I managed to attract his attention. Very discreetly, I might add. It didn't take much to arrange to meet the love-starved writer in his suite after the party."

"You minx," the smiling man said.

Among other things. Things that you will soon discover. "Why, thank you."

"So after your rendezvous you slipped this off his finger."

"Yes and no. First we held our own private party, and then, it seems that Mr. Desmond had to suddenly leave."

"I'm afraid you've lost me."

"Before he could finish his little celebration, I slit his throat." Christa watched his facial expression change with great joy. *I believe you Americans say "two points",* she thought, moistening her lips with her tongue before she revealed her shining white teeth.

She may be the one. Yes, I can see how much she enjoyed taking his life.

"After he finished his flopping and squirming I removed the ring. Unfortunately it was difficult to remove, so I had to sever the finger. For a few moments I toyed with the idea of leaving the ring on the finger. Then another idea occurred to me. I left him with his severed finger inserted in his anus."

"You left the body in the room?"

"Yes. Later, fearing complications, I had it disposed of."

Marsh placed the ring on the pointer finger of his right hand.

The ring of a king, and I am that king, he pridefully told himself, deeply admiring the gold Yellow Sign embossed upon a black base of onyx.

"I thought you might like to have the ring."

Rising, he walked to her and took her hand. "Your gift gives me pleasure. I shall enjoy wearing it," he said, lightly kissing her hand.

"*Ehn tehr Gor'ru Gr'xum Fng'i*," she whispered as she sank to her knees and kissed the ring.

As if choreographed his left hand reached out and stroked the side of her face.

Her head rose and her half-open eyes sought his. "My Lord," she said, as she unzipped his jeans.

His lust spent, he returned to the sofa and sat, in his egotism seeing himself as a king in repose, while she knelt beside him on the floor.

"I hope I please you, Lord?"

He stroked her hair as if she were a favored pet. "You do. Was that one of your gifts?"

"No. That was something I wanted for me."

"And the second part?"

"Another tale, Lord. If it will not bore you?"

"You may continue."

"This is in regards to the holy palace you wish erected for our Queen at Kashkash. If you recall, last summer I had sent you Randall Marsden's book of landscape paintings, *Erased Horizons*. It contained his Xothic Environments."

"The self-righteous dolt who refused our commission?"

"The very one."

"Yes. Marsden, he will labor for her in another manner when she returns. I have plans to serve him to her as a meal. As he dies in agony, we will see how well his moral values aid him. As his sanity flees from him, he will have a few real visions of horror."

"I have brought Thomas Brown's designs with me. I'm quite sure you will be pleased with his ideas. Roaker was delighted with them. Brown has incorporated all of your ideas and specifications

into the designs, which I feel strongly resemble Marsden's work. He
has even—"

"But he is not Marsden!"

"I agree, but—"

"It seems he'll have to do for now. Unless . . . perhaps there is still
a way to change Mr. Marsden's mind. The Holy Queen Mother will
command him to work in our service or face dire consequences. Now
that I think about it, I'm sure we can induce this person to do as we
wish. Faced with what would happen to him if he declines our offer a
second time, he would seem to have no other option. Yes, he will work
for us. I will have him design my personal chambers in Kashkash."

"There is a problem, my Lord."

"A problem?"

"I had him destroyed."

"When?"

"A few months ago. I thought you would be pleased."

"This is your *other* gift?"

"Yes."

"Tell me of his demise. Amuse me."

"Shortly after you had reviewed Marsden's work in the book I
sent you, Roaker informed me you wished me to commission him to
design Kassogtha's palace. Through his agent in New York I made
arrangements to meet with him and discuss the commission. As a
sign of good faith we gave him five thousand dollars, nonrefundable,
just to listen to our, forgive me, I meant your ideas. As you are aware,
Roaker and I met with him in London last May. We presented him
with your ideas, telling him he was working for an eccentric and out-
landish multimillionaire who had artistic ideas but no talent.
Marsden was told that this millionaire was a fan of his paintings and
Lovecraft's ideas, who wished a palace designed—more than a palace,
a vast, towering Xanadu of nightmare, poised above a cityscape."

Marsh closed his eyes and envisioned an oppressive Dracula's castle, or a brutal Frankenstein's tower—a vast spectral monolith, sur-
passing Babel—raping the bleeding sunset sky. The humid alto
breeze of her voice fanned him as the image morphed with landscapes
painted by Giger and Marsden.

Reveling, he found his feet on a half-mile-wide boulevard ending
in a circular arena where the *auto-de-fé* was reborn, pushed from the

womb of his desire with pained screams of fire. Dallying in a Brobdingnagian archway glorified in alien hieroglyphics, Marsh watched the bonfires of the apocalypse consume flesh and hope and dreams. He laughed as smoke streams stormed against the black clouded sky of blacker, suffocating night. Eyes glazed by rapture, he beheld savaged crowds pressed together in filth-caked pens, their panicked eyes cast skyward, fearful of swooping horrors. He bathed in the choked sobbing and fits of cackled laughter as the hurried prayers and pleas of the damned spurred his fantasies. There was no need to build ovens for his Holocaust. No, he would not waste flesh to indifferent fires, he would have thousands of hungry maws to forever banish their thin bright dreams to. Prideful and fulfilled, he saw himself, regally perched above, a lordly vizier, architect—Kassogtha's Torquemada.

". . . designed on paper, of course. We could not allow him to know that this design would actually be erected. The palace he would be designing was to become one of the seats of power for the Great Old Ones when they returned. Knowing he had painted Lovecraftian images before, we felt he would be easy to enlist. To lure him in we told him that the best-selling novelist Thomas Desmond was being approached with a very rough outline of a novel that this millionaire was interested in commissioning, and that if anything should arise from the novel, such as a film, Marsden would be the set and creature designer, if he so chose. Roaker and I felt he was very interested in the project when he began referring to it as 'creating a type of godly Devil's Castle.' He was also told that another designer was being consulted. That artist being Thomas Brown, with Marsden as the project's preferred designer. We told him that he could name his price, half when he accepted and the remainder upon completion, but there would be some restrictions. Such as general guidelines regarding size and overall appearance and possibly a timetable. He was also told that all hieroglyphic inscriptions and ornamental runes would be given to him and he would be instructed as to where they were to be placed. The primary restriction placed upon the project was that all designs would have to be approved by you. In regard to the timetable Marsden was told that he had three weeks to accept or decline the commission.

"Roaker and I left the meeting feeling Marsden would accept our proposal. Less than two weeks later we received a letter from his agent declining the commission. Marsden had also returned our check, uncashed. Somehow Marsden had discovered Roaker was linked to a cult which had been connected to sacrificial rites and three murders in Oregon in 1976. Marsden was quite adamant about not being connected to, or in any way involved with, 'persons involved in utterly villainous activities that wantonly disregard and insult the already trying and difficult lives of innocents.' Marsden's letter further stated that my name had been linked to 'cloven-footed witchcraft', along with my former husband's 'diabolical escapades' and other 'depraved occult activities' in and around Germany. We then contacted you regarding Marsden's rejection and moved into deeper negotiations with the ever-so-hungry Mr. Brown. After stewing for a while over Marsden's rejection I devised a plan to destroy him. I had Marsden followed during September, and then in October I performed the ceremony which left him dead."

"Exactly how was he destroyed?"

"Knowing he was involved in a new series of paintings, and had been working nights in his Fulham studio, also hoping it would please you, I invoked Ihsalüüd to deprive him of his worthless existence. Rumors concerning the tattered form the Wolf of Arcturus left in its wake were as wondrous as some of Marsden's paintings. From reports I have gathered his eyes were ripped from his head, and both his hands, as well as his eyes and heart, were missing. His torso was also ripped open from throat to loins, and his intestines were spread in a rough circle around the corpse. Most reports regarding his death state that parts of his organs were chewed upon by something. Something that could not have been human. The police were said to be baffled by the patterns of the bite marks."

Marsh's demon-echoing laughter filled the room. "A visionary without eyes. A painter without hands or heart. How marvelous. You have served me well. The painter lacked the vision to serve Her and you dealt with him in a fitting manner."

"Then you are pleased?"

"Yes. You have shown me you possess initiative and vision, as well as loyalty. You will serve me well."

"That is my only wish, Lord."

Cunning and deadly. She craves the taste of blood. I shall make her my Scheherazade. Spinning dark tales of death and blood for my private enjoy-

ment. A king needs a . . . . King. Yes. I will be a king, and a king needs a queen to bear his heirs. A king needs a son to continue his reign. I may have more uses for you than I thought. "Did you kill Marsden's agent as well?"

"No, I felt it too risky. He, after all, knows how to contact both Roaker and myself, and I though—"

"You thought!"

"Lord, his agent will soon be an appetizer for the Old Ones."

"True, but I dislike having loose strands dangling about. Were you or Roaker ever contacted or questioned regarding Marsden's murder?"

"No, my Lord."

Good. Then we are safe. "Hearing about his death makes me think of the others."

"The others, Lord?"

"Lumley, Campbell, Price, and their ilk. Especially Lumley! For a quarter of a century he has continued to pour his unholy filth into the marketplace. And the Reverend Mr. Price and that rag of his— I'll soon show him a little old-time-religion. When the Holy Ones have returned I intend to hold my own inquisition and try each and every one of these so-called writers for their literary sacrilege. And when the trials have reached their swift and just end, I shall personally sentence them to the fates they have brought down upon themselves with their lies and blasphemous heresy."

"Fates like Marsden's?"

"Exactly like the painter's."

"I would love to sit on that tribunal."

"I'm sure that can be arranged. Now, your last present, is it as fascinating as the others?"

"I am not sure," she said, removing a bag from her oversized purse. "When I purchased them I thought you would find them interesting, but now I am not so sure."

"The night is young and you have my ear. Please continue. You shall be my seductive storyteller, my Scheherazade."

Scheherazade? Yes, if you like. Very soon I will have more than your ear. "Scheherazade, Lord?" *Tread carefully! Not too dumb.*

"Do you know the tale?"

"Yes."

"Good. Your tales are as delightful. Spin another for me," he commanded.

"As you wish, Lord. This is my third gift. Roaker mentioned a recording you cherished by The Black Abyss. So I tried to find it on CD for you and found these instead."

He looked at the CD's. Erika Zann, *Beneath the Ancient Night Sky. I've heard of her. SYS? That's the Yellow Sign on the cover, but who is SYS?* "*Symphonie No. 3.* By who? Never heard of it. And *Massa di Requiem,* charming." *I vaguely remember Ida mentioning something about this opera. It will be a pleasure to finally hear it.* "Please tell me why you thought I would enjoy these. I know very little about classical music."

"Only one is classical. As I said, I was trying to find The Black Abyss recording for you, but unfortunately, had no luck finding it. During the course of my search, I discovered these recordings. Naturally, once I saw the names, I could not resist them, and because of my liaison with Desmond I could not resist the Society of the Yellow Sign's recording.

"I have seen them perform in Cologne and Stuttgart. Their concerts seem more Hasturian services then musical events. On stage they wear tattered yellowed robes and the Pallid Mask, and perform only by the light cast by dozens of black candles set in a pair of enormous candelabra. They are so secretive they have never appeared without the masks, not in public or in private. No one knows who they are or anything about the members. All their songs are devoted to The King in Yellow, Carcosa, and Hastur."

"Do you think they are believers?"

"Such a hellish joy could only be produced by the faithful."

"They play rock, then?"

"Of sorts, yes. I would call it droning rhythmic pulses beneath layers of guitar and keyboard white noise. The German music press has called them a demonic, distant cousin to Einstürzende Neubauten. There have been eight highly publicized *polizei* investigations concerning concert-goers disappearing from their shows in the last two years. Speculation abounds in certain circles regarding sacrifices."

"How many have disappeared?"

"Eight to date."

"One a season. They must be devout," he commented, toying with the ring she had given him. "You were discussing the music. Please continue."

"Yes, Lord. The vocals of SYS alternate between a clear sometimes almost tender soprano lamentation and the massed tortured
screams of the dying. Between songs they read the 'Inevir Decrees'
from the *Véniavd.*"

"Interesting. Go on."

"Their performances are beautifully chilling. I have witnessed
concert-goers flee from their shows. SYS have set 'Cassilda's Song' to
music. A woman, who seems to be their leader, sings it," she said as
she began to sing in a soft heavily accented soprano, "'Songs that the
Hyades shall sing, Where flap the tatters of the King, Must die
unheard in Dim Carcosa.' Please forgive my voice. I know I cannot
do it justice."

"Don't apologize. It was lovely. Perhaps later you would sing the
whole of it for me."

"If you desire it, Lord. The Erika Zann recordings were made
before she joined the Electric Commode. She had also recorded a
Satanic mass, but I felt that it would not interest you. If you look at
the titles of the songs on the back?"

Marsh read the song titles and brief credits on the back of the
two-disc set.

"He Rises" 7:19 (guitar feedback, bass, drums, organ, voice).
And soon he shall.

"Chaos Calls" 9:11 (feedback: Gibson Les Paul-Showman amplifier, solo voice). "Black Visions" 8:09.
Whose? The mad Arab's? Prinn's?

"The Prayer and Chant of Leng" 13:03 (percussion, voice).
Leng, wonderful.

"Necronomicon" 17:17 (quotes, electric wah-wah guitar, bass
clarinet). "The Haunter" 3:45. "The Feaster Walks" 4:09. "Bountiful
Nightmares" including "Noise Born in Silence" and "Black Robes In
The Distance" 6:35 (solo voice, Hammond B-3, sound effects).
"Dark Aeons" 5:10. "Necronomicon II" including "Invocation of the
Watcher" 49:13 (guitars, quotes, gongs, assorted percussion,
Hammond B-3, bass, found effects).

*Yes, Tätus will be invoked! From beneath eastern sands he will tri-
umphantly rise to greet his brothers.*

"You will notice they all refer to the Old Ones. Do you know of
Zann?"

"Yes. What about the music on these other CD's?"

"The *Massa di Requiem per Shuggay* is an opera from the mid-18th century, that is said to have only been performed only once. It was composed by Benvento Chieti Bordighera. This version was performed by a rock and roll band with a small orchestra accompanying them."

"I've heard of it, but how can a rock band perform an opera?"

"They took the opera's score and rearranged it. The vocal parts remain much the same, but the music is recast as a mixture of orchestral sections mixed with progressive jazz, avant-rock, and ambient textures woven into an electronic collage spiked with sound effects and noise. Overall it is said to resemble the original in much the same way as Emerson, Lake, and Palmer's version of Mussorgsky's *Pictures at an Exhibition* did. You would term it an adaptation."

"I understand. Go on."

"According to legend the score contains a spell woven into the notes; many believe that at an undetermined point in the third act Azathoth will appear. The opera revolves around themes of torture and incestuous rape."

"Interesting. Something like the Fried Spiders LP. Is the opera really a spell to summon Azathoth?"

"Certain sources believe that an insect from Shagghai had burrowed its way into Bordighera's brain."

"Shagghai. Yes."

"There is a story that you may find of interest regarding the recording of the opera. The group which recorded it, the German art band Knochen Maschine, which translates as bone machine, hired two Italians to sing the leads, which were written in Italian, but translated for this recording. Tiziana Salarezza sang Maria's role and Enrico Fabbri sang Pietro's role. During the recording sessions it seems they fell madly in love. As they were leaving the studio after rerecording the 'Duet Macabre' from Act One they stepped off the curb and were crushed by a bus. The irony of this is Manfred Joos, the record's producer, had them rerecord 'Duet Macabre' several times, as he felt there was insufficient emotion in a certain pair of lines. Maria asks, 'But why, my love, Must I die for you?' To which Pietro replies, 'Because, Alive I love you only for a day, But dead, I shall love you forever.'"

"You shall indeed be my Scheherazade. Your tales are bewitching. For countless nights you shall weave dark accounts of scandal, death, and lust beyond the pale, to enchant me. And does this last recording have a dark tale of woe or dismemberment behind it? Please, tell me it must. How many deaths does it encompass?"

"More than a few, my Lord."

"Then set my feet upon the shadowy road. Show me suffering and abhorrence."

I have already. "The tale deals with doom-fated lovers as well. This is the world premiere recording of this symphonie. Miroslav Capek, the owner of the Scherzo Recording Organization, says he paid one hundred thousand dollars for the only surviving copy of the original score. Capek, who, by the way, is a horror film enthusiast, only allows recordings of a horrific nature to be recorded on his label. Last year he was named European producer of the year for his recording of Julianne Hiller's *Screams of the Black Angel*. The symphonie is performed by the Saarbrücken Radio Symphonie Orchester, under the baton of Gerhard Christop Neubauer, whose wife is the acclaimed avant-garde vocalist Helen Briars. It was composed by Reinhart Aldric Knaup-Krötenschwanz, who was born in Stade in 1877. Although his works are rarely recorded or performed they have always held an attraction for me. You see, I was born a few short blocks from the home of Knaup-Krötenschwanz and St. Cosmae Church. St. Cosmae is the home of the famous ARP Schnidtger organ, which Krötenschwanz composed on. It is also the organ used in the symphonie. Before I continue, I should tell you about the symphonie itself, Symphonie Number 3 in D minor, Opus. 15, *Der Fall und Aufstehen von GorB Alt Eins*. The fall and rise of the Great Old Ones."

"This is about the Holy Ones?"

"Yes. The symphonie is programmatic."

"Programmatic?"

"The music follows a story line. Much like Strauss' *Don Quixote*, or Berlioz's *Symphonie Fantastique*. It could also be compared to Roussel's *Le Festin de l'araignée*, the 'Spider's Banquet', as it was originally conceived as a ballet. Each movement of the third has a title which describes its contents. The first movement, 'Out of the Black Heavens', allegro, represents the Holy Ones coming from Xoth to Earth, and the ensuing wars among themselves over territory. It concludes with the war between the Holy Ones and the Elder Gods. The second movement, 'R'lyeh Dreams', largo, which is written only for cello, organ, and percussion, are the thoughts, suffering, and dreams of Cthulhu as he lies imprisoned in R'lyeh. Throughout the work Cthulhu's voice is represented by the cellos. In the third movement, 'When Stars Align', scherzo, man arrives and the Holy Ones begin to prey upon him. This movement also deals with the mad Arab and the *Necronomicon*. There is a brief vocal part representing Alhazred's death, sung only in experimental vocalese by the English soprano Jane Ellsworth. She is renowned for her portrayal of the revenge-consumed and tormented Cassandra, who was hellishly disfigured by her lover in Byrne Merrill's *Chants of Evil*. And there are quotes from the *Necronomicon* itself, performed by the English tenor Thomas Christian Giles-Smith. As the movement closes all the barriers of their prisons are shattered and the Holy Ones are freed.

"The final movement, 'Cthulhu Supreme', allegro energico, finds Cthulhu and his brethren restored to their former glory. This is a work of great torment and impassioned anger, which ends in a joyous feast, as well it should. You should also be aware that in the symphonie each instrument is the voice of a certain entity or object. The cello is Cthulhu, while the double basses are the Outer Gods. The *cor anglais* and the brass are the Elder Gods, while man is represented by a single clarinet, and the oboes. The pipe organ and the bass clarinets are the other Holy Ones, and Alhazred's *Necronomicon* is represented by the concertmaster and Giles. There was also a fifth movement, but it was removed and recast as a separate piece. It became *Surrounded by the Sea (Threnody for Cthulhu) Opus. 19*. A symphonic poem for cello and wind instruments."

"Intriguing and quite fitting so close to Li-ure, but aren't there any deaths involved?"

"Yes, my Lord, a trio."

"Then continue."

"Thomas Giles-Smith and Jane Ellsworth were husband and wife. The lurid involvements and exploits of this pair could fill a novel. Giles-Smith was engaged in a two-year, torrid affair with the young mezzo Sharon Cross, whose sister Marion is head of the most powerful Satanic coven in Britain. It is unfortunate that she places no credence in our cause, as she is believed to be one of the most able and powerful sorceresses in Europe. My dead husband, Satan burn his debauched soul, often said that her powers rivaled those of the legendary Frau Wimmel.

"Now the trouble with this triumvirate of lovers began when the insecure Ellsworth, a woman of great cunning but little backbone, started to fear that her husband would leave her for his ravishing young lover. You see, Jane Ellsworth had signed what you Americans call a prenuptial agreement. At the same time Giles-Smith began to fear that his wife would publicly expose his dark tastes if he left her, so he broke off the affair. Now two things happened. The first was his lover, Sharon Cross, threatened suicide if he did not divorce his wife, saying she would name him publicly as the cause of her death. The second was when Ellsworth and Cross began a recording session together. While Ellsworth and Cross recorded together, Giles-Smith was in Milan, playing Calaf in an Italian production of *Turandot*, completely unaware of the hastily put together recording session."

"And then they plot to kill him. Right?"

"First the two women become lovers."

"Do they succeed?" he asked excitedly.

"We are not that far into the story yet. When the two women began to record together, his wife had no idea that Sharon Cross was her husband's lover. Jane Ellsworth was simply looking for a distraction. Cross, however, was aware of who Ellsworth was, and had entered the project only to tell Ellsworth of her husband's deception. So the two became romantically entangled and began to plot to kill the man who had, they felt, misused their affections. Unable to devise a fitting method of dealing with Giles-Smith, they approached Cross' sister, Marion, who sent them to enlist the aid of a woman who Giles-Smith had discarded years before, after a brief affair. Syndra Evans-Taylor, London's socialite dabbler in arcane affairs, was delighted to assist the pair. An occultist and collector with her fingers in every pie she happened upon, she gave them a spell said to call forth nightmare-spawned Dl'rasdus, the plague-infested reaver who guards the hundred wells of black Mrusucu.

"With their spell at the ready and their plot formulated, they awaited his return from Italy. Three days after he returned home, they killed him. His torn and dismembered body was discovered at his country estate near Bath. Some months after his death, Sharon

Cross, never a mentally stable woman, became distraught over what
they had done and hung herself. Jane Ellsworth's mind shattered
after her newfound lover's death; she was committed to the Sinfield
Sanatorium outside Kingswood. To this very day she resides there,
babbling about dark nightmares that visit her and the price being too
dear. Thus ends my trilogy of tales."

"Wonderful. I look forward to many more. Now come, I've
something to show you, but first would you sing all of 'Cassilda's
Song' for me?"

"If you like, my Lord—

Along the shore the cloud waves break,
The twin suns sink behind the lake,
The shadows lengthen
                     in Carcosa.

Strange is the night where black stars rise,
And strange moons circle through the skies,
But stranger still is
                     Lost Carcosa.

Songs that the Hyades shall sing,
Where flap the tatters of the King,
Must die unheard in
                     Dim Carcosa.

Songs of my soul, my voice is dead,
Die though, unsung, as tears unshed
Shall dry and die in
                     Lost Carcosa."

She must be the one I've been waiting for. Tomorrow should prove it. "Come,
Scheherazade. It's time you see Her shrine."

❦ Chapter Twenty ❦

"Hi, it's me."

"Chris. Thank God! Why haven't you called? I've been worried sick. Pat was here earlier."

"I'm okay."

"But Pat said—"

"Relax. He's like an old mother hen. Don't worry about me."

"He told us about the girl. You must be—"

"Lauri, could we not talk about this now?"

"Sure. Where are you?"

"At The Horror Corner. We've set up a stakeout. There's a good chance this asshole might try something after Beckett's article and the false news reports we're having aired."

"I didn't see the paper."

"I know. I had to buy it at Stewart's on my way in. You know, for someone who likes to read so much you'd think you would read the paper instead of watching the news on TV."

"Hey! Ed Dague's been bringing me the news for too many years to stop now . . . he's a fellow gardener, you know."

"I know."

"How long do you think the stakeout will last?"

"No way of knowing, but I think if he's going to try anything it will be soon. A week or two, tops."

"Who's working it with you?"

"It's just me and Willie Stanton. We're gonna be here until it's over. Rolly will be in and out."

"Just the two of you, that sounds dangerous."

"There's backup outside, and the whole is place is wired top to bottom. You'd think the Feds had set up shop. We're going to be fine. Lauri, there's something I want you to do for me."

"What?"

"I want you to call Pat and ask him to come over and stay with you for a couple of hours."

"I don't understand. Henri's here, and you said you didn't think that I would be in any danger."

"That's true, but I want Henri to come here, and I doubt he'll leave you alone. So maybe if Pat baby-sits—" *Shit!*

"Baby-sits. I'm perfectly capable of—"

"I know that, but do you think Henri will accept you being alone?"

"No. Why do you want to see Henri? Can't you come here?"

"No, the stakeout."

"Then I'll bring Hen—"

"No! I don't want you near this place. This animal could be watching the store." *He might see you and*—"Henri drives, right?"

"Yes."

"I want him to come alone. That's why I want you to call Pat."

"Okay, but—"

"No buts. Let me talk to Henri about this."

"Don't you dare hang up after you talk to him."

"I won't."

"Hang on, I'll get him."

"Christopher, *bonjour.* Laurinda said you wished to speak to me."

"Henri, I'd like to see you. I'm at The Horror Corner. Lauri can give you directions. There's some questions I want to ask you." Chris explained the situation.

"I cannot leave her here unattended."

"She won't be. Look, Pat might not look tough, but he's an ex-Marine who still works out three times a week. If he decided to, he could throw you around like a baseball. He knows more ways to kill a man with his bare hands than Sinatra's got records. If he wanted, you'd be dead in two minutes."

"If I come to this shop, will I be away long?"

"I don't think so."

"Then I'll come."

Henri handed Lauri the phone. "Do you want me to call Pat?"

"No, I'll call him, and call you back in a few minutes."

"I miss you."

"I miss you too. Bye," he said. He hung up and dialed Pat's home.

* * * * *

Willie sat by the front door waiting for Henri to arrive. When the Honda Accord pulled in front of the doorway and parked Willie stood. "Hooolly shit." *Chris said he was a big man, but that's bigger than big. This cat's nearly as big as Shaquille O'Neal,* Willie thought as Henri walked toward the door.

"Hello, my name is Henri Freniere. Is Detective Sergeant Stewart here? I believe he is expecting me," he said, wondering where and how Chris had come up with all the stones in the window so quickly, and why.

"Henri, right you are. C'mon in. My name's Willie, Willie Stanton. Everybody's upstairs waiting for you."

Henri followed Willie through the store. When he reached the midway point he paused and looked around. "May the loas preserve us."

"Sure is something, ain't it?" Willie commented.

"Yes. Something." Henri observed.

"When I was a kid, my father thought comics were bad for me. He'd go bonkers if he saw this stuff."

Henri followed Willie upstairs where they found Chris, Cosmo, and the Wizard sitting at the kitchen table.

"Henri, hi. Thanks for coming. Can we get you a drink?" Chris asked.

"Coffee would be nice," Henri replied.

"Sorry, we don't drink coffee. My name's Cosmo, and this is the Wizard."

"How do you do?"

"How about some tea?" Cosmo asked.

"Tea would be fine, thank you."

"Tea it is," the Wizard said.

"I'm sorry to drag you out in this weather, but we have a couple of questions about your grandmother's charm."

"Yeah, take a look at these," Cosmo said, handing Henri a few of the fake star stones. "They look like Chris' stone, as far as size, shape, and texture, but they're lighter."

"I saw them adorning the window when I entered your store. You are correct, they do appear to be the same. Yet there is a difference. *Grand-mère's* charms always feel warm; your imitations are room temperature. I would estimate the temperature in this room to be less than seventy degrees."

"What do you mean they always feel warm?" Willie asked.

"Allow me to demonstrate. Might I have the use of your freezer?"

"Sure," Cosmo said.

"Christopher, may I have your charm for a few minutes?" Henri asked.

"Yeah, here."

"Now we will place the charm in the freezer and give it time to cool."

"Are you trying to tell us that when it comes out it will still be warm to the touch?" Willie asked.

"Yes. If you would not mind me asking, why are the imitations in the window?" Henri asked.

Quick to impart his theory, the Wizard told Henri of his discovery and their scheme.

"Christopher, you said you had some questions. Perhaps while we are waiting, I could answer them for you," Henri said.

"Basically, we have two questions. One, what do you make of these fake stones, and two, what can you tell us about your grandmother's talisman? Do you know where it came from, or how old it is, things like that?"

"The charms were given to *Grand-mère* when she was nineteen years old by her Aunt Simone when she died in 1932. She was told that someday the family would have need of their power. There is not much known of the charms' origins. Aunt Simone told *Grand-mère* that the charms came from somewhere on the African gold coast. She said that her grandfather, Captain Rafael Serrat, had found them in a strange deserted temple, which was covered with unintelligible markings of some kind. *Grand-mère* places great faith in the power of the charms."

"Is there any kind of description of these unintelligible markings?" Cosmo asked.

"Family history says the temple was covered with carvings that resembled marine life."

"Hot damn! I knew it. See," Cosmo said, turning to Chris, "more weird coincidences. This just keeps building. The next thing you know, Cthulhu himself will start terrorizing our dreams."

Dreams. And headaches as well. Christ, a lot of the stories have narrators that are plagued by nightmarish dreams and headaches, and I've been having both. Nah. That's stupid. The headaches are from stress, and the bad dreams are from reading too much of this crap.

"I have read quite a few of Mr. Lovecraft's stories since I arrived here. Laurinda has several of his books at the house."

"What did you think of them?" Cosmo asked.

"I found some of his ideas interesting, but his style is not to my taste in literature."

"What do you like to read?" the Wizard asked.

"The classics—Twain, Mann, Fowles, and Steinbeck. That is not to say that I do not on occasion enjoy the work of some contemporary authors. Just recently I read and thoroughly enjoyed Umberto Eco's *Foucault's Pendulum*, and Anne Rice's *Cry to Heaven*."

"Well, if you're going to enjoy an Anne Rice novel that's certainly the one," the Wizard said.

"That is an interesting comment. After observing the horror paraphernalia that abounds here I would have surmised that her vampire novels would be more highly regarded."

"Can't judge a book by its cover," Cosmo interjected.

"Please forgive me for—"

"Forget it," the Wizard said. "Happens all the time. If I weren't me, I'd assume the same thing. See, I'm not big on vampires, I dig cannibals and ghouls, but I still think her vampire books are excellent. You really should read the first one. It's a superb piece of work, whether you enjoy the genre or not."

Opening the freezer, Henri removed the charm. "By now you might expect the stone to be cold, yet when you touch it, warmth still emanates from it."

Chris, Willie, Cosmo, and the Wizard passed the amulet among themselves. Each took note of the warmth that seemed to radiate from within.

"I had the same feeling when you first gave me the stone. What did you call the stone when you gave it to me?"

"*Le Pierre du gardien du ciel.*"

"What does that mean?" the Wizard asked.

"The stone of heaven's guardian. It has always been called that although no one in our family has any idea why it should so be described," Henri replied.

"The Elder Gods! Damn it! I should have made the connection before," Cosmo said.

"What connection?" Chris asked.

"When you first showed us the stone, you called it the stone of heaven's protector. Then the Wiz here said something about voodoo and I thought heaven's protector was some voodoo thing. Something like gris-gris or Damballah, but now Henri says it's not a voodoo name or term. This is the real McCoy!" Cosmo said.

"That's bullshit!" the Wizard exclaimed.

"Is it? Henri brings this stone from New Orleans at just the right time."

"Right time? What do you see, Cthulhu standin' outside?" the Wizard asked Cosmo.

"No, but some freak out there thinks he does. Look, Henri said this stone came from somewhere in Africa, some forgotten temple covered with strange hieroglyphics. I thought this was voodoo, but it's not. It's another Mythos-related coincidence, and they're starting to add up."

"To what?" Chris asked.

"To too much weird," Cosmo answered.

"C'mon, Cos, other writers have been contributing to Lovecraft's creation since what? The '30's? It only stands to reason that a few odd coincidences could, no make that would, occur over a period of sixty years. Look, you said it yourself, this sick fuck might know more about the Mythos than you do," the Wizard said.

"What coincidences are you talking about?" Henri asked.

Chris sat at the kitchen table and lit a cigarette as Cosmo and the Wizard related Cosmo's unsettling coincidences to Henri.

"They do not seem strange to me. Cults exist everywhere. Channeling is real. Some of the books Lovecraft and other authors have woven into their mythology are real. Rohr's *De Masticatione Mortuorum* and Glanvil's—" Henri said.

"See," Cosmo blurted at the Wizard.

"I'll tell you what I see. This psycho is the director on this film. We're just his audience. He's cast the roles and written the script. Hell, he's shot the film, and now he's looking for reviews. And so here we sit going over this film, frame by frame, line by line. What we're really starting to do is read things into this that probably aren't there. We're becoming fanatics. We want to see this asshole fry so bad we can taste it, so we sacrifice sleep and read so much Mythos shit it's running out our ears. Somewhere between our desire to see this freak burn and our total immersion in the stories we've lost sight of perspective," the Wizard said.

"Maybe everything can be explained. Except for one thing," Cosmo said.

"Which is?" the Wizard asked.

"Henri's stone. I mean a presumably real occult talisman that's an exact representation of the stones from Mnar. And what about the temple?"

"What about it?" Chris asked.

"The runes on it resembled marine-like creatures," Cosmo said.

"That's easy. The stone was found by a sailor in a different era. An era with different values, beliefs, and levels of education. This guy, we'll assume doesn't know shit—please excuse my discussing your ancestor like this," the Wizard said, turning to Henri, "—about archaeology or African history. He finds this temple, and it's got carvings on it. Now, was this temple near a coast? We don't know, but people who live near oceans or rivers often fish as a form of subsistence, and they might worship some kind of deity that we would call, what? A sea monster. Let's not forget how many mythological beings are theriomorphic. Here's my point. We don't have any descriptions of the carvings and we don't know where in Africa this stone was found, so all you're doing is reading something into it which may not be there. If we wanted to we could bend or distort almost anything to fit into the Mythos."

"Maybe, but it still seems weird," Cosmo said.

"Henri, this is your stone and your ancestor. Do you have any thoughts or comments?" Chris asked.

"I do not have the background in this matter that you have. Perhaps if I had more information, I might have some input, but at the moment all I have is what the cards have told me. And questions."

"Well, maybe we've got the answers. Ask away," Cosmo said.

"Do any of you believe in God?"

"Not since I was twelve," the dyed-in-the-wool atheist stated as he toyed with a guitar pick with a stylized W imprinted on both sides.

"Ditto," Cosmo seconded.

"Raised and married in St. John's—still go every Sunday with my family," Willie said.

"Guess I'm on the fence these days. Why?"

"First let me say I believe in the supernatural. I believe in God, angels, and the loas. Do any of these things exist? Can science provide us with documentation to prove or disprove their existence? No. To believe requires faith and perception. A perception that most of mankind has drifted away from in this century."

"I'll bite," the Wizard said.

Henri turned to the Wizard. Eye to eye, his tone deepened. "You are a musician. Where does your music come from? You simply close your eyes and open your soul."

"You might put it that way, but I still don't get it."

"Where is your soul? Is it in your chest? No. It resides in the human mind somewhere. A mind we know very little about. A mind with vast amounts of untapped potential. Was it always unused, or has man in his quest to harness and define his world stopped using that which propelled him through the ages? I come from a region that is hot, humid, and alive with spirituality. We are closer to our roots and to the earth and her mysteries. In New Orleans we believe in God, angels, saints, and spirits. You will also find many who believe in ghosts, werewolves, and vampires. As you walk the streets of the Crescent City you will still see tradition sitting on shaded stoops on hot afternoons, as the past strolls through the Garden District whispering secrets into the future's ear. Although the land here is old it is well trod and completely mapped in concrete and steel; it holds few mysteries to you, and so you have no need to use this part of your consciousness. The prayers and dreams of the past have become dying old men in a young world of too many answers and too few questions. Television, radio, and the print media's voracious lightning eye have replaced the wonder-filled pages of books, the church of the human heart, and the bedroom. Film director Oliver Stone put it succinctly when he said, 'The ancients had vision. We have television.' Morality and compassion are of little use to a contemporary urban society where random violence is perpetrated solely for fun, or out of boredom and petty anger. In this atmosphere of fear, your soul is becoming obsolete. In your hunger for security and order in a world going mad, you forget the pious light in the cosmos above you, and the song of Mother Earth, whose breast you once clung to for sanctuary and nourishment. Evil wins its war as everything becomes gray. You must not forget that some things remain black and white. What lies before you is darkness—evil. There is no gray to this monster. This beast, whose jaws are poised at your throats, is not born of accident or coincidence. The star has arrived here because it is needed. The loas, through the tarot, have told me you must accept divine assistance if you are to be victorious in this battle."

"But this violence is born from an insane belief in fiction," the Wizard interjected.

"Some think God is nothing more than a fictional concept."

"Wait a second," the Wizard said. "Are you saying man has outgrown God the way the Greeks and Romans outgrew Zeus and Jupiter?"

"In a way, yes. Man has discovered many things, things which have changed the world and how he views it. Through science man has demystified the universe. God is not tangible. His existence cannot be proven in a laboratory or with a formula, so prideful man begins to discount him."

"So?" the Wizard asked.

"You are dismissing the coincidences that Cosmo spoke of simply because you cannot explain them."

"Henri, do you really think there's something to this?" Chris asked.

"Yes."

"Got any ideas on how we can catch him?" Willie asked.

"Your idea about using the stones to lure him here seems sound. The stones are a real threat to his gods. You are dealing with someone who truly believes in this fictional mythology. I believe he will have to come here and deal with them."

"We're ready," the Wizard said.

"I'm not sure guns will be sufficient in dealing with this evil," Henri said, pointing at the Wizard's shotgun.

"You think there's a supernatural evil here? I think we're looking at the two-footed kind. The kind this will take care of real easily," the Wizard said, patting the stock of his loaded Remington.

"The loas have told me only through deep faith and sacrifice shall you be victorious in your confrontation with this foot soldier of evil."

God, how am I supposed to keep my faith? I'm not Job. All I've seen is death. Dad shot by a hunter. Me killing VC in 'Nam and putting kids I knew in bags . . . Mom being devoured by breast cancer. You want me to have faith when I had to watch her stripped of her dignity by months of soul-defiling pain, Chris thought, recalling images of his mother withering into a skeleton as she slid into the raw waiting arms of death. *And what about Sue and Merry dying like that. All that blood and half of Merry's face sheared away. Wanta tell me why I lost them? If there's some plan it doesn't make any sense to me. And now this. Faith! I'm not sure where mine's gone, but I have resolve. I hope that's enough. God, if you're there somewhere, do you think you could watch over me on this one?*

"Maybe we should all catch some sleep?" Willie accented his suggestion with a yawn.

"Tell the truth. If we're gonna catch this asshole it might be a good idea if we were awake when he shows up," the Wizard said.

"Don't you mean if?" Cosmo asked.

God, please make it when, Chris asked.

❦ Chapter Twenty-One ❦

A shadow breaking the rays of sunlight pouring through the windows, Ida walked into the library and stood over Gregory, who was immersed in his studies more intently than a half-starved dog chewing the marrow from a bone.

"You are doing well. In a few short weeks you have learned what took me years to digest and master. Perhaps we should take a break. I thought you might enjoy a picnic by the river this afternoon. There is a lovely spot a few miles upriver."

"That sounds wonderful. Maybe you could answer my other questions about the family."

"I'd be glad to. You deserve a reward for your hard work."

In Essex County, Massachusetts, beside the Manuxet River, Gregory and Ida sat on a checkered blanket with their picnic basket in the afternoon sunshine. Their laughter reflected off the white clouds hovering above them, until an old wooden rowboat piloted by two college coeds drifted by with the breeze. Unnoticed by the young women, the Marsh cousins watched the boat glide into a small cove a few hundred yards to the east.

Reaching out to touch his cheek, she whispered, "Could I interest you in dessert?"

Uncertain just what dessert might entail, but entertaining lusty ideas, he quickly breathed his response. "I'd love dessert."

Rolling over she took a bottle of wine and two knives from the picnic basket and stood. "Shall we go meet our neighbors?"

Two hours later they returned to the red checkered blanket that now matched the color of their clothing.

"What about the bodies? They'll be discovered."

"Leave them for the reef."

"But they'll float right through town."

"They won't reach the falls until dark. Now, I promised to answer your questions. What would you like to know?"

"I know nothing of the Marshes before Obed's time. I've seen the portraits, but—and I know nothing about my father. When I asked about him before you avoided my question. Do you know who he was?"

"Yes, and we'll get to him shortly. As to the family's history before Obed, our first ancestor, as far as we can trace the records back, was James Marsh of Kent. James was a captain in the royal army, a Puritan supporter of Oliver Cromwell and the Parliament who was beheaded by Charles I at Hedgehall in 1634. The year before he was beheaded, James' sister Mary took William and two other nephews by her half-sister and fled to America. Mary feared reprisals against their younger brother William, who was an outspoken college student. They settled in Salem, where William became involved in the fur trade and Richard, the younger of the nephews, served in the Indian Wars and eventually settled in what is now Redding, Connecticut to farm. Walter, Richard's older brother, came to Innsmouth in 1644 and married Rachel Martin. That same year John Marsh, Walter's older brother, also came from England to Innsmouth and married Sarariah Eliot. The two brothers, marrying into prominent Innsmouth families, founded our family. The Marshes of Innsmouth were sailors and fishermen until shortly after the Revolution, when they took over the shipyard and became seafaring merchants. For over three centuries the Marshes and their descendants have lived and controlled this region of Massachusetts, as well as the area around New Milford, Connecticut and Birchvale, New York."

"Birchvale. That sounds familiar."

"I believe it is only an hour or so from where you live. Ethan could be more specific, but I think it lies in the foothills of the southern Adirondacks. He was quite surprised you did not discover the link between the Marshes and the Hartwickes of Birchvale in your research."

"I remember Driscoll writing about them, something about the male Hartwickes coming to this region every twenty years or so in search of a Marsh bride."

"Correct as far as it goes. In 1673 Riverius Marsh's youngest daughter, Cornelia, using sorcery, enslaved and married young Byron Hartwicke. Cornelia's lust caused her to make a pact that no Hartwicke male has ever broken and lived."

"A pact with who?"

"Ut'ulls-Hr'ehr, the first-born daughter of the Black Goat of the Wood with a Thousand Young."

"Shub-Niggurath's daughter."

Nodding affirmatively, Ida continued, "Young Cornelia vowed to cover the earth with worshipers and sacrifices if she could have Hartwicke. The pact also charges that any male Hartwicke descending from her union must marry a Marsh woman or face the judgment of Ut'ulls-Hr'ehr herself. Cornelia also vowed these Marsh wives would continue the tributes to Ut'ulls-Hr'ehr."

"What if the women aren't interested?"

"The pact makes the option of refusal impossible for any Marsh woman chosen to marry a Hartwicke male. My mother's half-sister, Kathleen, is the current matriarch of the Hartwicke estate, Ravenscourt."

"I have another aunt?"

"Yes, but she has not spoken to any member of the family in over twenty years. Now, returning to the Marshes of Innsmouth."

"But—"

"My dear Gregory, I have never met anyone so full of buts. One item that you will not find in any of your fictional stories is how the Marshes became involved with the Holy Ones. Lovecraft and his followers have perpetuated the myth that Obed brought the family into contact with the Holy Ones when he discovered the legends in the south seas, but it was actually Riverius who came into contact with them almost two hundred years earlier. Riverius—a befitting name for a sailor, don't you think?—came across a body on the darkened streets near the docks of Marseille. Realizing the man was dead he picked up a leather pouch lying beside the corpse and took it. The pouch contained a book, a copy of *De Vermiis Mysteriis*. Riverius and those who followed became consumed by what they found in the book. This is why Obed was so taken with the Polynesian legends— there was much more than money to be attained. Obed sensed the power waiting to be gained by an alliance with the gods of family legend. Quite naturally, in the years between Riverius' discovery and Obed's, the family pursued the Holy Ones with a determined zeal. Many of the books housed in the family library were obtained in the early 17th century by Daniel and Zachariah Marsh. Obed's father, Partridge, spent many years in Europe and the Mid-East purchasing antiquities. Have you noticed the six figurines adorning the mantle in the study?"

"Yes, the jade Cthulhu is amazing."

"Those sculptures and a number of books are the fruits of his years spent abroad. Over the years many of our family members have gone to Europe and Asia seeking to enlarge the family's knowledge by obtaining books and artifacts. Mother herself spent a few years in Paris and Brussels in the late sixties. She is the one who located the copy of Ostane's *Sapentia Magorum* you were reading from yesterday. Although there are many anecdotal stories regarding the family and its interests, perhaps we should save them for another time."

"But—"

"Again these buts. You know the rest of our history and have met all the family, except your mother's sister, Marilyn, who has been a patient in Danvers Asylum for the criminally insane for almost twenty-five years."

"Three aunts! What's wrong with her? Can I see her?"

"I'm afraid there's not much to see. She's catatonic. The last time Aunt Marilyn communicated with anyone was over ten years ago, and then all it consisted of was incomprehensible babbling and a few broken moans. She tried to commit suicide a year before your mother ran away."

"That's another question I have. What caused my Mother's exodus from here?"

"Preserving our family's bloodline is extremely important to us. We strongly believe in racial purity. At least as far as the human blood in us goes. The Arab and his nigger cousin are nothing more than talking apes. And the Jews, well, clever mimics. The same applies to the orientals. That is how that vile Rhode Islander Lovecraft wormed his way into the family trust. All his talk of the mongrel races turning our cities into filthy dumps, the noble Ku Klux Klan, and Hitler's glorious *Mein Kampf*. White this family is, and so it shall remain. Our bloodlines are pure. And only the pure will serve the Holy Ones when they return. That is why for almost two hundred years we have, like the kings of great nations, practiced inbreeding. And there lies your mother's reason for leaving.

"The notion of bedding her father repulsed her. You must understand your mother was a weak-minded woman who developed fantasies of some lesser life in a mundane suburban environment. I fear Ernest's wife, Janet, the eldest daughter of Putnam Clapp in Kingsport, ruined your mother. Janet thought she was marrying into a life of style and money. And when she discovered otherwise, she placed her dreams in the head of her daughter, your mother. My mother, who knew Janet, has often said she was little more than a gold-digging harlot."

"Then I am—"

"A true Marsh. Yes. Your father was also your mother's father. Your blood is even purer than my own. Obed's daughter, your great-great-grandmother for whom I am named, and her descendants rarely coupled with the deep ones. At fifteen she was married off to her second cousin in Newburyport. It was her son Zebulon and his son Ernest, your father, who came back to Innsmouth and began restoring the town in the forties."

"But what about the things Derleth wrote about Innsmouth? Is there any truth to the statement of Abel Keane?"

"Derleth's tales are almost completely composed of literary fantasy. The family home has never been touched by fire, and no one in Innsmouth has ever heard of Abel Keane. Remember what I have told you about these blasphemers and their lies. The deep ones did in fact try to reassert their hold over us at one point and for a very brief period of time a schism split the family, but Ernest quickly reconciled everyone. How Derleth learned of these events has always baffled us, as they were never reported. In 1955 the family purchased both the dead Innsmouth *Courier* and the Newburyport *Correspondent* to ensure that we would be able to control the local media should the need ever arise again. We also purchased both local radio stations, WEDF and WPWB, in 1962. Outside of Arkham and Gloucester, we now completely own the media in this region of Massachusetts through offshore holding companies that cannot be traced back to the family."

"I would like to see Arkham."

"We never go there. Ethan had to attend college in Boston, simply because he was a Marsh. Although I doubt he would have chosen to attend Miskatonic University, even if they would have accepted him. You must realize the Marsh name is hardly revered in Arkham."

"Why?"

"Arkham is fast becoming a hot bed of studious blasphemers and fanatical terrorists who seek to destroy the Holy Ones. That damn university breeds them like cockroaches. Danger lurks everywhere. The Sutherland Foundation has a chapterhouse six blocks away from

the university, on the corner of Church and Sentinel. And we are fairly certain the Order of the Sword of St. Jerome maintains a residence
on Garrison Street across from the university. Witch-haunted and
shadowy Arkham may once have been, but it grows dangerous for us
as it collects ill-wishers to our cause, from all corners of the globe.
They enroll in the university's School of Medieval Metaphysics to
gain access to the library's copy of the *Necronomicon* and its companion volumes."

"Can't anything be done to remove these heretics?"

"It has been decided that leaving them to themselves is best for
now. When the Holy Ones return they will be severely dealt with."

"I understand."

"Do you? The Marshes have learned to prosper by camouflaging
themselves. We hide by not appearing to hide. We use tourism to
cover our activities. Over the years Lovecraft has developed a large
following, so we are using him and his Mythos to mask our under-
takings. The family is currently putting the finishing touches on the
boardwalk along the old wharf on Dock Street, and transformation
of the Gilman House was completed last July. You can now tour the
refinery and purchase imitations of the tiara you so admired in the
library, or enjoy an evening of cruising the harbor, complete with dinner and dancing. The menu is strictly seafood, by the way.

"At the Marsh Wax Museum on Water Street, tourists can be
photographed for a small fee, in the clutches of a byakhee, a deep
one, or a nightgaunt. Strangely enough, the most popular exhibit is
an altar surrounded by three hounds of Tindalos, which visitors lay
on; their torsos are then covered by a vinyl piece which makes them
look as if they've been ripped open by the surrounding hounds.
Imagine the fools laying there, paying four dollars apiece for a photograph of their disemboweled bodies! Another heavily visited attraction occurs at 9 p.m. every Saturday night during tourist season. We
hold a ceremony in the temple on the New Church Green. The lights
fail and deep ones roam the aisles as we immerse the cretins in our
own version of hellfire and brimstone. People have actually fainted
while attending our little theater performances—last June a woman
from Montreal had a heart attack and had to be taken to University
Hospital in Arkham. They come from far and wide, especially the

French and Spanish, to see and be frightened by crumbling, demon-infested Innsmouth."

"Why didn't you tell me these things before?"

"Forgive me. I meant to."

"It's okay. I have my answers."

"Good," she said as she rolled on top of him and licked a spot of dried blood from his chest.

"Do you know how much I love having you?" he asked.

Baring her teeth, she answered him with a deep salacious moan, before she began chewing on his nipple.

* * * * *

He sat at the work table in a brightly lit corner of his subterranean shrine singing "Cassilda's Song" quietly as Christa walked around examining the candlesticks and Kassogtha's altar. As her hands stroked the contours of the altar, she ahhhed smiles at the workmanship. Turning to gaze over her shoulder at him she smiled at her own craftsmanship and the control she'd held over his quivering loins thirty minutes earlier.

Seemingly engrossed in his own thoughts, his pen scratched across the paper as he prepared a list of things they must attend to in the coming days.

1 - One more. Whore? Black skin!

2 - Have Christa practice the incantations of the rite. Her timing and phrasing must be exact.

3 - Place the remaining candlesticks. Arrive tomorrow?

4 - Finish sewing robe.

5 - Contact the others and confirm their arrival plans.

6 - Call Beckett and the store. What should I say?

7 - Check out the stones at the store?

Hanging before him were his breast skins. Reaching fifteen inches to his left, his finger traced the dark edge of Donnalee O'Donnell's areola. His circular caress was as gentle as a mother's kiss on the dead flesh. He grew hard recalling the look in the dying woman's eyes as she had flopped on the white blanket of winter.

"Is this the material for the robe?"

"What? Yes," he said as he turned to her.

"How fitting. Donning the breasts of human females to give birth to the Queen Mother. Do you have enough material to make the robe yet?" she asked, pointing to the skins.

"I need another pair," he said, looking at her pert breasts. After a few seconds he added, "A black pair." The words danced across his dark smile. *Kassogtha, what a dumb bitch.*

Her momentary fright quickly turned into a composed smile. "Do you think I could join you on your next hunt?"

A man and a woman looking for kicks with another woman. That might be a good idea. The whores would certainly be a lot less wary of a couple out looking for fun than just me. Maybe she'd like to kill the next bitch herself. If she butchered that painter and Desmond that easily this could be stimulating to watch. "Maybe. Did you find yourself aroused when you cut Desmond's throat?"

"Yes. While I lapped at the blood coming from his throat after he died, I fantasized someone was mercilessly fucking me from behind."

"A fantasy I shall make real," came his royal decree. "You've given me an idea."

"About the next victim?" she asked with hope.

"Yes. What if you played vampire to a live victim? A woman."

After considering his question a moment she answered, "I'm wet just thinking about the possibilities."

"Good. It amuses me too."

"When, do you think?"

"In a few days."

* * * * *

"Hello. I have returned," Henri said as Laurinda and Pat walked into the kitchen.

"What did Chris say?" Laurinda asked.

"We discussed the stones and using them as bait to lure the killer to the store."

"What stones?" Pat asked.

"*Grand-mère*'s charms and Cosmo's fake stones."

"What are we talking about? I know that Moon's working a stakeout at the store, but how do these stones you're talking about figure in?"

"My grandmother had a premonition that something very bad was going to happen here. Do you recall me speaking of her? Remember I said she was a practicing voodoo priestess. She also places a great deal of importance in the tarot. She believes we're in danger of some kind and the stones are the only protection from the evil that she's seen coming. She sent Henri here with two charms to protect Chris and me. This is one of them," explained Laurinda, as she pulled the charm hanging around her neck from beneath her "FREE Your Mind! READ A Book" T-shirt. "They're shaped like stars."

"Sweet Jesus!" Pat exclaimed, crossing himself. "I've seen that stone before."

"You seen Chris'?" Laurinda asked.

"No."

"Where have you seen the stone?" Henri asked.

"In Ireland."

"That is not possible. There are only two charms in existence. This one, and your friend Christopher wears its twin," Henri said.

"Sorry, but now there's three. There's one of those stones in a frame above my grandmother's fireplace in Kilkenny. It's a legendary family heirloom that's been hanging on that same wall for two hundred years now."

Laurinda looked at Henri, who shrugged.

"I think I should contact *Grand-mère* about this new stone and we must also tell Chris," Henri said, beginning to wonder just what his *grand-mère* had been told by the spirits.

"You must be mistaken," Laurinda said.

"They look identical," Pat countered.

"But they can't be the same."

"Gran's stone is always warm. Even in winter, it's warm to the touch," Pat added as Laurinda looked at Henri for some response.

"That is true. The stars are always warm," Henri said, thinking of the holy number three. *Do we now have three real stones?* "Would you tell us about your family's stone? You said it was legendary. I assume there is a story or stories regarding the stone."

"Sure are. Why?"

"Let us term it curiosity for the moment."

"Curiosity? My family comes from Kilkenny in Ireland. Family legend says that sometime back in the 1790's my ancestor, one

Patrick Phalen, found the stone. Gran says that's why I'm Patrick.
She's a Phalen, by the way. Our family believes the first male child of
every generation must be named Patrick to preserve the family's
luck. If it's a girl she must be named Patricia. They think it was the
stone that protected the family during the great famine. Stone's got
a name, but it's Gaelic and I couldn't pronounce it even if I remembered it. The name means something like the stone from heaven that
fell from the sky."

"*Le Pierre du gardien du ciel*. The names are almost identical,"
Henri observed.

Laurinda pondered the significance of what Henri had suggest-
ed. *Heavenly wards? Can it be? If it's true what does their arrival signify?
Is Chris in spiritual danger as well? This is just a crazed lunatic. He's not
the Anti-Christ.*

"Please forgive my outburst, Mr. Price. Pat. Please continue."

"So this Pat was walking along the banks of the Nore River on
his way home one night and got waylaid by bad weather and holed
up in this cave near the river. Gran says that while he waited out the
storm he was confronted by one of Satan's demons. A horrible beast
with wings and tentacles. Half-octopus and half-dragon. Seems Pat
took the battle outside and while fending off this demon a stone fell
from the sky and scared the livin' shit out of this beast, which then
took off like the proverbial bat. So he picks up this stone and takes it
home. Where it sits today. You know it's funny, I haven't heard that
story since I was nine, yet I remember it just as if I were sitting on
Gran's knee right now. It was my first trip to the family's ancestral
home in Ireland."

"Dear God, what's going on here? My grandmother and her
voodoo and yours with old legends of demons, not to mention a
crazed butcher who believes in a demonic race of alien gods. Poor
Chris," Laurinda said.

"So what part do the stones play in the stakeout?"

Henri summarized his earlier conversation with Chris and the
others.

"Look, Moon's a real down-to-earth guy. He doesn't buy any cosmic mumbo-jumbo. Astrology, the occult, and the rest are all bullshit as far as he's concerned, but he's a stickler for details. If your

stones mean something, than maybe my family's might. So we better call him."

"I agree. Cosmo is starting to believe something odd is going on, and I am beginning to think he may be on to something."

"Do you really think one more stone could make a difference?" Laurinda asked. "I think we should wait until tomorrow morning to call. I'm sure he could use a night's sleep."

"I don't see any harm in waiting," Pat agreed.

"That might be a good idea. It would give me time to call *Grand-mère* and you could call your relatives in Ireland before we talk to him."

* * * * *

"Milk and cookies, huh. Not a bad idea," Cosmo said, walking into the kitchen and finding the Wizard dunking an Oreo.

"Couldn't sleep."

"Bad dreams?"

"Dreams, hell!—nightmares," the Wizard corrected. "What happened to eighteen, Cos?"

"Damned if I know. Remember what Guy Clark said about mistakes and horses."

"I know I wouldn't have rode it differently. Shit! I must be getting old. Used to be I'd get up in the middle of the night and play away my troubles, have a couple of beers, and—"

"'The ticking of the clock inexorably goes on, the howling of the stray souls of heaven,'" Cosmo quoted.

"Huh?"

"David Sylvian from 'The Devil's Own.'"

"Oh."

"Want some?" the Wizard asked, while pushing the box of cookies across the table.

"Thanks," Cosmo said, taking a couple.

"What fuckin' kind of reason can there be to butcher a seven-year-old girl? I went to that fuckin' school. I musta played on the corner where he grabbed her a thousand times. And what about those poor little kids that were raped and murdered last month? Wanna tell me why they're dead? What could a couple of kids that hadn't turned ten yet could have possibly done to deserve the horrors that were savaged on them?" the Wizard asked as he began ripping up the serial killer collectors' cards he had removed from the store's front window and the display case, and throwing them in the large clear glass ashtray in the middle of the table. With painstaking care he methodically worked his way through the cards, tearing each card into six pieces, occasionally tearing a Manson or Dahmer into smaller pieces, sentencing them to a more fitting hell.

"There's no reason for their deaths. It's like a cancer. People are dying and—"

"Bet your ass this motherfucker is a cancer. But who's got the knife to cut it away?"

"Chris has. He'll catch him."

"When? How much damage do these fuckin' freaks cause first? Gacy, 33 victims. Speck, body count unknown, maybe dozens. Bundy, 36 dead. Fish, another unknown. What a sick bastard! The son of a bitch was a goddamned cannibal, and he stuck needles in his balls so he could get off on the pain. And to top the whole damn thing off he practiced coprophagia. If that's not a portrait of evil, I don't know what is."

"Coprophagia? What's that?"

"Eating shit!"

"Really?"

"Damn straight. And while we're talking about freaks let's not forget about Roger Truman, the Dunwich Cannibal. That fucker enjoyed drinking milk shakes made of regurgitated matter with his meals. Did you know they uncovered the bones and pieces of a hundred and seventeen people on his chicken farm? Is somebody out there going to tell me there weren't any other entrees on the fuckin' menu? Or how about Dahmer, DeSalvo, and Manson, who are sitting around in prison jerking off and watching fucking TV. And that's just the top ten list."

"DeSalvo was stabbed to death in prison years ago. '73 or '74, I think."

"Good. Hope they pardoned whoever killed the bastard."

"C'mon, man, you're supposed to be the voice of reason around here."

"The hell with reason! This is Schenectady, not New York or L.A. We're twenty miles away from Albany. I thought Albany was supposed to be one of the safest cities in the whole country."

"True, but we've had a multiple murderer here before. Remember Mary Beth Tinning. What she kill—eight or nine babies?"

"How in the fuck can anyone kill a *baby*? And why do we let these monsters live?" the Wizard asked as he lit a match and tossed it into the pile of ripped up cards in the ashtray. *Why did we ever buy these horrible stupid things?* He grimly smiled as the colors sizzled out of the twisting cards. "Burn, baby, burn," he whispered. "In hell forever."

"I agree, but—"

"I don't want to hear it. We've got teenage-raping Satanists in Latham that drink piss, and this psycho-fuck killing women and children. Seems like there's a murder around here almost every day. Has the whole goddamned world gone ass over tea kettle? What happened to peace and love, or common decency and the golden rule? And more importantly, where the fuck is justice?"

"I wish there was something I could say to help . . . we're all as frustrated as you are."

"I know—ah, fuck! Maybe I'll try to go back to sleep," the Wizard said, chugging the last few ounces of milk, wishing it were a beer.

"Good idea."

"You know what we need here is Batman or better yet, Zorro. If you gave me five minutes alone with this asshole I'd carve a great big Z right in the middle of his heart. If he's got one."

"I don't think Batman or Zorro are gonna work this time. You're going to have to settle for someone like Judge Dredd or the Punisher."

"What do you mean?"

"Haven't you seen the look in Chris' eyes? I don't think this freak is going to live if Chris catches him."

"Good. I hope I'm there to see it."

"'Where do you want this killin' done?'"

"'Out on Highway 61,'" the Wizard coldly sang in reply.

Walking to the counter the Wizard picked up his shotgun and checked the safety. Pointing the weapon out the window above the sink into the moonless sky at an imagined shadowy featureless face, he hissed a fragment of a line from "Desperado", his favorite Alice

Cooper song. "'You're a notch and I'm a legend!'" As the word legend hung momentarily in the air his finger pretended to squeeze the
trigger. *Dead. That's where they all ought to be. Dead!*

* * * * *

"Morning."

"*Guten morgen*. I made coffee. I hope you don't mind."

"No. I could use some."

"I was looking at the list you wrote last night. I was thinking
that I could help you investigate the reputed Mnarian wards at the
horror shop."

"No need. The news is lying about Kthanid and the stones. The
store is a trap. Besides, it's far too dangerous at this point."

"That's what I was thinking. I agree that it's too risky for you, but
they would not be expecting a woman. With all the media coverage,
there would be curiosity-seekers going into the store. I could pose as a
fan of Lovecraft's tales. I have, after all, read most of the stories, and I
have even attended a few of Maurice Lévy's lectures on Lovecraft."

"They'd never suspect you. They're musicians and horror fans,
and you brought me music based on the Holy Ones. Maybe they'd
be interested."

"They're rare. They might not be unaware of the recordings,"
Christa said while handing Marsh a cup of heavily sweetened black
coffee.

"That may be our in. But you don't live here."

"I could be visiting a friend."

"Good. Do you know anything else about horror?"

"I've seen a great many horror films. I know a lot about Tom
Savini and I have seen all of Dario Argento's films. When I became
interested in the Holy Ones, I read everything I could find on the
subject, including fiction. I am also intimate with Anne Rice's vampire novels. In addition, I have also read most of Clive Barker's books
and quite a few of Stephen King's. I'm also well versed in the
German underground horror cinema, which they may have very little knowledge of, and don't forget I was a practicing witch and
Satanist before I discovered the true faith."

"This could work. You go in the store posing as a horror buff.
You've seen the store mentioned in the papers and you have these

discs you thought they might be interested in. You start talking about the music and Lovecraft, then you get interested in owning one of the stones."

"Maybe if one of the store owners is single and I could get him interested in me."

"If you could get a date with one and pump him for information. The papers have said they're working closely with the police. They must have information I'd find useful."

"What do we know about these two?"

"There was an article in the paper about them. It had their picture. I have it here."

She looked down at the grainy duo with cold and sparkling eyes. "This Wizard and Cosmo, they are certainly an oddball pair. One plays guitar and one sings. One tall and thin, clean cut, the other short, bulky, balding, and heavily bearded." *Look at his mustache. What century does he think this is?*

"The ape is the Lovecraft expert. The article says he is compiling an encyclopedia on Lovecraft's Mythos."

"Here is our way in. It says their store buys, sells, and trades horror items. I take in the CD's to trade or sell. I'm here visiting and I ran across the story in the paper."

"Good. But who are you visiting? It can't be me. What if someone checked?"

"In a way it could."

"How?"

"You are away in Europe, or so everyone believes. I am a known buyer of occult antiquities in Europe. We are acquaintances, and I have been thinking of buying a home in this region. Saratoga, the famous race track, is less than thirty minutes from here. I have just developed an interest in horse racing, that is why I wish to buy a home here."

"You've been studying."

"A little. So, while you are in Europe, I am using your home."

"That might work. You could call a realtor this morning and have them start looking for a place."

"I could also have my bank wire a few hundred thousand dollars to a bank here and set up an account. What about a motor vehicle?"

"You could use mine or rent one. Wait. We've no need of ruses this close to Li-ure. They won't suspect anything. You're walking into a trap set by men looking for a man. They'll never notice a woman."

"Which of these two do you think I should try to charm?"

"The Wop. He's the so-called expert."

"And if he shows no interest, should I try to attract the tall one?"

"Maybe. All we want to know is if the stones are real. You might be able to tell just by being close to them."

"Have you ever encountered a Mnarian talisman?"

"No!"

"If they have real star-stones, what do you think they would feel like?"

"How would I know?" he sharply hissed. "They might be painful to be near." *At least to me.* "There may be a chance that they won't have any affect on you at all. Maybe they only affect the Holy Ones and their inhuman minions."

"When do you want to go to this store?"

"If the other candlesticks arrive early enough, we could go there this afternoon."

"Are you going with me?"

"No. I meant you. I'll give you directions to the city. For a second I thought I might drop you off, but the police are probably watching the store, and there's a chance they might follow you."

"But that would mean they would follow me here."

"I thought of that. After you go to the store, you're going to go shopping. That should throw them off the trail."

"What am I purchasing?"

"Clothes, shoes, jewelry, anything. Maybe a couple of new horror books, whatever's currently popular, maybe something on the *New York Times* bestseller list."

"But if they follow me."

"I don't think they will, but if they do, all they'll see is a woman out shopping."

"Then we are all set."

"For now."

❦ Chapter Twenty-Two ❦

Still tired and a bit sore, he awoke alone. For a few groggy moments he sat, palms pressed to his dully throbbing forehead. Following a lengthy yawn, he surveyed the room.

Where am I? Ida's room! The events of yesterday came back to him as the sun poured through the windows. *What time?* The clock on the night stand read 4:05. PM. Showering and dressing quickly, Gregory Bradshaw Marsh went in search of his lover.

At the bottom of the stairway he heard strains of symphonic music coming from the living room. Hoping to find Ida, he went in.

Ethan Marsh sat in a dark leather armchair, a king in repose. Taking note of his cousin, he raised his finger to his lips to quiet Gregory's coming question. He extended his left hand in the direction of the sofa, gesturing for his cousin to sit. Gregory seated himself while the fragmented nightmares of the D minor scherzo of Mahler's *Seventh Symphonie* exhaled into the large room, tainting the late afternoon sunlight. When the unearthly waltz had concluded and the third movement ended, Ethan spoke.

"My dear cousin, thank you for indulging me. I have always found strains of Berlioz's *Fantastique* in Mahler's troubled, impassioned *Seventh*. I trust you slept well?"

"Yes. Have you seen Ida?"

"My sister had to briefly attend Mother. She will return for dinner, around six. She requested I entertain you in her absence. Might I interest you in a scotch?"

"No. No, thank you. But I would like some coffee. If it wouldn't be too much trouble?"

"No trouble whatsoever. Are you hungry?"

"A little, but I'll wait until dinner. I have a lot of questions."

"Ida was certain you would. She has asked if you would wait for her. As to your questions, she prefers to answer them herself."

"There is one question I would like to ask now. Ida mentioned a book, the *Zhou Texts*. She showed me four pages from it, and I was wondering what you knew about the book."

"I regret to inform you that Ida knows much more about the *Texts* than I. I have little interest in it and really would not be much help in answering your questions on the subject. When she returns, I'm certain your questions will be answered. In the meantime, I have a small private study upstairs, which contains a few paintings Ida thought you would enjoy seeing. I, as you may have noticed, have a certain fondness for the arts. Ida believes you will find them enlightening."

"I'm not much for art."

"I think these might interest you."

"Really? Do I know the artists or their work?"

"The painter's name is José Maria Estebañez. Do you recognize the name?"

"No."

"He was the lover and disciple of Meridiana Montevecchi, a sculptress of some note. We will discuss her further after you have viewed the paintings. Shall we adjourn to my study?"

In the shuttered and dimly lit study, Ethan Marsh freshened his scotch, after pouring his cousin's black coffee. On the table beside Gregory sat an expensively bound slim black book, whose cover bore a strange yellow emblem. "What's this?" he asked.

"A sentimental favorite of mine. It's a play entitled *The King in Yellow*. Are you aware of it?"

"No."

"The King is a Holy One. He appears clad in tattered rags of yellow, and wearing the Pallid Mask. At my eighteenth birthday party everyone wore a Pallid Mask and dressed in yellow, except Ida of course, who refuses to wear anything but her mourning black in honor of the imprisoned Queen. Mother had the book made specially as a birthday present for me. I often sit here and read from it. As your studies progress, I am certain that Ida shall instruct you on the King and Carcosa."

"I look forward to reading it."

"As well you should, but we shall discuss *The King in Yellow* another time."

Above the sofa that faced Gregory, Ethan switched on a lamp, which illuminated a painting that had been shrouded in deep shadows. Gregory rose from the chair and walked to the painting.

"An impressive work, wouldn't you say? Originally there were twenty-four paintings. Sadly, only three have survived," Ethan commented.

Gregory stood before José Maria Estebañez's painting of M'nagalah for two minutes before speaking. "I have never seen anything like this before. The style is . . . I don't have words for the painting's effect. This is one of the Great Old Ones, isn't it?"

"Yes, it's M'nagalah, once the master of Tethys."

"M'nagalah? Tethys? I've never heard of them."

"M'nagalah is Lord Cthulhu's right arm. The simpleton from Navarre describes him as a bulbous bloated mass with a thousand eyes and many tentacles of varying sizes and lengths. He describes the tentacles as resembling raw entrails. Estebanez has captured his image vividly in the painting, don't you think?"

"Yes. The eyes. They're—"

"Unlike any you have ever seen. Now, Tethys was a sea. Have you ever heard of the German geophysicist, Alfred Wegener?"

Without removing his eyes from the painting, Gregory replied, "No. What does geology have to do with the Great Old Ones?"

"Please allow me to explain. In 1915, Wegener hypothesized that the continents were once all one single land mass. He called this supercontinent Pangea. Slowly, over vast spans of geologic time, this supercontinent broke apart and spread. His theory is called continental drift. You will find a copy of his *Origin of Continents and Oceans* downstairs in the library. As to how this pertains to the Holy Ones, well, when they arrived here, some believe possibly as long as two hundred million years ago, the Earth was not as it is today. It is my opinion that they arrived around one hundred million years ago. At that time there were two major land masses, Gondwanaland and Laurasia. Tethys was a sea that once separated them. Today we would roughly place it where the Mediterranean is.

"There are a few points I would like to make. The first, man did not exist, so the Holy Ones preyed upon prehistoric life forms. Secondly, some believers in our holy deities, myself included, feel that there was a great deal of warring over territory by the Holy Ones. You must understand, dear cousin, that not all of our gods came here, nor did they all wish to. Before the great civil war that left them banished and imprisoned, some had perfectly acceptable hunting territories elsewhere in the cosmos. I myself believe that they chose the Earth as a base camp, which they would use as a jumping-off point to prey upon other galaxies in this portion of the Virgo Cluster. You

must understand that this opinion is based on the theories postulat-
ed by Professor Fredrick S. Blount in his self-published *They Travel the
Spaceways (Unraveling the Forbidden Secrets of the Cosmos)*."

"I'd like to read that. Is there a copy downstairs?"

"Yes, there is."

"His name almost rings a bell."

"That does not surprise me. Until he published his theories three
years ago, he chaired the astronomy department at a university not
far from where you live. Have you heard of Mohawk University?"

"Yes, it's not more than twenty minutes from my house."

"You should look through their library sometime. It is said to
surpass Miskatonic University's. A feat that is not easy to imagine."

"I didn't know they had any material dealing with the Great
Old Ones."

It seems there is a great deal you are unaware of. "As you know, our
holy deities savor fear as much as they savor flesh. Therefore, prefer-
ring higher forms of life to prey upon. The higher the level of intel-
ligence, the more refined the levels of fear. Thus the dawning of
mankind was a great boon to Lord Cthulhu and the Holy Ones as
man's emergence gave them something to prey upon while they're
imprisoned. There may be no flesh for them to feed upon, but they
have the stress, nightmares, and worries of billions to savor in their
dark slumber. And, more importantly, it gives them a means to flee
from damnation, to shatter their bonds. By divine vision and empow-
erment, they recruit humans to do their bidding. You and the members of this family are those chosen."

"Yes, Ida told me. I'm . . . the messiah, the deliverer. But—"

"Do not let Ida's age deceive you. She is the result of many
decades of this family's efforts to find a means to release the Holy
Ones. She knows more about this than I, and she is certain that you
are the gatekeeper. I have never seen her make an error in judgment,
and quite frankly, I do not believe it to be possible. But I fear I have
lost sight of why we came up here in the first place. The paintings."

Gregory and Ethan left the canvas that bore M'nagalah's image
and walked across the room to face Shudde M'ell. Ethan took great
joy in watching the look of awe that arose on his cousin's countenance. Before them hung a portrayal of a seemingly colossal, squid-

like horror emerging from the subterranean depths below the Earth. There was a wormish aspect to the elongated, slimy monstrosity.

"This is Shudde M'ell, the Burrower Beneath. I've read of him in 'Cement Surroundings.' It's in one of the books I told you about. He's the ruler of the chthonians. Lumley has written a great deal about him."

A dark vulgar laugh emanated from his cousin, "Please pardon my laughter, it's just that you remind me of myself at a younger age, when my boundless zeal for the Holy Ones produced many joyous discoveries. You have much to learn before your task is at hand. Let us look at the last painting and then I will tell you their story if you're interested."

Ethan went behind his desk and turned on the lights, illuminating a six by eight foot likeness of Cthulhu. "This is the master I serve. *Ph'nglui mglw'nafh Cthulhu R'lyeh wgah'nagl fhtagn.* Do you know the meaning of the phrase?"

"Yes. If Lovecraft translated it correctly."

Ethan continued without even hearing Gregory's comment, "Translated: In his house at R'lyeh dead Cthulhu waits dreaming. Often I just sit here and look into the painting, imagining what the world will become when he is restored as rightful ruler of this anthill. Is he not wondrous to behold?"

"Truly astonishing. Descriptions don't begin to do him justice."

"Look at him! The true monarch of this orb. Who could stand before him undaunted? Look upon the bane of man! His talons would make the teeth of a *Tyrannosaurus Rex* look like a child's. Would not the dragons of man's ancient legends envy those leathern wings? Is that not the true face of glory? Before you, Gregory, is the only true Lord of this Earth."

Gregory Bradshaw Marsh stared into the eyes of abomination, two demonic points of light centered in an octipoid head, set over a hideous mask of scaled tentacles.

No wonder the queen of red nightmare yearns for him. He is the quintessence of all darkness, Gregory thought. "You said there were originally twenty-four of these. Do you know what happened to the others? Were they all paintings of the Great Old Ones? You mentioned only these survived. Survived what?"

"They were all portraits of the Holy Ones, and although they were all destroyed, they are not completely lost to us. I possess a pamphlet of drawings, work sketches really. Each of the paintings is represented, except Kassogtha. Most of that page was ripped out. Here, let me get the pamphlet for you. While you look through it, I will tell you what I know of the history of the paintings and their creator."

Using a worn key Ethan unlocked a glass case. With reverence he lifted its contents. Three strides placed him and the sketches before Gregory. Handing it to Gregory, Ethan began his tale.

"José Maria Estebañez was born to a Catalonian whore named Teresa, sometime around 1875. During the civil war between the Carlists and the supporters of Isabella's son, King Alfonso II, Estebañez's mother left Barcelona for France. Can you imagine the humid streets and the smoky taverns filled with roasting sweet meats and the fervor of civil war? Even now I can see intrigue and death, sulking and swaggering through nearly black alleys by night, purloining secrets and blood. I can hear the disdainful murmurs and whispers that attended the balls alongside young maidens with bejeweled throats and the audacious power-seekers, their pride and their swords strapped to their sides . . . . Think of the docks and harbor filled with fortune and bright winged birds, hidden black flags, and hooded eyes. And in the taverns, dusky skinned serving wenches, bringing wine and trading their favors for gold coins and pearls. It must have been joyous to be alive at such a passionate time!

"Please pardon my digression. Teresa was taken to France and kept by a French nobleman, until he discovered that she was with child. In Paris, abandoned, left to her profession and the streets, she bore her only child, José Maria. A child she claimed was the product of a rape by an Italian sailor just before she left for Paris . . . ."

The wealth here; it all pours into my hands. The money, power. And Ida. Everything I need is here—all the information I require.

" . . . This version of Teresa's flight from Barcelona was disputed by Simone Jacqueline Delacroix in her commentary on occult art in late 19th-century Paris, and by Étienne Radiguet, who was Montevecchi's former lover and José Maria's drinking companion. Their story has Estebañez's mother fleeing reprisals apparently caused by thievery and blackmail. They say she found her way to Paris by providing her services to a young Spanish noble who was delighted to give her passage in exchange for her carnal favors. They also go on to state that it was this lusty young Spaniard who fathered José Maria. Apparently José Maria was a bright but troubled child, who spent his early years roaming the streets of Paris. It seems he was quite devoted to his mother, and added to her less than adequate income by petty thievery and pickpocketing. Some have said that the boy also found clients for her on occasion. On or about his fourteenth birthday, young José wandered into the Louvre, either looking for customers for his mother, or to pick the pockets of the rich. In the Louvre, he was introduced to his muse, painting. Here the stories abound."

He's a real piece of work; self-possessed, critical, and condescending. It's much easier to absorb this material from Ida. She appreciates my efforts, and when the work's done, my tasty reward, Gregory thought. He tried to concentrate on his cousin's tale, but his thoughts kept turning to Ida—her voice, her skin, and the dark pleasures they held.

"The first story says that while standing mesmerized before J. A. D. Ingres's *Grande Odalisque*, a gentleman approached Estebañez and inquired why he was staring at the painting. He said that the woman in the painting looked like his mother, who he explained was a beautiful flower that had been discarded by a disingenuous nobleman after she no longer served his purposes. From here, the story says that this kindly figure returned home with the boy, and upon discovering her to indeed be a great beauty, fell madly in love with her. This gentleman, rumored to be a high-ranking member of the recently formed provisional government, became his mother's benefactor until her death in 1893. A charming tale, but, I fear, completely false. First, Ingres' nude was not housed in the Louvre at any time during Estebañez's lifetime, although it currently resides there. And secondly, in Estebañez's portrait of his mother, she bears no resemblance to the woman in Ingres's *Odalisque*, other than the fact that both Teresa and the woman in the painting have dark hair. These are small points, but—"

The sound of breaking glass interrupted Ethan's tale.

"What was that?" Gregory asked, bolting from his chair. "Sounded like a window was broken downstairs."

"Please sit and be quiet," Ethan directed as he opened the drawer of the end table beside him and removed a pistol. "I don't have time to explain right now, but please remain seated until I tell you to move. No matter what happens in the next few minutes stay where you are."

"But I think someone's breaking into the house."

"We shall see."

What the hell is going on? Why isn't he worried? He must be concerned, he's got a gun. Yet he looks so calm.

Smiling an odd, dead smile, his hand resting on the pistol, his gaze fixed on the closed door behind Gregory, Ethan resumed his tale. "Now, the second story, which by the way I do believe, is not altogether different from the first. Again, this one says that around his fourteenth birthday José Maria went into the Louvre, and was discovered standing before a painting. This painting is said to be Theodore Géricault's *Raft of the Medusa*, a romantic piece, not Ingres' neoclassical *Odalisque*. I should point out here that there are many elements of romanticism present in Estebañez's work. Look at the emphasis he places on emotion and imagination. And in addition, the theme of hopeless desperation in Géricault's work seems to be present in the works of Estebañez. And if you look in the pamphlet you will see that some of the humans in the sketches are in nearly the exact positions that the people on Géricault's raft are in. I should mention that Géricault's *Medusa* was indeed hanging in the Louvre when Estebañez was an adolescent."

"I'm afraid that I don't know anything about art. I never—"

"Yes, yes. I understand. Now as I was saying, we know that as a young boy Estebañez attended the opera on many occasions. How does a young street urchin attend the Paris Opera House? There are four known paintings of operas performed during his youth. The most famous, if we can apply the term to Estebañez's work, is a scene from Saint-Saëns' *Samson et Dalilia*, which had its Paris premier in 1890. The angle of all four paintings is from the same box on the front right side. All the boxes in that area are reserved for the powerful and wealthy. How could this child of a poor street harlot gain access to a box held by one of Paris' affluent? Perhaps a kindly old French nobleman would take a small boy to the opera in exchange for a young woman's sexual favors. Or perhaps he was just trying to please the object of his ardor. It is at this time that José Maria begins to paint. It is possible that his dead mother's benefactor became his patron. But sometime in 1894 Estebañez met and became entangled with an Italian occultist. Her name was Meridiana Montevecchi. She said she was named by her mother, another Italian witch, for the fabled maiden lover of Gerbert of Aurillac, who became Pope Sylvester II, in Walter Mapes' *De Nugis Curialium (Courtier's Trifles)*. Again, it is difficult to peer through the thick mists of rumor and inaccuracies that surround her life." As Ethan spoke, his eyes, which appeared mightily angered to his younger cousin, never left the door, nor did his hand leave the pistol.

What is he waiting for? Why doesn't he go see what's going on? He doesn't seem afraid. Is the house being burglarized? In the middle of the afternoon? Is this some test? Why would Ida test me now?

"What is known of her is that around the age of thirty this witch divorced herself from a powerful Calabrian coven. Fleeing their wrath, she settled in Paris and took up with the much younger Estebañez. Why she left this coven is not known, but it is surmised that she discovered our Lord Cthulhu. How an expatriated Calabrian witch encounters Lord Cthulhu I'm not sure, but then how one of New England's oldest families encounters him sometimes baffles me as well. And I know that story. But encounter him she did, and became one of his most devoted followers.

"Here I should note that Montevecchi was also a sculptress of some repute. And it is here that her influence over her young lover becomes apparent. Prior to his relationship with her, he was the model, pardon my pun, portrait painter. Under her tutorage he became what you see here, driven, a mad genius. Whether this is due to visions, or because he had her sculptures as models we will never know. Her drawings are in the pamphlet you have. You will notice that Montevecchi's drawings resemble nothing in the history of art before them. Her merging of biological life forms with mechanics was considered at the time to be blasphemous. You must understand that the art world had yet to have even experienced the impressionists. Montevecchi's work is quite simply, at this point, other worldly. Like John Cage, Stravinsky, and Picasso after her, the world was simply not ready for her genius. As we speak, there is a young painter named H. R. Giger, another rare visionary, a magician of color and form, who has taken up Montevecchi's style, with brilliant modifications and ingenious additions. Nonetheless, her work became known in certain circles, and was much sought after. It is at this point that the noted British occultist Charles Bishop enters the picture."

"I believe I saw two or three books in the library by him," Gregory said as he again wondered how Ethan could remain so calm.

"Yes, they were purchased from a Mr. Jergens in Brussels by Mother in 1967. Now, as I was saying, while lecturing in Paris on the history of ritual sacrifice in the legendary all-female Parisian coven, Les Diables Prostituées, Bishop became enamored with young Estebanez. His attraction to dusky-skinned young men was quite well known. Bishop was a follower of His Holiness Cthulhu, as was Montevecchi. They greatly disliked each other and were only interested in their own self-promotion, each hoping for a position of power when Lord Cthulhu returned. Add to this their mutual lust for young Estebañez's favors and the fabric, as you well might imagine, becomes strained."

"I'd hate to be in that situation. But if anyone ever tried to come between Ida and me . . . I'd kill them."

Ethan momentarily considered shooting Marsh for his brash comment, but stayed his jealous hand and continued.

"Bishop promised the young painter fame and fortune if he would leave his rival's bed. It is said that young José Maria momentarily succumbed to Bishop's charms and stayed with him for a week. José Maria was quite tempted with Bishop's offer, but coming to his senses, or perhaps frightened of Montevecchi's powers, declined. It seems he was deeply in love with Montevecchi, who many remarked bore a striking resemblance to his mother. Comparisons of the portraits of Teresa and Montevecchi confirm this. After Bishop's favors were spurned, a war commenced between Bishop and his rival. At first, Bishop thought to frighten her with threats of punishment from her former coven. For years they had rattled their swords, demanding retribution for her desertion, but she felt secure, believing her newfound god would protect her. It is during this time she fell back into the dark arts, in an attempt to frighten Bishop into returning to England."

There was a muffled shuffling outside the door of the study. Gregory tried to quell his fright as the door burst open. Filling the open doorway, the sunlit hallway a brilliant backdrop, was a dark-skinned man in a black suit and a military haircut brandishing a knife with a curved blade.

"Luciferans, by the holy blood of St. Peter Martyr, I bring omnipotent God's vengeance down on you!" the intruder screamed as he stepped into the room.

Before the assassin could advance two steps Ethan expertly aimed the pistol and shot him twice in the chest. As he lay dying, he issued a whispered hiss, "We are a Hydra . . . th . . . Order will never rest . . . ."

"Cthulhu! He was going to kill us."

"They have tried before."

"They? Do you think there is another one in the house?"

"No. The members of the Order of the Sword of St. Jerome hunt alone."

"Ida mentioned them, but I had no idea they would attack you. Especially here."

"Perhaps you will now heed her warnings."

"I will. I promise I will."

"Good. Now as I was saying—"

"What about the body? You can't just leave it there."

"I will have it tended too later. These Christian irritants are nothing to fret over. There is a lesson here. The brothers of the Order can surface anywhere, at any time. Be alert, and never allow these zealots to divert you from your goal. Do you understand?"

"Yes."

"Now, I would like to finish my story. As I said, Montevecchi had returned to sorcery and through her dark arts she sent demons to inflict disease and injury upon Bishop. This may have some truth to it, as Bishop over the next two years apparently suffered many maladies. Still, he seems to have suffered more from his reported nightmares than from the sickness that assailed him. One wonders if these nightmares were not caused by the Holy Ones or their minions. Yet his obsession for Estebañez would not allow him to leave Paris. Bishop was often heard to say he would rather die than leave Paris without his heart's desire. It is at this point that Montevecchi seems to have decided that her best protection from Bishop, whom she felt was losing his sanity, would be to surround herself with converts to her master, His Holiness Lord Cthulhu. She began to lecture on the

Holy Ones and attracted quite a following. It has been reported that her flock grew to almost one hundred members. Bishop grew agitated upon hearing of her lectures. Imagine his rival for the favors of young Estebañez and Lord Cthulhu divulging the secrets of the Holy Ones. This was simply too much for Bishop to bear. He had lost the only deep love of his life, and now Montevecchi had usurped the position he desired as the next pope of Lord Cthulhu. Bishop's sanity was shattered. Upon hearing of her next lecture, Bishop went to confront her." Ethan paused and walked to a small bar at the side of the room. Freshening his scotch, he held the glass up to his cousin.

"No, thank you. I'll stick with coffee for now." *How can he just sit there with that body lying there?*

"As you wish. Now, where was I?"

"Bishop was about to confront her." *How does he do it? That body might just as well be a sleeping dog. Somehow I must acquire his distanced demeanor. I'm certain I'll find need for it in the future.*

"Fearing all was lost, he took a pistol with him. During a heated argument with her at the podium, Bishop drew the pistol and shot her dead before her followers. Miraculously, Bishop was not torn apart by her appalled sycophants. It has been said that Holy Cthulhu himself grieved over the loss of Montevecchi. There are those who believed she had been chosen to be His Michelangelo. They were convinced Lord Cthulhu wanted Montevecchi to erect statues—tributes—after his triumphant return. Angered, Cthulhu himself destroyed what was left of Bishop's mind. He was discovered the next morning near the steps of Notre Dame, unconscious and bleeding from the nose and mouth. Six months later, in his cell at the de Grandin asylum outside Paris, Bishop was found butchered in a manner akin to the mad Arab and von Junzt. What became of Estebañez over the next decade is not known, although many surmised he returned to his Catalonian homeland. The most common tale regarding his demise places it sometime in 1904, in an Andalusian monastery. He was reportedly quite mad and riddled with syphilis. I have heard it said that he contracted the disease at a young age from his mother. I personally place no credence to this, although I'm sure you will agree that liaisons of this nature do occur. What became of the works of art created by the pair of lovers is also a mystery. I, myself, believe they disappeared into the hands of private collectors like myself. All we have are the drawings in the pamphlet you hold. It and these few paintings are all that I have been able to acquire over the years. Estebañez's other paintings are rumored to have been burned by the Nazis in '41. Mother has spent thirty years searching Europe for the sculptures of Montevecchi."

Standing in the doorway, having viewed the body, Ida smiled at Ethan before gracefully stepping over it as if it didn't exist. "Ethan, I fear you will bore dear Gregory to death with your oft recounted tale. I merely asked you to keep him company while I was away."

"My dear, I had no idea that you had returned. Somehow my recounting of Estebañez's tale seems to have caused me to lose track of the time."

"It would seem so. Gregory, will you join me for dinner? Unfortunately Ethan will be unable to join us, as he has some pressing concerns to attend to. Perhaps after dinner you and I might walk in the gardens."

"That would be wonderful. Ida, we were attacked—"

"Yes, I can see you've had a bit of excitement while I was out."

"I know of no pressing matters that require my attention," Ethan said.

"Mother has requested your presence. She wants you to look over some documents for her. You should not keep her waiting." *I should like the unbroken attention of my student this evening. You would only be in the way of tonight's instruction*, she thought. *He'll be more relaxed if you're not here.*

Ethan finally realized Ida was trying to get rid of him for the evening. *What is she planning?* he wondered, while wishing he could be the proverbial fly-on-the-wall. *Some savage delight, more than likely. I'm sure I can find something to amuse myself. It's been a while since I enjoyed the company of Seton and Norma. Perhaps spending a quiet evening immersed in their carnal charms will prove entertaining.* "It probably has something to do with the salvage operation. Well, I shouldn't keep Mother waiting. Enjoy yourselves, I will see you both in the morning," Ethan said as he stood over the body before leaving the study. *Off to the ballet of flesh I go.*

"Shall we have dinner now?"

"What about the body? You can't just leave it there."

"This house has seen many bodies lying about at one time or another. I'll have it cleaned up shortly. Now, about dinner. Are you ready?"

"Yes, but aren't you curious about what happened?

"I'm sure you will fill me in."

"I will and I have a lot of questions. Ethan said—"

"The whole of the night rests in our hands, my dear Gregory," she said, taking his hand. "Enough time to discover answers and pleasure," her whisper promised, her lips an inch from his ear, her moist, heated breath inside it.

🍎 Chapter Twenty-Three 🍎

"*Bonjour*, Pat, please come in. Were you able to contact your *grand-mère*?"

"Just finished talking to her. It's late over there so she'll have my cousin Gerald send it tomorrow FedEx. We should have the stone in a couple of days. Did you talk to your grandmother yet?"

"Yes, I did."

"And?"

"She feels your family's stone is real, and I concur. I am certain the stones have arrived here at this specific moment for a reason. All we need do is determine how and when to utilize them."

"The way I see it, Moon's got point on this op, so let him figure out how to use them."

"Hi, Pat. Did you call your grandmother?" Laurinda asked as she came out of the bathroom.

"Yeah, she's sending it," Pat answered.

"Good. Let's call Chris. Maybe your stone will help. Besides, it will give me a chance to talk to him."

Laurinda dialed the number for The Horror Corner and spoke to Cosmo, who informed her that Chris had been up all night and was napping.

"Cosmo said he'd have Chris call when he wakes up," she told Pat and Henri.

"How about coffee while we're killin' time?"

"Perhaps we could have ham and eggs with the coffee," the always hungry giant asked.

"Coming right up," Laurinda said.

"Hold it. Who's the world famous chef here?"

"World famous?" Laurinda asked.

"Okay, city famous. You sit, I'll cook," Pat instructed.

* * * * *

Marsh placed the tip in the deliveryman's hand and quickly locked the door behind him. Like an impatient overseer he barked for Christa to attend him as he removed a crowbar and a dolly from a small room below the stairs. "Let's get these placed, and then we'll have time for you to check out that infernal store."

"I am looking forward to seeing these. When I was fifteen I had an interest in Eastern religion. Chaugnar Faugn has always reminded me of Ganesha."

A dark grin twisted his features as he pried open the crate that was labeled CF and removed the packing materials. "Here is your elephantine Buddha, although I doubt he will send anyone to Nirvana when he arrives," he said as the pair broke into laughter.

"I find it fascinating that Long could have described him so well without ever having seen him or read Navarre's text. You don't think he could have found a copy of Hurley's *Exiled Deities*, or S. Arnold Meyer's transcriptions of the *Three Gospels of Basolavma?*"

"Absolutely not!" Marsh said as he reverentially moved the granite figure and admired it. "Long must have certainly based his description on Ganesha. Always remember the fools thought they were playing a literary parlor game as they borrowed from virtually every nook and cranny of mythology, religion, and the occult. They never believed any of this was real. They constructed their lies from rumor and obscure reference. The fools knew nothing." Turning back to the figurine he began speaking to it as if it were a living being. "Are you ready to feast on human blood once again, my nightmarish Lord Buddha?"

"I still recall reading Long's description in 'The Horror From the Hills.' 'The ears were webbed and tentacled, the trunk terminated in a huge flaring disc at least a foot in diameter . . . its forelimbs were bent stiffly at the elbow, and its hands—it had human hands—rested palms upward on its lap. Its shoulders were broad and square and its breasts and enormous stomach sloped outward, cushioning the trunk'," recited Marsh's Teutonic Scheherazade.

"That sounds like an exact quote."

"I think it's very close. Could we open the others now?"

"Which one would you like to open first?"

"That one. ZM," she replied, pointing to a crate twice the size of the one they had just opened.

"Zoth-Ommog. Can you describe him as well as you described Chaugnar Faugn?" Marsh asked as he finished unpacking the jade sculpture.

Her hooded cold eyes reflected her eagerness to impress. "'The I-Kiribati whisper fearfully of a gigantic deity, Zoth-Ommog, who resides in the west with his lord, Cthulhu, at the bottom of the Pacific, in R'lyeh. In horror they tell of his massive, conically shaped trunk and relate tales of their fishing boats, sunk by four starfish like tentacles or appendages. These appendages are described as being larger than the coconut trees of their islands. The arms project from the upper portion of the body, just below a head which is vaguely reminiscent of a lizard, with teeth a demon would envy. Below the reptilian head is a great beard of serpentine or wormish appearing tentacles. Somewhere in this Medusan mane of tendrils rest two glaring, inhuman eyes.'"

"You quote Hurley well."

Marsh uncrated the remaining piece, Zhar, one of the tentacled twin terrors of Sung. Carved of graying wood which he couldn't identify, the mountainous mass of tentacles was gently set on the floor beside the crate as Marsh admired the craftsmanship of the four by two foot representation. "Now all we need is the skin to finish the surplice and we'll be ready to celebrate Holy Li-ure. Why don't you go get ready to impress this so-called Lovecraft expert while I place these."

"I was considering wearing all white in honor of Li-ure."

"Good. It will unconsciously suggest purity to this dabbler. He'll be so busy thanking his god for his luck in meeting you he won't suspect a thing. One other thing, do you have a necklace with a gold star pendant?"

"Yes. Why?"

"Simply for the effect the five points of the star will have on him psychologically."

"I had not thought of that. The star stones have five points."

"Don't forget the implied purity of the gold. And remove your fingernail polish."

"Yes, Lord," she said, sounding as if Marsh's every utterance were *lex scripta*. "It should not take me long to transform from Scheherazade into Snow-white."

* * * * *

"Why hasn't he called yet?" Laurinda asked as she continued to pace from the living room to the dining room and back.

"Maybe he's still nodding, or he's busy," Pat replied while pouring his third cup of coffee.

"Let's just go to the store. I'm tired of waiting."

"*Chère*, the fair one expressly stated you were not to go there."

"You don't think I'll be safe with the two of you?"

"She's got a point there, big fellow. You're armed with those shark's teeth, and yer average Joe doesn't walk around with four custom-made throwing knives. And if they can't stop someone this nine sure can," he said, patting the pistol he was wearing. "So I doubt anyone could pose much of a problem for us."

"Perhaps."

"Then it's settled."

"I'll be ready in five minutes," Laurinda said.

"Saddle up, Juma. I'll drive," Pat said.

* * * * *

Three coats were slung over the wooden chair cum coat rack near the door. Their owners, stripped to properly faded jeans replete with strategically placed holes, and baggy T-shirts (Led Zeppelin, the Cock Masters "Suck My Asshole", and Alice in Chains "Dirt", which bore suicidal lyrics jaggedly scraped across the back), stood pawing a VHS copy of Joel Reed's *Bloodsucking Freaks*.

"I heard this has got hundreds of naked twats these two guys use as furniture and toilets," the Led Zeppelin-clad leader said.

"It's got to be cool—every chic in the flick is naked. Look, it stars the Caged Sexoids and it's in Ghoul-A-Vision," the second added.

"There's like a thousand tits in this movie. I heard they use severed tits as poker chips," the Cock Masters fan excitedly commented.

"Yeah, they use bitches as dart boards, and at the end, one bitch cuts off a guy's cock and eats it on a hot dog bun," remarked the leering Zeppelin fan.

"What the hell do these idiots have to be angry about? Seems to me they've got it all now," the Wizard said as he left the store in disgust, ranting about the new breed of teenagers who seemed to have no moral sense whatsoever and far too many suicidal tendencies. "The bored little bastards should all be institutionalized."

Cosmo kept an eye on them as they ogled the copy of *Bloodsucking Freaks* which he was not going to allow them to purchase. "That's not a film for little piss-ants with no brains." He began to think he might have to put up a sign—No One Under 21 Allowed. *Don't these miscreants know they've got it back asswards*, he thought, looking at almost four inches of exposed underwear. *It's "Free Your Mind and Your Ass Will Follow", not the other way around.*

Against the biting curtain of blowing snow, a woman draped in white entered. As the stinging air and snow rushed in, four heads and a camera turned to observe her entrance. Cosmo exhaled and added his breath to the chilled circulating currents whirling into the store. The tallest of the three grunge aficionados, a thin, heavily pimpled seventeen-year-old in the Led Zeppelin T-shirt, mumbled something about showing her pussy no quarter, as the half-shaven mop atop the black Cock Masters T added, "I'd lick her ass. If she'd eat my cock first."

Unbuttoning her floor-length ermine coat Christa made a show of surveying the store. Walking to a shelf of books near the counter she removed a volume being a name she recognized, *The Hastur Cycle*. She sighed in relief. *I have made it through their wall of talismans unscathed.* After pretending to scan the table of contents she placed the book back on the shelf and picked up a copy of Michael Talbot's *The Delicate Dependency.*

Their stones hold no power. I am certain I would have felt something if they had been authentic. Marsh was right. It is only a ploy to draw him into their trap. Looking to her right, she smiled at Cosmo, who returned it, adding a nodding hello. *The man-ape Lovecraft expert smug at the center of his web*, she thought. *Shortly you will be bound in coils of another kind. Enjoy your comforts while you may. They shall abandon you soon enough.*

Who does she look like? Nico! Yeah, Cosmo thought, recalling photos of Nico he'd seen in *Creem* twenty-odd years ago. "Oooh, Mr. Wizzzz-ard. You better get your bony rear out here pronto. There's a customer that needs your special attention," Cosmo whispered into the intercom on his desk, wondering how long it was going to take the Wizard to fall under the spell of this pale beauty. *If this woman's intellect is anything like her looks, I give him five minutes at best.*

"Yeah?" the Wizard asked as he stepped through the curtained doorway that led to the stairway upstairs.

"Two o'clock," Cosmo said, gesturing toward the front of the store.

"'Wowie Zowie.' Just 'Tell Me You Love Me,'" said the ex-Zappaphile.

"'Floatin' like the heavens above, it looks like muskrat love,'" came Cosmo's musical reply.

"Don't call me Ray, and don't call me Zimmy, just call me Willis Alan Ramsey or Muskrat Sam, cause she's got my peaches doin' 'The Gumbo Variations.'"

"Whatever. Better hope you don't have 'Dog Breath.'"

The Wizard faked a scowl.

"Hi. Can I help you?" the Wizard asked.

"Hello," came the dusky, heavily accented voice. "I read about your shop in the newspaper."

She's got a voice right out of a noir film and reads the paper. Gotta be a sign.

"And I must confess to being curious. I am somewhat of a Lovecraft fan—"

So you can't have everything.

"—and I have two items I thought might be of interest to you."

"Well, I'm not the Lovecraft expert here. My partner Cosmo is the resident HPL enthusiast. Perhaps you'd care to speak with him."

"Then you are the Wizard. The musician."

She knows my name. Think, man, think. "Yeah. I play guitar." *That was brilliant, dummy. Any one of those three brain-addled morons could have come up with that*, he thought.

"Then perhaps what I have will interest you. I have two compact discs from Germany that are based on the Cthulhu Mythos."

"I'm always interested in music, and Cos, that's my partner, is always interested in anything dealing with Lovecraft."

From his desk Cosmo watched the pair exchange smiles and fidget as their conversation began.

Hot damn! He's smiling. Something's going on. 'And they whirled and they twirled and they tangoed.' If her name is Suzy I'll eat all my harps and the mike stand. Be nice if she turns out to be human. He could stand to meet someone decent after the way that fuckin' social vulture Aggie dug her talons in him. That self-serving witch was nothin' but death in red shoes, Cosmo thought as he began to sing a certain part of the Grateful Dead's "Casey Jones" softy to himself.

"Although the music is about Lovecraft's creations, only one is rock 'n roll," Christa said.

"I enjoy other genres of music beside rock. Doowop, r&b, folk. I used to be a big progressive nut. Henry Cow, Knights Templars, and Van Der Graaf Generator, but it didn't last long. I always keep returning to my first true love, r&b and the blues."

"Then you know of Can."

"You like Can?" asked the astonished Wizard.

"Yes. I once was interested in witchcraft and magic, and *Tago Mago* was named after a magician, so it became my favorite Can recording."

"Mine's *Ege Bamyasi*. Cos and I had a band in '74 that played 'Spoon' and 'Mushroom.' You don't by chance like Faust or Amon Düül II?"

"Yes I do. I used to play 'Luzifers Gholom' quite a bit. My older sister, Katrin, used to know one of the members of Amon Düül. That's how I became interested in progressive music. Before that I primarily listened to classical music. My father adored attending the symphony, and I often accompanied him on Sunday afternoons," came the words of deceit from the lightly shaded lips of the dark-souled Scheherazade. *This fool is so hungry for love, it's almost too easy.*

"I've been listening to a lot of classical stuff the last couple of years. Mostly orchestral. Scriabin, Stravinsky, Mahler. The Russians and the Germans. Kinda broadening my horizons. And I've developed a big thing for Janácek. I don't think he's capable of doing anything I wouldn't find charming."

This one loves to talk. I should be able to find out everything he knows before I leave here. "As I mentioned earlier, one of the recordings I have brought is a symphony based on the Cthulhu Mythos. It was composed by a fellow countryman of mine in the early part of the century. Sometime in the early '30s, I believe."

"First the German symphony has Leverkühn and his devil's juggling, and now Lovecraft and his demonology. Sounds interesting. I can't wait to hear it. Does it have a program?"

"Yes, it does. How did you know?"

"Just a guess. You said it was based on Lovecraft, so I made the jump to a storyline of some kind."

"You are very astute," she said, as her smile bloomed and radiated across his bemused countenance. "The program follows the Great Old Ones' journey across the cosmos to Earth and their ensuing war with the Elder Gods. We then are plunged into the dark dreams of Cthulhu and the beginnings of man. In the third movement there is a brief vocal part representing Alhazred and his black bible. Finally, in the forth movement, the seals that hold the Great Old Ones are broken and they return to reclaim Earth. Although the symphony is in D minor it opens with a B flat organ pedal, which fills the sound stage like a vast ominous curtain of gloom. Against this sonorous tableau a cello slowly rises to wander as if in a stark aimless dream, legato through chromatic fragments of the melody, then suddenly stopping. Moments later the violins, like poisonous blossoms, burst open completely, embracing the melody."

"Wow! Cos is gonna eat this up. He loves the cello." *I can't believe I'm talking to a woman who knows this much about music. I must be in a dream . . . and I think she likes me. God, look at those eyes. And she's intelligent. Maybe I should ask her out . . . she's not wearing a ring. That doesn't mean anything, this is the '90's. Maybe she's just being friendly. Well, come on . . . ask her, dummy. Ask! 'Muzzle to muzzle, now anything goes.' Later. So say something.* "Thanks." *Another brilliant response.* "You said you read the article in the paper and were curious."

"I have to confess I find many things here in America—peculiar. And being interested in Lovecraft you can well understand my surprise at the newspaper article. I hope you don't find my curiosity vulgar."

"Not at all. I'd be shocked if you didn't find the story unsettling."

"Thank you for understanding." *Change the subject. You cannot allow this one to become too curious; not about why you're here.* "I'm just visiting here, although I am looking to purchase a home in Saratoga. I love horses and I would only be a few hours by train from New York City. After London, I think New York is the most wonderful city in the world."

"Me, too. I've got a couple of friends that live there. I go down and visit as often as I can. I love the clubs and the museums. Shopping's great too. Tower, Smash, Forbidden Planet, and the

Strand—now there's a book store. I could probably live in the Strand if they'd let me."

"I agree about shopping, and I absolutely adore the city's clubs. It seems that there is never enough time to enjoy the city. There is always a dozen things to do . . . . Today must be my lucky day," she said, reaching out for a book on the shelf in front of them. "I have been looking for this for a while now."

Shit. The House of the Worm. *She would have to pick up one I don't know anything about. Why couldn't she want something of Barker's.* "That's one of Cos' favorites. Maybe you should talk to him. He might—"

Looking up, a fallacious expression of innocence appeared on Christa's face as she placed her fingers on his forearm. "If you wouldn't mind I would rather talk to you."

"Ah, I really don't know a lot about the Mythos, that's Cosmo's bag. I'm really the film buff around here."

"I adore horror films."

"You do?"

"Do you think it odd that a woman enjoys horror films?"

"Odd, no, but, somewhat uncommon."

"Years ago I had a friend who introduced me to the works of Herschell Gordon Lewis and Mario Bava."

"I have a copy of *Twitch of the Death Nerve*. Cos says it's a stupid embryonic *Friday the 13th*, but he says worse things about *Friday the 13th*, so—"

"Does he? Later I became fascinated with Fulci's ultragore. *The Gates of Hell* was my choice as the best horror film for quite a while, until I discovered Umberto Lenzi."

"Fulci's incredible, did you see *The House by the Cemetery*? And I loved Lenzi's *City of the Walking Dead*. Now there's a cannibal flick. Not to take anything away from *Night of the Living Dead*."

"I find cannibal films disturbingly erotic. Speaking of eroticism in horror film, Dario Argento's films are minor master works. After I discovered him, Argento quickly became my favorite director," she said, taking note of a poster for one of Argento's films behind the Wizard's right shoulder. "*L'Oiseau au plumage de cristal* is one of his best, and *Suspiria* was a dark delight."

"You're kidding. I loved the soundtrack to *Suspiria*. Talk about something I wanted to see come out on vinyl. It sounded like the

Devil had permanently engaged Hawkwind as the house band for Hell. The unrelenting pounding, those hellish synths, and breathy half-pained moans bent into tortured screams. Not that I didn't love the film, because I did, but the soundtrack really grabbed me. I always wanted to know who the Goblins were."

"They have quite a few recordings out on compact disc."

"You're kidding."

"I have seen the soundtrack to *Suspiria* and *Profondo Rosso*, as well as four or five others, unfortunately the titles escape me at the moment."

"They're out in Germany?"

"They were for sale, but they were German-made. The six or seven I saw were Japanese product."

"Figures. Sometimes I think every recording ever made is available in Japan. You don't happen to recall when you saw them?"

"It was only a few months ago. If you like I could contact one of my retainers and have them check on their availability."

Retainers? "That would be wonderful, but I hate to be any trouble."

Her hand found his arm again. "I cannot imagine you being any trouble to anyone."

Don't be a moron and start telling her tales of your misadventures, you were discussing horror films and things were going great, so get back to it. "I didn't care for *The Bird with the Crystal Plumage*—it's not bad, but *Terror at the Opera* is my favorite horror film, although under the influence of a couple of beers I might say *Pumpkinhead* is, but I would never compare the two. *Pumpkinhead* is only a guilty pleasure. Have you seen *The Opera?*"

"Yes. It may be his best film."

"Agreed. He's a true cinematic poet. A Hitchcock who's looked over the edge. Have you ever seen *Quatro Mosche di Velluto Gris?*" he asked without waiting for her to repl., "Whether it's a face pressed into a window or driving in the rain, his sense of atmosphere seems washed by the intimate details of reality and the vapors of the surreal. He shows us a single feather floating, or a hand slowly revolving, and we're sentenced by the unknown. That's what I love about *The Opera*. We see a woman bound by rope and terror; tears merge with blood as the rivulets seep down over the bewilderment and fear etched in her face, and we're transformed. It's as if we've become her. We sit there watching her watch, and we're bound by the horror before us just as tightly as she is. Then there's the ravens. Man, I love the ravens in *Opera*. I think it goes back to my early love for Poe. I'd kill to see the unedited version. All I have is a dub of a dub. It looks like a ham-fisted network editing job."

"I own an unedited copy. Unfortunately it is not here. I could send for it and you could make a copy if you like. I also have the uncut version of *The Church* I could have copied for you."

"I haven't seen it. Heard Argento wouldn't edit it down enough to please American distributors. *Fango* did a cover story on it a few years back, but even with that push it still didn't get released here. I guess Argento doesn't sell in America. People seem to give him tons of lip service as the master, but they don't buy or rent his work."

"I have all of his films and they are all uncut. Why don't I have copies made for you?"

"Really! That would be great! I've been trying to get my hands on real copies of his work for years, but every one I come across is chopped to shit. I can't thank you enough."

We will find some way. "It is my pleasure."

"Great! It'll drive Cos nuts."

"Doesn't he like Argento?"

"He hates Argento, Raimi, and gore in general. Hates just about anything that's not Gothic. All he wants is atmosphere and imagination. Says if you lead him to the edge of the cliff he'll jump himself, thank you. Thinks Coppola's *Dracula* is one of the only decent horror films made since Frank Langella played the role in '79. Cos goes bats for the first *Alien* film too. It's his personal favorite. Yet he's the only cat I know that ever saw *Raw Meat*."

"The film about the cannibals who dwell in the tubes of London?"

"You've seen it?"

"Yes. I own the film, if you would like a copy."

"Like a copy, hell, I'd sell my soul to see it!"

Would you now? "It is yours then. Do you enjoy the German horror directors as much as you like the Italians?"

"Offhand I don't know of any."

"We shall have to rectify that. It would simply be a crime if you did not get to see the works of Rainer Stangl, Vohrer, or Burkhard

Mengelberg. If you enjoy Argento I think you would adore Uli Bauer, and maybe Dieter Puschnig as well."

"I've never heard of any of them, although Mengelberg seems to sound familiar."

"You have to see Bauer's *Wake Him Not* and Stangl's masterpiece *The Butcher's Order*. Stangl is an Argento disciple, but his films deal with simple country peasants. They are stark and poetic religious metaphors that cast God as the true evil that damns the world to a living hell. Where Argento finds evil in the windows and hallways of the city, Stangl uncovers terror in open fields and the eyes of rabbits. Gardens become cemeteries, tomato stakes are head markers. Wells are doorways into nightmare, and the ragged curtains of dirty windows are little more than the swirling mists that cover the abyss. There is no hope of spring in Stangl's autumnal visions of dark harvests and the ever-returning razor hand of judgmental winter. In his films the land is a cursed hell because man has sold his soul for a few coins or to satisfy the heat of his loins, and so he is abandoned by God for having broken the covenant. I myself have invested in two of his films simply because I so adore his work."

Invested in two movies. Even if they're small budget films that must be quite a few bucks. Is she rich? And if she is, just what the hell do you have to offer a wealthy beauty like this, he thought.

"Allessandra Bellomo, his wife, has starred in all nine of his films. She has been offered parts in many, shall we say, mainstream productions, but refuses to work with anyone except her beloved Rainer. His sister is a ballerina in a small Viennese company, and he uses his love of ballet in every camera shot."

"His stuff sounds great. I'd love to see it."

"There must be at least ten classic German films you have to see. Reinl's *Die Schlangengrube und das Pendal*, *The Devil's Own*, the bloody carnival sideshow of *Welcome to My Nightmare*, Puschnig's classic *Enemy in the Mirror*, *Die Grabauber*, Bauer's gore-comedy *Satan Says*, Alfred Vohrer's *Creature with the Blue Hand*. Klaus Kinski stars in *Blue Hand*, by the way. Then there is Horst Kuhnlenz's bloody and bittersweet tale of a revenant haunted by familial betrayal, *Journey's End*, and Ursula Bruninghaus' gore-soaked psychodrama about a lesbian dance company of cannibals, *Bed of Black Ruin*."

"I've heard of that. Thought it was a Dutch film. Supposedly it one-ups *Re-Animator's* severed head performing oral sex on a woman by having a woman perform oral sex on another woman. Then wham a creature's head emerges from the woman's vagina and eats the other woman's face. *Fango* said it was banned."

"Not everywhere. A very close friend of mine is related by marriage to the cinematographer, so I managed to get a copy. And now so will you."

"Your incredi—thanks," *Why don't you just blurt out a marriage proposal?*

Incredible. Yes I am. "If I could be so bold, would you go out with me?"

"Would I? Sure. How about tonight?" The words were out before he could stop himself. "A friend of mine's band, the Smokehouse Prophets, are playing in Albany tonight. Maybe we could catch the show and have a couple of drinks, dance a little."

"That would be wonderful."

It would?

"Would eight o'clock be a good time?"

"Ah, eight's fine."

"Oh. I have completely forgotten about the compact discs I brought," she said, opening her handbag and removing the two CDs. "Perhaps I could trade them for the Myers book."

The Wizard looked at the discs Christa handed him, imagining Cosmos' scream of delight. "They're worth more than the book. I don't recognize either one and I'm willing to bet all my Phil Ochs recordings Cos hasn't either. If he knew about a Cthulhu symphony, I'd have heard about it. He'd probably play it in the store night and day. Hell, he's even got a Cthulhu For President bumper sticker on his car."

"For now why don't we call it an even exchange."

"Only if tonight's on me. What's this other CD?"

"The Society of the Yellow Sign. Have you ever heard of Einstürzende Neubauten or Knochen Maschine."

"Nochen who?"

"Knochen Maschine. It is German for Bone Machine."

"Never heard of 'em, but Cosmo has a copy of EN's *Strategies against Architecture* II on CD. Parts of it aren't bad. 'Z.N.S.' sounds a little like the Residents interpreting Faust."

"The two bands bear some similarities. They are both raw and contain metallic banging, as well as droning backgrounds. Some people might describe the recording as hellish noise with religious overtones."

"Hellish noise and religion! There's a combination Cos will go ape for. He's got this major league jones for Diamanda Galas, thinks she's a vastly underrated genius. You should hear him carry on about her range, something like four or five octaves I believe, her dedication and vision. He's currently going gaga over a reported recording project between her and Led Zeppelin's bassist, John Paul Jones. He went to see her perform a few months back, over at Union College—which is just a couple of blocks down the street. Thankfully I didn't have to go. Good godamighty, he musta spent three weeks raving about her performance."

"I had the opportunity to see her perform *The Plague Mass*. It was interesting, but I really didn't care for it."

Thank God. "Cos didn't get to see the Mass. She played stark interpretations of gospel and blues tunes. Cos would give his left eye to see the *Mass* performed—Christ, he fumed for a month after hearing, after the fact, she had presented it at the Victoriaville festival last year. I can't tell you how many times he's played *The Divine Punishment* and *The Saint of the Pit* in the store. I can't stomach the damn thing, but some of our customers eat it up. I'd bet he's personally responsible for selling a hundred copies of the thing. Sometimes I find some of his musical leanings, well, mystifying. Every once in a while he'll get into this mood and out comes the liturgical lamentations, things like Arvo Pärt's *Misèrere*. I don't like the stuff, but he has to put up with my doowop records." Suddenly realizing he had been babbling, he quickly changed gears. "Sorry for ranting. You were telling me about SYS."

"You needn't apologize. Lyrically the music of SYS is based on the King in Yellow. The songs, especially 'Cassilda's Song', are a cross between ethereal atmospherics mixed with postindustrial music and quasi-operatic vocals, often over a bed of indistinguishable, maybe blurred is a better word, whispers."

"Cos absolutely adores Chambers' King in Yellow stories. He's been hounding Mythos writers for years to write more King in Yellow material. He considers Karl Wagner's 'The River of Night's Dreaming' one of the best tales ever written. He's gonna go bats for this. If you don't mind I'd like to surprise him with these."

As the Wizard and Christa continued their conversation about the Society of the Yellow Sign's recording, the three pissed-off teens left muttering about censorship and taking their business to Fantaco, as Cosmo hadn't let them purchase *Bloodsucking Freaks*. Before they could slam the door, Henri stepped through the doorway with Pat and Laurinda. Turning to face the cold air rushing in, Christa saw Henri and Laurinda standing by the door. *Untermenschen!* she silently hissed, feeling her skin crawl. *They will be eradicated very soon, but unlike that egotistical bumbler Hitler, we will finish what we begin*, she thought, while continuing to maintain her soft, friendly mask.

Upstairs, casually observing the near-empty store in the security monitor Chris almost had a coronary as he saw Laurinda, Henri, and Pat appear in the store. "What the hell are they doing here?" he shouted to no one. "Christ almighty!" Wondering what the hell was wrong, Chris depressed the page tone switch on the intercom.

Cosmo pressed down on the talk button responding to the page, but Chris couldn't hear a word.

"Shit!" Chris said, realizing the intercom wasn't working. At an anger-fired pace he walked the length of the second floor and rushed downstairs. Forgetting his own rules regarding the stakeout he walked through the curtain and into the store. Laurinda immediately wrapped her arms around him and kissed him.

That's the policeman who was in the newspaper photograph Marsh showed me, Christa thought. *And that nigger bitch must be his wife or girl-friend. Marsh will love this. He said he needed one more pair of black tits to complete the robe, and hers are certainly large enough.* Christa quickly maneuvered a conclusion to the conversation, leaving the store to inform her master of the cop, his girlfriend, and tonight's date with the Wizard.

"What the hell are you doing here? I told you to stay away from this place," Chris said. "And you two. What the hell were you think-ing?"

"It's not their fault. We tried to call, but Cosmo said you were still sleeping," Laurinda said.

"I was going to call you back, but I needed to make some calls first."

"Simmer down, Moon. We've got something to tell you. You might find it useful," Pat said.

"It better be good. Real good."

"Yeah, yeah. You two guys better hear this too," Pat said to Cosmo and the starry-eyed Wizard. "Last night when Henri returned from meeting with you guys, he said something about these stones you guys got in the windows, and then Lauri shows me her stone, and pow, it hits me. I've seen this stone before. My grandmother has one over the mantle of her fireplace. Moon, don't you remember Pop telling you the story about the family's lucky stone?"

"Yeah. Something about your great-great-grandfather and some demon."

"Bingo. What if this demon was one of these alien things?"

"These alien things, as you put it, are only in books."

"Are they? I got the impression there was some talk here last night about strange things going on. Writers who don't write and stones from space."

"Christ almighty! Have you flipped out? I doubt there are any aliens floating around here."

"But here's another star-shaped stone, and another strange tale to go along with it. It must mean something."

"You're sure this stone is the real thing?" Cosmo asked Pat.

"As sure as you were born. I've held the thing in my own hands."

"That's three real ones," the Wizard said. "If this guy believes in the Mythos than he's got to believe in the stones' existence."

"So it stands to reason that the stones present a danger to his gods, and he will have to do something about them," Henri said.

"What do you think?" Cosmo asked Chris.

"Damn, I don't know. Even if these stones are real, and just for the hell of it we say they're magical or something, that doesn't mean that Cthulhu and his ilk exist. All it means is we've got some space rocks that have been carved into amulets. They're nothing more than lucky rabbits' feet from space."

"That's just it. They're lucky. Who are they lucky for? Whoever holds 'em. And that's us, and our freak must know that," Cosmo said.

"So how do we use this to our advantage?" Chris asked.

"Give it to Beckett and the rest of the media," the Wizard said. "They love shit like this."

"The stones are already in the paper," Chris said.

"Yeah, but we're not talking to the news magazines, like *Hard Copy* and *Prime Time Live.* If we start giving interviews to those sharks they'll blast this stuff all over the airwaves. It'll be on night and day, with updates," the Wizard said.

"Right. There must be a way to make this son of a bitch go crazy seeing all these stones on TV constantly," Cosmo said as he began to visualize sound bites on network television regarding Lovecraft and the Mythos. This could launch Lovecraft's works into the main-stream. King, Rice, and Lovecraft. The trinity of terror.

Cos could see the cover of the *New York Times Book Review*— Master of horror H. P. Lovecraft, dead almost 60 years, tops the charts with his atmospheric works of horrific wonder.

And then we'd get a big-budget Mythos film. None of this low-budget "loosely based on" shit. A real film with a world-class cinematographer and a real screenplay. There must be some baby-boomer director in tinsel town that couldn't get enough of Lovecraft when he was a kid. Wouldn't it be great to see a Coppola epic about Cthulhu? Now there's somebody who knows a few things about atmosphere. The Godfather *films have enough atmosphere for ten movies. And he seems to be in a horror vein these days; did a hell of a job with* Dracula. *Which reminds me, gotta find a part for Tom Waits. Like to see Ice-T in it too. Man, I'd love to be the consultant on that project. We could get Giger to do the set designs. Cthulhu painted by Giger. Man, that would be something to see. Goddamnit! It's too bad Marsden was butchered like that. What a horrible way to die. Wonder if they'll find out who did that to him? Damn shame; all those years of creativity lost . . . .. What else would we need? Industrial Light and Magic for the effects. Soundtrack by Danny Elfman, featuring vocals by Diamanda Galas. Closing theme played by John Surman on bass clarinet, with Bill Frisell's haunted guitar work floating under it. Somewhere we've got to find a place for Ken Nordine's voice, maybe he could read from Prinn or von Junzt—Alhazred! Yeah! Ben Kingsley would make a great mad Arab, and—*

"You still with us, Cos?" the Wizard asked.

"Huh? Yeah, sorry."

"I was saying maybe we should mention Henri and his stones. The voodoo connection might scare this asshole a bit," the Wizard said.

"Hey," Cosmo said, "there's an inherent racism that underlies Lovecraft's work. If our psycho is really into this stuff he might have picked up on it and taken it to heart, and I'm under the impression most serial killers are racists."

"So?"

"So, Henri's black. If you dangle a subhuman, a nigger—sorry, our killer's thinking, not mine—out there, one who's aiding us, well—"

"Sounds like a good idea. It might really piss this guy off. He'll think we've employed an inferior to aid us in bringing about his demise. I'm open to any ideas that will tighten the screws at this point. If Henri's willing," Chris said.

"But what about Laurinda?" Henri asked. "If you alert the killer to my presence it could somehow endanger her."

"I could assign a couple of men to watch her."

"No," Laurinda said flatly.

"How about if Pat here helps watch her?" Cosmo asked, recalling comments Chris had made regarding his Marine buddy's prowess and looking to Laurinda for objections.

Laurinda gave Pat a menacing scowl immediately followed by a smile. "If he'll behave."

"I will have to consult the cards and *Grand-mère*."

"Let's do it," Chris said.

As the others finished their dialogue, Cosmo sat down at his desk and again began thinking about filming the Cthulhu movie. *I'd open the film with La Mer playing as the camera pans a sunlit Pacific, and then the storm clouds would roll in as Elfman's score melts from La Mer into something dark and foreboding, then POW. Lighting and thunder claps, the ocean swells and the orchestra erupts, and there's R'lyeh, a towering black giant against the stormy sky. Then the camera slowly glides through a window, maybe through the main entrance. No, the windows better, we'll get a good look at the main entrance later. Picking up speed, the camera sharply wheels left as it tunnels down hallways bending and turning to stop on Cthulhu's sleeping form. Then a tentacle moves, or a wing flutters and an eye opens, and we're not in Kansas anymore.*

Lost in his daydream, Cosmo beamed as the others began pondering their forthcoming gamble.

❦ Chapter Twenty-Four ❦

While the plotters inside The Horror Corner held their hopeful discussion, Christa, warmed by her excitement, stood in the biting wind at a pay phone a block away, waiting for Marsh to answer.

"Yes," the cold commanding voice on the other end said.

"Lord, I have just left the store."

"Where are you?"

"At a pay booth, about a block from the store. If the weather were a bit clearer I think I would be able to see it from here."

"Hang up and call me from the car phone."

Inside the car, with the defrosters battling for clarity, Christa called Marsh back.

"Why did you want me to call from the car?"

"They might have a wire tap on the pay phone."

"Wire tap? You think they're monitoring calls?"

"Yes. Why did you call?"

"I saw something that I thought you should know about. While I was talking to one of the store's proprietors two niggers came in. One was a woman who hugged and kissed the policeman in the newspaper photograph you showed me. It was a passionate kiss."

"Stewart's married to a nigger."

"She might have been his girlfriend, I was not close enough to see a ring. While I watched them kiss, I remembered you said you need more skin."

"Are her breasts large enough?"

"Yes."

"Are you sure?"

"Yes. She was very well endowed."

"What a wonderful thought. Using her would drive him crazy. I'd love to watch his torment when he found her body. It's too bad we don't know where she lives."

"That is why I called. They are still in the store, I could follow them."

"It's risky, but it's tempting." Marsh weighed risks while Christa waited silently on the other end.

"The snow has stopped," she said. "I can see the store front. They are coming out. What should I do?"

"Follow them if you can, but be wary. This cop Stewart may be smarter than he seems. If you find out where she lives, call me immediately. And if anything seems odd or things become problematic, stop immediately and come back here. We're too close to the ceremony to blow it now."

"Here they come."

"Don't follow too closely. And be careful," he commanded.

* * * * *

"But why do they continue to resist when there is no way they can possibly prevail against what is inevitable?" Gregory asked.

Ida closed her eyes, exhaled, and composed herself before explaining. "Simply because they're alive, like the ant with his multichambered hill, or the spider and his woven tapestry of death, they build, then the hand of nature erases their efforts, so they build again, hoping against hope that this time they'll succeed."

"But the odds will be too heavily weighted against them."

"You must also take into account the insidious few, the leaders, those born as men which they transform into messiahs. Men who through deed or conviction drive them to dream with their speeches and ideas. They feed off the teachings of Christ and Muhammad. Their hearts become inflamed by the words of Churchill and that nigger, Martin Luther King. Lincoln and Jefferson are almost gods to them. Look at how the words of Hoffman, Lennon, and Dylan forge new hopes and dreams for today's youth. Their music is alive with hope.

"You must remember this: Even after the Holy Ones have returned, and humanity is shattered and disorganized, they will attempt to free themselves from the damnation they find themselves subjected to. To suit their own goals and ambitions they will pay any price. These human ants have a powerful spirit; not even Hitler could eradicate the Jews, although Cthulhu knows he tried. This race we find ourselves part of has endured for untold thousands of years, battling nature and what they perceive as evil. They have withstood the apocalypse of a thousand wars. Atlantis, Pompeii, plagues, and great earthquakes have not stopped their efforts to shape the planet to their needs and desires. Like cockroaches they live through famine, flood, and fire. Subject the fools to a thousand years of slavery and they will carry it before them as if it were a holy banner for the next thousand years. They will see the return of the Holy Ones as a new holy war, a plague of world-wide proportion, or some terrible new disaster that has been unleashed upon them. They will fight to survive. It is part of their being to survive and prosper. Tears and grief will become a forge. Oppression will be an anvil. You will offer them slavery and they will make a suit of armor from it. When God does not come to deliver them, they will create a new one. In the damp solitude of their rat holes they will plot and pray.

"To be victorious you must take the old first. They remember their triumphs, and remembering they imprint the young with hope. Weed the population down to immature and terrified youths. Keep the males at a minimum, and keep them young. This is the pool they cull leaders from. Use the greedy and the weak against them. Burn their cities and their books. Without shelter and knowledge they are little more than foraging packs. Immerse them in nightmare! Day and night grant them no rest. Scatter them. Then they will be weakened and manageable. And do not disregard the females. They are powerful, and when desperate, capable of great acts born of passion and sacrifice. Remember, she is life and inspiration to the race. The females are also teachers and more importantly, they are the nurturers. More than milk spews from their breasts as their young suckle. Never forget where there is a mother there is a she-devil, a primal demon, who will use tooth, claw, and indomitable spirit in defense of her offspring. She will willingly give her own life to save her child."

"It seems a daunting task."

"Not if you have faith in your ability to succeed. Take your vision and hold it out before you like a torch. Let the afflictions heaped upon Kassogtha and Cthulhu burn in your mind. Fill your heart with their agony, take their agony and turn it to energy unbound, harsher than the raw orb that bleaches the desert. Do you understand me?"

"Yes."

"Good. Now let's move on to the next subject of study, Shub-Niggurath."

"Why study her? I've already read a little about her in the *Necronomicon* and in Balfour's *Cultes des Goules*. It seems—"

"Apparently you have not read enough. She is not some lower-rung-of-the-pantheon godling, like E'tolvu. She is an Outer God; the bounty of creation. It is through her that our beloved mistress receives her sovereignty. To serve Kassogtha, you must also serve Ut'ulls-Hr'ehr and her mother, Shub-Niggurath. The heritage and lineage of the gods must be respected. Disrespect will only bring failure and death."

"I didn't mean to belittle Shub-Niggurath's importance."

"Then read the *Magnum Innominandum* and Thoephilus Merwin's *Four Tales Related by the Indian Shaman Chasqueneag*, then you may serve her properly."

"The Indians knew of the Holy Ones?"

"Of course." *Damnable twit! If we didn't need you!* "They inhabited this land for ten thousand years before we arrived. Do you recall reading about Cthulhu's cousin D'nüml in Winstone's *Legends of the Lakes?*"

"Yes."

"One of the Indian tribes that live near the Great Lakes, I cannot recall which one at the moment, calls her Nanabuta something, the demon spirit under the great waters."

"I remember. From a mountain of bubbling, swirling water she can arise and unleash destruction in a single moment and then disappear as fast as she appeared, leaving no trace in her wake."

"Exactly. To this day she continues to inexplicably take planes and ships without a trace."

"There was a list of lost ships in that book by Jeanrenaud."

"*Lost without a Trace.*"

"That's it. The *Griffin*, the *Cam Luc II*, the *Bannockburn*, and the *Edmund Fitzgerald*."

"Very good. While the fools try to explain the destruction she unleashes as a seiche wave or a UFO, she continues her activities unchecked and unnoticed. Soon enough they will be damned by their theories of agonic lines and UFO's. Now, back to your studies, and Gregory, while you are reading you might look at Reverend Ward Phillips' *Thamaturgical Prodigies in the New England Canaan*. Phillips also discusses the activities of certain Indian shamans and various legends that Merwin refers to. Reverend Phillips, by the way, was the third cousin of Merwin, on his mother's side, and her mother's mother Glyna was a Newburyport Marsh before marriage. There is also a book you should look at by Virginia Marsh-Lloyd, who lives near Witch Well, Arizona, entitled *Mother Born of a Thousand Tears*. It is a collection of Indian legend, Mexican, and American folklore from the southwest that deals with She Who Will Come."

"Arizona, New York, Vermont, Maine, Minnesota, Connecticut. It seems like there are Marshes everywhere."

"They are. One can find them from New Orleans to Oregon. After the Holy Ones have returned, you may find many of them helpful. Remember, as acting governor you will need a police force. Now, I have a few errands to run. We will have dinner together later and discuss Shub-Niggurath further. And if you're good, I'll bring you a surprise."

"I'll be good," he said, hoping the surprise would be young and unwilling to die.

* * * * *

Marsh's black felt-tipped marker flew across the page as he tried to compose another note to Chris.

dear boss (stewart) -
YOU DON'T MIND IF I CALL YOU THAT
DO YOU? AFTER ALL, WE DO SHARE A BOND NOW.
DID YOU ENJOY MY GIFT?

Beside him sat his portable Sony telephone and a heavily sweetened mug of steaming black coffee. *It's been twenty-seven minutes since she called. What in the name of the Holy Ones is going on? I should have told her to stay on the line so she could update me. Most Holy Kassogtha, hear me. Allow us to find out where this nigger bitch lives. If I could take her as the next victim the police would be so demoralized, their fear would spread like a full-blown cancer born on the fleet breath of the fourth estate.*

Anxious and impatient (forced into actions seemingly outside his direct control), the fingers of his left hand began tapping on the phone while his right returned to the note.

I'M WATCHING.
DO YOU BELIEVE THAT YOU ARE randolph carter OR titus crow?

DO YOU BELIEVE YOU COULD STAND BEFORE US AND LIVE?
SOON I SHALL DELIVER ANOTHER GIFT TO YOU.
I HOPE YOU'LL LIKE IT.
CEL GOR'RU GR'XUM FNG'I

P.S. I CAN'T WAIT TO BITE ON YOUR
BELOVED NIGGER'S TITS!
THEY'RE ABOUT THE RIGHT SIZE,
DON'T YOU THINK?

Laughter filled the chamber as he envisioned Chris reading the post-script. *It's too bad I can't tell him about those hapless fools Desmond and Marsden, but someone might be able to link her to their deaths, and we can't have that. Not when I'm this close.* Eyes fixed on the dark circle which had been Donnalee O'Donnell's right aureola, Marsh began to think about how the media was portraying him. *Small-minded fools! They have no conception of what they're dealing with. They think in terms of a lowly serial killer, street slime, uneducated trash, merely taking ten or twenty lives. Why can't they understand? I am not one man, alone and mad. What they face is a general. A leader with vision and power beyond dabblers like Khan, Hitler, and Stalin. I shall truly be the Earth's conqueror, ready to sweep it clean of vermin, ready to fill their holy larder with flesh and fear. Once I suckle from her holy teats I will become immortal, and my name will ring throughout the cosmos with theirs forever.*

* * * * *

On the phone with Rolly, Chris sat at a coffee table cum desk discussing the proposed media blitz and Henri's involvement.

"So, how's horror 101 coming along?" Rolly asked.

"You wouldn't believe how much of this crap there is. Don't suppose you have any good news? I could use some."

"Not really, but look at it this way, at least you don't have to sit here and talk to the looneys. Louie the Shadow has been here twice to confess."

"Lemme guess, Cthulhu took his Mad Dog money."

"Close. He's holding the Mad Dog for ransom."

"Ransom?"

"You heard right. I don't stutter, do I?"

"Ransomed for what?"

"Blood. Louie's so out of it, he doesn't even know our butcher is cutting off their breasts. He thinks the killer wants blood."

Chris shook his head recalling some of Louie's past confessions. "Guess every city needs a few."

"You missed a few good ones. I had one woman here yesterday afternoon who tapes her vagina shut with duct tape to keep this Cthulhu thing from escaping. Then, this morning I had the pleasure of talking to a fifty-two-year-old woman who told me she's the killer. And get this, she's made the pact with these beings because Elvis was an avatar of Cthulhu. Imagine, Elvis is coming back with tentacles. I thought when he came back with the white jump suit it was—"

"Christ, Elvis! I'd forgotten about the unzipped. Wanna trade places with Willie? He hasn't had the fun of interviewing many of these weirdos."

"Not a chance. I'll stay here, thank you. I actually had dinner with my wife last night."

"Anything good?"

"Hot antipasto, garlic bread with honey butter, and veal piccata."

"Tell Jan-Gee I'll be over for dinner as soon as this case is wrapped up."

"Will do, but only if you bring Lauri."

"Deal. Hey! If Jan-Gee decides to barbecue any of her marinated shrimp kabobs bring me a few."

"No problem," Rolly said, breaking into laughter. "By the way, the role-playing angle didn't turn up anything."

"Figures. I'll touch base with you later."

Hanging up, his thoughts and stomach focused on food, Chris started quietly singing, "'My neighbors grow their carrots, radishes, and beans. Me, I'm watchin' sprouts pop up from tiny little seeds, 'cause summer ripened cukes with mayo, are just about all I need.'"

Soon, Chris old boy, soon. You'll be out in the yard putting Miracle Grow on those little plants, watching 'em grow. I can smell them now. For the first time in days a smile came to his face. *Yep. Making love and homegrown cukes, the two best things in the whole damn world. And maybe tea. Think I'll try planting burpless this year.* "'Cause summer ripened cukes with mayo, are just about all I need'," sang the off-key tenor as he began to think about slicing up one and putting it with a little mayo between two freshly cut slices of seeded Russian rye from Mont Pleasant Bakery.

* * * * *

Pat pulled his a-season-away-from-a-full-blown-case-of-rust, four-door Chevy into the main branch of the library's parking lot on Clinton Avenue, four blocks from The Horror Corner. He parked in the first row. Three rows behind him and five cars to the left, Christa slid Marsh's Grand Marquis into an open slot. Letting the trio enter the building, she followed, pausing at the main entrance. While pretending to look over business cards and event notices tacked to a bulletin board near the front door she watched Laurinda walk into the center of the library and sit at a desk in the reference section. Quickly walking to the reference desk, she asked Laurinda where fiction was located, while taking note of the name plaque on the desk. Laurinda A. Sanders—Reference Librarian.

From her vantage point in the fiction section Christa watched Laurinda for ten minutes, until she stood and put on her coat. After Laurinda left, Christa walked back to the reference desk and asked the name of the helpful black woman who had assisted her. Miss Sanders was the reply.

As the trio exited the lot, Christa started the engine and followed them twenty-two blocks. Turning right on Hampton Avenue she quickly pulled to the side, waiting to see if they would stop or pull into a driveway. Fourteen houses down Pat parked as Laurinda and Henri got out of the car. When Laurinda and Henri were inside Pat's Chevy pulled away and Christa slowly drove by, taking note of the house number and the fact that Laurinda and Henri had gone in the right side doorway. Upper flat, she thought, as she drove four blocks before pulling over and calling Marsh.

* * * * *

"That's perfect! She must shop at the Price Chopper on Eastern Parkway. Where this one did her marketing," Marsh said, pointing to the tanned flesh of Donnalee O'Donnell. "Now all I have to do is watch her. But first we have to deal with your date this evening. You don't have any idea where he plans to take you?"

"He mentioned seeing a friend's band in a club."

"The police will be watching him, but I think they'd let him go to a club. It's public and they could easily put men in the place."

"Does it matter where we are going? I was under the impression I was only going out with this dolt to garner information from him. Were you planning on something else?"

"If the opportunity presented itself I thought it might be a nice touch if we killed this Wizard, but I'm still not sure we need anything more from him. You said you felt nothing when you passed by the stones, and that was really my only concern."

"I agree the stones seem harmless, but he still might have some information. Perhaps he can tell us something about this nigger and her cop lover that could help you."

"Maybe. You must be extremely cautious tonight. Play down the Lovecraft angle, at least for a while. Weave your web slowly."

"I encountered no problems with Desmond. I should not think this overgrown adolescent will be much of a problem for me. I also have been toying with the idea that I may be able to deal with him the way I dealt with the writer."

"No! Even though that's tempting I'm certain he will be followed, and you've no way of knowing by whom."

"What if I find out he is not being watched by the police?"

"How could we be certain?"

"I should think he would know. I might be able to find out directly from him."

"We'll talk more about this later. Right now I want you to begin practicing your part of the ritual. Time begins to grow short and I want no mistakes made. Read this well. Tomorrow we'll go over it in depth," he said, handing her a handwritten page of text.

Taking the page from Marsh, Christa sat beside him and began to read as he picked up two skins and began stitching them together.

With great attention to phrasing and pronunciation Christa practiced the rite.

Her priest will recite the following passage as the cantor chants the Incantation of Calling over the sacrifice.

Her priest will speak the following words:

> *Mother of demons, hear us!*
> *We offer this flesh to open the canal of your birth.*
> *Use its blood as a river to carry you to us.*
> *Use our prayers as a beacon.*

The cantor will chant the following passage after Her priest's benediction:

> *Iä! Kassogtha! Visoc curus noc g'ghna i'gaq!*
> *Ig'll pn'ghy ntils.*
> *Isg Hebyl'ctri nbeh'rt siv'lim.*
> *Ot'tiwo yrautcnas ry'msi.*
> *Cic'rl tuos gnis llirr'em Ncucurus dlr'um.*
> *Dlr'um yg'bss apu bt'hsew dlr'um scm'ifo.*
> *Bninc neleh Cau Mo!*
> *Kassogtha vti Vo'ddabr'xs,*
> *ytsi'mm cm'och bs'as m'ng G'uffr Iä! Iä!*
> *Cic'rl vm Vo'ddabr'xs!*
> *Cic'rl vm Ro'tmirp'ih!*

Her priest will carve the sign of Kassogtha into the lower torso of the vessel and speak the following words:

> *With this blade I open the way.*

The cantor will place her left hand in the opening of the vessel and after partaking of the blood will sing the opening command:

> *Cic'rl Kassogtha neleh vtiiv Cthulhu,*
> *Kashkash ubh'sotti R'lyeh!*
> *Bninc Cau Mo!*
> *Iä! Iä! Kassogtha!*

After the opening command Her priest and the cantor will take the holy blade and cut their left palms and join them together. After this they will place their hands on Kassogtha's altar and chant three times:

Iä! Iä! Kassogtha!
Bininc Cau Mo!
Cau Mo Kassogtha! Iä!

"Lord, what if the fools really possess Mnarian stones, and the ones they have displayed are only imitations made to lure you into the store?" Christa asked as she finished reading.

"If there was a real stone anywhere in the store I think you would have felt its vile presence. The stones merely represent the dreams of these sentimental ants. They're little more than a symbol, like the cross. These ants dream of crushing me, but they haven't the power or the vision to stop Li-ure. They see me as a nightmarish cancer growing on the edges of their milk and honey society. Their media has dubbed me Nightmare's Disciple. How little they understand this disciple's dreams of nightmare. Soon they will see the fruits of my prayers and preparations. Instead of a picnic feast to fatten them-selves on, they will see a great boot stomp down upon them. I live to watch them scurry about as they attempt to escape the damnation that awaits them.

"If they really possess the stones, we'll find a way to destroy them later, or we will use our newly acquired herd of slaves to collect the stones and place them somewhere where they will be no danger to the Holy Ones or ourselves. Besides, these infidels have no idea who the real enemy is."

"But if they stop the man they stop the ceremony. They need not believe in the Holy Ones to stop you," Christa observed.

"No, they need to be lucky or have us become careless. Neither of these things will occur," came his royal decree.

* * * * *

I wish we'd get a break. Sooner or later this asshole's got to make a mistake. Why couldn't it be now, before someone else is killed?

"What's shakin' Chris?"

"Not much, Cos. Not much. I was just getting ready to dive into the next batch of books."

"Which ones?"

"Let's see. Here's Robert Bloch and Frank Belknap Long. Houdon's *Death beyond Sunset.* She's the poet who doesn't write, as I recall. I can't wait to tell Lauri that I spent a Saturday afternoon reading poetry from some deranged hell. Man, she's gonna bust my chops for sure. I'm not big on poetry. And here at the bottom of the pile we have a couple more Lumley books and Aasterud's *Black Tales*. Too bad I can't get college credit for this stuff. Course if we could, you'd have a doctorate. How's the Wizard doing down there?"

"Nervous as a mouse at a cat's birthday party. He's been memorizing Mythos names and facts for over an hour. Man, I hope this evening goes down okay. He hasn't dated much this last year."

"Bad experience?"

"Bad! The bitch was a gold-digging vulture. She thought we were going somewhere. You know, big money rock stars; top-shelf coke and ambassadorial hotel suites. Once she found out we weren't interested in recording and touring, and all the bullshit that goes with it, she dropped him like the proverbial rock."

"I heard you guys play once and I thought you were good. I was under the impression that all bands want to record and make the big bucks."

"We just enjoy playing. It helps pay the bills and we get to have some fun. We had a deal working a few years back, but when the A&R man started spitting out names of producers—this cat from WEA told us he thought this twenty-something, hot-shit-guaranteed-hit staff producer could make us sound "really" great. Well, after ripping into this asshole, the Wizard told him to go to hell. Told him to be sure he took the express elevator. If you ask him to define music, he'll quote Thomas Carlyle, 'Music is well said to be the speech of angels', and then amend the quote with . . . and they don't get paid or prostitute themselves. All he wants to do is play what he feels, when he feels, and I'm in complete agreement. By the way, I wanted to thank you for calling off your baby-sitters. He was spitting fire over being out with her and being watched."

"I guess it would be a pain," Chris said, although he had no intention of letting the Wizard out of his sight unescorted. "But it was for his own good."

"He knew that, but thanks for backing off."

"No problem." *I hate doing this!*

"I called some of the news people to set up interviews. We'll start on Monday with WNYT and WRGB. They'll be coming in the morning, and then in the afternoon we'll start with the TV magazines."

"Good. By the middle of next week this story should be plastered on just about every channel."

"You know you're going to have to talk to some of these people."

"Yeah," Chris said.

"Can I ask you something? You see a lot of murders. How do you cope with seeing dead people all the time?"

"I guess the same way everyone else does. You put one foot in front of the other one and keep walking. A couple of times I tried to wash away some of the blood in beer. Mostly I rely on my friends. Pat tells the worst jokes and Lauri, well . . . and then there's my cukes. All summer I'm out there watering and weeding. I guess that's how I make sense of everything, standing there havin' a smoke and watering them while the sun sets. For ten or twenty minutes the world stops screaming and I find a little peace. I think it's those tender mercies that keep me straight."

"*Tender Mercies*. Did you see the movie?"

"Yeah.

"Duvall's one of the Wizard's favorite actors."

"One of mine too. Lauri says there's only two themes in movies that appeal to me, the cost of vengeance and the dream of redemption."

"Why does everything seem like it either deals with agony or ecstasy?"

"Maybe it's because we walk aimlessly through our timid, self-shackled lives afraid to really live, or because often the grandeur of our dreams exceeds the scope of our life spans."

"Who said that?"

"Me."

"Remind me to give you some Graham Greene to read when this is over."

"'Catholics and Communists have committed great crimes, but at least they have not stood aside, like an established society, and been indifferent. I would rather have blood on my hands than water like Pilate.'"

"Huh?"

"Graham Greene. Remember me? The guy in love with the librarian."

"Sorry. I never meant to imply you were a cretinous yahoo."

"Forget it, we're even. I wouldn't have thought you read him either."

"Cos! You fall in or what? I could use a hand down here," the Wizard barked into the intercom.

"Tell him I'm on the way. He always gets this way before a date." Three quick steps toward the summons Cosmo ripped into Jack Bruce's "Never Tell Your Mother She's Out of Tune." "'When I hear that big black whistle they blow, I feel inside it's time for me to be going.'"

❦ Chapter Twenty-Five ❦

The Wizard, with slumped shoulders and a frown, sat in a dark gray office chair behind the glass counter staring at a pair of Bob Murch's RAFM lead miniatures used for Chaosium's role-playing game *Call of Cthulhu*. In his lap sat an open copy of the fifth edition of the game, which he'd been browsing through trying to brush up on Mythos fact. After reading about the two barrel-shaped, star-headed figurines on the counter, Elder Things they were called, he memorized the Mythos prehistory of Earth and was working on the pronunciation of Mythos names.

Nyarlathotep, *NIGH-ar-LATH-oe-tep*. Nyogtha, *nee-AUG-thah*. *I'm never gonna learn the names of all these things before tonight*, he thought, as he finished the N's.

"What's shaking?" Cosmo asked.

"Brushing up for tonight. We were talking about horror films and music, and that went great. Man, she's into some deep gore and shit, but she's also a Lovecraft buff."

"Yeah. So?"

"So I don't know much about this Mythos crap."

"Relax. You know more about the subject than you think."

"How do you figure that?"

"Osmosis. You've been listening to me talk about it since what, '69, '70. You just don't care for it."

"Than how come I haven't heard of half of the names on this list?"

"It doesn't matter. The point is, you know the other half. The glass is half full, not half empty. Look, you know the basic history and a few dozen stories. I doubt you're going to spend the evening discussing Lovecraft. You're going to Pauly's, right?"

"No, Bogies. Gary's playing tonight."

"You're taking her to see the competition? If you're going to listen to them lowdown funky blues and hoist a couple I bet you won't talk about horror too much."

"Maybe not. Hey, I've got something for you," the Wizard said, taking the two CD's Christa had given to him from under the counter and handing them to Cosmo. Worry left his face as saw the ecstatic Christmas morning reaction he'd expected.

Cosmo flipped as he instantly recognized the Yellow Sign on the cover of the first disc. The wrapping was off the presents and the fireworks were exploding. Without even looking at the second disc he asked, "Where did you get this?"

"From? Shit! I didn't get her name. I've got a date with a knockout and I don't even know her name. Man, I must be getting old, or stupid."

Half laughing at his absent-minded friend, Cosmo said, "You don't know her name, and I thought I was bad." Looking at the second disc Cosmo recognized Cthulhu, Yog-Sothoth, and the Spawn of the Green Abyss on the cover. "What does *Auf-stehen von GorB Alt Eins* mean?" he asked as he read the title.

"The rise of the Great Old Ones."

"The fall and rise of the Great Old Ones. Someone's finally composed a Mythos symphony. Incredible!" Opening the jewel box and removing the booklet he scanned the liner notes. *"From the nightmare encumbered visions of American horror writer Howard Phillips Lovecraft (1890-1937) comes Reinhart Aldric Knaup-Krötenschwanz's apocalyptic third symphonie . . . The expansive textural sting of Gerhard Christoph Neubauer and the Saarbrücken Radio Symphonie Orchester . . . ."* "Yes! Eight pages of notes. In English." *"The cello, Cthulhu's voice throughout the eighty-two minute symphonie, slowly rises from the gloom to wander, legato through chromatic fragments of the melody . . . the passage's seamless dreaming abruptly ends as the winds deliver a dramatic glissando . . . ."* *Cthulhu is represented by a cello in this! Is this other one a symphony too?* "Where did she get this stuff?"

"Germany I guess. That's where she's from. And by the way, it's not new. It was composed in the '30's."

"The '30's! We gotta get some of these. I can sell a hundred of 'em just like that," Cosmo said, snapping his fingers. "If we can get some more of these I'll put 'em in the next flyer. Forty bucks each and I'll pick up the shipping. How much did you give her for these?"

Smiling, the expert horse trader said, "A copy of Gary Myers' *The House of the Worm*."

"That's it? It's still in print?"

"Yep. Saw it listed in the current Arkham House stock list."

"You dog. Anybody can buy that for less than fifteen bucks. These are worth thirty-five or forty bucks apiece. Maybe fifty."

"Hey, I'm buying tonight. That's all she wanted, except me of course."

"You better treat this woman right. I want to talk to her. Who knows, there might be more of this stuff."

"Before you get too hopped up you should look at the booklet for The King in Yellow CD. Based on what she told me about the band and the music, I think you'll find that one just as interesting."

"I will while I'm playing the symphony," Cosmo said as he turned and walked to his desk.

Placing the disc in the Denon DCD-1520 and pushing the play button, he adjusted the volume control knob of the Adcom GFP-555 II preamp and waited for what he hoped would be a chilling musical experience. Moments later the opening strains of Knaup-Krötenschwanz's aural nightmare began filling the store. Lighting a Kool, Cosmo smiled as a somber organ chord droned under the wavering notes of a single cello, which began swirling around the melody the double basses embraced. Just before three tympanis erupted, causing the Wizard practically to jump from his seat under the left channel speaker, the wavering melody played by the cello brought Ralph Vaughan Williams into Cosmo's soaring thoughts.

"Cthulhu's ascending all right," he whispered.

* * * * *

He was hairy when it was cool to be hairy, but not thin or fair. Amid the Apollonian physiques and blonde curls of his Aquarian peers he was dark, bestial, and brutish—outside. Inside he was light, a son of the water, an angel of the future—masked by skeptical misgivings and timidity.

As a youth he dreamed half adventures—great openings, full characters, but the middle was too fat, too cloudy, and the end was always missing. In the middle of his mental wanderings he often wondered why he hadn't packed batteries for the flashlight. There he'd be, halfway home on a isolated dark road, pursued by agents of some nefarious skullduggery, when the flashlight failed and his ideas left him.

So he watched, absorbed. Almost anything and everything. Sometimes he'd touch—Bonnie, Debbie, Mickey, Sharon; tall, thin, Jewish, glasses, short hair, curly, black, Polish, Rubenesque, it didn't matter. Only their eyes mattered. Only the light in their eyes. Dreaming about the light in Virve's eyes is how Willie found him, staring at a photograph of lost love, filled with ideas and the hopeful silly inventions of scared seekers.

"Hey, Cosmo, are you busy?"

"Not really, just daydreaming. Guess you could say 'I was walking a long dark road trying to create a map to the future with yesterday's broken dreams.'"

"Oh? Could I ask you to look at something for me?" Willie asked, handing a folded piece of paper to Cosmo.

"Sure. Whadaya got?"

"These are the words of a song I remember my father singing when I was young. I wrote them down a few months after he died. And I was thinking, you being a blues expert, you might know what the song is. If it helps, I remember him sounding something like John Lee Hooker when he sang it."

"Expert. Hardly, I just have an oversized interest, but I'll be glad to look at them." Cosmo read aloud—

> *'My heart's cold, my minds on fire,*
> *and the bottle's empty.*
> *Five empty rooms, six full chambers,*
> *and the clock's run out of time.*
> *I don't want to fight, I don't want to cry,*
> *Just give me an answer why . . . Then let me die.*
> *My woman's gone, took more than my heart,*
> *when she left me here to cry.*
> *Lord, seems I've lived it all,*
> *been troubled, tried, and tempted.*
> *All she's left me is my Smith & Wesson*
> *and this cold, cold resolve.'*

"Do you recognize it?"

"No, but I like it. Can I keep this for a while? I'll see if I can find out what this is. I have a couple of friends who know more than me. And the Wizard is going to see a friend's band tonight. Gary, that's his name, is a walking blues encyclopedia. If he doesn't know it we're going to have to call Alan Lomax or the Smithsonian."

"You really don't have to go through all that trouble," Willie said, not catching Cosmo's joke.

"Trouble? You hand me a blues number from at least twenty-five years ago that I don't know, that's not trouble, it's fun."

"I really appreciate your help. I've wanted to own this song since Pop passed away."

"I know just how you feel. Now, tell me everything you can remember about the tune. Think you could sing it?"

"Yeah, but I doubt you'll want me too."

"How bad could it be?"

"You'll probably wish you'd never met me."

* * * * *

"Henri St. John de Baptiste Freniere, got it," Beckett said.

"Front page Monday morning, right. And play up the voodoo." Chris commanded.

"I will. You know, after they read this they're going to climb all over me looking for comments."

"Cosmo's gonna give 'em plenty, so clam up and play dumb. I want this guy so mad he'll pop."

"Maybe he's stopped. Sometimes they do that."

"Not this one. He said we'd meet soon and I believe him. Look, I gotta run, so write me a winner."

"Will do."

* * * * *

As the car drove past the "Entering the City of Albany" sign, Christa put Marsh's plan into action. "Are there any raves or, what do you call them here . . . industrial dance, alternative clubs here?"

"Raves? Here? No. The Tri-Cities isn't quite that hip," he replied, lighting his third cigarette in twenty nervous minutes. "It's not really hip at all, but we do have one club that caters to the alternative crowd. It's small, loud, and garishly parades its hip pretensions. The music runs the gamut from techno to grunge to post-industrial dance and S&M infected goth. Typical crowd; flannel shirts mixed with the leather fetish crowd, and some nose rings, and from time to time a Count Dracula or two, and maybe a witch," the Wizard said with a clownish little smile.

Returning the smile with a faint laugh, the ex-witch, ex-Satanist said, "It sounds like fun. Industrial dance and trance are very big at home right now. My best friend, Malka, just adores Project Pitchfork and Yelworc. It has been years since I was in an American underground club. Would you mind if we popped in for a drink? I would enjoy seeing how today's American youth party."

"Sure. We're not too far from it." *Not far enough! Shit. Now she's gonna see just what a hard-ass you've become. If there's a band keep your mouth shut. You're way too critical of this angst-powered grunge. A denim jacket with a Pittsburgh Pirates' pin and a THE RING AT THE MET T-shirt—shoulda worn something different. Dumb idea to wear this—she's gonna think I think she's a Valkyrie or something.*

QE2, a converted hamburger joint turned club, was a noctuary of aural napalm and blastbeat riffery reflecting off rank gaunts in stream of consciousness voices and uniforms of preplanned anger. The self-concerned and the artsy, elbows and comments carelessly striking anything in their path, milled about like ghouls in sub zero weather. The Wizard began to wonder what he had gotten himself into. Turning away from a pale gaunt perfumed in body odor, the Wizard found himself toe to toe with a lone blue mohawk sporting a tattoo of a razor blade above its right ear. *Shoulda worn my ruby slippers*, he thought, wishing he were home, or just about any place else.

T-shirts expounding the religion of the young surrounded him; *What's Good is Gone—What's Left is Ours!* Edvard Munch's *The Scream*. *Free Mason* was locked arm in arm with *Jeffrey Dahmer All American Boy (Eater)*, while Radiohead "Creep" bought a beer for Lush. A thin girl wearing *I Blow Minds For A Living* held hands with *I Love Chicks With Big Tits*.

Man, you were through with this punk-ass shit in '78, the Wizard thought.

While the Wizard continued reading the proverbs and war cries of dissolution and resentment, Christa repelled the stares of two hungry males and thought about a deathly thin young Sex Pistols' fan she had devoured in more ways than one in '82. *This was once home*, she thought as the sweat and pheromones swirling through the hot club caressed her libido. For a moment her former nocturnal addictions returned and she was back in the clubs of London with a gram of coke in her purse, eyeing busty young girls with chained nipple rings and zealous tongues of sweet fire. An elbow and a wink jarred her from her flashback; a silent curse followed the fuck-off glare she hurled at the hard young cocksman with far too much swagger.

From every corner of the stale- smoke- and sweat-filled club the well over a hundred decibel *Boom-Boom-Boom-Boom* of distorted electronics repeated endlessly while a demonically-treated voice unrelentingly commanded, "Suck your Master, clean!" Twelve hurried loops of the command had the Wizard ready to beg for something a little more creative.

Can't they play "The Dominatrix Sleeps Tonight" or "I Eat Cannibals?" At least Total Coelo doesn't sound like a herd of methed-up dinosaurs slam dancing, he thought as the unrelenting pounding of Underground Kingdom of Cruelty's "Suck Your Master, Clean!" ended and was replaced by the much faster synthesized techno beat of Cannibal Coven's "Crackwhore." Above the techno-blitzbeat a woman's detached voice coldly asked "Have you ever fucked for a rock?" ten times in the song's first minute. *No melody and really snappy lyrics. Boy, am I in trouble*, the Wizard thought.

Cold bottles of Bud in hand, they walked through two pairs of heavy doors into the rear of the club to be assaulted by the deafening roar of Alice in Chains' "Sickman."

"So this is the music of America's youth," Christa yelled over the assaulting sonics.

"This be it! Anger directed at an enemy I don't see. Maybe I'm just gettin' old," the Wizard yelled back over the blurred power chords of slashing guitars and the Armageddon-stampedes-into-your-town bass. "It's little more than regurgitated bile from Spahn Ranch rejects."

Turning, he saw angst seated at a corner table with his finger in apathy's vagina. *Boring*, she yawned. *Show me death*, her cerebellum moistening as she began dreaming in red.

Alice in Chains faded into the Stone Temple Pilots' "Sex Type Thing." Hoping against hope, the Wizard wished this club would up and fly away as the song ended. *Be careful what you wish for, moron*, he thought thirty seconds into the next piece of music. Although he didn't care for the ethereal electronic soundscape (clouded with mysteriously haunted female vocals that seemed to evoke an almost religious sexual tension), he was more than a little thankful that the distortion-driven grunge of Alice in Chains and the Stone Temple Pilots had ceased temporarily.

God, I've gone from grunge hell to darkambient-goth hell, but at least these people have some sense of melody and structure. What the hell was that? Synthesized birds? Great, we're playing minimalist Messiaen from the dark side. Sounds like Black Tape For A Blue Girl or Jarboe on downs. Gimme strength and gimme shelter, he thought, as the dark ambient atmospherics faded and 7 Year Bitch kicked into the postpunk-metal college radio hit "Derailed." *Slash, burn, and a double shot of suicide, is that all they know? Thought Nirvana was bad, but they're fuckin' geniuses compared to this crap.*

"In '68 I loved the MC5 and the Stooges. I knew where to direct the anger of my youth. And in the '70's there was a bunch of punk bands I liked. I understood the Clash and the Damned, and I thought the Dead Boys and the Buzzcocks were great, but this. I just don't get it. They all want to get laid, but they think sex is boring, and they're mad, but about what? All the music seems to be about hopelessness and suicide. They're spreading some twisted death wish," he said as he brushed against drug-dead eyes above a Halo of Hate's *Lied To, Raped, and Left For Dead* T-shirt. He recoiled, as if he'd come in contact with a virulent disease, at the sight of the swastika-suggesting double H logo. *Race-hatred and self-hatred. These asswipes are the new storm troopers in a war of hate,* he thought, *but who the hell do they hate? Everyone? Themselves? Both?*

Tolkühn esel. Of course you don't understand these frightened calflings. They have no hope because they can sense the end approaching. They are not filled with your visions of gleicheit and brotherly love. Your generation's dreams have vergangen—Li-ure is almost upon you. "Rock and roll was always about anger and rebellion. This is how they express it. Given the chance these young people will grow out of their confused frustration and channel their anger into something positive," she said.

"But they're not rebelling against war or social injustice. Hell, they're not even mad about the environment. Seems to me they're just pissed because everything doesn't go their way. They're rebelling against reality and life. They're sucking on the cancerous tit of MTV as it spews the poison of gangsta rap and alternative-death-grunge down their throats. Christ, these kids don't like music, most of them don't even know who the Beatles are. I can understand that sex and drugs are part of rock 'n roll, but when did death enter into the equation?" *That was stupid. Death crept in the first time you heard Country Joe and the Fish sing "Not So Sweet Martha Lorraine" and "Death Sound" in '67. You went batshit for Mott and Lou. And you sure didn't have any trouble accepting Jacques Brel's dissolution or the Velvet Underground's decadence. And let's not forget Morrison. That fucker was on a death trip. I pick door of perception number three, Monty. Shit! Shut yer mouth and get right. Billy Joel was right, we didn't start the fire and neither did these kids. You're standing here with a woman that looks a like a cross between Marianne Faithful and Nico and you're having trouble dealing with decadence, dissolution, and death. Man you're getting old. Wish Cos was here, there must be a Dylan quote for this.*

"As a youth did you always walk the safe route?" she asked.

"Of course not, but—"

"But in your own way, and in your own time you grew."

"I like to think so."

"Then you should allow the misdirected energy of youth to find its own path to maturity."

"Sorry. I didn't mean to preach," the Wizard said, quickly reprimanding himself. *This is a date, dummy. It's supposed to be fun, so stop bitching about Gen X's mores before she thinks you're a jerk.* "How about another brew?"

"Thank you. I would love another."

"Comin' right up," he said as he walked to the bar and summoned the bartender with a pair of waving fins. Waiting for the beer he thought about the last time he had been here with Pattie. *What was that? Six, seven years ago? Too bad that didn't work, although it's nice not to have to put up with her playing that trans-euro crap all night. How many times did I hear Kraftwerk's "We Are the Robots", or Front 242. What the hell was that song by them she loved? "Headhunter!" Christ, I hated that almost as much as Bauhaus and Cab Volt. Who was that other weirdo she loved? Gaza X! "Mean Mister Mommy Man."*

"We're back," the Wizard said, holding up two bottles of Bud, "And I promise to contain the Agnewistic commentaries."

"*Gut.* Now as you Americans say, let the good times roll," she said as Classics Nouveau's "Guilty" began to fill the club.

"Hey, I love this song! Let's dance," he said.

"I'd love to."

And they danced as "Guilty" segued into the Beautiful People's trippy nod to Hendrix, "If 60's Was 90's". They sat out Nine Inch Nails' "Closer", returning to the overcrowded floor when Roxy Music's powerhouse, "Do the Strand", hit the hot air.

The Wizard joyously sang along with Brian Ferry, reveling in the highly favored oldie and Christa's promising smile. "The Strand" slashed to a stop and the DJ instantaneously kicked the thundering pulse on a stratospheric powerglide into the beyond with the "Hell Remix" of The Prophet's "The Techno God." Feinting softness, Christa slipped her arm through his and leaned against him as they walked back to the table.

* * * * *

Outside, Willie sat cursing the cold and having given up his weapon against boredom, cigarettes, while inside the Wizard baked and worked on his second beer. He'd already sat through Tommy James and the Shondells' "I Think We're Alone Now" and the Buckinghams' "Kind of a Drag" on WTRY FM. "Damn! What about Otis or Marvin?" The River 99.5 had played something he was glad he didn't know, and WFLY had just put him through "Whoomp There It Is" and Salt 'n Pepa. The rest of the radio stations had sounded even worse. "Why the hell can't we have one real r&b station here. Doesn't anybody remember James Brown or the MGs? This isn't a desert island or East Jesus, middle America. We're less than three hours from New York, for Christsakes."

* * * * *

"When we were discussing films this afternoon —"

"Excuse me for interrupting, but I did think of a film I've seen. A friend of mine showed me a film called *Bloody Kisses* by someone named Steinhauser."

"Matthias Steinhauser is one of Germany's best young directors. *Bloody Kisses* won two awards last year at the German horror film festival, best special effects and Karin Sunnarvik won for best actress. Steinhauser was also nominated as best director," Christa said.

"What a great film. That woman, Sun-ar-vik, was unbelievable. I don't ever think I've seen a more malevolent look on a human face than in the scene where she slips into her lover's bed before the alarm clock goes off and just stares at him. Man, when that clock went off I damn near wet myself. Talk about saved by the bell. Christ, I had the willies for days. And the camera work was fantastic. It was like watching a shark move, slow, almost imperceptibly gliding and then POW, off like a shot. Sometimes at strange angles. I love the way the camera dives, it's like gravity has suddenly increased a hundred fold. And then it ascends; no notice, just wham here we go like some bizarre roller coaster," the Wizard bubbled as if he were a kid telling a friend about a new toy.

"Steinhauser used that effect twice in his first film, *Zuwi'der*, and I suspect it will be in whatever follows."

"People find little touches directors continue to reuse in their films charming. Little things like Hitchcock being in all of his films or Scorsese's revolving camera shots. They're like old friends. I think of them as trademarks."

"Yes, trademarks. It's important to leave your signature on your work," she said.

Chapter Twenty-Six

"Box of Marlboro Lights please, and a book of matches."

"Got no matches. Buy a lighter."

Car's still there, Willie noted as he left the mom-and-pop operation. *Five twenty-nine for a pack of smokes and a light! No wonder everybody's got a foot in the poorhouse.* Coughing, he exhaled as he lit the cigarette. *I guess it's not like riding a bike*, he thought as he took his second puff and coughed again.

"Hey pal! Got a smoke?"

"Huh?" he asked, looking up.

Before he could raise his arm the scalpel pierced his throat, twisted, and pulled right. As his hands shot to his throat the figure in the black CPO jacket pushed him to the right, into a dim alley. As he lay there trying to halt the blood flowing from the gash he realized he had met Nightmare's Disciple. *It's him! My gun!* was the thought rushing to the fore as a steel-toed boot kicked him in the temple and into unconsciousness.

Marsh hurriedly unbuttoned Willie's coat and cut open his shirt. Bent over the dying officer, Marsh severed Willie's nipples before he left his semen and a note lying on the soon-to-be corpse. "Next it's your nigger girlfriend, then you, Stewart," Marsh said. Back in his van he checked his watch. *Almost an hour in there with that Wizard. She better be out soon.*

* * * * *

The Wizard sat waiting for Christa to return from the ladies room for nearly twenty minutes. Worried about her, he asked a girl to look in the ladies room for her, then circled the club three times. Fifteen minutes later he was standing on the curb of Central Avenue, cold, disappointed, and mad at himself, staring at the empty space where Christa's car had been parked.

"Me and my big mouth," he said, lighting a Kool and staring at the mocking pay phone.

Cosmo picked up the phone on the fourth ring.

"It's me, Cos."

"What's happening, my brother? Didn't expect to be hearing from you."

"Guess I scared her away. Can you come give me a ride? I'm at QE2."

"QE2? I thought you were going to catch Gary's band at Bogies," he said, as Chris cut into the conversation.

"Hi, it's Chris."

Shit. Now everybody knows I blew it. "Hi, Chris."

"Look, I know you're going to be mad, but Willie's been watching you. His car should be across the street."

"You said—"

"I know, but I couldn't let you go out alone. Too risky. See his car?"

"Yeah." *Shit.*

"Have him drive you back. We'll discuss having you tailed when you get here."

"Bet yer ass we will!"

* * * * *

"Gregory, I have not seen much of you. How are your studies coming along?"

"Quite nicely."

"Ida has told me you are an excellent student. She also says you will be leaving us soon. I assume you are looking forward to beginning your task."

"I am. But Ida told me that when I leave here I must never return. She says you will not allow it."

"Let us say that I would prefer you never return."

"Why?"

"Surely you know the answer to that. Once Ida has gone I will reside here and try to learn to live with my grief. If you were to return I would be confronted with her loss. I love my sister more than words can tell, and knowing you came here and captured her heart would only be a further reminder of my loss. You must understand that for years I thought that she and I would spend our lives here together. Then you came. Surely you can understand."

"Yes, but—"

"I am not strong enough to embrace my rival. You will have your work and my sister's love to carry you through darkness and doubt.

I shall have neither. So I wish you to leave me here in what peace I can find, untouched by reminders of her love for you."

"I'll respect your wishes."

"Thank you. There is another matter I would like to discuss with you. After you leave, if for some reason you need to contact me for money or information, please do so by contacting my law firm. I shall instruct my staff to aid you in every possible manner. If my staff is unable to assist you they will then bring the matter to my attention."

"Ethan, I never meant to—"

"Please don't apologize. I know you did not intend to hurt me. If you wouldn't mind, I would prefer not to discuss this subject any further. All I ask is that you honor your promise to me."

"I will. Can I ask you something else?"

"Of course."

"When They return don't you want to see them or be a part of their glorious reign? You could be a valued advisor to me."

You self-absorbed fool. "Thank you, but for now, no. If for any reason I change my mind, I will contact you. Now that we have concluded that bit of sticky family business, perhaps you would care to join me for a drink in the garden?" *It continues to go as we hoped. He suspects nothing.*

"It's a little early, and I've got a ton of reading Ida wants me to finish. Sure, let's have a drink," Gregory said, hoping he might be smoothing future tensions between them.

"Splendid." *Splendid indeed! More like brilliant. After that performance I could use a drink.*

* * * * *

Stepping from the club Christa looked to the right, where Marsh had instructed her to check for his signal. Not finding him, or his signal, she quickly walked to her car and drove away as instructed. *I do not know what he had planned, but it must have worked.*

She pulled into Marsh's driveway just as Chris was receiving the news regarding Willie's death from Rolly. Inside she found Marsh quietly rejoicing. Before Christa could say a word he was on her. Throwing her coat to the floor, his rough lips covered her. Tearing her blouse open and biting her hardening nipples, he quickly turned her over as she slid her jeans down around her ankles. His cock found her

anus and he began the hammering thrusts of his brutal pleasure-taking. Looking down he took great enjoyment in watching his pelvis
slam into the soft flesh of her ass. Untempered, his lust rose.
Whipped by the unconstrained beast in August heat, her moaning
quickened to match his fevered strokes. When his craving was sated,
he rose from the sofa and walked away.

"Have I displeased you, Lord?" she asked, knowing full well she
had not.

"Of course not." *You stupid bitch.* "We are celebrating another of
my victories."

"You killed the nigger bitch?"

"No. Not yet anyway, but I hope she will be mine soon. Tonight
I killed a cop. A nigger cop."

So that's what he had planned.

"I followed the cop following you and that Wizard. Did you get
him to talk?"

"Yes. Once he started, he would not shut up. I believe I now
know almost everything they know."

"Do they know anything important?"

"They have a description of you that could fit a thousand men.
And they think you drive a van. Of course they know of the Lovecraft
connection, but they believe it is some kind of madness."

"Perfect. I knew they would think me deranged. Anything else?"

"They have three real talismans."

"Real? How can that be? Where did they get real stones?"

"Stewart's nigger girlfriend. Her cousin, Henri, is here from New
Orleans. He brought the stones at his grandmother's behest."

"Explain!"

"According to the Wizard, her grandmother is a voodoo priestess
of some renown in New Orleans. She sensed trouble and sent her
grandson here with the stones to protect her granddaughter, the one
you so aptly call the nigger bitch."

"By the thousand holy vaginas of Kassogtha, damn them all!"

"Lord, they don't know how to use them and they don't know
who you are. The stones can't hurt you or your plans. This cop is only
using them to draw you out. If you forget the woman and take
another in her place they will never find you until the Queen Mother
has arrived, and then it will be too late."

"NO! NO! NO! I want *her*! The level of fear is not potent enough. She is the one."

"But that is extremely risky. After tonight the police will be watching everyone."

"Then she must die tonight."

"Lord!"

"Come! I want to see her house. One can't catch prey unless you know where and how it lives."

"But what of her cousin?"

"Do you know how to use a gun?"

"Yes."

"Then he is not a problem."

* * * * *

Laurinda put down the copy of Maya Angelou's *Wouldn't Take Nothing for My Journey Now* she had been trying to divert herself with since Henri had retired early. Her thoughts continually returned to Chris. Staring out the living room window into the clear night, she found the wind had stopped blowing dervishes of snow past her windows. As if quietude had been outlawed, her thoughts stirred again. "It looks like a mountain of clouds," she commented to the kitten napping beside her. "So carefree and still. It's a shame it has to turn black and melt, but's that's the life of a snowbank, I guess."

Picking up her almost empty tea mug, she walked into the kitchen looking for a snack. *No Swiss Cake Rolls, no Pop Tarts. Looks like I need to go to the market. There's nothing here. How am I supposed to watch* Good Morning America *without a cinnamon donut or a piece of coffee cake? Maybe I should pop over to the Chopper and pick up a couple things for breakfast. Hmm . . . only three eggs. Bread's low too.* "Let's see," she said, picking up a pen. *OJ, bread, eggs, milk, cinnamon coffee cake with and pecans. Coffee for Henri. Grapefruit to combat the sweets. Better get some bananas, Henri loves 'em. That should do it. I wish Chris could be here for breakfast. Better yet, I wish he were here now . . . . Probably wouldn't be hungry if he were, not for food anyway, Miss Sanders. Miss—Mrs. Christopher James Stewart. Mrs. Laurinda Allegra Stewart. I won't even have to change my initials . . . not that I'd mind, but still it's helpful. My suitcases are already embossed, but I'll still have to change my checks and my stationery, and my driver's license.*

That's after the honeymoon. Where should we go? Somewhere in the Caribbean. I want sea shells and sailboats, beautiful beaches and warm breezes. Barbados, or Bermuda, maybe the Bahamas. Bermuda! Sarah said Bermuda was beautiful. That's the place. I'll bet Pat tells him to go to Barbados. I know how much he likes those old pirate movies. I can just see Chris dressed up like Captain Blood. Drinking spiced rum by moonlight and making love in a hidden cove. Bermuda it is! "I'm going to the Chopper, little one," she said, bending down to gently stroke the newly adopted kitten. "I'll be back in a few minutes. You behave, and you too, Plato. Yes, I'll bring you both a treat."

* * * * *

On a melted/refrozen, black-stained, barely shoveled sidewalk in Albany, Chris was staring at the lifeless shell of his young associate in a partially unzipped body bag. To Chris' right Marlin Matthews was engaged in a scathing one-sided discussion with a high-ranking Albany police official.

"I don't want to hear any of this bullshit. Just get it done. There was supposed to be one of your guys here backing him up. So stick your 'we were busy/somebody slipped up' crap up your ass and get on this before I walk over there and make a couple of announcements to the fucking press," Matthews screamed over the wind.

As Chris finished praying for Willie's soul he pressed the tip of his finger to his lips before placing it on Willie's forehead, blessing him with the sign of the cross. "How in the fuck did this happen?" Exhaling smoke and moisture, his tight features appeared hellish in the tree-limb-fractured light.

Shaking his head the Wizard shrugged, as his fingers found the paper in his pocket containing the lyrics to Willie's father's song. *"Left me with my Smith & Wesson and my resolve,"* he thought. *Somebody's gonna pay for this!* "Look man, I—"

"Now do you understand why I couldn't let you go out unobserved?"

"Yeah."

"I can't believe I let you go at all. And for what?" *For what?*

"I'm sorry, Chris, I wish I could turn back the clock."

"I know. Look, it's not your fault." *This is my fault. Pat was right, this is an animal and I put this kid out here alone. I might as well have*

killed him myself. "Let's get out of here; they're not going to find anything." *I shoulda known he was watching us. It's all there in the tone of his
letters,* Chris thought as he reread the note found on Willie's body.

> My Dear stewart,
>
> It seems that your prey is the true HUNTER. Can't you understand
> your efforts are in vain? Nothing can stop LI-URE!
>
> You can watch all you like, but you will not find me. Remember I can
> find you whenever I wish.
>
> This is MY game we're playing, and you don't seem to have even dis-
> covered the rule book yet.
>
> There is no need to attempt to protect the frightened rabbits huddled
> in your warren. They will soon be stew meat for HER. I'll see you soon!

*I think you're gonna find the rabbits have moved out and the snakes have
moved in, so come taste our venom. I don't know much about the martial arts,
but I know one of its tenets is never underestimate your enemy, and you can
bet I'm through doing that. Can you say the same?* "C'mon, we've got
strategy to plot," Chris said to the Wizard.

"What are we going to do?"

"Spread our own propaganda."

* * * * *

"I bought presents," Ida said, putting down her bags. "One for me,
one for Ethan, and one for you."

"Thanks." Gregory beamed.

"Not so fast, I haven't even told you what it is. Do you dance?"

"No."

"I love to dance. It makes me feel . . . impulsive and reckless,"
she said, carrying a bag to the Linn turntable and removing an LP. "I
bought this today. It was playing as I walked past Barrett's Record
Shop and I found it irresistible."

As the music began she started to dance around the room. "Well
you're dirty and sweet, clad in black, don't look back, and I love
you," Marc Bolan purred and moaned as she whirled.

"This is wonderful. Come dance with me."

"I can't."

"Please?"

The riff swaggered and Bolan crooned, "You've got the teeth of a Hydra upon you, you're dirty sweet . . ."

"What is this . . . noise," an exceptionally agitated Ethan asked upon entering the room. "Oh," he said, luridly observing his sister's pagan swirling.

"It's rock and roll, darling! T. Rex. Isn't it intoxicating?"

"Yes," he whispered, watching his sister's pelvis pulsate to the rhythm. "Yes."

As the song ended Ida slithered to the record player while both sparrows ate the motion of the snake's firm buttocks. "That was wonderful," she hissed. "When I heard 'the teeth of a Hydra upon you', I had to stop and buy it. 'Dirty sweet', delicious. What have you two been up to while I was out?"

Yes, delicious. "Napping," Ethan responded.

"I was reading," Gregory said.

"And Gregory and I had a chat."

"Good."

"I'll check on dinner," Ethan said, leaving the room.

"And what were you reading?"

"*Exiled Nightmares.*"

"Tell me of Ut'ulls-Hr'ehr."

Delighted to be given a chance to impress her, Marsh launched into his description. "Hurley describes her as a grayish, egg-shaped, armored torso made of bone-like scales. Her crescent-shaped head is bearded by black pockmarked curved horns oozing a dark substance at the tips. No eyes, no visible mouth. There are two green-veined membranous blue appendages midface, one above the other. A heavily spiked appendage protrudes from the rear of her head. Below the torso is a black thorax, the underside of which is covered with reddish teats and hundreds of what look like fish fins lining each side."

"Very good. And who does Hurley ascribe his description to?"

"Von Konnenberg in *Uralte Schecken*, Navarre, and something I've never heard of, 'Visions in a Black Garden.'"

"It's the first part of the 'Oxia Obmina' in *Journeys across the Gray Lands.*"

"Is that here?" Gregory asked.

"Yes. The spine reads *Julianna's Diary*, although it is not a diary in any strict sense."

"Was she a member of the family?"

"No. She was a member of *Filiae Solitudinis*."

Marsh quickly translated the Latin. "The Daughters of Isolation."

"They were a little-known sect who worshiped Ut'ulls-Hr'ehr. Bishop makes veiled references to their existence in *Witchcraft on the Moors*, and *Commentaries on the Van Oortmerssen Monographs*. The Great Beast Crowley is said to have had a brief liaison with one of the Sisters—donating blood, sperm, and excrement to a failed ceremony. The Sisters experimented with and used narcotic substances, sexual pleasures, torture, and echoing as part of their ceremonies."

"What's echoing?"

"A process that begins with prayer and drug ingestion followed by an orgy. During the religious ecstasy found in sex magic certain members of the Sisterhood become open to the emanations of the imprisoned Mother, Ut'ulls-Hr'ehr, and Kassogtha. The drugs and the pleasures of the orgy were seen by the Sisters as a cleansing, a purification, the first step in unblocking their physically binding flesh as well as the remaining senses and mental faculties. By opening their awareness to the Mother's psychic vibrations the Sisters felt they could interpret her desires. When one of the Sisters became open or receptive to these vibrations, she would be removed from the assembly and the torture upon her unworthy flesh would commence. Torture, phase two of the echoing, was deemed vital in further opening the Sister's ability to receive the Mother's emanations. When the chosen Sister reached the proper plane of responsiveness her thoughts, feelings, and vibrations would then resonate or echo those of the tormented Mother. Julianna considered herself privileged to have been the chosen on eleven occasions, two of which were the most holy of holy ceremonies, the Mass of the Mother."

"Ahh. Are we recounting the story of Julianna and Leitanna? The sweet dark shrouded in the expansive arms of pain-induced rapture?" Ethan asked as he reentered the room and sat.

"Perhaps after dinner," Ida said.

"Why not during dinner? Gregory, certainly you wish to hear Julianna's story?"

"Yes."

"Ethan, you know a good story requires the right setting."

"Then we will sit on the terrace after dinner. You will have airy darkness and the fragrance of the summer garden to assist you as you ensorcel us with her tale."

"Perhaps."

❦ Chapter Twenty-Seven ❦

Cosmo stood in the kitchen leaning against the counter which contained the sink—which he was using for an ashtray—working on his second beer and hoping this wasn't going to be an all-nighter. "So," came Cosmo's gentle command to his no longer silent, but still badly shaken, partner.

"I don't know," the Wizard said, popping the tab of the night's fifth, wishing for the hazy oblivion of the twelfth. "You shoulda seen it. I never want to see another fuckin' gore flick again. Willie's throat was torn open. Blood was everywhere. It was the most . . . I never," his voice fading as he raised the can to his lips.

"Look, he was a nice guy and I'd give just about anything to change what went down tonight, but at least you're okay. This motherfucker coulda killed you both."

"I know that," the Wizard said as he began pacing.

"Maybe if you talk about it, get it out, it might help."

"It's not just that," he snapped, looking away as his words quickly dissipated. As if scored, the refrigerator's hum filled the troubled lapse. "I know this is a shitty thing to say, but I can't stop thinking about Veronica."

"Who the hell is Veronica?"

"The blonde who dumped me tonight. At least I found out her name. For all the good it does me now."

"So what happened?"

"So what happened? I opened my big mouth, that's what happened."

"Thought that was my specialty."

"Normally, but not exclusively. We went to QE2. And it was all nose rings and teeny bullshit, you know how that scene goes. So there I was knee deep in pathos and boredom, and POW! My mouth opens and out storms this tyrannical discourse encompassing everything from the irrationally misguided angst of Gen X to darkambient odes to razor blades."

"Christ! One of those."

"Yep. A big one. I couldn't stop ranting about the mentality and the slogans. Every goddamn T-shirt in the place screamed some Gen-X catchphrase. You should have seen them."

"Remember Zappa said we're all wearing a uniform of one form or another."

"Yeah, well. Next thing I know she goes to the bathroom, and home. All without a word, mind you. Just slid out when my head was turned. Not that I didn't give her a reason or six."

"Man. You're supposed to be nice on the first date. Best behavior and all that."

"I know that, Mom! I didn't plan to stick my head up my ass and come out covered in shit. Kinda just happened."

"No wonder we're single. Neither one of us has the social graces to have drinks with the Albany Street hookers, let alone with real women. Guess we're becoming the urban equivalent of mountain men."

"Got one of those I can have?" Chris asked, walking in from the living room.

"Sure," Cosmo said as he pulled three Pabsts from the fridge.

"I just spoke to my superior. He told me the Chief wants to pull the plug on this operation."

"That's fuckin' great! That motherfuckin' bastard was stalking me tonight and Willie's layin' on a metal fuckin' table with a toe tag waitin' for the M. E. to rip open his chest with a bone saw and you tell me some fuckin' political appointee wants to back off. Well, you go back and tell him to suck my cock! You see this?" the Wizard said, holding out his shaking hand. "There's blood on it! If I stayed home tonight, Willie would still be trying to figure out if *Frankenstein* was sci-fi or horror, or maybe he'd be standin' over there with that odd smile of his wondering what kind of lunatic I am. But no, I had to go out. So go tell your political marionette it's just a little fuckin' late. I'm already a flag pole rag, so we're gonna play this out!"

"It's not my decision."

"You're the Man!"

"I'm barely more than a pawn."

"Then get me the man! 'Cause this ain't over!"

"We can't make policy decisions for the cops," Cosmo said. "They're going to do what they want and we don't have anything to say about it. Hell, Chris just said he was overridden."

"I'm not! There's an army of reporters comin' here in the morning expecting interviews, and if we're out, than I'll give 'em interviews that will make CNN's top ten stories of the year. You tell 'em I know how to arrange a song for a particular audience, and I been playin' for local audiences for twenty-five years."

"Things are different now," Chris said.

"Damn straight!"

"Look—"

"I don't want to hear your cop-speak bullshit! I know what's different. You've got a dead cop. I've seen TV, I know when a cop dies that's worth, what? Ten, twenty regular people."

"That's not what I'm saying."

"The fuck it's not!"

"Let me talk to him, Chris."

"I don't need anybody to hold my hand."

"The fuck you don't! Now shut up for five minutes."

"Yes, Mom."

"I'll be in the other room," Chris said, leaving the heated kitchen.

"Later, Chris. Jesus Christ, bro! You were pretty hard on the cat. This shit ain't his fault. How about we have another brew and you chill a bit?"

"Make it two and hand me the JD."

* * * * *

The binding heat and humidity of the summer afternoon had given way to star-flecked darkness and a gentle breeze. The cold front that had touched off turbulent thunderstorms earlier had passed, leaving comforting dry air in its almost still wake. Sitting in the flickering illumination of candlelight in the light white cottons of summer, the trio was enjoying the soothing evening air and a bottle of Chivas Regal. Swirling and glittering in the dancing light, the ice in their glasses chimed along with their easy chatter and occasional laughter.

"Ida, grace those who your heart adores with the tale you tempted us with," Ethan requested.

"Please," Gregory added, sounding like a child begging his mother's favor.

She rose and stepped away, her back to them. As if considering the request, her eyes looked to the phantom sky of night above. Then she turned, like a great, singular lily illuminated by moonlight. Ida held their gaze and began, her voice a strange, enchanting flute of ancient tragedy. Receding from the reach of the candlelight's shadowy fingers, Ida's voice, a magnetic ballet of near song, danced for the thirsty pair. One moment her figure floated forward into soft illumination, her words a light soprano caress; the next, seemingly without movement, she suddenly retreated, vanishing in darkness, her voice a whispered assault of hissed pain.

> *"'Storms of darkness hold the cathedral sky,*
> *torrents of rapturous tears*
> *drown the feasting flesh lands beneath.*
> *The maiden and the mistress,*
> *one dancing beyond the pale mirror, drafting red runes,*
> *one beneath the serpentine caress of the lash.*
> *With the red coinage of a choked kiss, she, the vessel,*
> *freely enters the theater of desire*
> *and embraces the charnel promises of Teihmgoa.*
> *Standing in the realm of the sharp threshold and chaos tears,*
> *her lips quiver, her eyes entreat,*
> *her heart beats its prayer and melts,*
> *as her words enter the void to stand poised on the terrace of silence,*
> *and the echoes begin.*
> *Mind, beyond the boundaries of the flesh.*
> *Prayers, beyond the feeble inaccuracies of words.*
> *Soul, beyond the shroud of undead death,*
> *into the arms of the divine mother, Ut'ulls-Hr'ehr.'"*

Ida paused as the wind's breath gave momentary voice to the leaves. When stillness reigned again, she picked up her glass and resumed. "Before her name, before her story, these are the first words Julianna set to paper. Before she thanks Leitanna for showing her the grace that lies beyond physical pain, she reveals the joy of echoing the divine mother. Devotion and worship. These were the cornerstones of her life. A pious existence spent in the Mother's service."

"I was under the impression the Daughters of Isolation were lesbians who delighted in the pleasures of the flesh," Gregory said.

"I tell you this to illustrate a point I have mentioned previously. No life, even the pious one, may truly serve if it is not lived. Breathe, dear cousin. Those whom you seek to serve draw sustenance from worship and fear as well as from the flesh itself. If you cannot learn to enjoy earthly pleasures, you will fail them. Remember I said devotion and worship were the cornerstones, not the entire structure."

"Julianna found pleasure as well as holy requirements of service in the knife, the lash, and the passion-laced arms of her sisters," Ethan said. "In the tales you read you find pain feeding those who wait. Look deeper and see certain types of pleasure also sustain them."

"I'm trying."

"I know you are," Ida said, gently taking Gregory's hand.

"Gregory, please forgive us if we seem to preach. I am aware of how much material we are heaping upon your shoulders, but so much depends on your success," Ethan said in a believably concerned tone.

"Please don't apologize for your attempts to educate me. I know I'm thick at times."

"Enough of this. We waste the night."

"Patience, dear brother, the night is a young maiden who yields her treasures slowly. Your tale will begin soon enough."

And it did. As the candle wax traced molten rivulets downward, Ida spoke of the innocent but knowledge-thirsty young maiden Leitanna, always considered bright, exceptional, found in her father's library reading *Ater Monstrum*. Ida told the comfortably reclining pair of Leitanna's mother, a simple devout woman, shocked and sorely disturbed to find the girl reading the blasphemous text, and of the father's arrival home from Rome to be told of the girl's actions.

Appalled, and frantically certain his temptation-inclined daughter would succumb further if left unchecked, or even be thoroughly possessed, he sent her to a convent to have the evil expunged. As the scotch and Ida's voice captivated the drifting pair, she told them how Leitanna was seduced by the cloistered sisters' devotion to the Lamb of God, and, repenting, took her vows. Then Ida whispered of how under the tutorage of a domineering elder, obsessed with Leitanna's lithe, dusky form, the always curious young Leitanna (described by Julianna as a beauty with eyes that would shame the Aegean) was instructed in the teachings of Sappho and slowly exposed to the existence and sacraments of the Mother, Ut'ulls-Hr'ehr.

Her oration, at times almost a sermon, flittered and wavered as if dancing with the candlelight as she spoke at length of the small circle of nuns who were exposed by a shunned sister seeking admittance into the circle, and then sent from the nunnery. Ida, a deft storyteller, detailed the power struggle that splintered the small group of excommunicates, and how Leitanna and her faction of three wandered the French countryside while the other group sought haven in the forests of Germany. From the library Ida brought *Julianna's Diary* and read of Leitanna's travels south and east into Greece, and of the women who joined her order. The eldest was Eleni, whom Leitanna christened the salvation and the punishment, a dark-souled beauty who would become protector and punisher of the order, as well as Leitanna's lifelong companion. Her warm voice caressing the two rapt listeners, Ida read passages of Julianna's poetry regarding the delicate flower Christiane, Julianna's only love (whom the others called the lush garden), and the mute giantess, Elita, who betrayed the order in the bed of a man.

"From Greece they traveled to Africa seeking a talisman. There Kathleen, one of the excommunicates, was killed by a boomslang. Seeing Kathleen cut down by a symbol of male sexuality and dominance, Leitanna decreed that to be cut by the blade of male lust was a holy crime against the Mother. In honor of Kathleen's devotion, Leitanna decided that the order would leave the land of hot death for the northern lands of cold isolation, and to the moors of Wales they went."

Ida set down the handwritten volume and freshened her drink.

Gregory asked, "Can I look at that?"

"Certainly."

Marsh picked up the tome and began reading. "There seems to be a lot here I don't know of. Tautira, Urthoxia, the Eleven Shadowed Voices, Zr'ubia E'gl Sexualis."

"Do not trouble yourself, dear cousin, not even Azathoth himself knows everything," Ethan darkly quipped.

"Gregory, you have learned much and will continue to do so. Everything in Julianna's book you will soon know. When you are finished it will be as if you descended the Steps of Chaos and entered the Theater of Desire yourself. Now I shall finish my tale."

* * * * *

1:59 let the new hour take command, while twelve empty Pabst Tall Boy cans—as usual the Wizard was two up on Cosmo—stood like a cordon of sentries on the kitchen table.

"I still don't understand what the hell you were doing in QE2? You can't stand the music or the attitude," Cosmo said, again diverting the conversation away from Willie's brutal murder.

Shrugging his reply, the Wizard popped the tab of his eighth Pabst. Three up.

"That's where she wanted to go."

"Man, you had me scared for a minute. I thought we were gonna start doing covers of Alice in Chains or Nine Inch Nails material."

Eyebrows clenched and lips clamped, the Wizard glared at Cosmo. "Right! Just because I can't remember much of anything these days doesn't mean I've got a big hole in my head."

"Hey! Come to think of it, that might not be a bad idea."

"What's that?"

"Nine Inch Nails, Porno for Pyros."

"What the hell are you babbling about?"

"We could put a little boom in Generation X. Some kind of bizarre twist on the Big Daddy thing. Grunge played by Woodstock-era bands. Imagine 'Smells Like Teen Spirit' played by the Byrds, or if Canned Heat did 'Even Flow.'"

"Christ, you're whacked."

"No I'm not. Listen, all these bands are performing on tribute albums. We'd just be turning the tables. We could change the band's name. Call ourselves Jar of 1969's Lies, or Rage Against the Convenient Kitchen Appliances of Our Parents."

The Wizard burst into laughter as Cosmo continued.

"We could do parodies. Think of the material we could come up with. 'I-Feel-Like-I'm-Fixin'-To-Commit-Suicide-Because-Daddy-Canceled-My-Charge-Account-And-Mom-Made-Me-Eat-Her-Meatloaf-Rap', or 'We're All Brothers On Seattle.'"

"Or 'Smells Like Teens Are Stuck Inside Of Seattle With The Suicide Blues Again.'"

"'What's So Fun About Peace, Love, and Nirvana?'"

"'40,000 Pearl Jam Fans Couldn't Make Me Change My Mind If I Had to Make a Choice Between the Def Man and Blind Melon.'"

"'With a Little Razor Blade From My Friends.'"

"'Every Nose Ring Tells a Story', or 'Born To Be Dead And Bloated,'" the Wizard countered.

"'See Me, Feel Me, Kill Me' . . . 'Teach Your Parents/Shotgun/Carry On (With The Estate Money) Jam.'"

"'We're Not The Fugs Kids.'"

"'Ain't No Crack Pipe Full Enough.'"

"'No Crack Tonight/New Motherfuckin' Chrome-Plated Nine.'"

"'Everybody's Got A Convenience Store To Rob 'Cept Me And My Posse.'"

"'Say It Loud—I'm Dead And I'm Proud, Parts 1 & 2.'"

"'Takin' Eric Menendez Death Row Blues' . . . 'The Sound Of Silence Was Broken By A Drive-by Shooting.'"

"'Let's Jump Off Suicide Bridge (Feelin' Grungy)', and 'Eve Of Dissatisfaction (With My Parents).'"

"'The Liberation Of Manson Will Be Televised.'"

"Yeah! We'll sponsor a festival," the now well-oiled Cosmo said.

"We could rent an Orange County lumber truck and park it right outside the gates of Sing-Sing. But who'll play?" the Wizard asked.

"Ritchie Havens could open with 'Freedom.'"

"And Cream could reunite and perform 'I Feel Free.'"

"Yeah! Old Frankie and the Mothers doing 'Absolutely Free.'"

"How about War playin' 'The World is My Garbage Dump', and maybe the Stones could show up and do 'Sympathy for the Devil.'"

"We'll have the MC5 do 'The United States Is Burning.'"

"I got it, I got it! The Moody Blues. 'Roman Polanski's Dead.'"

"And Hendrix closes the festival with 'The Star Spangled Banner' as they give Manson the keys to L.A. and a gold-plated Mack-10. Empty of course."

"Don't forget the finale. We'll have the Black Panthers taking a bead on Charlie's head and giving him a twenty-one-gun salute."

"Now that's some real freedom."

"Straight up, my brother. Freedom for the whole angst-and-apathy generation. 'Free Your Mind And Your Ass—'"

"'—Will Follow,'" the Wizard chimed in.

"'Mommy, What's A Funkadelic?'"

"It's a parliafunkadelicment thang."

"It's a Byrd."

"It's a 'Virginia Plain.'"

"'It's the blimp. It's the blimp, Frank. It's the blimp'.'"

"It's two drunks with 'the drazy hoops'—"

"'The Animal Trainer And The Toad,'" Cosmo said, finding an opportunity to compare his and the Wizard's physical stature to Leslie West and Felix Pappalardi of Mountain.

"Who've made the *Mothership Connection*," the Wizard added, without commenting on Cosmo's overused heavy/thin likening.

"Bet yer *Motor Booty Affair*, Star Child."

The tab of a beer can popping and a match igniting brought pause to the game.

"Cos, I know you used to love my mother, and I know she thought of you as a second son, but what'd she do? Give you her secret for soothing my discomforts."

"Sorta."

"Thanks, man."

"Hey, what are friends for?"

"Thank you, Elton John."

* * * * *

Pushing her gray plastic shopping cart down aisle fourteen of the Eastern Parkway Price Chopper, Laurinda stopped and placed a gallon of 2% milk in the cart. "OJ, bread, eggs, coffee cake, coffee, grapefruit, bananas, and milk. That's it." At the checkout Laurinda wrote a check for $30.23 with an internal bellow. *What happened to ten dollars a bag?* "Thank you. You do the same," she said, fumbling through her purse for her keys.

Laurinda set the bags on the roof of her car and inserted the key in the lock. As she turned the key, the rear doors of the van parked behind her burst open. Before her stood a cold-eyed monster, scalpel and teeth bared.

"Nigger-whore, you're about to die for Kassogtha! Too bad your master Stewart can't see what I'm about to do to you, but I may send him a little present. Maybe he'd like a piece of your skin as a memento. Does he have a favorite spot?"

Enraptured by his blood lust and the night's previous success, Marsh moved too hastily and the icy surface below his feet extracted its payment. As his left foot began to slip and his arms desperately clawed the air at his sides for nonexistent handholds, Laurinda, vocalizing an earsplitting *"Yaih!"*, assisted his descent with a front kick to the chest, sending him sprawling backward and down. Marsh crashed hard, elbow and head smashing the icy pavement with a groan.

"Freeze, bitch!" Christa yelled, appearing at the lighted opening of the van's rear door and stepping down. "Get in!" she hissed, leveling a pistol at Laurinda.

Laurinda instantly assessed her situation. *She's standing on ice and she's mad. Maybe a little jumpy. Stay cool.* She lowered her gaze to ascertain Marsh's condition. *He's shaken. Head's bleeding. Wait for your opening.*

As Christa lowered her gaze to look at Marsh, following Laurinda's line of sight, a loud harsh voice to her right shouted "HEY! YOU ALL RIGHT?" Christa's head turned into it.

Now! Laurinda told herself, launching a second precise front kick. Fast and hard. Up, out, and pivoting right upon contact. Christa's arm and the pistol went flying as Laurinda followed the front kick with a knife-hand blow to Christa's lower back. Down she plunged, to share the icy hell of defeat with her master.

With the pair down and dazed, Laurinda grabbed her keys from the lock and jumped into the car, locking the door with her left elbow while starting the motor. In less than four seconds the car was moving, a sharp right, tires spinning, a sharp right again, leaving the parking lot, her groceries, and the two declawed predators behind. Through the red light and left; 20, 30, 40.

Think! She finally screamed to herself. *Don't go home! Chris! Go to Chris!*

* * * * *

Ida had finished her story and left with Ethan over an hour ago. "Some papers that require our attention" they'd said, leaving Gregory to bask in the cool evening air. She was surprised to find him sitting in the same spot when she came looking for him.

"What were you doing?" Ida asked Gregory.

"Screaming at deaf ghosts. Drifting in Charon's vessel considering the dream-driven steps of the madman."

"What madman?"

"The alchemist who yearns to make shadows solid."

"You're being plagued by doubts again."

"How could I not be. So many before me have failed. Just look what happened to Leitanna."

"Why do you waste time thinking about those who have already stood before Aeacus, Rhadamanthus, and Minos? Let them suffer the odious hell of defeat. The only abyss in your path is doubt; build a bridge with your desire and walk across. Do not make a mockery of my death with this talk of Charon and failure. You shall live after me, so the next time the shadows of uncertainty attempt to prey upon you, banish them. Remember Charon does not ferry the living. Waste no time in his boat," Ida commanded.

"I don't understand why the Fates deserted *Filiae Solitudinis*."

"Nor do I."

"The same could befall me."

"It won't, your lot is predestined. Atropos holds no shears before you." She left him, the trace of her fingers on his cheek lightly lingering like the memory of last night's perfume.

That night, alone in his bed of many longings, Marsh suffered a thunderous sleep. The ravenous denizens and lords of a dozen different mythological hells, the Jabberwockey, Grendel, the monsters Universal forever immortalized, Captain Hook, the Nazgûl and Mahars, the wicked witch of *Hansel and Gretel*, and a boiling horde of fangs and howls and poisonous claws from the night-shadowed dimensions of his cheerless childhood imaginings—all pursued him, tearing chunks of uncertainty from the fleeing boy clothed only in a cold cloak of fear. "Failure!" was the derisive bellow from every carrion-fouled maw.

❦ Chapter Twenty-Eight ❦

Henri was jarred awake by the two cats enjoying a late night game of catch-me-if-you-can. *"Qu'est qui ce passe? Ah, les chats."* Sitting up he gently scolded the pair of felines for using him for a hurdle. *"Vous n'avez rien a faire que chasser deux souris invisible a travers mon lit, maintenant aller. Aller!* Plato, you should not be teaching the little one such games. In the future act like your namesake and spend the night in contemplation, not leaving scratches on my chest."

As he tried to settle back into his pillow and the warm comforter he realized the dining room lights were on. Looking at the face of the Big Ben illuminated by the light cutting through the slightly open door he wondered why Laurinda was still awake. Rising from the bed he put on his deep blue terrycloth robe and went in search of his cousin, certain she was feeling troubled.

Walking through the flat, he found it odd that the living room, dining room, and kitchen lights were on at this hour. She was not in her bed. The door was open and the bed was still made. The bathroom door was also open and it was unoccupied. Standing in the kitchen, an uneasy tension began to grip him.

"Où est-ce qu'elle est? Chère, are you here? Laurinda!"

Once again he walked through the flat looking for her. He looked in the spare bedroom and checked the door locks. After checking the front door lock he noticed the stairway lights were on. He quickly went and looked out the window.

"Her car is gone. Laurinda? *Chère,* are you here?" *Where could she have gone at this hour? Christopher!*

Despite the late hour Henri went back to the kitchen and dialed The Horror Corner. On the second ring Chris answered the phone.

"What the hell do you mean she's not there?"

"I have thoroughly looked through the flat twice and she is not here. Christopher, her car is not here. I thought you might have telephoned her and she was meeting you somewhere."

Godammit! "I'm sending someone for you and a car's gonna sit outside all night. Leave her a note in case she comes back."

"I will."

"I'll see you in a few minutes. I'm putting out an APB on her and her car. Bye."

Chris held up his hand to stop Cosmo's question as he finished his phone call. "I've got to make another call. Can one of you guys grab me a beer?"

The Wizard returned from the kitchen with three beers and set one in front of Chris. "Well?"

"Lauri's not home. Her car's gone. Henri just called. She's gone out without him, and neither of us knows where she might have gone."

"How'd she get out without Henri knowing it?"

"He was asleep."

"Can't blame him for that," the still groggy Cosmo said.

"Seems I can't blame anybody for anything these days," Chris muttered under his breath as he stood and began pacing.

* * * * *

In the eight-hundred block of Eastern Avenue Laurinda's car hit a patch of black ice and did a pair of 360's, almost grazing a black Ford F-150 pickup and a red Chevy van parked in front of the Copper Keg. Two a-few-beers-over-their-limit patrons yelled bigoted obscenities into the bitter air.

"Damn it, slow down. You're halfway there, so don't get yourself killed." The word almost escaped as a scream. *Twice in the last five minutes. How can this be happening? Stop this! Find your center and breathe. You can fall apart in a couple of minutes. Just get to Chris first.*

* * * * *

As Laurinda's car cleared the parking space, Christa, on hands and knees, roused her dazed master. Helping him into the back of the van she quickly closed the doors and sped away as he collapsed again.

"Where are we?" he asked a few minutes later.

"Almost out of the city," she replied.

Rolling over, his head and elbow shrieking, he instantly noted he was alone in the rear of the van. "Where's the bitch?"

"I was unable to—"

"She got away? How the fuck did she escape? You had a gun on her."

"You were on the ground and I looked down to see how badly you were injured when a voice yelled, and I looked toward it, and she—"

"What? She what?" *Fucking worthless cunt! You'll pay for your bumbling.*

"She disarmed me, and then I was on the ground beside you."

"My scalpel! Where's my scalpel?"

"It's still there somewhere. There was not time to look around for it."

"And the gun?"

"With the scalpel."

"Fuck! Now they have our fingerprints. Does anyone have your prints on file?"

"No."

Mine either. "Where are we now?"

"We have just gone over the bridge."

"Take the second right. We'll go the back way," he said, holding his aching head. "I'm bleeding! That cunt drew blood." *She's dead!* "I'm going to carve her into a million pieces! Get me home!"

"Yes, Lord."

* * * * *

The police cruiser was stopped at the red light on the corner of Eastern Avenue and Nott Terrace waiting for it to turn green when Laurinda's white Honda took the corner too fast and did its third 360.

"What the fuck is that?" Officer Ike Lennear asked.

"Another drunk," Officer Paul Matolsi said, hitting the lights and siren. "Let's bag this asshole."

"Hey! That's the vehicle in the APB!"

Once Laurinda got control of the car, she was ecstatic to see the police car behind her. "An escort! And two blocks to go." *I'm safe*, she thought as she ran the remaining red light between her and The Horror Corner.

The brakes squealed and the Honda slid, with a slight fishtail, to a stop. The high beams of the car's headlamps threw a stark mechanical version of high noon through the plate glass windows of the store, as the horn Laurinda steadily depressed screamed its injured bellowing-beast cry into the cold night air. The police cruiser's rotating lights cut the harsh overbright illumination inside the store with sharp bands of red as Chris and the Wizard, weapons drawn, and Cosmo, his trusty old thirty-four-ounce Louisville Slugger skull-crusher in hand, ran into the unearthly glare.

"Wizard!"

"Yo!"

"Don't shoot unless I tell you!"

"But—"

"We don't know who's out there."

"It's obvious! Our freaky friend's come a-callin'," the Wizard said.

"With a patrol car on his ass? I doubt it. So keep your cool," Chris instructed, moving to the right to get a better aim at the driver's side of the car. "Shit! That's Lauri's car," he said as he ran for the front door. "Don't shoot!"

As he opened the door Laurinda ran into his arms.

"Jesus Ch—"

"It was him! It was him."

"Who?"

"The killer! He attacked me in the Price Chopper parking lot."

"The Chopper on Eastern?"

"Yes."

The woman on Londonderry Court, the girl at Zoller, and now the Eastern Ave. Chopper. This fuck's moved uptown. "Are you hurt?"

"No! But he might be."

"Huh?"

"I dropped him and his accomplice."

"Accomplice! He's got a partner?"

"A woman."

Chris shook his head in disbelief. "Woman? Christ! Why do you think it was him?"

"He called you and Kassogtha by name."

"Lennear!" Chris yelled.

"Yes, sir."

"I want you and Matolsi to secure the Price Chopper parking lot on Eastern until someone from the task force shows up. Haul it, son!"

"You got it."

"You're safe now. Let's get inside. I've got to make a call and we've got to talk about why you went out and what this monster said."

Inside and out of the January wind, the trio sat in the kitchen waiting for the tea pot to whistle and Chris to finish his call. While Cosmo poured the hot cinnamon stick tea, Laurinda broke down.

Setting his shotgun on the table the Wizard took Laurinda's hand and tried to comfort her. "You're safe now. Here," he said, offering her the box of tissues. "Dry those eyes and try to drink some tea. Cos boils some mean water."

"Thanks. I . . . I'm sorry for breaking down like that."

"Hey, you've got nothing to be sorry about. You just clocked that asshole and walked away," Cosmo said. "And as far as anybody knows no one else has done that. Right now the only thing that matters is that you're safe."

"Fuckin'-A right," Chris said, entering the kitchen, "are you sure you're all right?" he asked as she came into the loving secure hug he offered her.

"Yes, I'm sure. He never touched me."

"How the hell did you get away from him?" the Wizard asked.

"Chris made me take karate after my ex assaulted me. And to be honest, I think luck had a lot to do with it."

Honest, smart, and she don't take no shit. Chris is the lucky one here, Cosmo thought.

"Lauri, I need to know what happened. You said he mentioned my name."

"Yes. He said something like, you're about to die for Kassogtha, you nigger whore or nigger bitch. That might be why I reacted the way I did. You know how strongly I resent bigotry."

"I know. Go on."

"Then he said something about how it was too bad you wouldn't be able to see what was going to happen to me. As he came toward me, I don't think he was more than two steps away, he began to slip on some ice that was between us, so I hit him with a front kick and he went down hard."

"Then what happened?" Cosmo asked.

"The woman appeared in the doorway of the van."

"He had a van? What color was it?" Chris asked.

"White, maybe? Beige? I was busy. I didn't notice."

"What about the woman?"

"She had a gun and was pointing it at me and she said something, but I can't recall what she said. Get in, or something. Then she got out and looked down at him, he was bleeding and seemed dazed. Then someone in the parking lot yelled something at her, or us, and when she turned to see who yelled, I kicked her. After she hit the ground I got in the car and drove here."

God, she was lucky. They were both armed. "Lauri, I need descriptions."

"He was tall. Maybe six-two. Two hundred pounds. Black hair, cut short, no facial hair. And he had dark eyes. Clean-shaven and no glasses. I think he was wearing jeans and a black ski jacket," she said while Chris made notes. "She was blonde. A natural. Five-four, maybe five-five. A hundred and ten or fifteen pounds. No make-up, no glasses. She reminded me of one of Mick Jagger's old girl friends. Oh! Her voice. She had an accent. Maybe German, maybe eastern European."

Cosmo and the Wizard looked at each other and nodded.

"Damn right!" Cosmo said.

"It can't be!" the Wizard insisted, though he was as certain as Cosmo.

"Then why are you thinking it?"

"Thinking what?" Chris asked.

"Veronica," Cosmo said.

"Who?" Chris asked.

"The Wizard's date," Cosmo replied.

"Listen. Blonde. Right height and weight. German accent, and she shows up today out of the blue knowing a lot about Lovecraft and the Mythos," Cosmo replied.

"Fuck me!" Chris exclaimed. "And she was in Albany tonight when Willie was murdered."

"Bingo! Probably with her partner," the Wizard said, thinking about why they'd killed Willie. *Christ! They were after me!* "They were after me!"

"Why?" Chris asked.

"Information maybe? Or just to spit in your face,"

"That makes sense to me," Cosmo said. "She was in here today looking for information when Laurinda, Pat, and Henri came in. Then you came in the store," he said, pointing to Chris, "and she hotfoots it out of here. Holy shit! Laurinda, can you recall if she was wearing gloves tonight?"

"I don't think so. Why?"

"Because you said she had a gun and you disarmed her."

"Right. When I kicked her, the gun went flying."

"So?" Chris asked.

"So, maybe they didn't pick up the gun and if you guys find the gun, I've got something downstairs that I'd bet has her fingerprints on it," Cosmo explained.

"The CD's!" the Wizard exclaimed.

"What CD's?" Chris asked.

"She gave the Wizard two CD's that are based on the Mythos."

"If you're right, than she was in here today right under my nose, and he was probably close by. God damn it! Now what do we have?" Chris asked, hoping they would find the fingerprints on file somewhere and they'd match.

"Mr. and Mrs. Jack the Ripper," Cosmo answered.

"One kills 'em while one watches," the Wizard fearfully added, wondering how close the mister might have been earlier.

"Or maybe they're members of some cult," Lauri said.

"Cult? Why would you think cult?" Chris asked.

"There seems to be a lot of cults in the Mythos," Lauri replied.

"There's a lot of lone wolves too," Cosmo added.

"Let me make a couple of calls. We'll discuss this more when I'm done."

"Okay," she said, wondering when Chris was going to start railing about the fact that she'd gone out alone.

* * * * *

Christa had safely brought her injured master home. Parking the van in one bay of the three-stall garage of Marsh's mansion, she helped him into the house. She thought they'd been lucky to have eluded the police and capture. Thankful for their escape, she said a brief prayer to Kassogtha.

Inside, sitting at the dining room table, Christa tended to her master's wound as she wondered how things had gone wrong. *Cthulhu, that bitch was strong. I know nigger males are powerful, they were bred as beasts of burden, but I never thought their women were. I'm going to enjoy getting my hands on that bitch.*

"Ahhhhhhhh! Be careful! It stings."

"There. I'm done. The cut is small. We were lucky. Just a couple of cuts and some bruises. You will be fine after the swelling goes down."

"Fine! You call this fine?" he hissed, gently fingering the small egg on his right temple. "That bitch almost killed me. I won't be fine until I cut out her heart and make her drink the blood dripping from it. She's going to pay for this. They're *all* going to pay for what happened tonight. I'm going to keep her nipples in my pocket as a lucky piece. She'll die slowly. When I'm done, little miss librarian will think de Sade's games are as gentle as her mother's caresses. Before I finish with her, that nigger whore is going to beg me to kill her. She's going to beg me!"

"I'm sorry, Lord, I only meant that we escaped undetected and we are not seriously injured. That is all I meant by fine."

"No! Tonight has nothing to do with fine. That cunt got away from me and we lost my scalpel and my gun. Now they will have our fingerprints. Shit! Are your prints on file anywhere?" he asked, not remembering asking her twenty minutes earlier.

"No. I have never been—"

"Neither have I, but they know about you now."

"That will not help them. Even if they realize that it was me in the store today, they have a false name and nothing else but a description."

"You stupid bitch! They have your description, your prints, and they know, or suspect, you're German. And if they connect you with tonight's attack . . . they have the fucking CD's. They must have your prints on them. You've inhibited our freedom to move around unnoticed."

Me! You are the one who had to have this woman tonight. You couldn't wait. If you didn't stop to make a speech before you attacked her she might be dead now. Ethan was right about you. I should kill you tonight while you're sleeping and perform the ceremony myself. What do we need you for? We have everything we need except some skin, and I can obtain that. What a power-hungry asshole you are. You should watch yourself very carefully, the ice you tread upon is becoming very, very thin. "Try to rest, Lord. The troubled colors of weariness paint your face."

"Yes, yes. There's nothing we can do about what happened tonight. Tomorrow the others arrive, and then I'll teach these insects to fear me. Sing for me. No!—read something from Navarre while I rest my eyes," Marsh commanded as he swallowed two aspirins and walked to the sofa to lie down.

"What would you like me to read, Lord?"

"The Requiem," he whispered, closing his eyes. "Read it softly."

Thankfully the Spaniard included it, though it must have sorely galled him, Marsh thought as Christa began to read.

"'The servants of darkness blaspheme against God with our holy words. From the grace of the mass they cast a blight on the earth with their unholy theft. They torture and torment our ears and our souls with demonic usages of our holy words to God.

> *Dies irae, aeternam Dona eis. Domine Cthulhu.*
> *Dies irae, dies illa,*
> *Solvet saeclum in favilla.*
> *Quantus tremor est futurus,*
> *Quando judex Cthulhu est venturus,*
> *Cuncta stricte discussurus!*
> *Cthulhu! Rex tremendae majestatis,*
> *Exaudi orationem meam;*
> *Recordare, domine Cthulhu,*
> *Quod sum causa tuae viae:*
> *Et ab haedis me sequestra,*
> *Statuens in parte dextra.*
> *Exaudi orationem meam;*
> *ad te omnis caro veniet.*
> *Sanctus, sanctus, sanctus,*
> *Dominus Deus Cthulhu*
> *pleni sunt coeli et terra obscurum gloria tua.'"*

Sleep touched Marsh's eyes as she finished reciting the debased version of the Roman Catholic requiem mass.

Yes, sleep, while I decide what to do about you. I know what Ethan said, but maybe this is one of those times when it would be better to improvise, she thought.

* * * * *

"A nine-millimeter Glock. We might get lucky, we've got a decent set of partials and the serial number is intact."

"Don't forget Interpol."

"Got it covered. How's Lauri holding up?"

"Good."

"She was lucky, Chris. The Glock had a full magazine, and one in the chamber. They were ready to take her out one way or the other. This might be a good time for her to take a vacation. Her cousin could take her back to New Orleans until this is resolved. If this guy's ego is as large as we suspect he might try for her again," Rolly told Chris.

"Yeah, maybe. Damnit! I wish I knew what the hell was going on," Chris said, setting down the beer can. His hands shook while trying to light a cigarette.

"Look, Matthews has got everybody all over this. Wouldn't surprise me if we have to interview everybody for a five-mile radius. I'm amazed you can't hear him screaming down there. He's taking this personal. You know how much he adores Lauri. Christ, she's almost a daughter. If it weren't for Lauri, his daughter Sandy would have flunked out of Union, and don't forget those Super Bowl tickets she got for him two years ago. Talk about a debt."

"Yeah."

"Yeah? Is that all you can say?" Rolly asked, wondering if Chris was beginning to fall apart again. *He still can't shake the impotence he feels over their deaths. If he cracks, I'm going to kill this monster myself.*

"I'm just tired."

"Hold tight, man." *Don't fall apart on me now.*

"I will." *I will.* "Did you guys find the scalpel yet?"

"No, but we're sifting the whole goddamn parking lot. If it's here, we'll find it. I'm going to run. I'll have someone over there in a few minutes for those CD's. Hopefully one of these freaks has got a record."

"Don't count on it."

"Hey. Matthews wants to wake up Zyman. Wants something to plaster the streets with. Do you think Lauri's up to trying to construct a composite tonight? I could tell him to wait until morning."

"I'll check and get back to you."

"You take care of yourself. And tell Lauri I'm glad she's safe."

* * * * *

Gregory and Ida's ears caught the reverberating rantings and muffled sobs of a young woman they could not yet see below them.
Gregory's heart raced as he recalled his last little adventure in this
subterranean cathedral. Ida squeezed his hand. He grew hard imagining what was to come. As the pair neared the bottom of the stairway he took note of the fact that the chamber was much darker than
it had been on the previous occasion.

"This time you must catch your prey," Ida whispered in his ear.

"Hunting," he breathed, seeing a dark naked figure dart through
the shadowed edge of torchlight near the far wall.

"Yes, my darling. You must hunt this one. This one is an animal,
vermin. A nigger! Alone, unarmed, and frightened, but quite
strong," Ida said, placing the long-bladed ceremonial knife in his
hand.

"What—"

Ida covered his lips with her finger. "Ssssh. Do with her what
you wish. In this place you are the master. Whatever you conceive
is the law."

"I will make her blood a gift to you," he said, cupping her pert
breast in his right hand.

"Oh, Gregory," she moaned. "Bring the bitch to me!"

Leaving Ida near the stairway he ran into the darkness, away
from where he'd seen the dark-skinned shadow run. Slowly he
walked, silent step by silent step, toward the wall.

Ten minutes of adrenalin-edged silence passed as he crept further
into the blackness.

Standing motionless in the dark, he listened for the soft footfalls
of bare feet on the cavern's floor; straining, he listened for the
woman's breathing. He tilted his head back and tried to smell her
fear, but all he could smell was blood.

Blood!

He could taste it. He could feel it run over him.

Then he caught her scent. The scent of sweat mixed with crazed
hot fear.

"Come to me," he whispered to the dark-skinned maiden huddled in the inky depths. "I said come out, nigger-bitch."

"I'll see you in hell first!" came the maddened-by-fear growl.

"This is hell. Step into the light and see its master."

And she came—a frightened savage beast, claws and teeth bared—desperate to live, ready to kill. "Die!" she screamed at her human hunter as she leapt from the dark to meet the hilt of Marsh's blade crashing into the side of her skull. Her last thought before pain slammed her into the floor was that she'd not even scratched him.

Gregory dragged her, one hand tightly gripping her dark tresses, the other almost pulling the tiny nipple from her overabundant breast, to the altar.

"Here is your gift, my love," he said to Ida, dropping the body upon the holy altar.

"With this flesh you become the chosen of Kassogtha. Cut it open and let Her drink."

Gregory cut the woman open and began shattering the ribs with the knife's pommel, exposing the inner organs and her still-beating heart. Blood rained on the bestial pair as Ida, now naked, jumped on the corpse and lay down, spreading her legs.

"Fuck me now!" she screamed at the blood-covered beast.

* * * * *

Chris, Laurinda, Cosmo, and the Wizard were exploring the costs of the night's tribulations and their possible ramifications when Henri arrived. After explanations and apologies were exchanged they decided further discussion was pointless. All were exhausted, beaten down by frayed nerves and adrenalin. Cosmo, still suffering from the effects of one too many Pabsts, gave his bed to Chris and Laurinda, as the bed Chris had been using was only a single. Henri was given the old but quite comfortable sofa, while Cosmo opted for the futon on the third floor.

Twenty minutes later the building that housed The Horror Corner was dark, and its tenants, permanent and temporary alike, were desperately trying to find some solace in the arms of Morpheus.

The night was painfully spent. He had nothing left. Utterly exhausted and feeling impotent, Chris finally collapsed into the dark arms of fitful sleep. Beside him Laurinda lay quietly, while he twisted on the sweaty sheet. Hands clenched as tightly as eagle talons in prey he embraced the remaining hours of night, his arm choking a pillow.

Passing whispers fluttered in the softly lit, silver-edged clouds of his dream. Washed colors danced on the curved lines of the four winds as he soared, errant motionless movement, through the realms of sleep. Below him the dark floor of tree tops stirred under the sylvan caresses of moonlight. A moment's peace as billowy islands sailed by. Sweet and holy. He sighed, touched by grace.

A sudden chill clothed his body in goosebumps. *Something's out there, and it's coming. I can feel it. Why can't I see it?*

The breeze and its whispers lay still and grew quiet as the silvered light wavered and changed hue. Low-toned hurried murmurs and muffled growls arose around him as the wind shifted, carrying other inhuman sounds to his ears. Off to his right a series of sharp barks found a path to him. Somewhere to his left the high-pitched demonic cackle of hungry laughter clawed its way across the darkening skies.

Turning his face into the agitated winds, he looked toward the horizon which was no longer peaceful. Before his eyes could refocus a howling blade of hate shattered his dream. Boiling, a black-rimmed, gray whirling mass of cancerous apparitions advanced. Unshackled, unleashed, the demon horde arose from the blood pit of a nameless hell and galloped toward his rapidly dissipating Nirvana cloud.

Stewart! The sound bellowed from a thousand burning throats, skewering him. He felt as if he were lashed to a chain link fence woven of razor wire, bait for the apocalyptic horde. His soul was a light morsel for the clamoring black jaws of damnation.

And then he fell—plunging, buffeted by frictionless winds and fear. Instead of splattering against the impending ground he found himself suddenly, inexplicably, chained, several feet above the ground, to a deteriorated wall of dark slime-covered stone. Forced to face forward by a severely binding harness crudely fashioned of metal, his head fought for its freedom against the grating torture device.

Commanding his vision, perhaps thirty feet away, stood an ancient architectural construction of rough-hewn stone in an advanced state of disrepair. The temple of some villainous deity, or the dwelling of a hateful sorcerer, the structure seemed designed by architects whose geometry and sense of balance surely had been strained through half-formed visions stumbled upon in a grotesquely disjointed and misproportioned LSD cruise of demon-haunted vistas. Parts of the alien building were incomprehensible, while others seemed the half-finished work of deranged and less than poorly skilled craftsmen.

God, let this be a dream, Chris thought, although he was sure he was not sleeping but caught in a prophetic vision: the handiwork of some madman, one who had peered over the edge and had returned with new horrors to embellish his lunacy with. He strained to hold his reason in this blasted land where hellish choruses filled his ears and the putrid stench of the charnel house raped his nostrils.

Where am I? Somewhere on the road to the future. Christ, what a horrid place! The smell. And the color. It's like it's covered in . . . red dust? Rust? Oh my God! No! It's blood. Dried blood. How much blood would have to be spilled to cover this landscape?

As his mind fought the concept of oceans of blood drying and turning to sand, his ears picked out a new sound. Behind him, wet, tearing, sucking sounds mixed with choked cries. A renewed fear took him as he wondered what feasters sat gorging themselves on unknown but vividly imagined banquets. His fear and sweat perfumed the air of their dark dinner party.

"My dear Stewart! Greetings, and welcome. How nice of you to attend my little impromptu. I'm honored. And I see you've dressed for my party," said the mocking jester standing before him, its face a featureless smooth mask, its voice anger-sharp, harsh as the hungry jaws of a starving wolf, bitter as forced solitude. "In tatters. How fitting." Cavalierly postured before him, the figure in crimson tails raised its right hand and tapped the brim of the scarlet top hat tilted on its brow before bowing slightly. "You'll be happy to hear you've an excellent chance at winning the door prize for best costume."

"Fuck you!" Chris screamed, straining to reach his gun in the limiting chains and finding it missing.

"Feeling a bit impotent without your metal cock?"

"I still have my hands."

"Hands, guns, and desires will not help you here."

"And where is here?"

"Here is where you are too afraid to believe exists. It is the world, your sweet comforting earth after Li-ure."

Li-ure? "You're insane."

"Was Hitler insane? Or Columbus? Must you always see visionaries as crackpots or dangerously insane madmen?"

"Interesting that you'd mention Hitler, 'cause you're another demented piece of shit."

"If you're so bent on seeing insanity please allow me to show you some."

Turning, the master of ceremonies, with soulless eyes and a frozen smile, clapped his red-gloved hands together, and a gallows of barbed wire nooses and iron maidens appeared beside him.

Incomprehensible atrocity pierced Chris' vision and soul as he saw the murdered prostitutes, hung by their tongues, sway beside the broken and mutilated bodies of his friends. Laurinda, Lindy and her daughter, Anne, Sue and Merry, caged in iron maidens, eyes, mouths, breasts, vaginas, and anuses pierced by rusty penises of bloodied iron. Tears further distorted his vision as he saw Henri and Pat castrated, their entrails hanging like mock genitals, slowly revolving like sweetmeats on a spit. Rolly and Willie, handcuffed to each other around a burning monolith of protruding oversized nails, harmonized with banshees as their flesh seared and the fat of their bodies turned to grease and oozed from their pores. Joni Holland was hog-tied with barbed wire and hanging like a piece of meat for sale in some hellish bazaar. The remains of Cosmo and the Wizard, two battered and bloodied torsos, crushed heads and broken limbs strewn beneath them, were little more than a battlefield of maggots and grave worms. Beside them Plato, Misty, and Bast, hung by their tails, dangled mere inches from the ground while rats feasted on their dying bodies.

"Perhaps I could offer you a mirror so you could view the so-called insanity reflected in your face? No? You unpitiable fool, you know nothing. Your bland, blue-collar imagination cannot stand before my holy vision. Soon this peek at the future I have granted you will become a reality. What do you think of my carnival of atrocities?"

"I think if I get my hands on you, you're fucked."

"Tsk, tsk. My dear Stewart, we've no need for vulgarities," scolded the nightmare-spawned knave while admonishing Chris with his wagging finger.

"Don't talk to me about vulgarities. This surpasses things even Satan would call vulgar. This place you call Li-ure is worse than—"

"Than what? What would you call it?"

"I'd call your psychotic little jihad and its sick accouterments the products of a mind eaten away by the cancer of insanity."

"I caution you to—"

"Didn't your Mommy love you?" Chris barked, attacking with the only weapon at his disposal.

"MY MOTHER WAS A COLD REPULSIVE WITCH WHO IS HOPEFULLY ENJOYING HER STAY IN HELL!" His balled fists shook as if possessed by lighting.

"With you for a kid how could anyone blame her for being repulsed?"

"You try me with your lack of vision and your petty retorts."

"I'd like to try you out back of the barn. No lawyers, no judge, no jury. Just you and me and a bat."

"I can see you're not enjoying your brief visit to my little paradise. What a pity. Perhaps when you've relocated and become one of our permanent residents, you'll begin to appreciate the stunning vistas and the luxurious accommodations."

Someone get me outta here!

"Use the sign," came the gentle glowing voice.

Who?

"I am Kthanid. Use the Elder Sign."

The Elder God Cosmo spoke of? Where are you? How?

"I am far from you. I speak in your mind."

How do I make the sign?

"Simply think of it, then project it with your mind. I must leave you now."

Wait!

"Have you left me, Stewart? Perhaps I bore you?"

As the blathering taunts and terse admonitions continued to be hurled at him, Chris took the outrage that filled his eyes and the remorse that filled his heart and focused it. In his mind the Elder Sign took shape and began glowing until it burned forge-hot. When it seemed too much to bear, he unleashed it. His mental arrow of justice flew true, finding its mark in the dark heart before him.

His heart was pounding as he awoke from his nightmare. A headache the Excedrin plant couldn't dent pummeled his temples as a lingering whisper hissed death promises in his ear. *Is there something here? Has some specter crossed over with me?* he thought, reaching for the light. The dimly illuminated room held nothing but the ghosts and

fear he'd brought into it—fear of failure and the ghosts of the innocent dead. Every molecule in the universe carried their cry as his
cheeks carried his tears. Turning, he saw Laurinda lying beside him
softly breathing.

Lauri! Thank God! You're safe! It was just a bad dream.

Quietly, so as not to disturb her peaceful slumber, he rose and went
into the bathroom. Standing in the claw-foot tub, his chin supported
by his chest, he stared at the black maw by his feet and watched the
water spin downward into the drain. *Life sucked into the black void.
Death*, he thought. *We waste life the way we waste water, needlessly.*

Razor-sharp hot water tried to burn the tension built by fitful
sleep from his neck and shoulders. His right arm hurt from sleeping
on it and the muscles of his legs and back faintly screamed from too
little sleep. Reaching for the shampoo bottle, dark pink strawberry
something, his hand slipped and he dropped the bottle, which
bounced, sending splatters flying, to cling like oozing blood on the
plastic shower curtain.

Wasted blood. Wasted life. "For what?"

"Because I decree it!" came a hissed whisper through the stream
of near-scalding water.

"Now I'm hearing shit while I'm awake." *Gonna need a long break
from this one.* "Hey, you still listening?"

No reply.

"Go fuck yourself."

❦ Chapter Twenty-Nine ❦

Gregory Bradshaw Marsh sluggishly rolled onto his back and opened his eyes. As the glaring morning light of winter, intensified by the icy mirror of frozen snow, pierced his eyes, pain, quickly followed by anger, hit him hard. *The bastards will pay!* was his first thought. Coffee and aspirin were the second. Looking at Christa, sleeping beside him, his anger escalated. *You stupid cunt! You should have shot her! It's your fault she escaped.* "Fuck you," he hissed at her as he left the room. "I've things to do today."

* * * * *

Chris leaned against the dresser and lit a cigarette. Through the coils of blue smoke he watched Laurinda sleep, her breathing soft and even. *Thank God you weren't hurt. I've got to get you away from here.* Looking up, he saw a painting of Kassogtha hanging above the bed. *Jesus Christ! No wonder I had nightmares, sleeping under that damned thing. It looks a little bit like one of Marsden's paintings. Wait a minute! If Kassogtha is such a small-potatoes deity why did someone paint her? Cthulhu, I can see, but Cos never said anything about being a painter.* Walking to the painting, Chris looked at the signature. Katy Prior. *Who the hell is Katy Prior and how does she know about Kassogtha? I'll find out when Cos gets up. Shit! The note! I've got to ask him what Li-ure is, or means. It's gotta be a Mythos name. I just hope it's one he knows, and it means something useful.*

Butting his cigarette in the black ashtray on the dresser, Chris looked at the items neatly arranged upon it. In the rear corners stood two small black gargoyles. Fangs bared, wings outspread, the forever-vigilant guardians of the polished walnut chapel seemed poised, ready to administer their charge. Safe within the sphere of their protective gazes were two inlaid silver framed photographs of Cosmo's departed paramour Virve, her imaginative dark eyes shining in the warm professional-looking portraits.

Guess he's not over her yet, Chris thought, lighting the morning's second cigarette. "Does anyone ever really recover from the loss of love?" he whispered as he stared into the silver window frames of Cosmo's heart.

Placed in the center of the immaculately kept shrine of remembrance lay a cigar-box-sized, cut-glass box with a small, snow-white likeness of the Dailbutsu Buddha meditating atop it. Resting safely in the transparent sarcophagus on a deep maroon layer of velvet lay a slim black leather book with the title embossed in gold leaf, *Visions of Yaddith and Other Poems* by Ariel Prescott.

Yaddith? I think that's a Mythos name. Does this have anything to do with Kassogtha? Something else I'll have to ask him. 7:15. Better get some tea, and a couple aspirins wouldn't hurt. Today's gonna seem like getting battered by a hurricane with all the razor-toothed assholes barking their endless, unanswerable questions.

* * * * *

The sun was pouring through her window at 7:30 a.m. and Claudia Richards was still awake. She had been having a great deal of trouble sleeping since her roommate Angela had been butchered on New Year's Day.

Fifty-five bucks last night. How the fuck am I goin' to get out of this dump on scratch like this. Cheap asshole johns don't seem to be nowhere. Pieces of shit are more afraid than we are, with all those fuckin' cops everywhere. And they want free blow-jobs, while they're busy makin' my business hell. Another grand and I could be in Florida. All those nice old retired guys would be quick, easy pickings. Bet the old fucks would pay a bundle for head. Bet they'd pay for just a smile and wiggle—not like the fuckin' assholes here who think you should work your ass off for a couple of bucks. I hate this fuckin' cold. Standin' out in wind and snow for twenty lousy bucks. I want to be where it's warm. Good old Florida. Close to the water. Shakin' my ass at the beach. Maybe by the end of the week I can make enough bread to blow this ratty shithole. Just a few more tricks and it will be fun in the sun.

Claudia Richards pulled the covers tight, and tried to go to sleep. *A few more and I'll be gone.* "Just a few."

* * * * *

Marsh parked in the short-term parking lot of the Albany County Airport and immediately entered the terminal. He stood rigid for ten minutes waiting for the passengers to deplane.

Before him stood his new vassals, two with heads tilted reverentially, the remaining four greeting Marsh with calculating and hungry eyes. Cautiously, he looked them over with the judgmental eye of a steel-handed SS general.

Roaker, you transparent cretin, I see your tiny machinations. Boot-licking toady, you'll do exactly as I instruct you. You'll be too afraid not to.

Vernon McClellan. Our southern gentleman. Roaker says he's the cruelest man he's ever encountered. Certainly looks it. Cold, unreadable eyes, scarred skin like old leather.

Marsh scanned his mental bio of McClellan: three tours in Vietnam commanding some spookish Special Ops coterie which floated, like unseen wraiths, through the jungles of Cambodia and Laos dispensing their highly stylized species of death and psychological terror. Heir to a sizeable petrochemical fortune, and almost revered as a god in the Southeast Asian antiquities underworld.

He should make a good lieutenant, but he'll bear watching, Marsh warned himself.

Charles Atherton Selby and his wife, Sela Astley. Cthulhu, what an ugly old bitch! He mentally winced at the pale, skeletal woman, who the years had harshly worn. *Her face is meaner looking than McClellan's. Why did Selby marry her? All that wealth, or was it her connections to the Starry Wisdom sect and the Brotherhood of the Beast? Doesn't matter. They'll serve their purpose.*

Motohiko Yano. Filthy gooks are little more than a nigger subspecies. Look at those eyes—no color. They're not human, they're the eyes of an animal. I'll deal with the slant-eyed dwarf after he's served his purpose . . . although he could prove to have long-term value to me. I'll need someone to watch over the Asian herds. And who more fitting to lord over the Chinese than a Japanese. Almost imperceptibly, he bowed in greeting to Yano.

Marsh recalled the bat-winged rumors he'd heard on three continents regarding Yano. How a young Yano, to show his devotion, had had his body completely covered with a lavishly detailed octopoid tattoo, and then spent the next two decades of pious instruction under Darius Pschenischnikova. Roaker believed Pschenischnikova had given Yano the fabled *Scythian Scrolls* before his death two winters ago—Marsh wondered if they might be in the attaché case Yano gripped in his right hand. And then there were the unsubstantiated whispers Yano had attended, as an honored guest, a Tcho-Tcho conclave ten years ago. Also whispered about were Yano's two voyages to the Antarctic. Henryk Deuber in Bremen had personally disclosed to Marsh the exacting sailing arrangements he'd made on Yano's behest for the second expedition—"Yes, that is correct. The vessel's destination was McMurdo Sound."

This one may prove far more valuable than I previously anticipated, Marsh said to himself a second time, envious of Yano's experiences.

"Hatred is a tool. Sharpen it, but do not soil the blade needlessly," Ida had told him. *Perhaps her instruction should be applied here*, he thought.

As of this moment all their knowledge and networks are mine, Marsh thought, allowing himself to smile. If his new lieutenants could have heard the tone of his self-obsessed thought they would have fled or cowered in terrorized supplication.

Moving two steps to his right Marsh extended his hand to the venerable figure standing before him.

Smartly dressed in an expensive, hand-tailored charcoal gray suit, sartorially topped by penetrating gray eyes a shade lighter than the suit and by a cascading silver mane, Bennett James Meadow met Marsh's gaze. While fingering the solid platinum octopus that crested his black cane, which seemed an extension of his willowy arm, Meadow assessed the young warlord he had been invited to attend.

Bennett James Meadow, the famed occult power broker known from out-of-the-way and avoided cobblestone alleys, grimly shaded under ancient towers and quickly whispered rumor, in Edinburgh to the perilous, luxuriant private rooms of certain establishments in Bangkok. Bennett James Meadow, the London-born necromancer fearfully esteemed in a dozen power-laden, secret societies common men were more than ignorant of. Bennett James Meadow, scandalously dismissed Oxford professor, banned author, once-favored student and, rumored trusted confidant of Crowley himself, introduced in glowing terms to Gregory in a letter bearing Ethan Marsh's signature. That letter, arriving early last summer, highly unexpected and seemingly out of the blue, was one of a scant few pieces of correspondence between the cousins since Gregory had received word of Ida's passing early in 1973.

Marsh knew this man moved easily through elegant and exotic worlds. He'd be equally at home in exclusive clubs where the bouquet of debate and cigars permeated high-ceilinged rooms of richly oiled paneling and accomplished dialogue, as in indulgence-lacquered chambers where the dancing bullwhip caressed breast and buttocks in ornately framed, antique full-length mirrors as it drew blood. On how many occasions had Meadow's expensively booted feet padded the hard, worn floors of hidden caverns, to observe, or participate in, mystic rites of primal worship?

"Mr. Meadow, I have looked forward to meeting you," Gregory said in a crisp pleasant tone.

"And I you, Mr. Marsh," the tall elder man replied, returning Marsh's firm handshake with a vital grip Marsh was surprised to encounter. "You are about to make my last seventy years seem little more than a poverty-stricken child's meager birthday celebration."

"Very true. We should be going. After you, Mr. Meadow. It's only a short drive to my home."

"Thank the spawn of the Mother," Meadow responded. "The flights were quite tiring. I am not quite as young as I once was," he said with a demon-humored smile that caused Marsh a slight shudder.

* * * * *

"Morning, Chris," Cosmo said as he reached for the aspirin bottle. "Sorry about last night. The Wizard gets passionate at times. He means well, it's just this thing is getting to him. Not that it's not affecting me."

"Don't sweat it. I'd be pissed if I were him. I wish I hadn't involved you two in this."

"Part of me wishes the same thing, but the other part, the Mythos fan, wouldn't miss this for the world. I mean, I wish this fuck never killed anybody, but having a Lovecraft story kinda coming to life like this, well, I'd hate to read about this after the fact. Does that sound sick?"

"A little, but I understand," he said, thinking about the intellectual versus emotional wars of homicide investigation. "Just so you know, we've been granted a reprieve. Chief gave us seventy-two hours to work a miracle or . . . . There's a couple of things that came up last night we never got around to."

"Like?"

"There was a note on Willie's body that had what I think is a new word. I mean we haven't come across it before. Ever heard of Li-ure?"

In the painful mental fog caused by too little sleep and too much drink Cosmo formed the word Li-ure. "No. Can I see the note?"

Chris handed Cosmo a copy of the note. "Any guesses?"

"Yeah. Li-ure is when the GOO are coming back. Brian Lumley called it 'The Fury' in *The Transition of Titus Crow*."

"The Fury, name makes sense. They've been imprisoned for millions of years and they're pissed when they get here. Nothing can stop Li-ure. This maniac thinks nothing can stop his gods from returning. Why didn't I see that?" Chris said.

"A lot happened last night. Emotionally you musta been on a roller coaster ride through hell."

"True. Li-ure isn't a Mythos word?"

"Not that I know of."

"Then where did he get it?"

Cosmo shrugged.

"I keep thinking you know it all."

"Not even close. Even though I follow it, there's stuff I miss, and there could be stories in German or Japanese, might be stuff in Portuguese or Russian I've never heard of. And I wouldn't doubt there's a ton of unpublished stuff out there that's privately circulated. Remember me saying this freak might know more than me? He could have made it up."

"Could be. He's living in a fantasy world, and you thought he made up his title."

"Bingo. He's adding to the Mythos just like the writers. Makes sense. It's part of the game."

"Great. Something sensible about the behavior of a psycho. Couple of other things I wanted to ask."

Cosmo's head was beaten and burnt, it wanted an anti-Cthulhuvian vacation—a long one—but his heart wanted revenge. "Okay," he said. It sounded more like a groan than a word.

"There's a painting over your bed."

"*Kassogtha Supreme*. Great painting."

"If you say so. One, who's Katy Prior, and if Kassogtha is hardly known where'd you come up with a painting of her. Two, there's a book in a glass box on your dresser called *Visions of Yaddith*. Is it a Mythos book?"

"Katy Prior is a girl I went to Mont Pleasant High School with. She moved to Frisco after graduation and became a painter, noteworthy in some circles. About ten years ago she was in town and we ran into each other. While she was here we dated. Seems she had a crush on me in high school, although I didn't know it then. So, while we were dating she developed an interest in the GOO and did a series of paintings. I told her about Kassogtha and she painted that one for me. Does that cover it?"

"Yeah, I guess so. Does she still paint Lovecraft stuff?"

"Only the five she did ten years ago. Why?"

"I'm not sure, just curious. I thought there might be something here, something we've overlooked. What does she paint now?"

"Landscapes made of metal, partially inspired by the work of H. R. Giger and Randall Marsden, but her interest in metal developed when she was a teenager. Her father was a welder and she used to hang around his shop."

"Prior's. I remember that shop. Ten-hundred block of Strong, near Brandywine. They fixed my bike once."

"Bingo. Katy's father welded extended forks on my Sting Ray. Wizard hated the thing, but . . . sissy bar, hand brakes, black banana seat, and extended forks, man I thought I was a biker. Cut the sleeves off my denim jacket—my mother pitched a fit you could hear up and down the block."

"How about the book?"

"First edition. Charnel House, London 1927, and I'm 99.9% positive it's the only copy in existence."

"Is it a Mythos book?"

"Yeah. Half of it anyway, the other half is Dreamlands-based. Do you remember me telling you about Lovecraft's Dreamlands?"

"Do I ever," he responded, covering his ears.

"Christ, another comedian. Well, these poems were written before 'The Call of Cthulhu', Lovecraft's first real Mythos story. Some of Prescott's poetry even predates 'The Festival', which was '24, and 'The Hound', which was '22. "

"Why's it the only copy?"

"Prescott died screaming about dholes in Oakdeene Sanitarium in '27."

Cosmo's statement hit Chris like a cold shower. "Oakdeene's a real nuthouse?"

"Yep. Near Glasgow. Lumley mentions it a lot."

"Christ! Another real Mythos occurrence."

"Hey, I didn't choreograph this ballet—I'm just a dancer."

"Glad to hear it! You'd make a shitty Diaghilev," the Wizard sarcastically commented upon entering the kitchen, last night's rage no longer tattooing his haggard features.

"Thanks."

"Don't mention it. Mornin', Chris."

"Hi. About last night—"

"We'll discuss it later. Give me a few minutes to sensitize my brain to the fact it's still among the living."

"Sure. By the way, Carroll gave us another seventy-two hours before he pulls the plug. So how'd you get the book, Cos?"

"Prescott's family—Prescott isn't the real family name by the way—had every copy destroyed after her death. I guess they were trying to find a way of erasing the pain of her insanity and suicide. It's gotta be tough on a family to bury someone so brilliant and so young. She was only twenty-four. The copy you saw in my room was discovered in '76 by her grandnephew. I managed to purchase it before it could be destroyed, thanks to the efforts of Tom Desmond."

"She died screaming about dholes before the Mythos existed." *Only one copy in the world.* "If you've got the only known copy in the world . . . would our freak want the book?"

"Bet yer ass he would. If his whole fantasy world consists of the Mythos, then he'd want anything that has to do with it. The son of a bitch must be obsessive, and collectors, at least most that I've met, will often stop at nothing to obtain items they deem vital," the Wizard said.

"Have you read it?" Chris asked Cosmo.

"Sure. Just once though, actually read it aloud into a tape recorder, and later transcribed it onto a computer file. It's fragile," Cosmo replied.

"Talk about your obsessive collectors—you're looking at a hall-of-famer. And one who's in good standing to boot."

"Could we use anything in it against this psycho?" Chris asked.

"Not really," Cosmo replied.

"Could we lie about what's in the book?" Chris asked.

"Yeah! I'd bet the farm, or in this case the store, that this freak has no idea what's in the book. We could probably say it contains anything we want."

"Then I think it's time we wake the others up and have a little meeting before the press arrives."

"But what about your boss? What's he going to say about this?" the Wizard asked.

"Fuck him. I want this bastard, and I've got a feeling we're getting real close," Chris said, holding up his thumb and his forefinger a quarter of an inch apart. "Cos, I want you to cook up a believable lie or two about the book, something we can feed to the media. Something that our boy can't dispute, and more importantly something so alluring he can't resist."

"I'll get on it as soon as I wake up my darker half here. How you feelin' bro, or shouldn't I ask?"

After popping three aspirins and taking a long pull off of a forty-ounce bottle of Dole Orchard Peach Juice the Wizard, attempting a friendly scowl, grumbled a line from Scrapper Carr's "Tomorrow Is A Long, Long Day": "'Can't get it goin' this morning, not even sure it's worth tryin'.'"

* * * * *

How can she make me do this, Gregory thought, letting the events of the last four months replay in his mind. "Kassogtha damn Ethan! This is his fault."

"I trust you will honor your promise." He could hear Ethan's voice, half-plea, half-command, as he looked down at the bags of luggage sitting by the door.

Gregory was still juggling thoughts and emotions ten minutes later when the Marsh family retainer, Douglas Whatley, knocked at the open door.

"Good morning, sir. Mr. Ethan sent me for your bags."

"They're ready."

"Very good, sir. I'll take them to the car. Miss Ida instructed me to tell you that she is waiting for you in the library."

"Tell her I'll be down shortly."

"Very good, sir." Whatley removed the two bags and left Marsh in the empty bedroom.

Marsh stared after him into the doorway where Ida had first appeared as if he were waiting for a reprieve or a miracle, but nothing came to break the silent hopelessness of his thoughts except the soft Westminster chimes of the anniversary clock on the mantle. Reining in his fears, Marsh embraced the cold brass doorknob. Closing the door, he began his journey homeward.

As he walked down the hallway and descended the stairs, he nodded his goodbyes to the portraits of long dead Marshes he had often engaged in one-sided conversations. At the bottom of the stairs he exchanged detached polite good-byes with a Marsh he occasionally wished dead—his rival, Ethan.

"Please honor the promise you have given to me," Ethan said in closing. Then like Marsh's hopes he was gone, the weight of his final command hanging from Gregory like a chain, binding and limiting his last and most important goodbye.

Ida rose from her chair, a spring flower blooming, sending its color and bouquet skyward, as Gregory entered the library. And like the prisoner of winter released to behold the first crocuses of gentle spring, Marsh held the treasure offered him. His eyes, the searching eyes of a child looking to his mother as he boards a school bus on the first day of kindergarten, loving, afraid and pleading, asked to be released from the fearful uncertainty of the canvas that the future considered with brush and paints at the ready. She came across the room, taking his hands and whispering promises and instructions. Embraces, words, and tears mixed, forming memories his eyes, ears, and mouth would later replay as if they were favorite melodies. Then, like a lover's revelry, too intoxicating and far too short, the goodbye ended. Fingers withdrew from his grasp as she bestowed a last, faint, momentary kiss on her dark prince.

Marsh found the waiting black limousine and entered its dark interior. As it turned left onto Washington Street he thought to turn, to take one final look, but did not. What was there to see? Someone had turned the page.

* * * * *

The media, bored with nonrecord-breaking snow falls and the doldrums of winter, were little better than frenzied sharks as they fell upon the interviewees. The Wizard, never comfortable in public except when before small thankful audiences, contained his revulsion of suits, painted-on smiles, and sensationalized questions, while skillfully disseminating the predominantly erroneous information. True to their nature, the media swallowed the chunks whole. Beside him Cosmo, usually appreciative of an audience willing to endure his rambling Mythos minilectures, found the interviewers, especially the national media dolls, underresearched and highly insensitive.

Chris, Henri, and Lt. Marlin Matthews fleshed out the panel, which by three o'clock had finished their performances. Now all they had to face was the clock and their fears. None were patient fishermen.

After Matthews left, Henri collected Laurinda, who had been upstairs observing the proceedings on the surveillance monitors, and took her and her protests, both the rational and irrational alike, home, where they would be placed under constant police protection.

* * * * *

Cosmo lifted the receiver from the cradle on the third ring. "Horror Corner. Can I help you?"

"I want to speak to stewart," the harsh voice demanded.

"Can I tell him who's calling?"

"A close friend."

"Your name?"

"I've no time for games. Tell him it's his nigger whore's dance partner. Tell him she was lucky and be quick about it." The command lashed at Cosmo, fast as an arcing razor, coarse as sandpaper.

"I'm here," Chris replied in a tone as hate-riddled as the death he wished across the phone line.

"So we meet. Unfortunately not face to face. But soon."

"How do I know this isn't a prank?"

"You require proof? The nigger cop didn't get to finish his smoke. Marlboro as I recall. How's that? Not enough yet? Ask the guitar player how he liked his date with Veronica."

"You fuckin'—"

"Now, now, stewart, adversaries should be civil."

"After what you've done?"

"Done? I have yet to start. Holy Li-ure is almost upon you and you've run out of time. While you have the chance, you should pray to your hollow god."

"Fuck you and your Li-ure shit! Why don't you come here with your bullshit goddess and we'll do this right. Just you and me, you chickenshit asshole."

"Detective Sergeant. Temper, temper."

Although the tone of Marsh's admonishment was rigidly polite, Chris felt he had been spat upon.

"I see my time is up. Stewart, everything is ready! I wish I could make you see. You think I'm mad and the Holy Mother is just some dark manifestation born of insanity, but you're wrong. She's real and tomorrow you will see. Did you hear me, stewart? Tomorrow!"

Tomorrow . . . tomorrow . . . tomorrow . . . . The cries of the dead reverberated within the echoing word. Chris closed his eyes, hoping it would seal his ears. He couldn't bear the thought of another victim harmonizing with the anguished cacophony.

The connection severed, Chris quickly asked if they'd traced the call.

"Got it, but you're not going to like it," came the reply.

"Where?" Chris asked.

"Colonie Center concourse."

"Shit! A mall pay phone on a Saturday afternoon. He's probably halfway to his car by now. Thanks, Ron."

"Sorry, Chris."

Christ! This bastard's smart. He could be from anywhere. He said everything's ready and it's happening tomorrow. Shit!

* * * * *

Beaming, Marsh opened the door and got in the car. Beside him Bennett James Meadow asked how his call had gone.

"Like a charm. The cop's pissed off—I could hear the anger and frustration in his voice"

"Excellent. Then we are finally ready for the greatest moment in history to occur."

"When this is done we will have had a larger impact on humanity than Buddha, Mao, Hitler, and Jesus Christ combined," Marsh said.

"Everything in history, except perhaps the asteroid which crashed into the Yucatán peninsula, will pale before what we are about to accomplish. With one stroke we shall irrevocably change the face of the Earth."

"Yes, a fitting destiny for these insects," Marsh agreed.

"Evil permeates this charnel house man calls the cosmos. It is only fitting that that which once held dominion over the Earth is called home," Meadow said. "The world is waiting. As we speak, the seams rip apart, exposing the hatred and violence which prowls the hallways of the human soul. Everything is ready for the glory of the Holy Ones. *IÄ KASSOGTHA!*"

"*IÄ KASSOGTHA! HPTUGN! G'GCHNA NI'ZOS I'GAQ!*"

"*G'GCHNA NI'ZOS I'GAQ!* There will be a new order when they have returned. Even the shark, lord of the seas, who has lived for almost a hundred million years unchanged and perfect as he has no natural enemies, will flee in terror as the oceans swell with a new master."

A new master indeed. A king ordained by a goddess. And I am that king. The Lord Fng'i, *chosen of the Queen Mother, soon to be shepherd over all the flocks of Earth.* "Do you know what I'm most looking forward to?"

"No."

"The nursery. Does that sound strange?"

"Not at all."

"Over the years I've spent a great deal of time wondering what her holy offspring will look like. Gods sired by gods. Years ago my cousin and I discussed what her children might look like."

"I'm certain they will be wondrous to behold."

"Yes, they will. They certainly will."

* * * * *

The sun had set four hours ago and now darkness covered the blanket of winter white. Beyond the cemetery's gate the wind sounded like rushing water in the whipping limbs. From inside The Horror Corner the meager light shed by a few lamps escaped the windows, cutting thin pale splinters into the bitter gloom that held the building in its grasp.

Like moistureless leaves torn from limbs and held prisoner in swirling tunnels of blustering autumnal wind, Cosmo and the Wizard spent the hours locked in the gray desolation of another's dark longings. As the blues men sat over their long cold cemetery tea watching the inchworm clock track into the unknown, ifs and whens performed mock ballets to the blurred melodies of maybe.

"Did it ever occur to you we're getting too damn old for this?" Cosmo asked, breaking a lengthy silence.

"Huh?"

"All these bogies and chimeras," he said, gesturing toward the store's merchandise.

"You just need a beer," the Wizard commented, realizing it was again his turn to play sounding board and mother.

"No, really."

"Really what? Sell insurance? Maybe you'd prefer a nice little office job? Two or three plants on the desk, and FLY 92 playing mindless, overproduced feelgood dance crap in the background while we stuff papers into gray file cabinets. Maybe we'd get lucky and not have some frustrated wannabe as a boss. Look around. This is the life those people dream of."

"Not all of 'em."

"Okay, so it's not a nightclub on the beach in Maui or a fishing cabin in the Adirondacks, but there's no clocks or interoffice politics picking our pockets, and we don't have to raise our hands to go to the bathroom."

"Want a brew?"

"In a minute," the Wizard said in a fast, serious tone. "You weren't born to live behind a picket fence with Rockwellian collectors' plates depicting scenes plucked from a forty-year-old version of the American Dream decorating the walls of some quaint suburban bungalow. Think about it! You wanna wind up sitting in a paneled basement with a Naugahyde bar and shag carpeting watching a football game with a black velvet portrait of Elvis for company? If you chuck this, how many women with intelligent eyes and thirty-eight-inch busts in halter tops are going to ask to buy you a beer, slip you their number, or tell you how great you sing 'I Want to Be Loved' and 'Mannish Boy?' Do you think perks and adoration like that just come driving down the identically manicured streets of suburbia? Don't let this shit bring you down."

"Thank you, Neil Young."

"That's right! He had the right idea. Just let it pass."

"Oz has spoken."

"I guess you could put it that way."

"Gimme strength and gimme shelter! You win."

"Good. I'll have that beer now."

* * * * *

Chris sat in another corner of the building fidgeting, wrestling frustrations and a room full of ghosts adorned in the rags of his guilt. Looking up at one of Cosmo's gargoyles he asked, "Aren't you guys supposed to keep the demons outta here? And you," he said, picking up a model of Thor, "you're a mythological hero with super powers, why don't you fix this mess?"

"Thor, huh," Cosmo said as he entered the room.

"Sorry, I was just admiring how well it was painted. Musta been tough. Did you paint it?"

"Yeah. Sometimes when I'm bored I work on models. It's a kind of therapy, I guess."

"You did all these?"

"Yeah. I pretty much do the monsters for the Wizard and the superheroes for me. I'm still big on comics—not fanatical, mind you, but interested. We've considered branching out into comics on a couple of occasions but the competition's too stiff in this area, what with Fantaco and all."

"I loved comics when I was a kid."

"Yeah, you mentioned it. Did you like the heroes or the villains better?"

"The heroes. Didn't everybody?"

"No. I loved the villains. Marvel's of course, DC's villains were little more than cardboard cutouts as far as I was concerned. Man, Stan and Jack were brilliant. Did you have a favorite villain?"

"The Red Skull."

"He was one of the Wizard's. Mine were Dragon Man, Baron Zemo, and Loki. And I loved Hydra, and Dormammu. Guess that's where my love of horror got its roots."

"I don't recall him."

"Archenemy of Dr. Strange. He was a demon sorcerer—had a head that was a ball of fire."

"He must have been after my time. Other than the Red Skull, the only other villains I remember are the Mole Man, Dr. Doom, and Galactus."

"Dr. Doom was great—driven by loss, vengeance, and egotism. That's one of the things that made Marvel so great, the bad guys were three-dimensional—they had depth. They weren't just petty criminals looking to pick up a few bucks. Hell, it's stupid to have Superman with all those powers fighting bank robbers. I've always felt a hero is only as great as the obstacles he has to overcome. The greater the evil and the struggle, the greater the hero."

"Guess we could use a superhero to clean this mess up."

"Don't need one. I told the Wizard you were our superhero. Our own personal Judge Dredd. I think you're going to do fine."

"Thanks."

"You're welcome. Funny how things go, the Wizard discovered *Playboy* and left comics behind, which is normal I guess. Me, I stayed with 'em all these years. Wonder what that says about my personality? Probably some kind of Peter Pan complex."

"What it says, Cosmo, is that you're just interested in a good story where the good guys win."

"Amen to that! How 'bout havin' a beer with me and the Wiz while it's quiet?"

"Let me give Lauri a call first."

"Sure thing."

* * * * *

"Good afternoon. How are you feeling?" he asked, setting his briefcase down beside the sofa.

"As well as anyone could be expected to after suffering the cruelest joke of all," she replied. *We manage to convince Gregory I had a brain tumor to get rid of him, and then I suffer two strokes. Why? Have I not done everything she required?*

"You look tired, dearest. You know what the doctor has said about driving yourself so hard. Have you been overexerting yourself again?"

"Perhaps, but Seth needed my assistance. Do you have time to sit with me for a while? You seem so busy these days."

"I have the rest of the day to spend with you. Would you like to sit in the solarium?"

"No, I would rather sit here by the fire, if you don't mind. The house seems so cold these days. I can't recall a winter this harsh."

"I think '88 was much worse."

"It brought us more snow, but the temperatures were not anywhere near this frigid."

"I had a letter waiting for me at the office this morning. It was from our long departed cousin in New York."

"And what does he have to say?" Ida asked as she adjusted the lap throw covering her wheelchair-bound legs.

"It's really nothing more than another invitation to attend his approaching ceremony," Ethan replied, taking a seat beside his fragile sister.

"Have all the participants arrived?"

"The letter says in two days, which should be today."

"And does he mention your German *whore*?"

"Ida, I wish you would—in passing, yes."

"I don't understand what you see in her. I never did." *I should have never let you go to Brussels alone. If I had been there, you would have been far too busy to notice that power-hungry slut.*

"Please don't be jealous. She is merely a dalliance."

"A five-year dalliance?"

"No one will ever replace you," he said, taking her hand and pressing his lips softly against it.

"Nor should they try! I still have a great many methods for dealing with bothersome situations at my disposal. You might remind her of that again. I have only tolerated your little witch out of my love for you. I am more than aware of the emotional and physical activities you require, things I can no longer provide you. My body may be failing me, but my eyes still behold a vital man. A man of vast desires—one I shall not lose. I would warn her if I were you, I will not be completely replaced."

"How many times must I tell you, I would never allow another to push you aside. Don't you understand I love only you?" he said, gently squeezing her pale hand. "How many times must I say the words."

"You know full well I will never tire of you telling me." *Trapped within this delicate shell, what else have I left? What I wouldn't give for one night in your arms.*

Ethan rose and kissed her forehead before wrapping his arms around her. "You know I would pay any price to change your lot, but—"

"It was a small price for Her freedom, and there have been rewards."

"She should make you a living saint when she arrives. At times I wish I—may she feast on my living flesh, but I sometimes regret what you did for her. Was it truly necessary?"

"I know, my darling, I too hold regrets, but it had to be done. What use is a door without a key?"

"Perhaps we could have unhinged the door with the use of force."

"Countless others have tried and failed; this was the only way. In your heart you know that to be true."

"I only wish there had been another who might have taken your place."

"Ssssh," she whispered, placing her tremor-inflicted finger to his lips. "Has there been any communication from your witch?"

"No. I do not expect to hear from her until after the ceremony has occurred," he said, taking her hand in his to quell the shaking brought on by overexhaustion and excitement.

"And then?"

"We shall review our options. Now, I think you should rest. Come, let me tuck you in and rub your back for a while."

"At times I think you believe me to be an old woman," she said, smiling—wishing her body would allow more than just his hands gently massaging her back.

"I am only looking after your health. I almost lost you twice and I am not about to take any more chances."

"Can we stop and look at our blossoms for a moment before you put me down?"

"Whatever you wish."

❦ Chapter Thirty ❦

"Is there anything we've overlooked? Any last detail we need to tend to before the ceremony?" Bennett James Meadow asked Marsh.

"Everything is finished and in place," Christa answered for Marsh, who seemed too deeply lost in himself to reply.

"All we have left to do is procure the sacrificial material," Roaker excitedly interjected.

"I can take care of that," Vernon McClellan said. "It will be a simple matter for me to pick up some dimwitted streetwalker."

"It might be better if I did it," Sela Astley said. "After all, who would suspect anything injurious from an unattractive woman of my stature seeking lesbian sex from a whore."

"They probably suspect Christa's involvement in the other killings," McClellan said, staring at Astley and thinking that no one, not even a whore, would consider bedding her emaciated and repulsive form.

"She is young and beautiful. I fit neither description."

"They are not looking for women," Marsh said, coming to life in the edgy air. Air warmed by their collective anticipation—thin as a revenant and as heavy as the charge Marsh shouldered. "They are looking for me. Christa, you and Sela will both go. I'm sure a thousand dollars for spending the night with two lesbians will be more than sufficient to tempt whatever whore you deem fitting. I doubt the nickel-and-dime whores of Schenectady will be able to resist that kind of money."

"Yes, you're right," Meadow said. "The police will not suspect two women."

"Thank you," Marsh said. "It will also make it easier to control the bitch once you find her. Besides, Christa knows the route into the city."

"What if she's seen?"

"In a dark vehicle on a snowy night? That I doubt. She goes!" came the command from Marsh, who knew in a few hours he would have the Earth as his toy, to play briefly with and then smash.

"But she might—" McClellan started to interject.

"I am the law! You would be unwise to question my decisions."

"Of course, Lord Marsh. Please forgive me." Scowling, but unwilling to test Marsh, McClellan retreated a few steps.

"They will leave at six to procure the offering. The rest of you make sure everything else is ready," Marsh ordered, leaving the room of fearful attendants.

* * * * *

Chris' morning seemed to be moving at an impossibly slow pace until Jack Beckett called saying there was another black envelope sitting on his desk, and that Rolly and Marlin Matthews were already on their way to inspect it.

"You hear that?" Chris asked Cosmo.

"Sure did. The freak said today was the day. Do you think it's an invitation?"

"Of sorts. Better fire up your computer. When Rolly calls I want to pump whatever we get in there."

"I hope this one's useful in some way."

"Not half as much as I do." *Shit! That came out wrong.*

"RPI just read the weather report, looks like we're gonna get that storm they've been predicting."

"How much?"

"Twenty-four to thirty inches and blizzard-strength winds, we could get gusts of up to forty-five or fifty miles an hour. Maybe this SOB won't be able to come out tonight."

"I don't think the flood itself would stop this lunatic."

On the phone Rolly and Chris briefly discussed the note while it was being faxed from Beckett's office to The Horror Corner. Chris watched Cosmo read the note, looking for a spark to ignite. None did. Cosmo shook his head and silently mouthed the word "sorry", as Chris read the words "your nigger girlfriend's tits" on the fax.

"This son-of-a-bitch is all over our shit," Rolly said. "How the hell can he do it? He's placed an accomplice in the store, butchered Willie, and stalked Lauri. What else does he know about us?"

"A hell of a lot more than we know about him."

"Ask Cosmo if he recognizes the two names mentioned in the letter, Randolph Carter and Titus Crow," Rolly asked Chris. "They seem familiar."

Chris put Rolly on the speaker phone. "Cos, Rolly wants to know who these two people are."

"They're both Mythos characters, good guys, who have battled and defeated, or at least held at bay, various members of the GOO and/or their minions. He's taunting you."

"I'm going to get this to the lab. I'll call you as soon as I know anything," Rolly said. "One thing, Chris, when we catch this racist bastard I've half a mind to make him strange fruit."

"Rolly, I promise when we meet this fuck we're giving him a pre-paid, nonrefundable, nontransferable, one-way ticket straight to hell." *After what he tried to do to Lauri we won't be sending this piece of garbage to some loony bin on the insanity plan.*

"I'll make sure he boards that flight. I'm glad you're back with the living. I thought you were going to crack on us the other day."

"Sorry I shook you, but don't sweat it . . . I'm here for the duration. Talk to you later."

* * * * *

"Is there anything I can do to make you more comfortable, Lord?" Christa asked her expectant, pacing lord.

"No. Yes—have they updated the weather report?"

"Yes, Lord. We are definitely getting the storm."

"Then Fu-Shen's prophesy will be fulfilled. The blizzard heralds her arrival. Come here and please your Master, my soon-to-be-queen! We shall celebrate my ascendancy early."

I will be the queen, but not yours. And after I destroy you, that feeble bitch in Innsmouth is next. She thinks she can keep me from Ethan. With one snip I'll sever her tenuous hold over Ethan. He'll require a queen who is capable of truly ruling beside him, not some broken shell who cannot even share his bed. She can have her former lover Marsh, in death. You're correct in thinking the ascendancy is here, but it's not yours. Kassogtha has no use for you, she'll have Ethan and me to serve her. "Yes, Lord."

"Have you discontinued using birth control as I instructed?"

"I have, my Lord." She lied.

"Excellent. Soon I wish you to bear me an heir. A son!"

"I exist to serve you."

"Then disrobe!"

* * * * *

"Gonna be a slow night for peelin' bananas," commented Jerry Silk, the owner/bartender of the Honey Pot Club (once the Hill's seediest strip joint, now little more than an umbrella for hookers on inclement nights), looking out the broken-in-too-many-fights-to-count front window. "We could go in the back and you could polish my knob if you're bored."

"Jer, why don't you stick your head up your ass, where it belongs? And while yer doing that get me another one," Claudia Richards snarled while waving her empty glass at him. *Fuckin' asshole! First the cops want freebies and now the bartenders, next the johns are gonna want me to pay to suck their cocks. Fuckin' snow! Why couldn't I have got enough coin last week to get to Florida? The only friggin' money I'm gonna see tonight is if I walk that old fuck Hank home after he's blitzed, and clean out his wallet. My luck, he's broke.*

Claudia Richards, after two fortifying highballs, walked the short quarter-block and leaned against the Albany Street side of the bank. Lighting a Winston on the fourth match, she wondered why she was even out here.

Fifteen minutes later, while she was lighting her second Winston she found out.

"Kassogtha be praised!" Christa exclaimed. "Pull over there!"

Sela Astley stopped Marsh's Grand Marquis in front of the bank and Christa got out and flashed ten one hundred dollar bills as she began her negotiations with the buxom black prostitute. "Just us three girls having a little fun. We'll bring you back in the morning."

This one I can do, but that old bitch is too fuckin' ugly. Think of the money, and Florida.

"We have tons of booze, champagne if you like, and some coke if you're interested. I have, shall we say, an interest in black breasts, and she loves black pussy. If you're really good there might be a siz-able tip," Christa smiled. "We'll give you half up front."

"Just a simple three-way job. No fuckin' weird stuff. I don't do showers and that shit, got it?" *A fuckin' grand and a tip. Girl, you're on your way to Florida!*

"We understand," Christa answered, turning to open the car door for Claudia. *Ethan, my darling, soon our labors will be over and we will be together. I wish you could be here to see the seals shattered, and witness her glorious return into this vermin-infested world.*

* * * * *

Pat wasn't in a good mood. Big things he could handle, but little things aggravated him to no end. On one of the worst nights this winter he had to drive back to the restaurant to let Joe back in after he'd locked himself out.

"Maybe I'll stop and check on Moon while I'm down this way." *Wouldn't surprise me if he needs a pep talk, with all the bullshit on TV. I've got half a mind to call Channel 13 and tell Bob Kovachick when it comes to storms like this don't be so damn accurate. Look at it come down. Man, he must have a crystal ball.*

After unlocking the door for Joe, Pat decided not to bother Chris and just to go home. Ten-odd minutes and five blocks later, sitting at a red light, he saw Christa holding a car door open for a hooker.

"Christ, that's the blonde from the store!" *Why the fuck didn't I listen to Lindy and get a car phone? If this bitch is helping Chris' spook, I'd better follow 'em. Maybe that's their next victim. Wish I had a way to contact Chris.* "Well, Patty me boy, looks like your keister is back in the bush, and yer the point man for this op." *So get your head on straight and open your eyes. At least you got a few smokes and you're strapped if things go in the crapper.*

When the traffic light turned green, Pat drove past and pulled in a driveway. Turning around, he began to follow the car with Christa and her soon-to-be victim.

"Wish I knew who was driving," he said while fishing for a smoke. *Guess you'll find out soon enough.*

Pat smoked and wondered where he was being led as they drove past The Horror Corner. "Fuck me! I'm this close to Chris and don't have any way to signal him." As he drove past Union College, and out Van Vranken Avenue, he began to doubt himself as he passed the city limits. *Maybe that wasn't her? No, that was her all right, but why are they leaving the city? Is he killing them somewhere and then dumping the bodies in the city? I don't like this . . . Christ, here comes the snow again.*

Pat followed them over the Rexford Bridge and right on River Road, drawing back a few times to avoid being seen. *Where are we going? Rexford? Clifton Park? What else is out this way? He lives out here! It's only fifteen, twenty blocks from the city limits to where he's been hunting. Son-of-a-bitch doesn't live in the city, he creeps in the back way.*

Ten minutes later he watched the car pull into a driveway on Moe Road in Clifton Park. *Christ! We're less than a mile from Lindy's folks.* He drove past quickly and pulled in to the volunteer fire department parking lot and watched the driveway two hundred feet back.

For ten tense minutes he watched and smoked. *Time for some recon*, he thought. *Ain't got all night for these freaks to work on that girl.*

* * * * *

Twenty hours of nothing can shatter nerves frayed by frustration and desire, and tensions in The Horror Corner were pressurized if nothing else. The stale, overly warm air, dead from lack of circulation, reeked of five and a half packs of cigarette smoke, one minor argument, and guilt. Outside the wind roared. Inside impatience and rankled impotence warred for elbow room with ill temper.

When the phone rang three faces looked to one another. All wore the same expression—it's heaven or hell. None of the edgy trio were gamblers, but they were beginning to understand the true scope of odds, and prayer.

* * * * *

For almost two decades, Gregory Bradshaw Marsh, always the deft manipulator, had managed the dangling pawns bound in his web with the steel-handed finesse and exacting precision of a *keiretsu oyabun*. His multipage phone bills recorded frequent calls to the continent and Southeast Asia in the late '70's, and a blitz of urgent calls to North Africa and the Mid-East in '81 and '82, while his Visa and American Express cards asked after payment for his extended stays in Istanbul, Alexandria, Khartoum, Kanpur, Rangoon, and Bangkok during '85, '86, and '89.

Crates and packages of varying size and configuration, most secreted across the Mexican and Canadian borders, found their way by truck and plane to his home. Heavy wood crates bearing unlawfully procured antiquities, which had ridden the backs of camels striding cooling sands by moonlight, or had been poled in hand-carved boats down the twisted, shadowy rivers of two continents, were opened in the dark recesses of his basement. When the *Zhou Texts* was finally delivered to Marsh, the last, and most vital, piece of his crusade was in place. Now all he had to do was wait.

* * * * *

Pat finished his recon and hot-footed it to his in-laws, where he was dripping on Lindy's mother's two-week-old carpet while dialing the phone. "Cosmo? That you? Let me talk to Chris, it's urgent."

"What's up?" Chris asked.

"Is this line secure?" Pat asked in response.

"Everything's monitored, you know that."

"Clear it!"

"Pat—"

"Give 'em the word, Moon. Now!"

"Ron. Are you there?" Chris asked.

"I'm here, Chris," Ron answered.

"Give me a clear line."

"Chris, that's against regulations," Ron said.

"I know. I'll take responsibility. Clear it."

"It's your ass, Chris. Call me when you're done"

"Okay, Pat, shoot," Chris said.

"Saddle up, bro'. I'm deep in the shit and I don't have much time."

"What?"

"I've got your boy."

"Huh?"

"I was just sittin' outside his place, and the fuck's got a hooker in there."

"Holy shit. You sure it's him?"

"Yeah. Look, we're running out of time here. She's in there bound and gagged. They're gonna do her, Moon. Now haul your ass."

"Slow down."

"Fuck that! This ratfuck kills kids—you know what that means. Look, I already looked the place over and I'm going in. This ain't gonna wait, so get yer ass here."

"Where are you?"

"First things first. You're coming alone."

"You're outta your mind!"

"Either that, or I'm going in alone."

"The fuck you are!"

"This piece of shit don't deserve to live and we both know it. So you come alone and we handle this, or it's just me."

"No way!"

"Later, bro'."

"Wait!"

"For what?"

"I'll come. Where are you?"

"First promise me you're coming alone. No other cops!"

"Pat!"

"Promise. Swear on the immortal souls of Sue and Merry."

"Goddamnit, Pat."

"I'm waitin'."

"Okay. Now where!"

"Know the red brick school house on the way to Lindy's parents?"

"You're in Clifton Park?"

"Yeah. At the school, turn right, you'll see my car. I'll meet you by the road in twenty minutes, unless it gets bad and I have to go in."

"Don't go in there without me!"

"Don't worry. I'm strapped, and I got great connections with the man upstairs. Now haul it!" Pat said, severing the connection.

Chris' hand was shaking as he cradled the receiver. *Headstrong son of a bitch!* "Goddamnit!"

"We were listening—and we're going," Cosmo said, holding his Louisville Slugger.

"Bought my ticket a while back," added the Wizard, standing beside Cosmo with his Remington.

"No fucking way!"

"You've got no choice," Cosmo told him.

"I haven't got time for this."

"So let's go," Cosmo said.

"What the hell has got into you people?"

"I believe Professor Fether and I have come to our senses," the Wizard answered.

"I couldn't take you two if I wanted to."

"You can't leave us here unattended, and if you do we'll just run outside screaming murder and tell the cops what's going down. You're stuck," Cosmo said. "Be tough to erase this piece-a-shit with an army of cops there."

Realizing he was fucked, Chris agreed. "You do exactly what I tell you, and nothing else!" *But you're gonna sit in the fuckin' car.*

"We'll talk about it on the way," Cosmo said. He looked at the bat in his hand. Could he use it? Stepping through the doorway he realized that after years of reading about it, he was about to go doom-faring. He tried to decide if the chill that racked him was from the cold or fear.

* * * * *

The snow resumed five minutes before Chris pulled up behind Pat's car. After Pat voiced his adamantly negative opinions about Cosmo and the Wizard's presence ("You brought a pair of FNG's on this op. What's the last fucking thing they've killed? A mouse? Maybe a spider?") and Chris had calmed him down, they spent two minutes running down the layout of Marsh's lair and tactics.

"First off, I think we've got some time. I've seen two of them walking around looking at their watches. If you ask me they're waiting for midnight. The house is about two hundred feet back in and to the left. The driveway bends right seventy feet back or so. When you get back there, you'll see the garage on the right. One car outside, with two flats," Pat said with a smile, waving a hunting knife, "and get this, there's a van in the other stall. Over on the left side is a huge terrace with a low railing. There's plenty of cover till we're about ten feet away. We can enter through the French doors. Look like old things—simple lock, and the glass will break easily if the lock won't pop. We'll be through them quick as a rat through a New York City sewer. Cos, you're third man in. Stay back twenty feet or so, just in case. Is that all you brought?" Pat asked, pointing at the bat Cosmo held. "Didn't you see *Indiana Jones* or *The Untouchables?*"

"You trying to tell me I brought a knife to a gun fight? Don't worry, she's got a little extra sweet in her sweet spot," Cosmo said, slapping the barrel of the reamed-out, lead-filled bat in his left palm.

"Wizard, you're the caboose. If either of you get lost or hurt in there, sit tight. We'll find you. Questions?"

"Yeah, who made you top?" Chris asked.

"Once we go through that door you're the man."

"Thanks. Seen anything inside?" Chris inquired.

"They've got a hooker hog-tied on a couch to the right of the doors. I saw the blonde—the woman from the store."

"Veronica," the name burst from the Wizard edged with anger.

"That her name? She slapped the hooker a couple of times. There's also an older woman; doubt she's five feet tall. I saw the spook, by your description of him, and at least one other male, a big guy, maybe six-two, two-fifty. I haven't seen any weapons, and I'm hopin' we're the cats with the firepower. All but your psycho are wearing red robes with strange black designs. There's a circle on the chest and stripes here and here. Nothin' but some twist on Satanic crap, if you ask me. Probably gonna pitch a group grope after they dust the hooker. One more thing; only the hooker walks out of there. The rest go down," Pat commanded.

"You mean like in the movies? Terminate with extreme prejudice," the Wizard asked.

"That's exactly what I mean. Completely fuckin' erased! You think you're going to be able to pull the trigger? And while you mull that around, remember one of our lives may depend on you having the nerve to shoot. So you'd better be ready. Dig?"

"I'm in," Cosmo said, still uncertain he could kill.

"Ditto, and don't worry about me. After what these bastards did I don't think they qualify as human," the Wizard added.

Chris added his affirmative by removing the safety and sliding a shell into the chamber of his pistol.

"All right, let's block the driveway with the cars and take a walk on the wild side. Chris said you guys play the blues. Well, it's time to switch gears 'cause we're gonna rock 'n roll here in a couple minutes," Pat said, giving Chris the once-over. *He's locked and loaded. I guess we're ready.*

Cosmo sang a phrase Chris couldn't make out. Imitating Lou Reed, the Wizard's strangled tenor repeated the line, musically continuing a long-standing argument over whether Mitch Ryder or Lou Reed owned the definitive version of the Velvet Underground classic, "Rock and Roll."

Hearing Cosmo and the Wizard quietly sing, Chris shook his head. *What a pair*, he thought, *probably sing in their sleep.* Yet he understood the pair were simply trying to banish their fears with their own particular variation of whistling in the dark.

Pat and Chris moved the cars. As the quartet began walking up the driveway, the snow stopped and the wind died down. Reaching the tree line surrounding the estate they paused. Before them lay a white field of star-lit snow, a pair of monolithic pines—appearing to them as dark foreboding sentries—and the predominantly unlit mansion. *Almost looks a Christmas card*, Chris thought. As they stood there, thoughts of Christmas, light, and birth sparkled briefly in Chris, before darker thoughts soiled his momentary brush with contentment. *And what lies beyond birth*, Chris asked himself, his thoughts flying to newly made memories of Laurinda before darker images blotted out the scene of passion he'd fixed on. Death was the answer he settled on.

Five minutes later the justice seekers were crouched by the terrace railing peering through the French doors. Hurried breathing slowed as the Wizard wished for a last smoke. Tension gripped them as if it were a weapon to be armed and then unleashed. Adrenalin flowed, giving them perceptions of power. And the wind rose, echoing their thoughts. *Soon*, its cold breath whispered.

"Soon," Chris whispered back, certain of what lay inside. While he fenced with murderous scenarios, the faces of the dead filled his thoughts. As if it were a zombie, pieced together from misappropriated body parts, the anguish of the slain assembled and rose up as a solitary entity. Before him stood the resurrected dead, a seething monster, reanimated not by electricity but forged of vast desire and a single demand—vengeance. Before the cyclonic battering of bloody images could split his temples Chris unleashed fourteen months of anger. He let the pleas and command of the dead wash over him as he embraced their thirst. Grasping the tarnished silver crucifix which hung from his neck through three layers of cloth he wondered if he'd ever be forgiven for what he was about to do.

Beside Chris, Cosmo fell prey to dark musings. Years of suggestion, in the form of dark literature and macabre film, began circling a single thought—something was coming, and it was not something wonderful. A dim chant, a repeated thought, began its needle-stuck-in-a-groove mantra: Something wicked this way comes. Cosmo understood it wasn't a carnival, not even Bradbury's eerie carnival.

"Looks like our little congregation of cockamamie Satanists moved their little party to another part of the house. It's cold out here. Let's take care of this little king of fear. I'm gonna pick the lock. Wizard, Chris, if something happens I'm going left, so try not to shoot me," Pat said, hopping the railing.

"Cos, watch your ass in there," the Wizard instructed.

"Same goes for you, bro'."

Before the Wizard stood the entrance and something he'd never bargained for. Turning, he looked at his best friend's face—he hoped he'd see it after this was concluded. *What in the hell are we doing?* No firm answer materialized, but he hoped it was the right thing. *And how'd you manage to get so far from home?*

"Listen up, and do just what I tell you. This is my ass and I don't want to wind up in Dannemora with some three-hundred-pound bodybuilder hoping I'll drop the soap," Chris said to the musicians as Pat inched open the door.

* * * * *

Smoke from dozens of sticks of incense, hashish, and opium filled Marsh's stiflingly hot, unvented cement shrine. The robed celebrants awaited Marsh's command to begin. Thick black candles, held by representations of the gods Marsh awaited, shed flickering light into the dim cavern, and upon the naked, squirming woman bound to Kassogtha's blood-encrusted altar.

Marsh, a ghoul now clothed in hellish vestments made from the human skin he'd acquired by butchery, seemed intoxicated, almost blissful. "Are you ready?" he asked the group.

"Yes, Lord," came the unanimous response.

Marsh walked to the wall near the door and pushed a button. A section of the shrine's roof rolled back, revealing the sky above.

Christa took note of the now clear sky above her. "It stopped snowing," she said. *This is a bad omen.*

"I can see that!" Marsh barked, also taking the clear sky as a bad portent. "Close the damn thing," he ordered, storming out of the shrine.

* * * * *

Once inside the four quickly decided not to separate. They'd check the house floor by floor, ground floor first, then work their way up. "Stay quiet," Pat reminded them. "We want to to surprise 'em."

Chris was the first to enter the next room, a large living room that was as empty as the one behind. *Clean and well maintained,* thought Chris looking around. *Looks like we've got a tidy killer with deep pockets.*

In the fourth room of the ground floor, the dining room, Chris noticed Cosmo's absence. "Where's Cos?" he asked instantly, worrying that Cosmo might have been silently grabbed from behind. *Fuck. I knew I shouldn't have let these two come.*

"I thought he was with us," the Wizard said. "I'd better go back and look for him."

"No. We'll backtrack after we finish in here."

Unaware the others had gone on, Cosmo paused before a lectern and stared at the leather-bound tome it held.

It drew him. He couldn't believe what he was seeing. It bound him. The more he struggled to move on the harder his eyes remained fixed on the words before him. "Beware sons of light! Beware! She waits! Her jaws are the open gates to hells not yet imagined by men."

All these years, and all his fantasies regarding Lovecraft's wondrous mythology lay before him. Was it—real? Could it be? or had this madman created it to serve his own dark purpose? Cosmo had to know; twenty-four years of adoring the Mythos demanded it. Like the heated touch of an ardent lover, possibilities whispered to him. "Bah!" he snorted loudly, nearly walking away; but he didn't. Like a young man staring at his first live, uncovered breasts, his eyes were transfixed by the book.

The book appeared ancient, a real relic. All he had to do was take it. Here was the dreamer's Oz, King Solomon's mines, and the Floridian fountain of youth. Here was one man's winning lottery ticket and another's Avalon. Here was revelation and promise. Finally, finding his resistance to leave the book impossible to overcome, Cosmo picked it up and placed it in his backpack along with two others that bore legends Cosmo recognized. For the first time since he had been seven Cosmo took something that was not his.

He suddenly realized he was alone in the room. To his left he noticed wet footprints on the carpet. *That way*, he thought as he quickly followed the trail of prints on the off-white carpet from the room.

"Where the hell were you?" the Wizard asked.

"Just looking around a minute," Cosmo hesitantly replied.

"Stay with us," the Wizard ordered. "This ain't an amusement park."

"No shit," Cosmo replied with a shaky smile.

Pat walked the two steps that parted Cosmo from him. Face to angered face, Pat hissed, "Fuckin' around in this place could get someone killed. Catch my drift?"

"Yes."

Finishing their search of the ground floor they decided to hit the second floor next. Pat wanted a sentry to "cover their asses." The Wizard and his shotgun were chosen for the assignment—Pat was going to keep close tabs on Cosmo. "You stay in the middle, and take everything slow and silent," Pat firmly instructed.

While the others searched the second floor the Wizard anxiously stayed below. "You'll be covering our tails, just in case," Chris had said. So the Wizard waited, something the always-in-motion musician couldn't tolerate. Wondering how the others were faring he was about to follow them upstairs, when his ears caught the sound of creaking hinges beyond the dining room in the kitchen.

Looks like it's my at bat, thought the Pirates fan as he walked through the dining room toward the door. Before he could enter, the door swung open and Christa walked into the room. Both were stunned by the other's presence.

"You? How did—"

"Maybe we're not as stupid as you thought."

"You don't understand. I did not mean to mis—"

"Save the bullshit! You had Willie killed! Now it's your turn."

"Please listen to me. I can help you. He made me!"

His features hardened.

"I couldn't—I have feelings for you. He wanted to kill you, but I interceded; he took the cop instead."

"Can it! I'm about as interested in your lies as a rock is in the wind chill factor."

Lips parted, beckoning—moist, hinting a smile, eyes softly pleading—Christa took a tentative step toward him. Her hands moving as if to form a question, her swaying hips presenting a firm promise. To check her advance he leveled the shotgun at the black circle on her chest.

"There's only a few feet between you and hell. Don't think I wouldn't be happy to use this. God, I can't believe how *stupid* I was! You and your sick little friend intended to kill me! Won't be much of you left if you take that step." "*Muzzle to muzzle now anything goes*", he thought. *Where'd that come from? Guess I had a different idea in mind the last time that lyric reared its head. Am I always gonna be so damn foolish when it comes to attractive women with brains?*

Understanding she would be unable to talk her way around him, Christa reached for the ceremonial knife hanging from her belt. As it cleared the sheath the Wizard responded in a manner he'd have thought utterly impossible a few weeks ago: He took a life.

Lying at his feet, lips still parted, eyes still pleading, Christa tried to speak.

"Don't bother. Whatever hell you wind up in, I hope you reap what you've sown. Suffer forever, you bitch!" he said as she groaned and exhaled her last breath.

Looking at the pained mask of her face he recalled another time. A time when he felt her face was angelic. He recalled her laugh, and . . . "Fuck that noise!"

As his thoughts warred, he tried not to look at the shotgun's handiwork, but couldn't help himself. Although the results were gory, some part of him found satisfaction. He found justice filling and sweet. Momentarily appalled by his feelings, he wondered what he'd become; an avenger, he decided.

* * * * *

Hearing the roar of the shotgun blast below them the trio, who hadn't found anything, ran downstairs to find the Wizard standing over Christa's body.

"Wearing robes with big circles on the front is kind of stupid . . . you don't need a target that precise with this," he commented, cradling the shotgun and turning to the others as they entered the dining room.

"There's our first confirmed kill," Pat stated flatly.

"Where'd she come from?" Chris asked.

"Through there," the Wizard replied, pointing the shotgun barrel toward the kitchen door.

"Just great. We were already in there, and the only thing there is, is a doorway to the basement," Cosmo said, wondering if all psychos found it more comforting to be physically closer to hell. *Why's it always attics and basements with these monsters? Must have something to*

*do with the musty smell. Maybe these assholes think it smells like a grave?
Just once it would be nice if one of these freaks had a second-floor walk-up.
Shit! Isn't that what Dahmer had?*

"Looks like the elevator's going down. Lingerie for the dead, *Ka-ka-cut-lery,* and mortuary services," Pat wisecracked, gesturing toward the open door.

"Guess if there's a hell below, we all gotta to go," Cosmo fearfully whispered.

Reentering the kitchen the four found the basement door ajar and a light on below, beckoning them. On nervous feet they began their descent, Pat and Chris on point, waving Cosmo and the Wizard down once they'd reached the bottom. Across an empty fifty-foot expanse stood a large steel door set in a concrete wall. After a cursory look around the sparsely filled basement, they knew where they were headed. Hearts and ears pounding, they approached the door and looked to one another. *Ready? This is it. All for one and one for all! Let's do it!* their expressions said.

Pat reached out, cautiously testing the door handle. It turned. "Unlocked," he whispered to the others. "We'll go on three." With great caution he cracked the door open. With silent words accompanied by fingers he counted out *one-two-three!* and yanked the door open.

Near-darkness lay before the four in the form of an empty, dimly lit tunnel with another door at its end. Guns leveled, glances exchanged, four keyed-up faces turned to face the fifty feet of tense questions that lay before them.

"Fuck me," Pat quietly hissed as they all began breathing again. "Looks like we've got to try it again."

Shit. Looks like there's a few more steps left on the way of sorrows, Chris thought. *And more blood, before we discover damnation or—if this goes bad. How the hell did I let these guys get stuck helping me carry this cross? Pat's been in the shit before; he knows there'll more than likely be a price. But these two haven't thought that far. Maybe if I wasn't so scared, or so . . . what? Committed? I oughta be committed for being so stupid.*

Adrenalin, as wanton as barreling flood waters, coursed as the edgy quartet, like slow-motion automatons, silent except for their heartbeats, moved into the tunnel. Pat, still on point, wired and wary, scoured the cement corridor as they inched along its dark length.

Pat caught his breath when they reached the second door. No booby traps. Slowly, with a firm grip, he reached out and tried to turn the handle. It was unlocked. "Here we go again," he almost silently mouthed the words to his compatriots. "On three," came the sharp whisper.

1! Pat's pointer finger flashed.

2! Cosmo suppressed a fear-born laugh as Pat's two fingers formed the peace sign. *Doubt we're about to meet anything peaceful,* Cosmo thought as an image of a sssshing Miles Davis, finger gently pressed to his lips, flashed.

3! Pat wrenched the door wide open. The panthers sprang, fangs bared, ready to judge.

Wavering candlelight, smoke, and a scene from some Friday night late-late Satanic blood-feast discharged into the tunnel as the vengeance-hungry justice collectors poured into Marsh's sanctum of debauchery. John Wayne, Rambo, and Judge Dredd (all rolled into one) had arrived. Let God sort 'em out.

* * * * *

Marsh, emotionally unable and unwilling to wait for Christa's return from the bathroom, began his ceremony early. *Just a few small strokes,* he thought, holding the blade above the bound woman's bared torso. Marsh needed to see blood—just a taste, something to tide him over.

The sound of a single hand drum hammered its aural beacon under layers of swirling smoke rising from three-legged silver braziers of pungent incense and opiated hash. Above the sonorous din, the prostitute's gag-distorted screams further stimulated exhilarated ears.

Ringing the sacrificial table, the drug-energized conclave of robed worshipers danced (deeply bending at the waist, jerking left and upward, then stomping their right feet down and pulling themselves back to an erect position, torsos centered over both feet) to the primitive eight-beat syncopation, as they chanted—guttural inhuman sounds colliding in a hurried chaos of call and response speaking in tongues—while their demonic Pope, his dagger bloodied, cut red runes of alien design in the black flesh of the oblation bound before him.

Sela Astley's not quite high-pitched, grating voice rose, fell, and swooped above the repetitive drum rhythm like a vulture anticipating its prey's impending death. Her hotly colored cheeks contorted as her lips and tongue worked to reproduce the inhuman sounds of the ceremony's holy incantation. A song of hell issued forth as her jaw shifted right, then left (her throat tightening, her nostrils pinching inward) to accommodate the formulation of the harsh sounds. Every dark passion she had engaged in over the last decade filled her; this was the moment she had yearned for. Soon the well connected and self-absorbed somebodies in Maryland would pay for their demeaning looks and their disgusting thoughts about her as she cut through them like the poisoned blade of a jagged knife. Between phrases of the holy litany, she smiled, thinking about her second coming-out party before Maryland's high society.

Like a hyena rearing up to protect looted prey, Marsh's head rose from its bold rune-carving at the sound made by the opening door and the voices that surged through it. Bestial eyes burned the quartet of intruders. They faced a mask of hate and war, painted in mania and blood, crowned by the freshly peeled black skin of the woman's left breast, her nipple a spire pointing to the stars above. Before the loathing in the quartet's souls could be conquered and the beast felled, the ghoulishly twisted apparition of debauched madness plunged the dagger into her chest.

Bathed in blood from the female bodies he was butchering in his opiated fantasy, Vernon McClellan was sitting with a hand drum nestled in his lap, tattooing a doomfaring pulse, when the shrine door flew open. Roused from his bloodsport, he sluggishly heaved the percussion instrument at the bearded barbarian who appeared before him.

In the teary, blurred vision of the smoky room, shots were fired and curses exchanged. Cosmo, with the reflexes of a cat, quick and lucky, sent the small hand drum launched at his head flying with a swing that the Wizard would later term "a line-drive double", while the other three emptied their weapons into the robed demon-worshippers.

Pat's first shot entered McClellan's brain via his left eye.

Infuriated by the interfering infidels, Sela Astley, in midword, paused to look at the three holes which had suddenly appeared in the front of her robe. Shocked by the pain that permeated her chest, she fingered the wounds. *I have been denied*, she thought. *On this day! How could this happen today?* Utterly frustrated and confused, she expired.

Realizing his master's plans were ruined, Bennett James Meadow launched his silver-tipped cane at the unwelcome intruders. It fell short of its mark as he hit the cement with Chris' bullet lodged in his throat and a second burning in his abdomen.

Roaker was stunned. Fully aroused by expectant abandon, he'd been swirling, head back, eyes closed, as he prayed for the miracle awakened, when the disapproving bark of gunfire interrupted. Startled, he turned, saw the intervention—men, a terrorist assault, emphatic bullets not words asserting their demands. Gaping in utter disbelief he watched Meadow's cane sail past, watched it impact nothing. The priest of M'nagalah looked up from the cane and gazed into devouring eyes harboring only loathing. His hands, so used to meticulously arranging placements and issuing directions, made vicious fists. All Roaker's prayers and promises and hard-hearted schemes were swiftly delivered to darkness by four rounds effectively dispensed—two biting high, a good pair side by side in the left lung near the heart, two penetrating low, violating kidney and liver.

Roaker's flashing eyes, as if in a fever, wrestled with the unconscionable crime. A man who had slaughtered with words, an impulsive seeker who had avidly picked through every outpost of visceral intrigue and each narrow back-alley marketplace, embracing brutality with delight—loving the tortures harvested, he found himself with no time to examine the war which had erupted. He, at the end—vanquished and bitterly perplexed—found no words to sway or understand this violence.

The remaining Marsh attendant, Motohiko Yano, was hidden from view behind a large, smoking brazier. Lost in prayer and high from opium and expectation, he was jarred back from the realm of religious obsession by the gunfire. Three years of servitude and another decade of training and purification had been ruined by the blasphemers. To his goddess, Kassogtha, he vowed they would pay for their intrusion. Rising up, a shadow in a mist of smoke after Pat walked past where he was hidden, Yano eased the blade from its scabbard. Before Yano could plunge the blade into the small of Pat's back, the Wizard's shotgun took its second victim. Startled, Pat turned at the sound of the blast. A vision of 'Nam flooded Pat's sight as Yano's headless corpse collapsed against its intended victim.

Crouched behind Her altar, Marsh, on fire with rage over having his holy rite fouled by heretics, hurriedly uttered the final section of the mass. *"Cic'rl Kassogtha Neleh Vtiiv Cthulhu! Kashkash ubh'sotti R'lyeh! Bninc Cau Mo Iä! Iä! Kassogtha!"* his strained voice bellowed.

In the subterranean theater of horror, his hands in motion—rising, expanding circles—he poured his energy into the invocation which would nullify the accursed seals. "Holy Mother, I your devoted servant offer you these insects. Come to me! Return to your kingdom. Resurrect Cthulhu, your beloved. Most Holy Kassogtha, eraser of light, womb of darkness. One thousand years I pledge you my soul. Allow your devoted servant the pleasure of carrying out your holy judgment against the blight of purity that fouls your earth. Let feast and funeral be the law of the land."

As the smell of gunpowder wafted in the hot blurry air a new smell, a fetid mixture rank with damp decay and burnt flesh, accosted their nostrils. Behind the altar where Marsh crouched hidden, the four thought they were viewing a magical illusion, hallucinations, or the act of some mystical deity as wall and roof dissolved. There lay the stars, and—

Fear and bile clawed their way up Cosmo's esophagus. The Wizard's stomach turned to a caldron of tense fire, while his brain screamed obscenities of disbelief at his eyes. Pat and Chris reached for the prayers they believed had carried them through the humid hell of Vietnam.

Before them, slowly revolving in an ocher-veined nimbus as if a deformed fetus floating in a uterus of chaos, the leviathan of diseased coils appeared.

As if turned to stone before this god, their eyes were accosted by a vision the rational mind only encounters behind the safe walls of sleep, and even then rails against. Forced into facing the truth floating before them, desire evaporated and expectation took flight. Stumbling Catholic and atheist alike desperately tried to understand what neither credo had allowed or conceived.

"Sweet mother of God!" Pat exclaimed, staring at the insanity that choked his vision as it floated in the abyssal void before him.

"Jesus save us!" Chris yelled as he recognized the mountain of flexing, knotted coils poised before him. "It's her!" Reason, religion, and science fled before the hovering brobdingnagian madness. He stood immobilized, his mind screaming, terrified of the asylum his eyes abandoned him to.

Cosmo and the Wizard stood paralyzed in a state of stupefaction, as recognition of the form instantaneously ensorceled them.

She exists! That means . . . Cthulhu and the others really exist! Cosmo thought. *Lovecraft knew!*

It's one big snake pit, constantly slithering in between itself, thought the awed and unnerved Wizard. *It's almost beautiful.*

For the briefest moment, or for an hour, they knew not which, beyond the reaches of space and the hands of time they stood at the brink of some unnamable vista facing a new reality—one no longer born of insanity, but truth.

Hearing Chris' voice proclaim Kassogtha's arrival, Marsh whirled to behold his queen. Twenty-two years of obsessive fanaticism and prurient desire had not prepared him for the prophecy-fulfilling phantasm he beheld. She was here. His truth, hidden throughout the ages of man, had arrived. The Messiah, enduring the holy labors of devotion and prayer, had born a god into existence. Slowly, reverently, he rose to stand and pay tribute to her sacred form. Hurried, half-formed, half-spoken prayers streamed from his lips. Rapturous tears lined his face.

Breaking the jagged grip of terror that held the quartet, a warm golden voice filled the frigid room. *"The sign. Cast the sign if you would live!"*

Kthanid! "Form the Elder Sign in your minds and project it at Her," Chris ordered the other three.

"What?" Pat asked.

"The shape of the star stones—the Elder Sign. Form it in your mind and propel it at her!" Cosmo said.

With sweating brows and petrified hearts they mentally formed the wards and sent them forward at the living form of evil hovering before them.

As the projected conjurations hit their target a blurred cacophony of pain scraped at their minds.

Chris reached for his Mnarian talisman. *Will this really affect that?* he asked himself, tearing the amulet from his neck and casting it at the nightmarish god before him.

In a moment slowed almost to motionlessness, Marsh saw the Mnarian ward fly toward Kassogtha's constricting, spasming form. "Not this close!" he cried as his long-prayed for moment of blissful epiphany soured and metamorphosed into merciless despair. "*Nooooo!*" The echo of his final wail was half death cry, half plea for a second chance. Tainted by the anger of failure, it hung, a dim pulsating ring, then lay still as Kassogtha, in a fit of rage only a god could actualize, encompassed his essence and devoured him mind and soul.

Striking her, the stone dispersed in an explosion of light, painfully bright but heatless. The pure brilliance momentarily blinded the unhinged quartet. Then with a motion beyond human conception, part twist which seemed to fold into itself, part bounce, Kassogtha vanished, fleeing the conflagrant emblem of the star.

As sight returned to them, they found the wall, now embossed with the Elder Sign, reformed before them. In the center of the seven-foot-tall bas-relief symbol, fused to the cement barrier, lay Chris' small gray talisman.

* * * * *

The four stood smoking in the cold, exhaling tension along with nicotine. One face frightened and still scarred by its confrontation with incomprehensibility; one astounded, feeling asylum-bound; one embittered, deprived of vengeance and filled with the aftermath of righteous anger; and the last held a hint of nervous guilt.

"What do we do now, Chris?" the Wizard asked, finally finding his voice.

"Burn the fuckin' thing! Erase this place!"

"Can we do that?" Cosmo asked.

"Look, Cosmo, there isn't anybody, sane or otherwise, who's going to believe what we just saw, and there's no way to explain away our actions."

"We just saved the fuckin' world!" the Wizard exclaimed, still badly shaken by what he had been forced into believing.

"True, but just because we were justified it still won't mean shit. Nobody is going to believe us. Christ, I saw that thing and I don't believe it. We just killed seven people, and we didn't even save that poor woman. As far as anyone's gonna be concerned we're vigilantes, murderers, justified maybe, but still killers, and they've got laws against that."

"Let's do what we have to do and get outta this hellhole," Pat ordered.

"Chris, what do you think is going to happen to us," Cosmo asked minutes later as the building burned.

"I don't know. We'll discuss that on the way back," Chris replied.

"What are we going to say? There'll be questions," the Wizard said.

"We'll lie like hell," Pat said. "And the politicians will cover our asses, 'cause we took the monkey off their backs. People didn't want those freaks caught. They wanted them dead!"

"There's still the media," Cosmo said.

"They'll get so much smoke blown up their asses they'll be too teary-eyed to see straight."

"That's the truth," Chris said, recalling the faith-shattering images he'd just witnessed. *God forgive me. I wonder if there are other truths we've yet to experience? And how the hell do we go on knowing we're nothing?*

❦ Chapter Thirty-One ❦

Jack Beckett didn't believe word one. Not one fuckin' word. *An internal power struggle within some bullshit cult? Where the hell did the other weirdos come from? A fire caused by a gas leak and a bullet? Bullshit!* he thought as the press conference concluded. *I made a deal with Stewart and he better keep his end.*

"Hey, dipshit, I don't like it any more than you do, but I can't do anything about it," Chris told Beckett in a more than believable tone.

"This bullshit you're feeding us doesn't add up."

"You hear stranger shit on the news."

That's true, Beckett thought.

"Face facts, Beckett, the only thing about this that bothers you is it didn't play out the way you wanted. Well, stand in line, because I wanted that motherfucker too. And if you think I'm happy because I didn't get to blow his brains all over hell and creation, then you're missing more things than I can explain."

Beckett accepted Chris' pent-up, angry truth. How could anyone not have? It was huge, hard, and ugly; it encased him like a diseased second skin. Chris had wanted to kill that monster himself and he'd been denied—robbed. "What would you think if you were me?" Beckett asked.

"What did you think—they were gonna get some handsome young stud to play you on the movie of the week? Not every story ends with the cops breaking down the door and saving the day. John Wayne ain't in the department, and Bruce Willis makes too much money to quit Hollywood and sign up with the Schenectady PD. Christ, you know the score. Most of the time we just come in and clean up the garbage. You're gonna have to live with the way this played out, same as everybody else."

"I guess," Beckett said, walking away like a kid whose disappointment had become anger.

I hope something comes along quick to turn his nose away from this. If he gets wind of what we really did, or the Fed-Sutherland Foundation connection, he'll bury us. Course if the details came out and people believed it, we'd all be better off.

* * * * *

Henri had finished his errand in Orleans Parish and had returned home with his package.

"You have de book?" his grandmother asked.

"Yes."

"And everything else is *finis?*"

"Yes. The dean accepted my resignation this morning, and all my accounts have been closed. Laurinda says I can have her flat."

"Good. Watch over them for me."

"I will."

"Now come and please an old woman, I have made de shrimp creole for you. It may be some time before you taste it again," Henri's grandmother said, regretting her necessity-forced decision to send him to live in New York. *If there were some other way*, she thought, *but others need him now.*

* * * * *

Cosmo sat on the third floor of The Horror Corner in a room which housed his comics, photographic images of a family life dead years ago, and a pantheon of memories—many too intimate, others too crushing—he didn't care to share, not even with his closest friend. The small room was Cosmo's personal attic. The Wizard's makeshift attic was next door. Neither friend ever violated the other's dusty memory galleries.

Guilt knotted with self-loathing and fear coursed through Cosmo as he smoked his third cigarette. Beside him sat an end table of empty beer cans and an overflowing ashtray. Spurred by a firm decision he rose. This time he was going to look through the books. "Damn the torpedoes!"

Twenty minutes later he still stood before the books he'd pirated from Marsh's mansion. He'd taken them out, but that was as far as he had gotten. Too fearful to open them, he stared down in disbelief; this was the third time he'd taken them out of their hiding place below a stack of read-only copies of *Tales to Astonish* and *Strange Tales* and tried to look through them.

Tottering at the precipice of desire and indecision, behind him the great beast of his fear, below and before the unquenchable mouth of madness, he wondered if he was to become Prometheus or Victor Frankenstein. As if they were clouds too heavy to bare their charge, questions stormed within him. Would he deliver fire and freedom, or rain down aberration by opening these pages? Like a child frightened of thunder he turned away from the storm front, certain he was Pandora, about to open something better left sealed and dead to the minds of men.

Time seemed on sabbatical, or irrelevant.

Shrouded in a haze of cigarette smoke, he stood paralyzed, as seemingly lifeless as hardened statuary. Arrested by the cold mire of indecision, he fought to grasp rationality, but found himself buffeted by a thousand plagues of doubt—some slow-footed, moving on spider-light feet, their journey in tiny increments, while the others, the many, savage as a firestorm, howled, demanding to be heard above the din, as they suddenly burst into existence and spread like a panicked mob.

I've got to tell them about these books. Even if it means they'll destroy them. No! I can't let them be destroyed! Not yet. We might need them. Those things are still out there. "Ahhh! If I could just work up the courage to look inside." *Maybe I shoulda told the guy from the Sutherland Foundation about these. He, they might know how to use 'em. Are you stupid? There was something wrong, maybe it was odd, about him. Aw, Christ! Anybody who inhabits the world of those things is bound to seem strange to ordinary people. Ordinary? Fuck me, I stopped being ordinary the moment I saw Her!*

As Cosmo warred with his desires and apprehension, the Wizard sat in Pat's grill working on a steak sandwich with onions and cheese and his second beer. "Do you really think we're going to get away with this?" he asked Pat. "I've never been involved in anything . . . *covert* before."

"Those guys are connected all the way to the top. You met 'em. They didn't impress me as just yer average walkin'-around Joes."

"But—"

"Hey, something went on. We've all been interviewed by representatives of the Sutherland Foundation and that pair of snakes from the NSC. Scares the shit outta me thinkin' they've got the president's ear. This thing's reached high up for some reason." *A damn good one as far as I'm concerned.* "But I think we're in the clear. It wouldn't surprise me if they gave us medals. Not that they could; they'd have to admit these things exist. And you can bet your ass that ain't gonna happen. Not in this life."

"Guess you're right. Damn, it's impossible to make sense of this. At times it seems like we were caught in an episode of *The X-Files*."

"We were, but who said man is supposed to understand? You're a smart guy, maybe we were created by the great alchemist in the sky, but so were ants and dogs and trees and they don't understand, so why in the hell should we?"

"It's just this thing's really got to Cos. I'm startin' to think he should see a shrink. He still refuses to talk to anybody about it. Told the cat from the Sutherland Foundation to fuck off. And he still won't perform. We've almost been reduced to instrumentals. I'm really worried. He's, I don't know, shaken up. Haunted. Tormented. He's always looking over his shoulder."

"Ain't we all! I sure don't sleep too well anymore."

"Me either. Think there's more of these disciples floating around?"

"The spooks from the Sutherland Foundation sure think so, and I bet they know a hell of a lot more than we do."

"That's what scares me. We're like fish in a barrel; talk about this island earth. What the hell are we going to do?"

"Get on with our lives as best we can, because we still gotta get up in the morning and face ourselves in the mirror." *Maybe not for long, but.* "And one other thing."

"What's that?"

"Leave this Cthulhu business to the experts."

That's fucking great. "They can't even run the goddamn government and you want me to let them handle this?"

"What do you want to do, join the Sutherland Foundation?"

"That's an idea. Maybe I could help 'em find a way to stick a nuclear firecracker up Cthulhu's ass."

"Don't get too tempted. It's better to leave crawling through the slime to those trained to do it. We got lucky once, I wouldn't want to bet on our chances a second time."

"I'm not so sure we got through it, not as long as those things are out there."

"Tell the truth."

* * * * *

This is where you've wanted to be for years, Laurinda told herself as she unpacked some of her books and placed them in the sparsely filled bookcase of Chris' living room. *He'll shake this off. He just needs time after what he's been through. At least he's not drinking.*

"Hi. How's the unpacking coming?" Chris asked.

"All I have left are some books and knickknacks. Have you noticed how much Plato seems to love it here? You're not feeling crowded, I hope?"

"No. Place's starting to look homey. Lauri, I wish things were different."

"It's okay. We'll get through this together. You just need some time."

"But it's not fair."

"You've never thought life was fair. You've always felt it was a forge. Look at it this way, people learned to live under the threat of nuclear annihilation. We'll learn to live with this," she said, taking his hand and smiling.

"Guess you're right."

I have to be.

❦ Epilogue ❦

Ida Louise Marsh summoned her son to the library. "Seth, I have been informed your biological father has died. Your studies now completed, your vigil commences. Nightwalker, once I tended you as if you were a rare flower. Now I command you to be stone! Lovecraft said there was a shadow over Innsmouth. Sentinel, I charge you to lengthen it until it eclipses this clockwork orb of insects."

"I shall, Mother," Seth Gustav Marsh pledged. "Perhaps you'd like me to convey the news to Cassilda?"

"I have already informed your sister of his demise," Ida replied as Cassilda Emeline Marsh, Seth's seven-minute-younger identical twin, entered the study. With a triumphant glow, she set a sterling-silver ice bucket before her mother. Beads of water upon the bottle of Dom Perignon shone like gems. Before her hand left the ice bucket, her pale, slender fingers gently caressed the engraved family crest and the two marine-like creatures flanking it.

Soon our crest will be engraved upon the world, Cassilda thought.

"Mom, you knew he would fail, didn't you? How did you know?" Cassilda asked.

Her mother looked up—her eyes moist with pride—and lovingly considered the young woman who might have been considered bewitching in contemporary society, if not for her complexion which many considered almost ichthyic in some intangible way.

"Because, my dearest blossom, he was never meant to succeed."

"I see Father's hand written all over this," Seth commented. It had only been a week since he'd discovered the man who had raised the twins as if they were his own issue, the man the twins had thought to be their biological father, was unable to sire children. *The family must have been beside themselves with joy when that buffoon showed up in '72 with his fertile sperm and genetic purity intact. At least we know I'm not sterile*, he thought, images of the two infants upstairs sleeping warming his heart. *I shall succeed and my heirs shall reign after me. The Marsh dynasty has been born.*

"Have you ever known your father to be remiss, or in error, when it came to dealing with matters regarding this family and its concerns?" Ida asked her son.

"Of course not. I can't conceive of a Marsh being more devoted to the family, or to Their release, than Father," Seth replied. "Perhaps we should wait for him to return from Danvers before we toast Gregory's demise?"

If I know Father he'll have another form of celebration in mind. "Mom, will you tell us how you and Father arranged all this?" Cassilda asked, looking forward to her father's return from Danvers Asylum with Aunt Marilyn. *I love watching her racked with pain when she Echoes. If she'd been a true Marsh—spiritually committed to the cause—her feeble mind would have been able to accept the holy gift.*

Ida raised her glass. "After we've celebrated the fool's demise with a bit of your bubbly."

* * * * *

Spring's ascending radiance arrived to melt the embedded memories of winter. Guilt and pain, in stark faded rags, slowly retreated as green's promise of renewal began taking back the landscape. Crocuses, followed by tulips and daffodils, filled the warming breezes with their fragrant song. Garage doors flew open as children in bright T-shirts, voices loudly triumphant, took to the streets on blazing bicycles and rollerblades, and a smile, still periodic and somewhat faint, returned to Chris' face.

Three months later, as the lords of the barbecue held their fiery weekend courts, Pat held a hardly-a-surprise birthday party for Chris while "The Entertainer" blared from a white truck where the children traded quarters for ice cream. The sun in his brilliant summer regalia had reached the zenith of his reign, shortening dark nights of choking doubt, and lessening the hold on Chris' soul slowly fading nightmares had enjoyed. Things were trying to get better one day at a time.

Shortly before seven on a picturesque July evening where the breeze and temperature were almost a song, Chris popped the tab on his second beer and set it on the picnic table, while his other hand maneuvered a garden hose which gently watered his fattening cucumbers. Softly, as if not to break the moment's simple serenity, he sang his favorite summer song to himself. "'My neighbors grow their carrots, radishes, and beans. Me, I'm watchin' sprouts pop up from tiny little seeds. 'Cause summer ripened cukes with mayo, are just about all I need.'" As his words faded he heard Laurinda's comforting voice floating softly through the kitchen window as she washed the dinner dishes.

"'Perhaps, at least in our hearts . . . one day . . . we'll all . . . be . . . free,'" she quietly sang. Her soothing alto softened the warm evening.

Free? Never again, he thought. *Not completely. This is just a moment of calm. That . . . thing's still out there waiting. They're all out there waiting. Sooner or later, another disciple will come along and—*

"Hey! Thought we might talk you into a cold brew," the Wizard yelled from the gate.

Pat smiled and held up a twelve-pack of cold Pabsts.

"And a game of horseshoes!" the Wizard enthusiastically added.

ABOUT JOSEPH S. PULVER, SR.

Joe Pulver was the jazz/classical/new music reviewer of *The Music Advocate*. He is currently the music critic for *Crypt of Cthulhu* and the editor of *Midnight Shambler* and *Cthulhu Codex*. His poetry and fiction have appeared in *Midnight Shambler, LORE, Tales of Lovecraftian Horror,* and *Cthulhu Cultus*, and will soon appear in *En Compagnie du Roi en Jaune* and the upcoming Chaosium collections *The Book of Eibon* and *Nameless Cults: The Complete Mythos Fiction of R. E. Howard.*

Additional Acknowledgements

The succeeding acknowledgments are an extension of page iv.

A musician whose work I sometimes enjoy once wrote a piece entitled "Life's a Long Song", to which a friend of mine added, "made of many colorful notes." I'd like to express my deepest love, gratitude, and praise to those "colorful notes" listed below for their many contributions to my first song.

Love and thanks to Joe Jr. for never tiring of my bedtime stories and continually checking on the page count.

Love and thanks to Tom for the French lessons, and to Jon for the energy to kill so many.

Many, many thanks to Lindy Jones for "I want more!", the software and tarot lessons, and her tireless dotting I's and crossing T's.

Special thanks and a case of brew (ice cold Tall Boys) to Chris Grey, the real Dr. Frankenstein: friend, ad hoc shrink, captain of the cheerleading section, brother in arms, and patient—beyond measure—sounding board.

Many thanks to Donnalee O'Donnell for allowing me to use her name, and for being an enthusiastic and gentle reader and kind, tireless editor.

Thanks to Marlin Norris and family for not laughing and the names.

Thanks to my brother-in-law, Paul Whittam, for the voodoo.

Love and thanks to my sister Carol for lunch, the cartoon, and the bottle of '62.

Thanks and praise to a real 20th-Century visionary, H. R. Giger, the true originator of the biomechanical style, for the stunning works he has given us, and for his kind permission to refer to his works and borrow his name.

My deepest gratitude to musical poet David Sylvian, for his kind permission to quote from his restless and beautiful gem "The Devil's Own."

Special thanks to Alice Cooper (and his representatives) for kindly allowing me to quote from "Desperado", and a hell of a lot of damn good rock 'n roll.

DC Comics is the owner of all rights, including trademark and copyright, in and to Batman® and Superman®. The Metal Men and Platinum are DC Comics' copyrighted properties.

Marvel Comics®'s the Hulk®, Galactus®, the Grey Gargoyle®, Thor®, Mentallo and the Fixer, Nick Fury®, The Avengers®, The Fantastic Four®, Captain America®, Spider-Man®, Dr. Strange®, Benjamin J. Grim/Ben Grimm, the Thing®, The Trapster, the Red Skull®, the Wizard®, Dragon Man®, Loki®, the Mole Man®, Dr. Doom®, the Punisher®, Chrusher Creel the Absorbing Man®, Dormammu, the Dark Dimension, and the expression "It's clobberin' time" are properties of Marvel Comics/Marvel Entertainment Group, Inc., which is the owner thereto of all rights, including copyrights and pertinent trademarks.

Many thanks to Frank Belknap Long for "The Horror from the Hills," and to Kirby MacAuley for kindly allowing me to quote from it.

Thanks to Thomas Ligotti for his kind permission and his truly without peer nightmares of lyricism.

Thanks to Ramsey Campbell for his kind permission to use his name and his marvelous creations on these pages.

Extra special thanks and praise to Brian Lumley for directly inspiring me to play Lovecraft's literary parlor game, and for very kindly allowing me to use his name and his many wondrous creations on these pages.

Undying thanks to Lin Carter, both as writer (the critics be damned!) and editor, for steering me in so many directions.

My deepest thanks to Lynn Willis who overcame his "dread" and read it. And then to my delight and amazement, well . . . . thanks for believing!

My undying and deepest gratitude to Robert M. Price, masterful chronicler, scholar, editor, and vigorous advocate of all things Cthulhuvian, for his seeming magical aid, time, enthusiasm, and introduction. I hope I can live up to it in some small way. Like Gleason used to say, "You're the greatest!"

And finally, thanks and more than my lacking words can convey, to J who put up with this crazy idea and its lengthy birth.

Keep singin'!

— JSPsr

WIZARD'S ATTIC

Missing a few *Call of Cthulhu* fiction books from your crypt? You can now order them all from Wizard's Attic, your source for Cthulhiana and more. To order by credit card via phone call 1-800-213-1493 (1-510-595-2443 outside the United States) or to order via the net, visit our web site at http://www.chaosium.com/wizards-attic/

CALL OF CTHULHU FICTION BOOKS IN PRINT

The Complete Pegana $12.95
    The fantasy fiction of Lord Dunsany
The Cthulhu Cycle $10.95
Cthulhu's Heirs $10.95
    New Cthulhu stories for the modern-day
The Disciples of Cthulhu $10.95
    A second edition of the classic Cthulhu collection
The Dunwich Cycle $10.95
Encyclopedia Cthulhiana, Second Edition $14.95
    The mythos codified, A-Z
The Hastur Cycle $10.95
The Innsmouth Cycle $12.95
The Ithaqua Cycle $12.95
Made in Goatswood $10.95
    A tribute to Ramsey Campbell and the Severn Valley
The Necronomicon $12.95
    Stories about the book and translations of the dread tome itself
The Nyarlathotep Cycle $10.95
Scroll of Thoth $12.95
    The collected Simon stories, by Richard Tierney
Singers of Strange Songs $12.95
    A tribute to Brian Lumley, the Chthonians, and more
The Xothic Legend Cycle $10.95
    The collected Mythos fiction of Lin Carter